Stadium ADVENTURE Series
BOOK #2

3000 FEET OVER LAMBEAU

ROGER D. HESS

stadiumadventureseries.com

AUGUST IN
AU TRAIN
PRESS

For bonus puzzles and quizzes,
new releases and fun all day long,
visit *stadiumadventureseries.com*

Dedicated with love
to the one and only Sawyer Street Gang...
Kristen, Tim, Kara and Chris.

And to the more-than-amazing Alliance...
Chris, Sarah, Brandon and Amanda.

ALSO BY ROGER D. HESS

Freaked Out at Wrigley Field
Stadium Adventure Series #1

3000 Feet Over Lambeau
Stadium Adventure Series #2

by Roger D. Hess

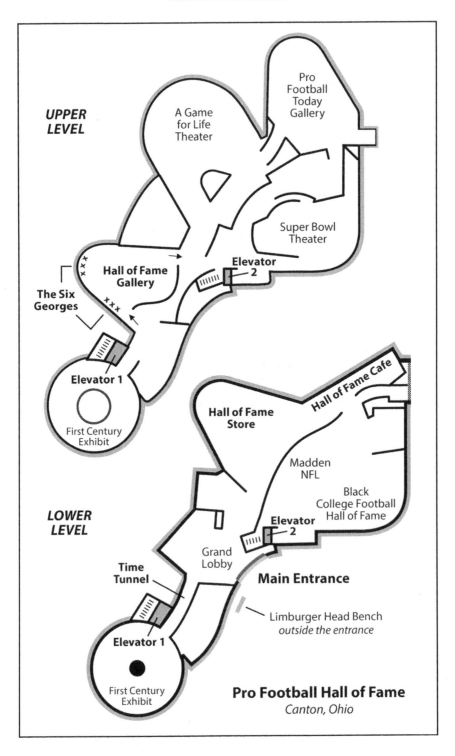

UPPER LEVEL

Pro Football Today Gallery

A Game for Life Theater

Super Bowl Theater

Hall of Fame Gallery

Elevator 2

The Six Georges

Elevator 1

First Century Exhibit

Hall of Fame Store

Hall of Fame Cafe

Madden NFL

Black College Football Hall of Fame

LOWER LEVEL

Elevator 2

Grand Lobby

Main Entrance

Time Tunnel

Limburger Head Bench
outside the entrance

Elevator 1

First Century Exhibit

Pro Football Hall of Fame
Canton, Ohio

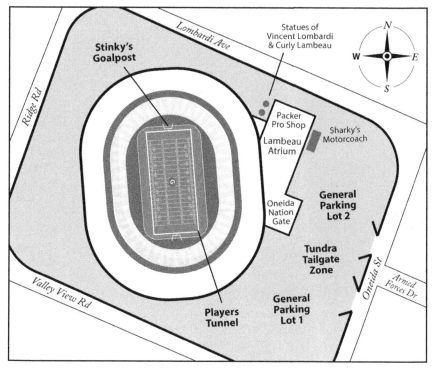

Lambeau Field
Green Bay, Wisconsin

- Lambeau Field opened in 1957 with a capacity of 32,500. With the 2014 completion of its ninth addition, Lambeau's seating capacity grew to 81,441.
- Of all 31 NFL stadiums, Lambeau Field has been in use the longest.
- Lambeau Field's nickname, *The Frozen Tundra*, came as the result of the Ice Bowl, December 31, 1967, between Green Bay and Dallas. The game was played in temperatures of 15-degrees below zero, the coldest NFL game on record. The Packers defeated the Cowboys 21-17.
- The first *Lambeau Leap* occurred December 26, 1993 when LeRoy Butler leaped into the stands after scoring a touchdown. Later popularized by Packer receiver Robert Brooks, it's become a fan favorite and a ritual players still celebrate today.

August 18 - 2:55 pm Central Daylight Time (CDT)
Monroe, Wisconsin

Big Dairy Dan Elliot lumbered out of the barn and headed toward his house painted in Packer green and gold. Inside, he settled down at the kitchen table with his afternoon snack, Limburger cheese with crackers, and he flipped open the newspaper. The headline sang to him. His favorite time of year had finally arrived!

THE MONROE TIMES
PACKERS TO PLAY IN HALL OF FAME GAME SUNDAY
Regular Season Kicks Off September 2

National Football League training camps are in full swing and our beloved Green Bay Packers have the honor of playing this Sunday at the annual Hall of Fame game in Canton, Ohio.

Packer Backers interested in attending the game should contact Irene Onufry at Packer Fan Tours. Packages include transportation via deluxe motor coach, hotel rooms, tickets to the game and passes to the NFL Hall of Fame.

The Packers have 23 players enshrined in Canton, second only to the Bears who have 28.

The Green Bay Packers and the Chicago Bears, two of the league's most storied franchises will face each other on national television September 2 at historic Lambeau Field in the first regular season game ever played on a Tuesday night.

"Packers second to the stinkin' Bears," grumbled Dairy Dan, his massive hairy hand trembling. Throwing the newspaper toward the trash can, he picked up the knife he had been using to spread his smelly cheese on a crispy rye cracker.

"That needs to be fixed and I mean...like...NOW!" shouted Dan.

Raising the knife over his head, he slammed it down hard, stabbing the blade deep into the tabletop to punctuate his feelings with an angry exclamation point.

CHAPTER 1

August 18 - 4:05 pm Eastern Daylight Time (EDT)
Port Clinton, Ohio
6 Days to Hall of Fame Game | 15 Days to Kickoff at Lambeau Field

Hawk Hapburn was trying to not to be scared as old Dr. Bartlett walked toward him with an electric saw in his hand.

"Now, hold still," warned the man in the white lab coat. "I'd hate to cut off your arm." Hawk wanted to laugh at the doctor's joke, but when he got a good look at the bright blue saw with sharp metal teeth, he wasn't sure the doctor was joking.

"But I guess I shouldn't worry," said the doctor as he plugged in his hand-held American Orthopedic Cast Cutter. "This saw blade has a PTFE coating. Nothing sticks to it. If blood or chunks of skin get on it, it washes off real easy."

Hawk closed his eyes when he heard the high-pitched whir of the saw as it started.

Since breaking his arm playing baseball, the hard cast on his arm had served as a powerful club when he found himself locked in hand-to-hand combat with brothers.

The sound of the saw changed as it began ripping into the plaster cast. The air was suddenly thick and heavy with a dry taste to it. Hawk grit his teeth and waited for the pain that never came.

"There," said Doc Bartlett as he laid his saw down on the examination table all covered in white powder. "You were one of the lucky ones. Look! No blood!"

Hawk opened his eyes to see his doctor splitting the autograph-covered cast in two and removing the protective layer of cotton.

"Can I have that?" asked Hawk, pointing at his busted-up cast.

The doc handed Hawk the two pieces of plaster, picked up his blood-free blue saw and put it back on the shelf.

"It feels funny now," said Hawk, rubbing his arm.

"You've had a cast on it for more than 8 weeks. It'll feel funny for a few days. In the meantime, take it easy. No rough-housing with your brothers."

"What about football?"

"Football?" Dr. Bartlett frowned.

"Yeah! I missed baseball this year 'cuz of my arm. I don't want to miss football season, too! First practice is this afternoon."

The old doctor scratched his chin. After a long pause, he walked over to a large white cabinet against the wall and began digging through a box. Finally, he pulled out a piece of thick, black fabric.

"Here...put this on," the doctor handed the cushy, black object to Hawk. "It's a padded arm sleeve."

Hawk slipped the spandex-polyester pad over his forearm. "Does it come in red? Our team's colors are red and white."

"Wear it during practice for a couple weeks," said the doc, ignoring Hawk's question. "It'll give that arm some protection."

"So, does this mean it's okay to play?" asked Hawk, excitedly.

"It means you should take it easy for a little while. Try out for kicker or water boy." Then Dr. Bartlett paused and pointed at him. "Remember, be careful!"

"Don't worry! I'll be careful!" Hawk jumped off the examination table and waved at the Doc. He turned quickly and took off, running beak first into the closed door. Hawk staggered backward and fell to the floor.

"Lucky, I had this pad on my arm," smiled Hawk as he scooped up his souvenir cast and scrambled to his feet. "That didn't hurt a bit!

August 18 - 3:27 pm CDT | Monroe, Wisconsin

Dairy Dan picked up his phone and dialed. While holding the phone with his right hand, he tried pulling the knife out of the table with his left.

Ten rings into Dairy Dan's struggle to remove the knife from the maple tabletop, Einstein Wozniak answered.

"What took you so long to answer your phone?" growled Dairy Dan.

"I was assisting Mama measure and mix the ingredients for her cabbage rolls," replied the voice on the line.

"Well, as soon as you can, I need you to get the 'heads together. I'm calling an emergency meeting tonight at 7. Baumgartner's basement. We've got serious business to discuss."

Then, finishing the phone call, Dairy Dan blurted out, "Seize the cheese!" He slammed the receiver down and went back to his struggle to extract the knife he had planted deep in the dinette.

August 18 - 4:29 pm EDT | Port Clinton, Ohio

In the waiting room, Hawk's Mom, Audrey Hapburn, was scanning a bulletin board covered with photos of Dr. Bartlett's patients.

Her eyes stopped on a picture of three boys, an Asian-American, an African-American and Hawk, the white kid in the middle, sitting in the stands at Wrigley Field with big grins on their faces.

"There they are," she said softly. Slowly placing her finger one at a time under each smiling face, she said her adopted sons' names with an affectionate whisper, "Nestor…Hawk…Michael."

Audrey was pleased to see that the picture she had sent of her three boys' recent adventure in Chicago had already been added to Dr. Bartlett's photo gallery.

"C'mon, Mom," yelled Hawk, as he burst into the waiting room and ran past the Port Clinton music teacher toward the exit.

Audrey reached out to grab her son as he whizzed by.

"Hold it a minute, young man," demanded Audrey, stepping away from the bulletin board. "What did the doctor say about football?"

Hawk screeched to a stop halfway between his Mom and the door that led to freedom (aka the parking lot). "Well, he was happy he didn't cut off my arm with his saw," offered Hawk. "And he gave me an arm pad to wear for the first couple weeks of practice."

"So, he said it was okay to play?" asked Audrey, as she pulled the keys to the blue Malibu out of her purse.

"We gotta hurry," insisted Hawk, grabbing his Mom's hand and pulling her toward the door. "First practice and parent meeting are both at 5:00!"

"We've got 30 minutes and it's a six-minute drive," said Audrey, looking at her watch.

"It never hurts to get there early," shouted Hawk over his shoulder as he dashed out the door.

Outside, Hawk found his brother, Michael, leaning against the blue Malibu, eating a chocolate power bar. His other brother, Nestor, was standing on the sidewalk with Stinky Smothers. They were laughing, while Stinky Smothers' brother was smashing into the wall on the side of the office building with his football helmet on backward.

"Hey, Stinky! What's your brother doing?" asked Hawk.

"He's running into that brick wall," giggled Stinky. Hawk winced.

"Make him stop..." Nestor said to Stinky. "Here comes my mom!"

A dull clunk greeted Audrey, as she walked out of the medical clinic. Turning in the direction of the sound, Audrey saw Stinky Smothers' brother laying face-down, face-guard up in the grass next to the building.

"Oh, dear!" shouted Audrey, rushing over to the crash scene to offer aid. Hawk, Nestor and Stinky followed behind, strictly in an advisory capacity.

"How awful!" moaned Audrey as she bent down. "Nestor, run in and get the doctor! This poor child's head is on backward!"

"It's okay, Mom," answered Nestor as he motioned to Stinky. "Help me get him up."

"Don't!" warned Audrey. "He could have a concussion."

"No, really, Ms. Hapburn. It's okay," reassured Stinky. "He usually lies there a second or two after he hits the bricks."

"He does? Who is he?" asked Audrey, thoroughly confused.

Nestor, with Stinky's help, flipped the younger Smothers over, got him to his feet, unstrapped the helmet, pulled it off, announcing, "Stinky Smothers' brother, mother!"

Helmet off, and a little wobbly, Stinky Smothers' brother whirled around to face his audience. "Did I do it? Did I bust through?"

"Bust through?" Audrey bent down and got face-to-face with the 11-year-old. "What do you mean: bust through?"

"You know, through the wall!" answered Stinky Smothers' brother. "Stinky and Nestor told me the football coach wants guys who can run through brick walls. So, I was practicing!"

"C'mon, Mom...we've got to get going!" squawked Hawk as he walked over to the Blue Malibu to join Michael, who was digging through his backpack in search of another snack.

Audrey turned to face Nestor and Stinky, her eyes flashing fire. "You boys told him to run into that brick wall?"

"We didn't really tell him to do it, Mom," said Nestor, his head down.

"No, we didn't tell him to do it, Ms. Hapburn," added Stinky. "We just sort of suggested it."

"Yeah, they also suggested turning my helmet around so I wouldn't know when I was about to slam into the wall," chimed Stinky Smothers' brother. "It was a good 'jestion, too, 'cuz that way, I could smash into it at top speed!"

"Nestor, we'll talk about this later," snapped Audrey, visibly upset. "And Richard, you know I'll have to tell your mother."

"Yes, Ms. Hapburn." moaned Stinky, kicking at a pebble.

"Richard? Who's Richard?" asked Stinky Smothers' brother. "Is that you, Stinky? Is Richard your middle name or your front name? Are you Stinky Richard Smothers or Richard Stinky Smothers?"

"Ms. Hapburn, could me and my brother ride with you to practice?" Stinky kept his head down and continued to talk. "Our mom is still at the library. She's coming to the field after work."

15

"My brother and I," corrected Audrey, picking up Stinky Smothers' brother's helmet and herding the boys toward the blue Malibu. "Yes Richard, you and your brother can ride with us."

"Your name's really Richard?" asked Stinky Smothers' brother. "I think I like Stinky better."

August 18 - 3:36 pm CDT | Monroe, Wisconsin

Sliding the cookie sheet filled with cabbage rolls toward his mother, Einstein Wozniak hung his apron on the hook in the closet.

"Dziekuje," said Henrietta, thanking her son in her native Polish. She patted her son on the top of his clean-shaven head.

"Zapraszamy," replied Einstein. *You're welcome.* Kissing Henrietta on the cheek, he ran upstairs to his bedroom.

Einstein lifted the corner of his mattress and pulled out a green folder he had hidden there. The folder was labeled in bold print.

The Pasteurized Brotherhood of Limburger Heads
TOP SECRET!

Opening the folder, he shuffled through the pages until he came to a list of names and telephone numbers. Putting his finger on the first name on the list, Einstein picked up his cell phone and dialed.

"Hello-eo-eo-eo-eo," yodeled the voice on the phone.

"Knock it off, Floyd. We've got serious business," interrupted Einstein. "Dairy Dan wants an emergency meeting at seven tonight. Baumgartner's basement."

"Emergency meeting, you say? Stinkin' Bishop!" replied Floyd

"It's required you call Helmut, Nick, Rick and Papa. If Papa doesn't answer, send a text. Do you comprehend your assignment?"

"You betcha! Done deal, Albert!"

"Not a word about this to anyone else," ordered Einstein. Then, before hanging up, he added, "And don't call me Albert."

August 18 - 4:49 pm EDT | Port Clinton, Ohio

The drive over to True Lay Stadium was short and tense. No one made a sound, except for Michael, who finished off an apple and was now opening a bag of Cheetos in the front seat of the blue Malibu.

Nestor was worried about what Audrey was going to say to him. Stinky Smothers was worried about explaining the brick wall incident to his mom. And all Hawk could think about was getting to practice. Stinky Smothers' brother wasn't worried at all. He just didn't have anything to say.

The blue Malibu pulled in five minutes early. Kids and parents were already on the football field on the other side of the chain link fence.

"We made it!" shouted Hawk, tumbling out of the car.

"Hold it!" demanded Audrey, stopping Hawk in his tracks. "I just want to say one thing to you boys before we go through the gate… you guys are going to be teammates and teammates need to have each other's backs. You look out for each other. Understand?"

"Mom, I didn't do anything," complained Michael, shoving in the last Cheeto, crumpling up the empty bag and tossing it away.

"Exactly," shot back Audrey, motioning for Michael to throw the bag in the trash can. "Instead of stopping it, you just stood there watching."

"And eating," added Hawk, under his breath.

"Hawk!" snapped Audrey.

"Sorry, Mom," said Hawk quickly.

"Me too, Mom," added Nestor.

"Me three, Mom," chimed in Michael.

Stinky Smothers patted his little brother on the head. "And I'm sorry I let you keep smacking into that building."

"Okay. That was good," said Audrey, taking a deep breath to calm herself down. "And what did we learn from this?"

"Stinky Smothers' brother raised his hand, "Bricks are hard?"

"That's true," smiled Audrey.

"All for one and one for all?" offered Nestor.

"Yes! That's it. And since no one got hurt, I'm going to overlook this incident this time, okay?"

Relieved, the boys nodded and picked up their gear.

Now, let's all get in a huddle," said Audrey, using the only football word she knew. "And we'll have a group hug."

"You want me and...ah...Richard to hug, too?" asked Stinky Smothers' brother.

"Absolutely!" shouted Audrey. The brothers, who knew better than to resist this public show of solidarity, converged on the sidewalk, hugged and shouted, "All for one and one for all!"

Then, quickly breaking the huddle, they turned to run through the gate, past the small, white cement-block ticket booth and onto the natural grass turf of neighborhood True Lay Stadium.

August 18 - 3:55 pm CDT | Monroe, Wisconsin

Turning down the alley off 11th Street, Dairy Dan parked his Ford pickup at the back door of Baumgartner's Cheese Store & Tavern. In the bed of the truck, there were three large wooden boxes with **DANGER** stenciled on them in big black letters.

One at a time, he lifted the boxes off the truck and wrestled them down the three steps and into the tavern's cold, gloomy basement.

Wet with sweat, Dairy Dan looked at his watch. It was almost 4:00. Only three more hours before he revealed his dark and evil plan.

August 18 - 5 pm EDT | Port Clinton, Ohio

With his two skinny assistant coaches, Jekyll and Hyde, at his side, Coach Carl Yakunshenko filled his lungs with as much air his 400-pound frame could hold and blew his whistle long and loud. It was time to start the meeting.

A former Ohio State offensive lineman, Coach Yak was almost as wide as he was tall. Standing at the 50, he occupied the space from 49-yard line to 49-yard line. In his four years as a Buckeye, he never allowed a sack because it was impossible to run through him. And, because of his immense size, it took too long to run around him.

After the three coaches introduced themselves, Coach Yak pulled a stack of papers from his clipboard and handed them to his assistants.

Adjusting the Buckeye ball cap on his head,
gave his whistle a quick, sharp blast, which sent
scurrying out to the parents with the handouts.

"We have good news and bad news," bellowe
tone. "This year, the annual NFL Hall of Fame
the Green Bay Packers playing the Denver Bror
is…the Port Clinton Braves have been invited t
halftime!"

The parents gasped in amazement while the
cheer.

Yak raised his beefy arm in the air to signal

"The bad news? The game is Sunday. That gi
days of practice."

The players let out another loud cheer, which
assistants silenced with a quick double whistle b
notes on his clipboard.

"The team will board the bus to Canton at 9:
We'll tour the Hall of Fame, have a team meal,
scrimmage with the Olmsted Falls Bulldogs in
Fame Stadium."

With jaws dropped, Hawk looked at Nestor,
Michael and Michael looked at Hawk. They cou
were hearing.

"After we play the Bulldogs, we'll watch the
NFL game from the stands."

Lifting his eyes from his clipboard, Coach Ya
please fill out the permission slips Coach Jekyll
handed out and have your son…" Coach Yak sto
sentence as he noticed a girl mixed in the group
boys.

Clearing his throat, he picked up where he le
bring them back tomorrow before practice."

Hearing the word *daughter*, Nestor scanned t

er there, next to Ray Ray McKay," whispered Nestor, pointing
ght. "It's Killer Kopecky!"

ill shot up Hawk's spine as he blurted out, "She's on our team?"

little dark-haired girl standing beside Ray Ray McKay snapped
d around. Audrey, who was standing behind her boys, gave
shoulder a firm squeeze. "You be nice!" she demanded.

k sheepishly nodded and then glanced over at Kathy Kopecky
er giving him the death stare.

ng to swallow the lump in his throat, Hawk quickly turned
Coach Yak, who was pulling a football from an equipment
is feet. Holding the football with both hands, he lifted it high
is head as if it were some rare and precious object of worship.
at is this?"

)otball!" shouted Stinky Smothers' brother.

ght..." replied Yak, lowering the pigskin to eye level.

ky Smothers' mother, who had just joined the meeting, smiled
ounger son. "Very good!" she said, beaming with pride.

most people, it's an ordinary football," acknowledged the
coach. "To me, it's much more than that. To me, it's passion...
age...it's the blood that runs through our veins."

k leaned over toward Nestor and Michael. "He scares me more
ller Kopecky."

or and Michael giggled, prompting Audrey to give them a poke.

tball is the greatest team sport ever invented," continued
Yak. "How do you spell team?"

ky Smothers' brother raised his hand, but Coach kept talking.
-A-M. T is for TOGETHERNESS. E is for EFFORT. A is
TITUDE. M is for MENTAL TOUGHNESS. There is no
m!" bellowed Yak. His red face was puffed up even larger than
d seemed ready to explode. "Football is...all for one and one

ring this, Stinky Smothers' brother let out a loud cheer and
at Audrey, "Hey! That's what she said!"

Now, in a full blast motivational rage, Coach Yak sucked in as much air as his lungs could hold and bellowed out the conclusion of his pre-practice speech.

"Just like being successful in life, FOOTBALL demands you to give it your all. To go ABOVE and beyond. AND…if the situation requires it, RUN THROUGH BRICK WALLS!"

Cheering again, Stinky Smothers' brother pointed at Nestor, Michael, Hawk and Stinky, happily shouting, "And that's what they said!"

Although his face was tomato red and he was totally out of breath, Coach Yak's head did not explode and make a mess out on the field.

Needing a moment to recover, the big crimson-cheeked coach tossed the football to Coach Jekyll, who then thanked the parents for taking the time to attend the meeting and instructed the kids to stick around for a short practice.

"We'll do some conditioning, then hand out playbooks and the uniforms," said skinny Coach Jekyll, smiling and tossing the football to his fellow assistant.

"I've gotta go to Billy DelSesto's piano recital. See you boys later," said Audrey with a wave. "And Hawk, you be nice to that little girl, understand?"

"Sure, mom," replied Hawk, as he watched her turn and walk off the field with Stinky Smothers' mother.

Hearing a sharp whistle blast, Hawk's head turned back toward the coaches on the field.

"OK, TEAM!" yelled the also skinny, but menacing Coach Hyde, who now held the football which apparently entitled *him* to speak. "20 times around the football field. We're gonna run you 'til you puke!"

August 18 - 7:11 pm EDT | Port Clinton, Ohio

Running through the front door and up the stairs to the bedroom he shared with Nestor and Michael, Hawk grabbed a marker off the desk and circled Sunday, August 24 on the Cubs' calendar taped to the wall.

Nestor, a few seconds behind Hawk, pulled his laptop out of his backpack and googled Tom Benson Hall of Fame Stadium.

"I can't believe we're gonna play on the same field pro players play," said Nestor, his fingers flying over his keyboard.

"And we're gonna see a real pro football game!" Hawk added.

Finally, the last brother trudged through the bedroom door. "It's a pre-season game," corrected Michael.

After bowing to the life-size cardboard cutout of Hot Dog Eating Champion Joey 'Jaws' Chestnut, he flopped on his bottom bunk.

"I can't believe you puked on the first lap around the field," laughed Hawk, looking around the room for a place to display the cast that had been on his arm the past few weeks.

"Not funny," moaned Michael. "Practice...not fun. Coach Hyde... NOT nice."

"Do you even chew what you eat?" asked Hawk, placing his cast on the dresser, right next to the baseball Jagdish caught on Opening Day at Wrigley Field. "Some of those Cheetos you upchucked were whole!"

"Cheetos. I need some. I'm hungry," Michael rolled off his bunk to see if he had stashed anything to eat under his bed.

"Wow! It says here that the capacity of Hall of Fame Stadium is 23,000," shouted Nestor. "The game starts at 6:30. Our game's at half-time, so we'll be playing under the lights!"

"Cool!" said Hawk, as he unzipped the duffle bag the coaches handed out at the end of practice. "Do you think we'll be any good?"

"We'll be okay once we get some practice," answered Nestor, who was now going through his duffle, too. "I wanted to try out for quarterback, but when I saw how far Killer Kopecky could throw that ball, I decided I'd have a better chance at receiver."

"She scares me," said Hawk, recalling the death stare she gave him just a few hours before. "You know, she killed Jim Woody."

Nestor shook his head. "She didn't kill Jim Woody. She punched him at recess because he was picking on her little brother."

"Well, I never saw Jim again after that," argued Hawk.

"Because he moved! Jim's dad got transferred to Columbus," replied

Nestor. "Besides, whether we like it or not, she's on our team. She might even be our second-best player, next to Michael."

Unwrapping a Hershey bar he found stuffed in one of his dirty socks, Michael voiced his opinion. "She's the best player on the team because I'm going to quit!"

"Quit?" shouted both Nestor and Hawk, lifting their heads out of their duffle bags.

"Yeah, quit. I hate it. All that running around."

"Everybody hates that part," admitted Nestor. "They make you do the hard stuff first and, then you get to have some fun."

Michael took a bite of his candy bar, "See what I'm doing right now?"

"Eating," answered Hawk.

"Right! Food going down. That's fun. It's NOT fun when it comes back up," explained Michael.

Nestor kicked his duffle bag toward the bottom bunk and sat down next to the eating machine. "Michael, think about this. We'll have lunch in the cafeteria at the Hall of Fame. After our game, we'll get to eat dinner at the concession stand in the stadium. Steaming stadium brats smeared with mustard."

Michael closed his eyes and imagined a concession stand tray with a couple of juicy brats and a pile of nacho chips smothered with cheese.

"Maybe I'll stick it out this week," said Michael, shoving the other half of his Hershey bar back in his sock. "I don't want to upset mom by letting the team down. You know, all that talk about all for one and blah, blah, blah."

Hawk reached into his duffle and pulled out a red jersey with large white numerals on the front and back. "Look. I got 23."

Nestor held up his jersey. "I got number 1."

Michael licked the melted chocolate off his fingers and unzipped his duffle bag. Spreading out his number 99 jersey on the bottom bunk, he sighed, "What time is practice tomorrow?"

"8 in the morning and 5 in the afternoon," said Nestor cheerfully.

"Twice?" Michael's head dropped in despair. "We practice twice?"

"Yeah! Double sessions all week," nodded Nestor.

"I'm quitting," grumbled Michael.

"Hey, guys! Look!" Hawk stood in front of his brothers wearing his jersey. Then, pretending to take a hand-off, he ran into the dresser, bounced off and dove on top of his bed.

"Touchdown! Port Clinton Braves!" shouted Hawk, trying to sound like a sports announcer. "Horace Hapburn, *Nuuumber 23!*"

August 18 - 7:11 pm CDT | Monroe, Wisconsin

"23!" shouted Dairy Dan Elliot, holding up the newspaper article from the Monroe Evening Times as he addressed a room filled with grown men wearing yellow foam Cheesehead hats on their heads. "That's how many Green Bay Packers there are in the Hall of Fame."

The meeting of the Pasteurized Brotherhood of Limburger Heads in the damp, dark basement of Baumgartner's Cheese Store & Tavern was getting angry.

"The Chicago Bears have TWENTY...EIGHT! **FIVE** MORE players than we have! HOW is that possible?" screamed Dairy Dan at the top of his lungs.

"That's so wrong!" shouted Nick Monroe, pounding on the table in front of him.

The Bears stink!" yelled Nick's son, Rick.

"The Bears stink!" shouted the room of angry Limburger Heads.

The veins in Dairy Dan's neck were popping out, his eyes bulging out of his skull.

"So...I ask you my fellow Packer backers: "WHAT ARE WE GOING TO DO ABOUT IT?"

Floyd Dowler, the fourth member of the Taleggio Trio Polka Band, immediately stood up and started choking a stuffed bear he'd brought to the meeting.

The Limburger Heads cheered loudly!

"Good job beating up the teddy bear, Floyd, but that doesn't do anything to fix the problem," complained Dairy Dan.

"How about I make a statue of Max McGee out of Gorgonzola and

we ship it to Canton, Ohio?" volunteered Helmut Lunquist, Cheese Master at the Chalet Cheese Co-op, just north of the city.

At the mention of Max McGee, wide receiver for the Packers who scored two touchdowns in the very first Super Bowl, the Limburger Heads removed their Cheesehead hats and placed them over their hearts.

Old Army Cargo Plane Pilot Demetri Papadopoulos, grabbed his walker, struggled to his feet and, with tears in his eyes, he started singing, "Go, You Packers, Go".

Seconds later, all the Limburger Heads were singing and crying, including Henrietta Wozniak, who sang the song in Polish.

Drying his eyes with a Packer bandana, Dairy Dan nodded in Helmut's direction. "That's a very good suggestion. That's the reason we broke away from those regular Cheeseheads in the first place...they don't give a hoot about getting McGee enshrined. But even if he was in, there would still be more Bears in the Hall than Packers."

A grim, uneasy quiet settled over the group. Sounds of laughter from the diners in the tavern above drifted down into the basement onto the sad and desperate group.

Bending down to the floor, Dairy Dan lifted one of the large wooden boxes he had delivered earlier and placed it on the table.

Upon seeing the word <u>DANGER</u> stenciled on the pine boards, the Limburger Heads gasped in unison.

With a snarl, Dan grabbed the newspaper again and waved it above his head. "After reading this trash, finding a way to fix this horrible wrong is all I can think about. So, Wozniak stopped by my milking parlor this afternoon and we brainstormed."

Using his Packer bandana to wipe perspiration from his forehead, he continued. "Let me just say: Sometimes getting what you want in life demands you to give it your all. To go ABOVE and beyond. AND...if the situation requires it, RUN THROUGH BRICK WALLS!"

Taking a deep breath, Dairy Dan grabbed a wooden pointer from the table. "Executing the game plan we came up with won't be any picnic, but if we work as a team, we will be victorious!"

Giving the pointer a twirl, he handed it off to Einstein, who stood up just as Dan was sitting down. The choreography was beautiful and acknowledged by the Limburger Heads with a smattering of applause.

Einstein reached up and pulled a white sheet off the wall. As the sheet fell to the basement floor, it revealed a chalkboard with these words scribbled large: **OPERATION GEORGIE PORGIE**

"Operation Georgie Porgie," Einstein read aloud, underlining each word with the wooden pointer.

"Who's Georgie Porgie and what kind of operation is he having?" asked Floyd, with a great deal of concern in his voice.

Ignoring Floyd, Einstein continued.

"We could not determine a way to get more Packers *into* the Hall of Fame, so...."

The Limburger Heads were dead silent, waiting to hear what was coming next.

"...we shall journey to the Hall of Fame in Canton, Ohio and take some Bears *out*."

"Steal some Bears? You mean like carry the statues out of the Hall of Fame?" asked Helmut Lunquist.

"Yes, but they're not truly regulation statues," explained Einstein. "They're more half-size."

"Less than half-size, really," added Dairy Dan, trying to making it sound easier. "You know, just the head and a little bit of the neck."

"Whoa, way cool," squealed the young, twenty-something Rick Monroe, who was sitting next to his worried-looking dad, Nick. "Which Bears are we going to steal?"

"Mitch Trubisky!" yelled Floyd Dowler, jumping up again.

"Trubisky's not in the Hall of Fame, Floyd," said Helmut softly, not wanting to embarrass his friend.

"Good!" responded Floyd, sitting back down.

Baumgartner's basement was buzzing as Einstein Wozniak opened his TOP SECRET folder, pulled out a piece of paper and held it up over his clean-shaven head for his friends to see.

Pointing at the HIT LIST Einstein was holding, Dairy Dan stood up smiling. "To answer your question, Rick...the plan is to steal all the Hall of Fame Bears named George."

OPERATION GEORGIE PORGIE HIT LIST
George Halas
George Trafton
George McAfee
George Connor
George Blanda
George Musso

We did the math," said Einstein, handing Dairy Dan a piece of chalk. "28 Bears in the Hall of Fame..." As Einstein spoke, Dairy Dan scribbled the arithmetic on the chalkboard. "...minus six Bears named George...equals 22."

Dairy Dan circled the number 22. "This is our goal. If we can do this, the Packers, with 23, will have the most players in the Hall of Fame!"

The Limburger Heads jumped to their feet and roared approval. After a full five minutes of high-fives and back-slapping happiness, Nick Monroe, the only Limburger Head who didn't seem completely pleased, interrupted the celebration by raising his hand.

"I hate to be a party pooper..."

"Bathroom's upstairs, Nick," interrupted Floyd.

Helmut gave Floyd a quick elbow to the gut and Nick continued.

"...but this whole Operation Georgie Porgie sounds more like Mission Impossible. Believe me! I love Packer football more than life itself. Our family has been on the season ticket waiting list since the day Rick here was born 25 years ago. But I just don't see how we can do this without getting caught."

"It would be just our luck we'd get called for Packer season tickets and there we'd be, sitting in prison! Huh, pops?" laughed Rick.

Smiling, Dairy Dan walked back to the table and gently put his hand on top of the large wooden box with <u>DANGER</u> stenciled on it.

"Believe me, Nick, there's no need to worry. With our secret weapon, stealing the Bears will be a piece of cake. A piece of CHEESEcake."

August 18 - 10:30 pm EDT | Port Clinton, Ohio

The brothers' bedroom was dark, except for the glow from Nestor's laptop. Too excited to hit the sack, Nestor and Hawk were digging up information about the Hall of Fame and the teams they were going to see play, the Broncos and the Packers.

Michael, knowing he'd need all his energy to survive the scheduled two-a-day football practices, was in his bottom bunk, trying to sleep.

"Look at this!" said Nestor, squinting at the computer screen. "There are 105,000 people on the Green Bay season ticket waiting list. This says if you sign up now, you'd have to wait a thousand years."

"That's crazy," laughed Hawk. "Hey, go to the Packer website and see if we can get on the list!"

"We can't get on the list. We're just kids," argued Nestor.

"Go to the website and see," begged Hawk.

Reluctantly, Nestor logged onto packers.com and clicked on Season Tickets.

"There!" chirped Hawk. "Season ticket waiting list form! Print it!"

"Knock it off you guys," groaned Michael, pounding his pillow. "I need sleep."

Nestor hit the print button and handed the form to Hawk.

"Look, Nestor! It doesn't say anything about how old you have to be. All I gotta do is put my name and address and stuff," said Hawk, filling in the blanks. "How many tickets do we want?"

"I'm a Browns fan," yawned Michael.

"How much do they cost?" asked Nestor.

"Doesn't say," answered Hawk. "Anyway, we won't get to the top of the list for 1,000 years, so we've got plenty of time to save up the money."

"I'll put down three, just in case you guys change your mind and want to go to the games with me."

Hawk finished filling out the form, folded it, then went to the desk the brothers shared and dug through the drawers for an envelope.

Finally, getting a little sleepy himself, Nestor closed his laptop and climbed into the top bunk as Michael snored loudly on the bottom.

"Why'd you shut down, Nestor? I wanted you to check and see how much a Cheesehead hat costs."

"I'll check it out tomorrow," promised Nestor, pulling the covers over his head.

"Find out how much a cheeseburger costs, too," added Michael, talking in his sleep.

Then silence blanketed the room. Hawk dug around and found an envelope, addressed and stamped it. He wanted to mail the Packer season ticket application in the morning on the way to practice.

Placing the envelope on the dresser, the flourish of words scribbled on his discarded cast caught his eye. *Live your dreams! Roger Ringwelski*

Immediately, an image flashed in his mind of his friend rolling out a sleeping bag inside the scoreboard at Wrigley Field. Smiling, Hawk pulled off his #23 jersey, hung it carefully on the hook in his closet and jumped into bed.

A beam of light from the street lamp outside landed directly on the date circled on the Cubs' calendar taped to the wall. Hawk smiled, closed his eyes and drifted into his dream. In six days - Sunday, August 24 - he would be playing football in the NFL's Hall of Fame Stadium.

August 18 - 9:53 pm CDT | Monroe, Wisconsin

"Sunday, August 24," said Dairy Dan, tapping the date written on the chalkboard with the wooden pointer. "That's when we go in and steal all the Bears named George."

"Stinkin' Bishop! That's only one-two-three-four-five…six days away," objected Floyd, counting on his fingers. "Why so soon, Albert?"

"With the Packers participating in the game, it's our perfect window of opportunity," declared Einstein. "By traveling on the tour bus out of Green Bay, we will blend in with the other Cheeseheads on tour in the Hall. Just prior to closure, when everyone is vacating the premises…"

"Then, WHAM!" interrupted Dairy Dan, slamming his hand

down on top of the large wooden box marked <u>DANGER</u>. "That's when we make our move! There are six George heads to carry out, which means it'll take a half-dozen Limburger heads to do the job. So, who's in?"

Einstein nodded his bald head at Dairy Dan and they both raised their hands. "Dan and I are the initial volunteers for Operation Georgie Porgie. We will require four more...uh...."

"...heroes!" interrupted Dairy Dan, adding some shine to their 'help wanted' ad.

"Yes, very good," said Einstein, indicating his approval. "We will require four more *heroes* ...daring to face danger, death, or even worse."

"It's over the weekend, so nobody has to miss work," added Dairy Dan, happily.

Quickly, Rick Monroe raised his hand and then gave his dad a friendly jab. "C'mon, Pops! Danger...death...it'll be fun!"

"Okay, count me in," said Nick, raising his hand reluctantly. "But I'm only going to keep an eye on you, son."

With a firm grip on his walker, Demetri Papadopoulos rose to his feet, "I go. I am old. Death...I spit in its eye. We go to game? Yes?"

"Yes! Yes, Papa," reassured Dairy Dan, with a vigorous nod. "Once we load the Georges on the bus, we'll all go watch the Pack play!"

"However," interjected Einstein. "Because the removal of the Georges will run concurrent with the beginning of the game, you might miss the kickoff."

"No see kickoff? Okay," said Papa with a dismissive wave of his hand. "Sign me down for Georgie Porgie."

"Great! That's five! We just need one more!" exclaimed Dairy Dan, looking at Helmut and Floyd.

"I'll tell ya, fellas. I want to help in any way I can, but I can't go on this mission," said Helmut sadly. "Our Maddie Rose is getting baptized at Saint Victor's Sunday and grandma and me gotta be there."

"Understood, Helmut. It's close, but family is the only thing more important than Packer football." Dairy Dan gave his cheesemaking

friend a reassuring pat on the back. All eyes shifted over to Floyd, except Henrietta's, who was in her chair snoring loudly...in Polish.

"All right, I'll go," sighed Floyd. "I just wish it didn't have to be THIS weekend."

"As I clearly outlined previously," snapped Einstein, getting cranky from fatigue. "It is the perfect opportunity."

"Yeah, yeah, I hear ya. It's just I was planning on having a birthday party for myself, ya see?"

"Your birthday isn't for another six months," protested Helmut.

"I know, but I'm starting to get excited about it," explained Floyd. "I guess I can put the party off for now."

"Okay, great! We have our six," exclaimed Dairy Dan, with a little extra volume so he could be heard over Henrietta's loud Polish snoring. "Now, here's the plan!"

"Excuse me, but I'd propose we table the topic for the evening," offered Einstein. "The hour grows late and, considering its importance, we might be well advised to postpone this discussion until tomorrow when we're better equipped to focus properly."

"I wished he'd speak English," grumbled Floyd. "I understand what his ma says better than I do him."

"We could meet at my residence at 1700 hours to dine on cabbage rolls and digest the intricacies of Operation Georgie Porgie."

"Good idea," Dairy Dan agreed, clapping his hands. "Limburger Heads, we meet again tomorrow at five at the Wozniak bunker."

"Wait a minute! Don't leave us hanging like that," protested Nick Monroe. "If we're going to face danger and death, at least give us clue. How do we get away with this? What danger is in that box? And if you have a secret weapon, WHAT IS IT?

"Relax, Nick," smiled Dairy Dan, holding up both hands. "You want a clue? Here it is."

Patting the wooden box on the table ever so gently, he whispered, "Stink bombs."

CHAPTER 2

August 19 - 8:08 am EDT | Port Clinton, Ohio
5 Days to Hall of Fame Game | 14 Days to Kickoff at Lambeau Field

Michael was surprised when he opened his eyes and found himself at the bottom of a pile of players holding a football.

Minutes before, at the start of practice, Coach Yak had divided the players into two groups: offense and defense. Coach Jekyll huddled with the kids on offense, while Coach Hyde was placing his players in various defensive positions.

Kneeling in the middle of his offense, Coach Jekyll flipped to the first play on his clipboard, Fullback Power-Dive Middle. He explained each player's assignment and then gave them the snap count.

Breaking the huddle, Kathy Kopecky, playing quarterback, got behind the center. Yelling out the signals, she took the snap and stuffed the football hard into the middle of Michael's gut. His reflexes responding, Michael's arms automatically wrapped themselves around the ball tightly, but he never moved his legs.

The defense swarmed on the motionless running back. One after another, players jumped on top of him. Until finally, after all eleven kids on the defensive side covered him completely, Michael's knees buckled and Coach Yak whistled the play dead.

"What's going on? Where am I?" yelled Michael from the bottom of the twelve-player mound.

Hawk, who was playing safety, rolled off the pile and reached down to help his brother to his feet. "You're at practice."

"Practice?" Michael looked around the field, eyes blinking, "How

did I get here?"

Noticing Michael's confusion, Coach Jekyll ran over to him and led him back to the huddle.

"I'm wearing a football jersey?" asked Michael looking down at his chest. "What happened to my pajamas?"

"Maybe you better go over to the bench and sit out a few plays," said Coach Jekyll, unstrapping Michael's helmet.

"He's okay, Coach," reassured Nestor, who was just getting back from running his wide receiver route.

Worried, Coach Jekyll bent over, getting eye-to-eye to his full-sized fullback. "I don't know…he seems a little groggy…could be a concussion."

"Oh no, he was asleep. He was snoring the whole time we walked over to practice," laughed Nestor. "In the summer, Michael doesn't like getting out of bed before 10:30!"

"Nestor! What about breakfast? Did I have breakfast?"

"Yes, Michael," answered Nestor. "Mom fixed us French toast. You ate ten pieces and some bacon."

"Oh, man! I LOVE French toast! Why didn't you wake me up?"

"We better play it safe," said Coach Jekyll, turning Michael toward the sideline. "Go stand by Coach Yak for a while."

The assistant coach then scanned the rag-tag group of substitutes standing a few yards away. After giving them a long, hard look, he sighed and called Stinky Smothers' brother's number.

"Twenty-five! You're in!"

Looking down at his jersey to double-check, Stinky Smothers' brother gave a happy shout and roared head down onto the field at full speed. Halfway to the huddle, he ran smack into Michael, who was lumbering toward the sideline.

The collision sent the smaller player into a backward somersault.

From the ground, he called to number 99, "You all right?"

Never stopping, Michael gave a little nod and kept plodding in the direction of the sideline and Coach Yak, who was waving him over.

"What's the matter? What was going on out there?" demanded

Coach Yak, never taking his eyes off the field or his whistle out of his mouth.

"I just found out I had French toast for breakfast," said Michael, sadly.

The massive 400-pound coach shot his player a quick look and then gave a couple of sharp blasts on his whistle. "C'mon! Let's see some action out there!"

The rest of the morning practice did not go well. Aside from a long pass by Killer Kopecky to Nestor and Hawk recovering a fumble and lateraling the ball to Ray Ray McKay who ran 80 yards for a touchdown, the rest was a comedy of errors. Except no one was laughing.

Players were tripping over each other, dropping the ball, missing tackles, even running in the wrong direction.

The coaches - worried something was wrong with Michael because he wouldn't stop talking about French toast - kept their big fullback on the bench for the rest of the AM session.

Looking at his watch, Coach Yak blew his whistle and walked out on the field. "All right everybody...SIT," he yelled, pointing a meaty finger to the ground in front of him. "This afternoon, conditioning with Coach Hyde...Hapburn, number 99, you're excused. Study your playbook. Come back in the morning. The rest of you BE HERE at 5!"

Then, wanting to end on an encouraging note, he grumbled, "Good practice," under his breath.

"Okay...huddle up!" ordered Coach Jekyll, preparing for one last morale-boosting exercise. "TEAM on three! Ready? One...two... THREE..."

"TEAM!" everyone shouted in unison, except for Stinky Smothers' brother who was still yelling *EAM* after everyone else had finished.

The players, sweaty and tired, groaned and headed off in different directions.

"We're pretty bad," moaned Hawk, walking off the field between his two brothers. "We can't block, we can't tackle...half of our guys can't even tie their shoes!"

"Plus, no snacks," added Michael.

"Snacks?" questioned Nestor.

"Yeah! Snacks," grumbled Michael. "Who wants to bust their butt just to hear a coach say 'good job' or 'atta boy'? I need snacks."

Suddenly, a light bulb flashed in Nestor's head. "Keep walking, I'll catch up with you."

Clutching his helmet by the face mask, Nestor turned and took off running toward the three coaches who were talking together as they dragged equipment bags to their cars.

"Excuse me, Coach Yak..." interrupted Nestor.

The trio of coaches stopped and turned around.

"I studied our playbook last night," said Nestor nervously. "And it's pretty good. But I just got an idea for a few modifications."

"Modifications?" Coach Yak scratched his head and gave the short, thin, energetic kid in front of him a hard look. "You want to make changes to the team playbook?"

"Just minor alterations, really, on what is already a brilliant tactical strategy," replied Nestor, trying to be as polite as possible.

"Alterations...modifications...quite a vocabulary you have there, Number One," scoffed the crabby Coach Hyde. "How about you think of more big words to say while you're doing 20 extra laps?"

"Okay!" said Nestor, "Anything to help the team!"

Nestor quickly dropped his helmet and took off running.

"Hold it, Hapburn," shouted Coach Jekyll. He winked at Coach Yak and Coach Hyde. "You guys go. I'll take care of this."

The other two coaches picked up the equipment bags and trudged toward the parking lot as Nestor trotted back to where Coach Jekyll was standing.

The young coach picked up Nestor's helmet and handed it to him. "You don't have to run extra laps right now...you'll be doing plenty of conditioning this afternoon."

"I don't mind," said Nestor, cheerfully. "I just want to help the team any way I can. That's why I wanted to talk to you about changing some of the plays."

"Well, just let me say, we appreciate your commitment," assured

Coach Jekyll. "But you have to trust us to do what's best. Between the three of us, we've got a lot of football experience.

"I know the team doesn't look like much now, but this is only the first day. I think we have a pretty good group of guys, including you! That was a nice catch and run you made out there this morning!"

"Thanks, Coach," said Nestor, disappointed his offer to help was being rejected.

"Go home and rest," ordered the coach with a smile. "You're gonna need plenty of energy at practice this afternoon."

Coach and player turned and jogged off in opposite directions. A few minutes later, Nestor caught up with Hawk and Michael standing among a bunch of lawn gnomes in Mrs. McChesney's front yard.

Mrs. McChesney lived a couple of houses down from the Hapburns and she'd invested a small fortune in her collection of lawn gnomes.

Gnomes with wheelbarrows, gnomes with tennis rackets, kissing gnomes, gnomes of all sizes covered practically every square inch of her front yard.

The chess set gnomes were the Hapburn brothers' favorite. It was always Hawk and Michael versus Nestor. Nestor always won.

"Hurry up, Nestor," yelled Hawk as he put the gnome chess pieces into position on the lawn. "Let's play a game!"

"Not right now! I need to get home and figure out some new plays for the team."

"C'mon!" pleaded Hawk. "Just a few moves."

"Yeah, Nestor. Five minutes, that's all," proclaimed Michael. "I wanna get home, too and see if there's any French toast left."

"Okay," agreed Nestor, grabbing a red gnome pawn in front of his queen gnome and moving it one space forward. "Five minutes."

Hawk and Michael huddled up to discuss their strategy. After a few seconds, the brothers moved the black pawn in front of the king's bishop gnome forward.

Without hesitation, Nestor lifted the pawn two spaces in front of his king.

Smiling, Hawk bent over and whispered to his big brother. "Look!

He exposed his king! Move our pawn in front of the knight, then attack with the bishop."

Michael nodded and moved their pawn in front of the king's knight up two spots.

Pleased, Hawk and Michael both folded their arms and waited to see what Nestor would do next.

They didn't have to wait long. Nestor immediately grabbed his queen gnome and slid her four spaces diagonally, placing her beside the pawn Michael had just moved.

"Checkmate. Game over," declared Nestor. He turned and ran toward home.

"He beat us again," said Michael, scratching his head. "In three moves."

"Yeah, but we're getting better," said Hawk, congratulating his brother with a pat on the back. "Last time, we lost in two moves."

Bending down to pick up their helmets, the brothers looked up just in time to see Nestor zoom up the Hapburn front porch steps and into the house. He was on a mission. An all-important secret mission that would make the Port Clinton Braves the greatest youth football team Ohio had ever seen!

August 19 - 5:15 pm CDT | Monroe, Wisconsin

The seven Limburger Heads seated around the Wozniak dining table looked up when the swinging kitchen door flew open.

"Więcej?" asked Henrietta, offering her third platter of steaming cabbage rolls as she entered the dining room.

"No more," laughed Dairy Dan, patting his bloated belly. "Another bite and I'll explode."

"I'll have another, Mrs. Wozniak, please," called Floyd Dowler from the other end of the dining room table. "But six is my limit. I need to save room for some of your babka cake!"

"Dobry!" squealed Henrietta. *Good!* She waddled toward Floyd and scooped another cabbage roll onto his plate.

Licking his plate clean and then wiping his mouth with his napkin,

Einstein Wozniak pulled out his TOP SECRET Pasteurized Brotherhood of Limburger Heads folder and stood up to address the group.

"While you gentlemen complete the consumption of your cabbage rolls, I will commence with the purpose of this gathering."

"What's that you say, Albert?" mumbled Floyd, with his mouth full.

"He's going to start the meeting while we finish eating," translated Cheese Master Lundquist.

"I don't know if that's a good idea," blurted Floyd, spraying bits of cabbage roll everywhere. "It's hard to chew and concentrate."

"Floyd, if at any time, you find you're having trouble understanding, maybe you could put down your fork for a minute," suggested Dairy Dan as he joined Einstein at the head of the table.

Dairy Dan and Einstein quickly collected the dirty dishes in front of them and handed the stack of plates to Henrietta, who then teetered back into the kitchen.

Bending down, the pair of Limburger Heads lifted the large wooden box marked <u>DANGER</u> up on the tabletop. Dairy Dan pulled a screwdriver from his pocket and pried open the lid.

Reaching into the box, Dairy Dan and Einstein pulled out ten glass mason jars filled with a variety of moldy, yellow-green goop and lined them up across the table in front of their crew of curious conspirators.

"What you are observing in these containers are the world's top ten cheeses most offensive to the human nostril," proclaimed Einstein, holding up a jar with the #10 taped to it. "Ten: Taleggio; Number Nine: Blue Stilton; Eight: Stinking Bishop…"

"Stinkin' Bishop! My favorite," mumbled Floyd between mouthfuls.

"…Number Seven: Limburger," continued Einstein, touching each jar as he said the number. "Six: Roquefort; Five: Brie de Meaux; Four: Epoisses; Three: Munster; Two: Camembert … and Number One: The Crown Prince of the World's Smelliest Cheeses…Pont-l'Eveque!"

The Limburger Heads gasped in unison. They had all heard of the powerful and pungent properties of Pont-l'Eveque, but none of them had actually smelled, touched, or tasted it.

Dairy Dan carefully picked up the mason jar labeled #1 and passed it to Cheese Master Helmut, so he could get a closer look.

"Each of these cheeses has a smell that is super strong," said Dairy Dan, waving his hand over the jars.

"In fact!" interjected Einstein. "For most of the world's inhabitants, outside the state of Wisconsin, the intense odors of these cheeses preclude an individual from even being in close proximity to them… let alone, considering them suitable for consumption."

"Wow! Do you think his brain ever overheats?" marveled Floyd.

"Separately, the cheeses are completely safe, but, mix them all together…what you get is a dangerous and - possibly deadly - stink bomb," Dairy Dan stated in a serious tone. "So, we need Helmut to figure out what would be the perfect combination to knock a person out, but not knock 'em out for good. Do you follow?"

Helmut inspected the jar of Pont-l'Eveque and nodded. "I am honored to help in this important mission in whatever way I can," said the cheese master. "I'll get working on it first thing."

"Great!" replied Dairy Dan, carefully placing the containers of smelly cheeses back in the wooden box. "I'll deliver the jars to the cheese co-op in the morning."

"So we'll have these stink bombs Helmut is making, but what the *heck*…excuse my French…are we supposed to do with them?" asked Nick Monroe, nervously.

"Wow, Pop!" laughed Rick. "I didn't know you spoke French!"

"Gather 'round," said Einstein flipping open his laptop. "I detailed a plan on how to execute Operation Georgie Porgie."

The Limburger Heads crowded around the computer as Einstein read his daring, ten-step plan out loud.

"Step One: Saturday. Board tour bus leaving Green Bay, Wisconsin at 11:45 am. Arrive in Canton, Ohio at 10:57 pm. Check into Ramada Hall of Fame Hotel.

"Step Two: Go to bed.

"Step Three: Sunday morning. Get up."

"Brilliant," grumbled Nick. "Good thing you put that in there."

"Step Four," continued Einstein. "Place stink bombs in backpacks, put on Cheeseheads and board tour bus to Hall of Fame. Scout out Hall of Fame and identify the location of all requisite Georges.

"Step Five: Synchronize watches," Einstein pointed at his Packer wristwatch, "so at precisely 4:30 in the PM…"

"30 minutes before the Hall of Fame closes," added Dairy Dan.

"…each of us, positioned strategically in a selected zone, will activate our individual stink bomb at exactly the same moment, causing security and all civilians in the building to pass out on the spot, rendering them temporarily helpless.

"Step Six: Proceed to the Hall of Fame Gallery on the upper level and each of us procures our assigned George bust from the wall. We then bag the heads in potato sacks, exit the Gallery via the elevator, depart the building and immediately secure the Bears on the bus…"

"Babka cake! Babka cake!" chanted Demetri Papadopoulos, rapping his fork on the table.

"Time out! Papa wants his dessert," declared Dairy Dan, sensing the Limburger Heads were becoming bored.

"But what about the remainder of the plan?" objected Einstein.

"Remainder?" questioned Dairy Dan, as Rick and Floyd began pounding their forks on the table, too and joining in with Papa's chant…

"Babka cake! Babka cake! Babka cake…"

"You know, the last steps of the plan!" shouted Einstein. "I haven't explained the manner in which we will covertly transport the Bears back to Wisconsin…"

"Babka cake! Babka cake! Babka cake…"

"Or how we will conceal the statues until the night of the Green Bay-Chicago game…"

"Babka cake! Babka cake! Babka cake…"

"And what about the portion where we implement sledgehammers and…" frustrated, Einstein stopped himself in mid-sentence and waved his hands above his bald head, crying, "Cease banging your forks and listen to me!"

But the Limburger Heads kept chanting, "Babka cake! Babka cake!"

"You better get Mama out here with the babka cake," instructed Dairy Dan, pushing Einstein toward the kitchen. "Before they stick a fork in you!"

August 19 - 6:58 pm EDT | Port Clinton, Ohio

"TWEEEEEEEEEEEEEEEEEEEEET!"

The sharp, shrill sound of the whistle sent the exhausted Port Clinton Braves running toward the end zone on the last forty-yard sprint of the day.

Letting the whistle fall from his mouth and dangle around his skinny neck, Coach Hyde looked at his watch. Two more minutes before the afternoon conditioning session was over.

Nestor and Killer Kopecky were the first to cross the goal line, while Hawk and the rest of the team stumbled into the end zone a few steps behind, dripping with sweat and struggling to breathe.

"Running is fun, right?" shouted Coach, seeming quite pleased at the sight of his players scattered along the goal line, gasping for air.

The team answered with a long, painful groan.

"That's good," said Coach Hyde, smiling for the first time that day. "Because this is how all our afternoon conditioning sessions will end."

"Ugggggggggggggh," groaned the players with their heads down.

Coach Hyde gave two short whistle blasts and barked, "Huddle up!"

The players struggled to their feet and crowded into a tight circle to listen to their coach's final instructions.

"Go home and study your playbook. You're all back here on the field at eight in the morning! Remember! We've got a game to play in front of 23,000 people in five days! Okay...TEAM on three! Ready? One...two...THREE..."

"TEAM!" everyone shouted in unison except - again - Stinky Smothers' brother who was a little behind and still yelling *EAM* in the time it took Nestor to run a few feet away and return with a red folder.

As the players turned to drag themselves home, Nestor tapped Coach Hyde on the shoulder and held the red folder up.

"Excuse me, Coach," said Nestor, trying to be as polite as possible. "I drew up some special plays for the Braves I think will work great."

"C'mon Nestor! Let's go!" pleaded Hawk, tugging on his brother's jersey. "You're asking for trouble."

Nestor swatted Hawk's hand away. "I've got to do this. It's for the team."

Hawk shook his head and moved slowly away, mumbling to himself, "This isn't going to be good."

Looking down at the player in front of him, the crabby Coach Hyde scratched his chin.

"You drew up some special plays there...ah...ah..."

"My name is Nestor. Nestor Hapburn."

"Right...Hapburn, Nestor," said Coach Hyde, reversing the order. "Well, how about you give me that folder with those...uh, special plays, Heartburn...and then you can run five extra laps around the football field while I give this some SPECIAL consideration."

"Oh, sure! That's great! Here!" said Nestor. He handed the assistant coach his red folder. "Oh, and my name is Hapburn...not Heartburn."

"Fine, whatever. Just get going now and run those laps," barked Coach Hyde. Then he turned Nestor around and gave him a little push. "Go!"

Without hesitation, Nestor trotted off to the running track that encircled the football field. As he ran past Hawk, who had moved down the sideline away from the unpleasant coach, Nestor called out cheerfully to his brother.

"Coach is going to look at my plays while I do extra conditioning. Don't wait for me. Go home!"

"I'm not waiting," Hawk shouted back. "I'm resting."

Nestor gave a wave as he jogged toward the far end zone.

Hawk watched him for a couple of seconds, then turned to leave. In front of him, Coach Hyde was heading toward his car with the red folder in hand. Without opening it up to see what Nestor had given him, he dropped the folder in a trash can.

Hawk let out a gasp and whipped his head around to see his brother still happily running. Then, looking back, he watched as Coach Hyde got in his car and drove off.

Angry, Hawk kicked a Mountain Dew can to the curb, then trotted over to the trash can and lifted the lid.

There the red folder laid, resting on top of a greasy, empty bucket from Kentucky Fried Chicken and a sticky, squashed drink box. Holding his breath, Hawk stuck his arm into the smelly garbage receptacle and rescued his brother's hard work.

Sitting down on the curb, Hawk opened the red folder and flipped through the pages.

"Wow! These plays are great!" he whispered excitedly to himself.

Helmet in one hand, red folder held tightly in the other, Hawk stood up. He needed to make one stop before he could go home. Bending over to pick up the Mountain Dew can, he threw it in the nearby recycling bin and took off running through the parking lot and down 6th Street.

Out on the track, Nestor (unaware that his special plays had just been pulled from the garbage) was running, too. He had four more laps to go.

August 19 - 7:12 pm EDT | Port Clinton, Ohio

Hawk stepped up onto the porch of 603 Grant Street. Calming himself with a deep breath, he knocked on the front door.

After waiting a few long seconds, Hawk lifted his hand to knock again when the door suddenly opened. There in front of him stood a tall, dark-haired man with hedge trimmers in his hand.

"Sorry, Mr. Kopecky. I hope I'm not interrupting you," stammered Hawk.

"No, not at all, Horace. I was just about to give Little John here a haircut," chuckled Big John Kopecky.

Hawk saw Little John Kopecky peeking around the leg of his father.

"You cut hair with those things?" asked Hawk, pointing at the large, pointy pair of shears.

Mr. Kopecky laughed. "No, I was joking! LJ and I were just out back cutting bushes, but I can give you a little trim. No charge!"

Little John Kopecky giggled behind his dad.

"That's okay. My mom cuts my hair. She does it for free, too," Hawk explained nervously. "Ah, is Killer...uh, I mean...your daughter home?"

"You call Kathy...Killer?" asked Mr. Kopecky with a grin.

"Yeah, but not to her face," answered Hawk, sheepishly.

"That's probably a good idea," said Mr. Kopecky, nodding. "Well... ah...Killer IS here. She got home from practice about 10 minutes ago. She's upstairs changing. You want me to call her down?"

"Yes, please, if you don't mind."

"Sure," smiled Big John and he turned and called up the stairway. "Kathy! Can you come down, please? Horace Hapburn is here to see you."

"Horace Hapburn?" replied a female voice. "What does he want?"

"I don't know, sweetheart...why don't you come to the front door and find out?"

Big John and Little John stood together and waited as Hawk fidgeted uncomfortably on the porch.

"Would you like to come inside?" asked Mr. Kopecky.

"No thanks. I'm fine out here," answered Hawk, preferring to keep a safe distance from the hedge trimmers.

Seconds later, they all heard the sound of footsteps coming down the stairs. Then, suddenly, at the front door, stood the quarterback of the Port Clinton Braves in a bright pink top and pajama pants with hearts on them. Her short, dark hair was still wet from her shower.

"Hello, Hawk. What are you doing here?" smiled Kathy, curious why a boy she'd never said more than two words to was at her front door.

"He calls you Killer," giggled Little John.

"You better get out of here before I kill you, you little pest!" snarled the suddenly-surly older sister.

"C'mon, LJ," laughed Mr. Kopecky. "Let's go out back and finish our trimming and we'll let these two talk."

Big John and Little John turned and disappeared, leaving the two Port Clinton Brave teammates at the front door, staring at each other.

Haw was suddenly struck by the fact that Killer Kopecky was pretty and he found himself tongue-tied. Without a word, he held up the red folder, hoping she'd take it.

"What's this?" asked Kathy, wrinkling her nose. "Do you want me to have this?"

Still unable to speak, Hawk nodded so hard and fast, he was lucky his head didn't roll off his shoulders.

"Okay, okay," replied Kathy, quickly grabbing the folder to prevent a bloody scene on her porch.

Realizing Hawk was having some sort of problem, she maneuvered him over to the front step. "Here, let's sit down and I'll look at what you brought over."

In a daze and weak in the knees, Hawk settled down on the top step next to the cute QB and tried to collect himself.

She flipped through the pages of the red folder and, every so often, she would murmur, "Oh, this is good!"...or..."I like this one!"

Once, as Killer was turning the page, their elbows touched, causing Hawk's heart to suddenly start beating at double speed.

After a few minutes, she closed the folder and turned toward Hawk.

"Wow! These plays are great!" gushed Killer. "Are these your ideas? Have the coaches seen them? Are you some kind of Einstein?"

Hawk, still struggling to find the ability for basic speech, blurted out his first word since Kathy Kopecky appeared in her doorway.

"NESTOR!" shouted Hawk, producing a big blast of air that nearly blew the red folder out of Killer Kopecky's hands.

"Nestor came up with these plays?" she asked, blinking.

Hawk started nodding his head hard and fast again.

Acting quickly to prevent any serious damage, Killer Kopecky placed her hand on Hawk's forehead and applied pressure.

"With these plays, we'd be unbeatable," said Killer Kopecky, after successfully bringing Hawk's head-bobbing to a complete stop. "You need to show them to the coaches!"

Taking a slow, deep breath, Hawk was finally able to string a few sentences together. He managed to explain what had just transpired at the football field and how Coach Hyde had tossed the folder in the trash, without glancing inside.

"He threw it away without looking?" snapped Killer. "What a rat!"

"Right!" agreed Hawk feeling both mad (about Coach Hyde) and glad (seeing Killer Kopecky angry) at the same time.

"So that's why I came over. I thought maybe you could somehow sneak one of Nestor's plays into our practice tomorrow."

"Great idea, Hawk!" replied the Braves' QB.

Hawk blushed as Killer opened the red folder again.

"Here! This one!" she said, pointing at the first play on the page. "It's pretty easy. I can quickly explain it to the guys in the huddle!"

"Okay, so what should I do?" asked Hawk, looking deep into Kathy Kopecky's big brown eyes.

"Tell Nestor what happened and what we're going to do, but don't tell anyone else, not even Michael. I'll see how practice is going and when the time is right, I'll call the secret play."

Hawk's head started nodding fast again, "Sounds good!"

Killer put her hand on Hawk's forehead one more time to stop his vigorous nodding and added one last instruction.

"Be sure to bring the Snickers bar."

"Got it!" replied Hawk, suddenly filled with happiness.

As they both stood up, ending their emergency meeting, Hawk was struck by a sudden impulse to kiss the little brown-haired girl. Scared at the thought, he took a shaky step backward and tumbled off the porch and rolled onto the sidewalk.

"I'm not hurt!" he exclaimed, jumping back to his feet quickly. "See you tomorrow!" He took off, without waiting to see Killer wave and go into her house.

Running toward home, Hawk worried about what had just happened.

"There's no way...no way..." Hawk mumbled to himself. "No way I want to kiss our quarterback."

Then, trying to leave that thought behind him, Hawk ran faster.

August 19 - 8:28 pm CDT | Monroe, Wisconsin

Floyd Dowler was face down on a dessert plate, snoring loudly in the Wozniak dining room. With each snore, he'd suck in some air and blow it back out, causing the babka cake crumbs to dance around his dish.

The meeting to discuss Operation Georgie Porgie was over and the rest of the Limburger Heads had headed home, leaving Einstein and Dairy Dan in the kitchen to clean up.

"They don't know the plan," complained Einstein, as he scoured a pan with baked-on tomato and cabbage. Steam rose from the sink full of hot water, creating an angry fog around his face.

"I have serious doubts about the success of our mission. Papa is old. Nick is fearful. Rick is a kid and Floyd..." Einstein paused and shook his head hopelessly. "Floyd is the worst. He chatters nonsense non-stop, he is constantly engaging in foolish games, and he does *not* pay attention...he is a ticking time bomb."

Rinsing the pan and handing it to Dairy Dan to dry, the unsettled Limburger Head continued his rant.

"In order to confiscate these statues, it is essential we operate as a fine-tuned machine. Everyone must be committed to their respective responsibilities and they must perform them with precision. Absolute and total concentration from every member of the team is paramount. One false move and the entire endeavor could blow up in our faces."

"Relax. The only things blowing up will be the stink bombs Helmut is making. With those, Operation Georgie Porgie will be so easy, a bunch of monkeys could pull it off," laughed Dairy Dan.

"I would prefer monkeys over the group we have now," muttered Einstein.

"Move over and let me finish washing those pots and pans," said Dairy Dan, pushing his short, stocky friend away from the sink. "All the steam from that hot water has your brain boiling. Stick your head in the refrigerator and cool down."

Einstein dried his chubby fingers on the towel and grumbled, "I'll go check the table and make sure we got it all cleaned off."

Hands dry, he shoved the swinging kitchen door open and looked around the dining room. His eyes stopped on Floyd, still face down on his dessert plate and still snoring.

"WAKE UP, FLOYD!" shouted the steaming hot Limburger Head. "Take your plate into the kitchen and go home!"

Without a word, Floyd popped out of his chair, picked up the dish on the dining room table and carried it into the kitchen. He dropped his plate in the dishwater, splashing Dairy Dan at the sink, and walked out the back door.

"Good night, Floyd!" called Dan as the door slammed shut.

A few seconds later, they heard Floyd's Chevy start up and drive away.

"What happened?" asked Dairy Dan as he placed a pan on the dish rack. "Did you make him mad? He didn't even say good-bye."

"That was extremely strange," answered Einstein. "No jokes, no smart remarks. He just did exactly as I instructed. And did you notice his eyes? They held a mysterious glaze as if he were…"

Dairy Dan jumped in and finished the sentence. "…like he was tired of listening to you yell and wanted to get out of here."

"I've got it," said Einstein, snapping his fingers. "Judging from the blank expression on his face and the fact that he left without a word, I believe he was in some sort of somnambulistic state."

"No. No, he's not," argued Dairy Dan. "Floyd lives in Wisconsin like the rest of us!"

"I'm not referencing a *state* state," said Einstein. "A somnambulistic state refers to somnambulism or noctambulism. It is a malady of the parasomnia family."

"What family?" asked the totally frustrated dairy farmer. "English, Einstein. Please, tell me what this is about in plain, ordinary English."

"Okay, in layman's terms," Einstein paused for a second and took a deep breath. "I believe he was sleepwalking."

Dairy Dan's jaw dropped and he mumbled, "Incredible," as he drained the water from the sink.

Einstein nodded. "And you know what is even more incredible?"

Dairy Dan blinked his eyes, waiting and wondering what his fellow Limburger Head would say next.

"Not only was our friend, Floyd Dowler, sleepwalking … he got in his car and he is now sleepdriving."

CHAPTER 3

August 20 - 7:37 am EDT | Port Clinton, Ohio
4 Days to Hall of Fame Game | 13 Days to Kickoff at Lambeau Field

Audrey Hapburn gave Hawk and Michael a kiss on the forehead and walked out of the kitchen to prepare for her first piano lesson of the day.

Once he was sure his Mom was a safe distance away in the living room, Hawk reached across the breakfast table and grabbed a chunk of Michael's arm between his thumb and index finger and squeezed hard.

"Ouch!" complained Michael between scarfing down spoonfuls of Count Chocula. "Cut it out before I knock your block off!"

"I'm just making sure you're awake," explained Hawk. "We've got to get going to practice in a couple minutes."

"Why didn't you make sure I was awake yesterday when Mom fixed French toast?"

Wiping his mouth with his napkin, Hawk ran out of the kitchen and up the stairs, leaving Michael at the table to finish his cereal.

Hawk burst through the bedroom door, with a loud bang. The noise startled Nestor, making him jump and bump his head hard on the bottom of the top bunk.

"Next time, yell before you come busting in like that," said Nestor, his heart pounding fast. "You scared me! I thought it was Michael."

"Did you get 'em?" whispered Hawk.

"Yeah, two snack-size Snicker candy bars, a package of peanut butter crackers and a strawberry fruit roll-up," answered Nestor as he zipped up Michael's backpack. "I had to sneak them out of his pantry."

Nestor handed the treats to Hawk. "Hide 'em 'til we get to the field."

"Okay, got it!" chirped Hawk. He tossed the goods in his helmet and then threw a couple of hip pads on top.

Nestor grabbed his equipment and gave Hawk a nudge. "Let's go before Michael shows up and finds out he's been robbed."

The brothers bounded down the stairs and into the kitchen where Michael was about to pour himself another bowl of cereal.

"Hey, stop!" shouted Nestor, grabbing the Count Chocula box out of Michael's hand. "We gotta go."

"Give it back! I'm still hungry," growled Michael.

Hawk grabbed his brother's helmet and handed it to him. "C'mon, Michael! If we're late, Coach Hyde will make us run extra laps."

"Okay, but first I'm going to grab a couple snacks out of my backpack," said Michael, turning to head upstairs.

At that moment, the three Hapburns heard the sound of scales being played on the living room piano.

"Too late!" said Nestor, turning his bigger brother and pointing him toward the back door. "Piano lessons have started. You know what Mom says: No running up and down the stairs during lessons."

Michael let out a groan and followed Nestor and Hawk out the door.

Catching up with his brothers out on the street, Michael lifted his nose and sniffed the air like a scent hound. "I smell snacks. Which one of you guys has candy?"

Pretending they didn't hear him, Hawk and Nestor walked faster.

Driven by his powerful appetite, Michael refused to be left behind. He blurted out the word "chocolate" and picked up his pace.

Seeing that Michael was gaining on them, Nestor gave Hawk a quick jab with his elbow and whispered with quiet urgency, "Run!"

Michael took off after his brothers, shouting, "Stop now and nobody gets hurt!"

The five-minute walk to practice turned into a two-minute sprint.

The three Hapburns ran onto the football field at top speed a full ten minutes early. Some of the other players who were dragging themselves to the 8am session stopped and stared as the brothers roared by.

"That's what I like to see," applauded the gigantic Coach Yak. "Kids excited to get to practice!"

Holding up his massive hand, Coach Yak waved Michael over, forcing him to give up the chase.

Hawk, his heart beating fast from his pre-practice run, quickly scanned the group of players by the sideline. There, sitting on the bench, he saw Killer Kopecky with the red folder open on her lap, studying Nestor's secret plays.

Walking over to her, Hawk's heart started beating even faster.

"Kathy, we've got the stuff," gushed Hawk as he held out his helmet.

"Call me Killer," she said without looking up from the folder. "I like that better."

Hawk, still finding it difficult to speak to the cute QB, blinked and struggled to start over. "Okay, ah, Killer…we've got the stuff."

"Dump it in here," she instructed, throwing the red folder into her pink duffle under the bench. Hawk took the hip pads out of his helmet and dumped the snacks into the duffle.

She zipped it shut, put her hand on Hawk's shoulder and whispered in his ear. "When the time is right, tell Nestor I'll sneak the Snickers to him and we'll run the play."

Hawk, woozy from their heads being so close, nodded weakly and tried to breathe. Killer's hair smelled like cotton candy.

On the other side of the field, Nestor was waiting for Michael to trudge back from his pre-practice meeting with Coach Yak.

"What did coach want?" asked Nestor.

"I think he just was checking to make sure I wasn't still talking about French toast." Then, shifting his eyes to the sideline, he saw his brother with the team's quarterback. "Why is Hawk over there with Killer?"

"Hawk's with Killer?" replied Nestor blankly, trying to come up with an excuse. "I don't know…maybe he likes her."

"Her? No way," said Michael, shaking his head. "She's a girl!"

"TWEEEEEEEEEEEEEEEEEEEEEEET!"

Standing at midfield, Coach Yak let the whistle fall from his mouth.

"Okay! Offense over there with Coach Jekyll. Defense on this side with Coach Hyde. We'll do some stretching first, then some running and then, we'll start banging shoulder pads!"

Ninety minutes into the morning practice, the team wasn't looking any better than it did on the day before. There were dozens of dropped balls, more sloppy tackling and multiple penalties on every play.

Time after time, the defense would line up wrong, causing Coach Hyde to throw his arms up and yell at the sky.

"Linemen should be lining up along the LINE of scrimmage... that's where LINEmen belong. Linebackers should be BACK behind the linemen, BACKING them up. That's why they call them line-BACKERS!"

On offense, Coach Jekyll was trying to be patient despite the fact that every play he tried to call - *"Let's run Double Wing-Full Back Wedge-Dive Right on three!"*- was met with twenty questions.

"Am I supposed to block 36? What if he's on the bench?"

"I studied Wishbone Z Motion-Tight Left! Can we run that one?"

"My favorite flavor of ice cream is chocolate. What's your favorite flavor, Coach?"

On the sideline, Coach Yak was occupied in a life-and-death struggle, swatting all the bees swarming around the Gatorade table.

"Land, you sucker, so I can put an end to your miserable...OUCH! He got me!"

Finally, with less than a half-hour of practice remaining, Killer pulled Nestor aside.

"It's time," she whispered, slipping him the snack-size Snickers bar.

In the huddle, Killer changed the play called by Coach Jekyll. "Pay attention, everybody! We're going to run Snickers Halfback Sweep Right," she announced with authority.

Everybody in the huddle began talking at once.

"Snickers Sweep?" asked Frankie Fitzwater, the flat-nosed center.

"But we're s'posed to run Right 32 Dive," objected Stinky Smothers.

"That's not in our playbook. What's my assignment?" whined Ray Ray McKay.

"Snickers? I'm hungry," moaned Michael.

"Quiet!" demanded Killer. "It's a new play and it's going to work! Now, listen up!"

The huddle fell silent as the plucky quarterback took control. She got face mask-to-face mask with her running back.

"Michael, one of our three receivers has a Snickers bar…"

Immediately, Michael's eyes lit up as he looked around at the huddle. "Who's got a Snickers?" asked the hungry Hapburn.

"When I call the signals, the third number I shout…*that* will be the player with the Snickers. Understand?" asked Killer.

Michael nodded and the Braves' QB continued explaining the play.

"I'll take the snap from Frankie and hand the ball to you. Then you chase whoever has the Snickers and when you catch up to him, you can trade the ball for the candy bar. But if you get tackled, Michael…"

She paused a moment to make sure this next point was completely understood. "…you do not get the Snickers. Got it?"

"Yep! I've got it and I'm going to get it. Let's go!" shouted Michael.

"What should the rest of us do?" asked Ray Ray McKay.

"Everybody else can just block or not. It doesn't matter," Killer replied. "Just stay out of Michael's way." Then, again speaking directly into her running back's grill, "Remember: listen for the third number I call. Snap count's on two! Ready…"

"Break," they all shouted in unison.

The offense marched up to the line of scrimmage. As Killer took her place under center, she studied the defensive set on the other side. Then, after a quick glance at her receivers on her right and left, she shouted out the signals.

"OMAHA…eighty-nine…eight…ONE…"

Standing behind Killer in the running back position, Michael quickly scanned the jerseys in front of him. Number 89……8…… then his eyes found the prize……number 1, spread far to the right.

Michael licked his lips and whispered to himself, "Nestor has the Snickers!"

"READY…SET…HUT-HUT!"

As soon as Frankie Fitzwater heard the second HUT, he snapped the football between his legs, slapping it hard into Killer Kopecky's hand. Turning to her right, she held the ball out for Michael, who roared forward to take the hand-off.

With both arms firmly around the ball, Michael looked up and saw Nestor streaking down the right sideline toward the end zone. Like a bull, Michael broke three tackles and busted through the line, dancing around defensive players trying to trip him up.

Charging past midfield, middle linebacker Moses Kupperman made a desperate dive at Michael's knees, but the suddenly-unstoppable running back hurdled over him in hot pursuit of the Snickers bar.

At the twenty-five, Hayes Herman and Bobby Kargosian each latched on to a meaty thigh and tried to slow him down. But before reinforcements could arrive, the monster truck-sized Michael executed a surprisingly-graceful 360-degree pirouette, which sent the pesky little DBs flying off in opposite directions.

Up ahead, Michael saw Nestor cruising into the end zone. Now, all that remained between him and his snack was twenty yards of green grass and number 23, Hawk Hapburn.

Even though Hawk wanted Michael to score to prove to the coaches Nestor's plays would work, he still had his job to do. And his job was to stop the ball carrier before he crossed the goal line.

Both players were tearing up the turf at top speed. The lighter, faster Hapburn had the angle and caught up to his bigger brother at the ten-yard line. Then, with the running back locked in his sites, Hawk launched his body *like a rocket* at his target.

At that exact moment, Michael stopped dead in his tracks letting the human missile fly past him and explode harmlessly on the field a few yards away.

Hawk, on the ground with a hunk of sod stuck in his face mask, looked up in time to see Michael roar into the end zone and straight over to Nestor who was standing under the goalpost.

"Here!" shouted Michael, handing his brother the football. "Now, give me the Snickers!"

A split-second after Nestor tossed the treat to Michael, he had it unwrapped and was biting down.

Ten-thousand taste buds in the running back's mouth immediately started cheering and a split-second after that, they were joined by the surprised and happy Port Clinton Braves team.

"What a run!" yelled Stinky Smothers' brother.

"That'll be the #1 play on ESPN's Sports Center!" exclaimed Ray Ray McKay, pounding on Michael's shoulder pads with excitement.

"Hit the rock!" laughed Frankie Flat-Nosed Fitzwater, offering his teammate a fast fist bump.

That's when Coach Yak came huffing and puffing into the end zone.

"Where did that play come from? That isn't in our book!"

Killer held up her arm like she was answering a question in class, "I called the play, Coach," she said. Then turning, she pointed at Nestor, standing between his two brothers, "but he's the one who invented it."

The heads of all three coaches, Yak, Jekyll and Hyde, swiveled in the direction of the three Hapburns.

Hawk, thinking they were in trouble, spoke up.

"It's my fault. I'm the one who talked Killer into trying that play."

"Killer? Who's that?" asked Coach Yak, scratching his head.

Nervous, the players stood around choking on their chuckles as Coach Jekyll leaned and whispered something in the ear of his boss.

"Kopecky?" blurted out the head coach, directing the question at Hawk. "You call Kopecky...*Killer?*"

"Ye-ye-yes sir," stammered Hawk. "She said I could."

Coach Hyde leaned in close to his two coaches and whispered, "It's a pretty good name. Maybe we should have her play defense, too."

"Excuse me, Coach Yak..."

The trio of coaches lifted their heads in unison again, and, this time, it was Nestor speaking.

"If anyone is to blame, it's me. I'm the one who came up with that play. If you want me to run extra laps..."

"Blame?" laughed Coach Yak. "I don't want to blame anyone! That play was great! I want to know more about it and why it worked!"

Coach Jekyll snapped his fingers and jumped into the conversation.

"Coach! Remember yesterday when Nestor stopped us and wanted to make a few modifications to our scheme?"

"Oh, yeah," replied Yak wiping the sweat off his forehead with his sleeve. "So, you told him to go ahead?"

"No, I told him not to bother and to trust us to do what's best for the team. But it's a good thing he didn't listen to me because look! That was a pretty good play he drew up!"

"It was a GREAT play," shouted the large and suddenly-inspired head coach. "What do you call it?"

"That's Snickers Halfback Sweep Right…it's like the regular Sweep Right in the playbook only with the Snickers added to it."

"Snickers?" asked Yakunshenko.

"Yeah, that's the important part," explained Nestor. "See, I thought if Michael had a reason to run - some motivation - he'd be impossible to stop. And nothing motivates my brother more than food."

"Oh, sure. I understand that," said the 400-pound ex-Ohio State lineman. "So, do you have any more of these tasty plays?"

"Yeah, I do! A whole folder full! I gave it to…" Nestor's excitement came to a screeching halt. He realized if he called out Coach Hyde for throwing the red folder in the trash, the crabby coach might make him run extra laps until Thanksgiving.

Coach Yak waited a few long seconds for Nestor to continue, then Coach Hyde, deciding he couldn't hide what he had done any longer, finally spoke up.

"Well, yesterday after practice," started Coach Hyde sheepishly. "Ah, Hapburn, I mean Nestor, gave me the folder and I threw it…"

"…to me!" interrupted Killer, saving Coach Hyde from revealing his secret.

Running quickly over to her pink duffle bag, she pulled out the smudged red folder and handed it to her head coach.

"Here it is, Coach!"

Yak licked his thick index finger each time he flipped a page and muttered quietly to himself, "Wow…these plays are great."

Smiling for the first time since recovering a fumble in the fourth quarter of an Ohio State/Michigan game during college, he passed the folder to Assistant Coach Jekyll.

"Make copies and pass them out to the team at this afternoon's practice."

"Yes, sir!" saluted the skinny offensive coordinator.

Coach Hyde, realizing he wasn't in any trouble for tossing the folder, quietly heaved a sigh of relief and clapped his hands as the big Coach Yak happily barked, "Huddle up!"

The twenty-five teammates gathered around him in a tight circle.

"Be here for conditioning with Coach Hyde this afternoon at 5. Tomorrow, we'll start practice with…" Coach Yak paused and looked in the red folder, "…Peanut Butter Crackers Reverse.

"TEAM on three! Ready? One…two…THREE…"

"TEAM!" yelled 24 players in unison. The 25th player, Stinky Smothers' brother, was still yelling *"EAM"* after everyone else had turned to walk away.

....

Dairy Dan was shoving the last bite of a grilled cheese sandwich in his mouth when his cell phone started ringing. Looking down at the display, he recognized the number. It was Helmut Lundquist calling from the Chalet Cheese Co-op.

"Hello, Helmut! I was gonna call you after lunch. What's up?"

"I've been working on the stink bombs all morning and I think I finally got it," came the excited reply. "I'm afraid I killed a few grasshoppers trying to come up with the right combination of smelly cheese. Now I'm ready to test it on the neighbor's cat."

"No need to waste time testing it on a cat," declared Dairy Dan. "Let's go over to Baumgartner's and try it on the lunch crowd."

"Experiment on live people? I'm not ready for that," replied Helmut nervously.

"Oh, don't worry! It'll be fine! Meet me over at the Tavern in ten minutes and bring the stink bombs."

Shoving his cell phone in his pocket and piling the dirty dishes in the sink, Dairy Dan ran out of the house and jumped in his truck. If the stink bombs worked, the Limburger Heads would be off to the Hall of Fame to go bear hunting.

....

Cheese Master Helmut Lundquist was pacing up and down the sidewalk in front of Baumgartner's Tavern when Dairy Dan pulled up in his truck.

"It's pretty busy in there. Maybe we should just come back later," suggested Helmut.

"Are you kidding? This is the perfect time!" laughed Dan. "The Hall of Fame will be busy like this. We need to know whether or not these work in a crowd. Did you bring the stink bombs?"

"Yep, two of 'em," said Helmut, holding up a brown grocery bag.

Dairy Dan smiled and gave the fidgety cheese master a reassuring pat on the back.

"Great! Let's go stink up the joint!"

The two Limburger Heads walked in the restaurant and sat at an open table in the front room near the door. The place was jumping, just like Helmut had reported. In the back room corner, the Taleggio Trio was adding to the commotion by playing the Flying Car Polka.

"Look! Floyd's over there, playing the tuba," shouted Helmut, trying to be heard over all the noise. "Should we let him know we're conducting an experiment?"

"How come it's called the Taleggio Trio? There are four people in that band," wondered Dairy Dan out loud.

"When Floyd joined, they already had three guys in the group and they didn't want to change their name," answered Helmut with tears in his eyes.

"What's the matter? Why are you crying?" asked Dan, handing his friend a handkerchief.

Helmut wiped his eyes and blew his nose. "I can't help it. Flying Car Polka always makes me cry," replied Helmut as he handed back

Dairy Dan's snot rag.

Dairy Dan slid his now-slimy handkerchief in his pocket, reached into the grocery bag and pulled out two mason jars filled with a yellow-green ooze.

"How should we do this?" asked Dan, holding up a jar.

"Here's what I think: You take a stink bomb over to that corner," instructed the cheese master, pointing to the back of the restaurant. "I'll take a stink bomb to the opposite corner and when I hold up my hand, we'll take the lids off the jars, which will activate the bombs."

"Sounds simple enough," smiled Dairy Dan. "I'm ready!"

With a worried look, Helmut sighed and handed Dan a clothespin.

"What's this for?" laughed the leader of the Limburger Heads.

"Before you activate your stink bomb, clip it on your nose. That way you won't pass out from the fumes," explained Helmut. "You want me to give a clothespin to Floyd, too?"

Dairy Dan looked over to where Floyd was happily huffing and puffing on his tuba. The Taleggio Trio now had the entire tavern tapping their toes to the lively Wiener Schnitzel Polka.

"No, no time for that. Besides, using Floyd as a guinea pig might be good. When it's over, he might be able to tell us something important."

This appealed to Helmut's scientific brain. "That's true," he said nodding his head and clipping the clothespin on his nose.

***Instructions to the reader:* When the dialogue is <u>underlined</u>, hold your nose with your thumb and index finger and read the <u>underlined words out loud</u>. This is how the Limburger Heads sound when they talk with clothespins on their noses.**

<u>"Okay, let's take our positions. When I give the signal, we unscrew the lids to our stink bombs."</u>

Dairy Dan clipped on the clothespin to his nose and the two Limburger Heads got up from the table and squeezed through the crowd to opposite corners of the restaurant.

The loud and lively mob was so busy dancing, singing, eating and having fun, they didn't even notice Dairy Dan and Helmut roaming the room with clothespins on their noses.

Ready to give the signal, Helmut took a deep breath through his mouth and waved his arm.

Floyd looked up from his sheet music that exact instant and saw Helmut waving in the corner.

Thinking his friend was waving at him, Floyd was about to wave back. But before he could lift his hand, Dairy Dan and Helmut took the lids off the stink bombs and a powerful and foul odor exploded through Baumgartner's Cheese Store & Tavern, attacking the nostrils of every living and breathing creature inside.

Everyone eating lunch went face down in the food on their plate. The dozen or so people kicking up their heels on the dance floor collapsed on the spot. The four members of the Taleggio Trio, who were joyously making music, went suddenly limp, slumping over on their instruments. Even a mouse, munching on a few crumbs in a dark corner of the restaurant, passed out mid-munch.

The only people still awake and alert were the two Limburger Heads with clothespins on their noses.

Dairy Dan looked around the suddenly stone-cold silent restaurant and clapped his hands.

"You did it, Helmut! The stink bombs worked!"

Walking to a table in the middle of the restaurant, Dairy Dan grabbed a Pastrami and Swiss sandwich off a customer's plate.

"Hey, that's Mayor Barney's sandwich!" protested Helmut as Dairy Dan took a big juicy bite.

"That's the Mayor? With his head down in that bowl of potato salad, I didn't recognize him," laughed Dairy Dan wiping his mouth with his sleeve. "When he wakes up, I bet he doesn't even notice."

"If he wakes up," answered the cheese master, not yet ready to celebrate success. "Maybe we better deactivate the stink bombs."

"Okay-okay...quit worrying," said Dairy Dan, putting the Pastrami sandwich back on Mayor Barney's plate. "Let's screw the lids back on and open up the door to let some fresh air in."

Helmut nodded and, quickly, the two Limburger Heads sealed the stink bombs and carefully placed them back in the bag. They took one last look around the crowded and completely quiet restaurant before walking to the front and propping the door open.

Out on the sidewalk, they removed the clothespins from their noses and then peered in the window to see what would happen next.

Nervously, Helmut checked his watch, "it should only take 15-seconds or so and they should start…"

"Look! They're waking up!" interrupted Dairy Dan. Congratulating the cheese master with a slap on the back. "See! You did it!"

Helmut let out a sigh of relief as people started opening their eyes and yawning as if they were waking up from a nap. A minute later, it was as if nothing had happened at all. Baumgartner's customers went back to eating, including the mayor. Everyone on the dance floor was back up off the floor and twirling around. And all four members of the Taleggio Trio picked up where they left off, huffing and puffing at their instruments.

Smiling, the two Limburger heads walked back into the restaurant. Besides being a little stuffier, nothing was different from the first time they'd come in fifteen minutes before.

Just as they were ready to sit down, the music stopped and Floyd Dowler was waving and walking toward them.

"We're on break…let's go outside for a few minutes. It sort of smells like stinky socks in here," said Floyd, turning his friends around and nudging them toward the front door. "Hey, what's with those red marks on your noses?"

CHAPTER 4

August 21 – 8:48 am EDT | Port Clinton, Ohio
3 Days to Hall of Fame Game | 12 Days to Kickoff at Lambeau Field

The Port Clinton Braves were forty-five minutes into their morning practice. The team was in high spirits and looking sharp.

Every time they would run one of Nestor's trick-treat plays…Fruit Roll-Up Flat Curl;Peanut Butter Crackers Reverse; Snickers Right… Michael would score. As long as he knew he could exchange the football for a snack, the hungry Hapburn was unstoppable.

The last play of the day, Hawk latched on to Michael at midfield and the 12 year old, 200-pound running back refused to be tackled, dragging his brother 50 yards for a touchdown.

For the last twenty yards, Jimbo Banks and Moses Kupperman piled on, too, but that didn't even slow him down. After crossing the goal line, Michael simply tossed the football to Nestor and demanded his Twinkie.

Watching the incredible show from the sidelines, the coaches were amazed. Just the day before, the Braves were a stumbling, bumbling bunch of bums. Now all of a sudden, they were playing like Super Bowl champions.

Coach Yak was shouting encouragement and patting the players on the back after every play. Coach Jekyll was jumping up and down with excitement and fist-bumping everyone on the field. Even the horrible Coach Hyde was a lot less horrible since Nestor, Killer and Hawk saved him from revealing his embarrassing secret about the red folder.

"TWEEEEEEEEEEEEEEEEEEEEET!"

Standing at midfield, Coach Yak let the whistle fall from his mouth and motioned for the team to gather around him.

"Great practice today! We're looking good," boomed the happy head coach. "And because you've worked so hard, Coach Hyde says we're skipping afternoon practice."

"No running?" blurted out Stinky Smothers.

"No puking?" added Frankie Flat-Nosed Fitzwater.

"That's right!" laughed Yak. "You guys…and ah, gal…you have the rest of the day off!"

The team let out a loud cheer. Some of the players even patted Coach Hyde on the back, including Hawk, who was glad his aching body would have a chance to recover from the beating it had taken trying to tackle his brother all morning.

"We'll see you here tomorrow morning…only two more practices before our scrimmage with the Bulldogs on Sunday," barked big Coach Yak in his serious voice. "Use your extra time today to study your playbook. Know their assignments frontwards and backwards."

"TEAM on three! Ready? One…two…THREE…"

"TEAM!" yelled the members of the now powerhouse Port Clinton Braves. And this time, even Stinky Smothers' brother shouted it out with everyone else.

There was a lot of chatter and energy as the players picked up their football gear and headed off in different directions.

Hawk rushed to the sideline, kicked off his cleats and reached into his duffle bag for his sneakers. Quickly tying his shoes, he stood up and looked around. His eyes darted back and forth from the field to the parking lot until finally, they stopped on Killer Kopecky hugging her dad next to a white mini-van.

He watched as she shoved her little brother out of the way and jumped into the front seat.

"Rats! He picked her up," sighed Hawk, shoving his cleats in his bag.

"What's the matter?" asked Nestor as he caught up to his brother on the sideline.

"Nothing," groaned the unhappy Hapburn.

Up ahead, Michael was waving and shouting to his two sibs, "C'mon! We have time to play a game of chess at Mrs. McChesney's before lunch!"

"Great practice, huh!" chirped Nestor. "We're going to destroy those Bulldogs on Sunday!"

"Sure, you can say it's a great practice. YOU don't have to get run over by the runaway truck up there," complained Hawk, pointing in Michael's direction.

"I'm glad about that," admitted Nestor. "But at least we don't have practice this afternoon. That's a good thing. And Coach Hyde sure is being nicer right now!"

"That IS good," agreed Hawk, allowing Nestor to help him out of his funk about missing the chance to walk home with Killer. "I can't wait 'til the game on Sunday. When those Bulldogs try and tackle our brother, they won't believe what hit 'em!"

"And we get to tour the Hall of Fame! It's gonna be great!" said Nestor, giving Hawk a playful shove.

"Ouchhh! Don't touch me, I am one big bruise," grimaced Hawk while managing a painful chuckle.

Nestor and Hawk stopped walking at Mrs. McChesney's house and watched as Michael finished setting up the lawn gnome chess pieces in the front yard. Energized by all the extra snacks at football practice, Michael buzzed quickly back and forth in a blur.

Picking up the smiling red queen gnome that had wandered over to sniff the roses near the front porch, Michael placed her on the brown square of mulch next to her red king resting on a green square of grass.

"Ready," proclaimed the Braves star running back, waving for Hawk to join him. "Today is the day we beat Nestor!"

Nestor smiled as Michael and Hawk put their heads together to discuss their strategy.

"Ready! One...two...THREE...TEAM!" they shouted as they broke the huddle and moved the bishop's pawn two spaces forward.

Nestor quickly responded by moving his King's pawn two spaces. A fast and ferocious back and forth flurry of activity followed, ending with Nestor surrounding Michael and Hawk's King with two knights and a bishop.

"Checkmate!" said Nestor, wiping his hands together to punctuate dusting off his adversaries. "Game over."

"Wow!" shouted Hawk. "We lasted seven moves!"

"Yeah! Seven moves!" laughed Michael, pumping his fist in the air and taunting his lightweight sib with a chant. "Seven moves! Seven moves! Seven moves!"

"Yeah, so? I still won! How do you like them French fries?" sneered Nestor.

"I like my fries with chili cheese, thank you," replied Michael happily as he turned to head home for lunch. "I also like waffle fries, curly fries, sweet potato fries, shoestring fries, steak fries, crinkle-cut fries…"

Nestor and Hawk stood among the lawn gnome chess pieces in Mrs. McChesney's front yard and watched as their brother walked away, naming French fries. After he bounced up the front steps and into the house, the other two Hapburns picked up their gear on the neighbor's lawn and started down the sidewalk.

"Coach Yak wants me to make a list of the trick-treat plays so he can pick up the snacks we need for the game on Sunday," said Nestor. "I'm thinking I should write down some healthy stuff like maybe… raisins or granola bars."

Hawk wrinkled his nose, "Granola bars?"

"Yeah! You know Michael, he'll eat anything. And we don't want him getting fat," said Nestor.

"Too late for that," laughed Hawk.

"Well, if, you haven't noticed, with all the running Michael's been doing, he's in pretty good shape."

"He's harder, for sure! He's like that brick wall Stinky Smothers' brother was crashing into. At least that's what it feels like when I'm trying to tackle him," moaned Hawk, rubbing his sore shoulder.

"Hey, I know! Maybe I'll run over to Killer's house later and see what she thinks. I bet she knows about healthy stuff you can eat."

"That's a good idea," nodded Nestor as the brothers walked across the lawn toward the Hapburn front door. "You know, at first I wasn't sure I liked having a girl on our team, especially playing quarterback. But now, I don't even think of her as a girl … just my teammate."

"I think she's pretty," gushed Hawk, skipping up the front steps close behind his brother.

Suddenly Nestor stopped and Hawk crashed into him. With a loud THUD, they both rolled into the house in a heap on the floor.

"Killer? Pretty?" asked Nestor, rubbing his head from the bottom of the two-body pileup.

Hawk blushed as he fumbled around to pick up his helmet and duffle bag. "I mean, she's pretty…uh, smart. Yeah, pretty smart."

"Lunchtime" called Audrey Hapburn from the kitchen, saving Hawk from any further explanation.

Immediately, the brother's bedroom door upstairs flew open and Michael came thundering down the stairs and past Nestor and Hawk.

"Outta my way!" shouted Michael with a push and a shove. "I'm hungry!"

....

Dairy Dan's Ford truck was kicking up gravel as it thundered down the bumpy dirt road toward home. He was supposed to meet Einstein there at one o'clock and he was late. Buckled down on the seat next to him was a case of Helmut Lundquist's special stink bombs.

When he pulled in the driveway of his Packer green and gold farm house, Einstein was waving a large envelope over his shiny, bald head.

"I have procured the vouchers for the Packer motorcoach excursion to Canton," shouted Einstein.

"You got the bus tickets?" asked Dairy Dan as he walked around to the passenger side of the truck to unload the stink bombs.

"That's an affirmative," said Einstein with a salute. "I also obtained six additional vouchers for our special guests on the return trip."

Dairy Dan patted the top of Einstein's smooth noggin. "Good thinking! We can sit the statues on seats at the back of the bus where they won't get noticed."

"My thoughts exactly," agreed Einstein. "And what about our secret weapon? Was the cheese master able to concoct the correct combination of malodorous cheeses to incapacitate a crowd for a specified period of time?"

"Touchdown!" crowed Dairy Dan raising both arms up above his head. "Helmut and I tested the stink bombs at Baumgartner's yesterday and as soon as we unscrewed the lids…WHAM! Everyone was out like a light! It was amazing!"

"And the question of side effects?" queried Einstein.

"Side effects?" repeated Dairy Dan as he hoisted the wooden crate loaded with stink bombs out of the truck and up on his front porch. "Whaddya mean?"

"Did you perceive any harmful or detrimental results from your experiment?" explained Einstein.

"Oh, you mean did anybody need to go to the hospital? Nope, nothing like that. After we put the lids back on the jars, everybody woke up like nothing happened," answered the head Limburger Head. "In fact, Floyd and his Taleggio Trio were at Baumgartner's jammin' and he never knew what hit him or that he had even been hit!"

"Excellent!" said Einstein smiling broadly. "Speaking of Floyd…"

"Yeah, what about him?" sighed Dairy Dan, wondering what his bald-headed friend would say next.

"Do you recall how troubled I was about him as well as his ability to carry out our plan?"

Einstein paused, allowing Dairy Dan time to give a nod.

"Do you also recall the other evening after his large dinner, he slipped into a somnambulistic state during which he followed my instructions precisely without arguing or uttering a frivolous remark?"

"You said he was sleepwalking. So what?" responded Dairy Dan.

"I believe upon arrival at the Football Hall of Fame," continued the big-brained Limburger Head, "If we provide him with a sufficient number of cabbage rolls to render him somnolent, I am convinced Floyd can successfully sleepwalk, as you say, through our entire mission!"

Dairy Dan scratched his head and chuckled. "Okay. I think I agree with everything you said. Tell them to be at Baumgartner's tomorrow night at eight for a final walk-through. Oh, and don't say anything about this sleepwalking stuff to anybody. That's between me and you."

Once again, Einstein straightened up and saluted his leader. Then, after handing Dairy Dan the envelope containing the tickets, he shouted: "Seize the cheese!"

Marching down the steps, he jumped in his car and drove off.

Dairy Dan watched until Einstein turned onto the gravel road in front of his farmhouse. Once his friend was out of sight, he rubbed his hands together in excitement. Everything was falling into place.

Pulling a screwdriver out of his back pocket, Dairy Dan pried off the lid to the wooden crate on his front porch and grabbed one of the stink bombs. As he held the jar close to his face for inspection, the light caught the gold and green ooze just right causing it to sparkle.

"Beautiful," he whispered.

....

Michael was lying on his back in the middle of the brother's bedroom floor, tossing a squishy football up toward the ceiling and catching it.

Nestor was at the computer, working on the list of snacks for Coach Yak while Hawk peered over his brother's shoulder to supervise.

"Can you think of anything else?" asked Nestor.

Hawk put his beak closer to the screen and read the list out loud.

Top Secret Trick-Treat Plays *(Property of Port Clinton Braves)*
Snickers Halfback Sweep Left
Snickers Halfback Sweep Right
Peanut Butter Crackers Reverse
Fruit Roll-Up Flat Curl
Twinkie Off Tackle
Oats & Honey Granola Bar Blast
Raisins Right 34 Slam

"It's good. Print it out and I'll run it over to Killer and see what she thinks," Hawk announced.

"Get rid of raisins and put chili dogs on the list!" shouted Michael, still playing catch on the floor with the squishy football.

"I'll go over to Killer's with you," said Nestor, ignoring Michael and hitting *Print*.

"It doesn't take two of us to deliver a list," moaned Hawk.

Nestor pulled the list of plays off the printer and shoved it in his pocket. "Yeah, you're right. You chill here and I'll go."

"Why you?" asked Hawk in desperation.

"You know…in case she has questions," explained Nestor.

"Or how about barbecued chicken wings?" suggested Michael, making yummy noises.

"On second thought, maybe we should both go," said Hawk, heading toward the bedroom door. "Since we don't have practice this afternoon, we can jog over to her house and get some exercise."

"That's a great idea!" agreed Nestor, following Hawk out of the room and down the steps. "You wanna come, Michael?"

Michael stopped tossing the football to consider the invitation. "Exercise?" he mumbled. He shook his head no.

Nestor and Hawk rushed out of the house and started jogging down Look Out Drive toward Taft Street. On the corner of Look Out and Taft, they waved at Mrs. McChesney who was on her front lawn, moving her gnomes around.

Turning right on Taft, left on Adams and then right again onto Grant Street, Nestor slowly picked up the pace. "C'mon, Hawk! Let's race the rest of the way!"

"Let's not," objected Hawk. "I don't want to get too sweaty."

"Since when are you worried about getting sweaty?" asked Nestor, slowing back down to an easy jog.

"I heard Frankie Fitzwater is digging for buried treasure at Portage Park," said Hawk, trying to change the subject. "He says there's a pirate grave over there."

"If you don't sweat, you're not exercising very hard. Sweating is good for you," said Nestor. "It creates an invisible force field against germs."

"I bet Frankie's gonna get sweaty digging for that treasure. It's kind of hot today," said Hawk as Killer's house came into view. "Okay, that's enough running. Let's walk the rest of the way and cool down."

"Cool down? We didn't heat up!" complained Nestor.

Hawk pretended to wipe perspiration off his forehead with his sleeve, patted down his hair and gave his brother a cheesy smile. "How do I look?"

"You're asking me how you look?" Nestor shook his head in disbelief. "Oh wow, you're scaring me."

The brothers turned on the sidewalk and stepped up on the porch of 603 Grant Street. His heart beating fast, Hawk knocked on Killer's front door.

A couple of seconds later, the door opened and Little John Kopecky was standing there with a shovel in his hands.

"Hi John," said Hawk, greeting the young Kopecky with a wave. "Is Killer...I mean, Kathy home?"

From deeper inside, they heard a man's voice. "Who is it, Johnny?"

"It's that kid again and another kid," shouted Little John Kopecky over his shoulder into the house. "From the football team."

Little John was joined at the front door by his dad, Big John, who was also holding a shovel.

"Oh, hi Horace! Hi Nestor!" said Big John Kopecky with a smile. "Do you guys want to come with us and dig for buried treasure at Portage Park?"

"No thank you, Mr. Kopecky," answered Nestor politely. "Horace doesn't want to get sweaty today."

"Mr. Kopecky, we're here on official football business," explained Hawk. "We need to talk to Kathy, if it's okay."

"You mean Killer?" questioned Big John with a chuckle. "She went shopping with her mom to buy a new dress for the team trip to the Hall of Fame. They probably won't be back for another two hours."

"Gone shopping?" repeated Hawk, his voice full of disappointment.

"If it's important, I can call Mrs. Kopecky on her cell and tell them to come home now," offered Mr. Kopecky.

Hawk's face suddenly brightened, "Yes, could you do that?"

"No, no…you don't have to do that," interrupted Nestor. "But could you give her this when she gets home and have her call us?"

"We sure can," smiled Big John as Nestor handed him the list of plays and snacks.

Nestor turned away and tugged on Hawk's arm. "C'mon, Horace. Let's go."

Head down, Hawk sighed and slowly followed Nestor down the front porch steps.

"Good luck at the Hall of Fame game on Sunday! We'll be there watching!" shouted Mr. Kopecky as the brothers moved along the sidewalk.

"Good luck digging for treasure," shouted Hawk in return with a sad, weak wave.

The two Hapburns were both in deep thought as they walked back down Grant Street toward home. After a couple of minutes, Nestor finally broke the silence.

"Our quarterback is out buying a new dress," said Nestor shaking his head. "I hope the other team doesn't find out about this."

"I hope it's pink," whispered Hawk. "She looks pretty in pink."

Nestor's head snapped around. "What did you say?"

Hawk, realizing he may have whispered a little too loud, gave his brother a playful shove and a challenge. "Race you home!"

"You'll get sweaty," warned Nestor.

"Since when has getting sweaty bugged me?" crabbed Hawk. "Ready?"

"Sure," shrugged Nestor.

"Okay…1-2-3…GO!" shouted Hawk.

Hawk and Nestor took off like they were shot out of a cannon as they flew over the pavement, running side-by-side. Turning on Adams Street, Hawk managed to take the lead. On Taft Street, Hawk was a good ten feet ahead of his shorter-legged brother.

As Hawk rounded the corner of Look Out Drive, he glanced back over his shoulder to see how far behind Nestor was.

He never noticed that Mrs. McChesney, who was still in her yard moving lawn gnomes around, had left the King Gnome in the middle of the sidewalk.

"Look out!" Nestor yelled to warn his brother of the impending danger.

Hawk turned his head forward a split second before he crashed into the two-foot tall monarch blocking his path. Popping up in the air, Hawk did a complete somersault and skidded to a stop, face down on the cement.

Nestor arrived at the accident first and, a moment later, he was joined by the plumpish Mrs. McChesney.

"Oh, Horace! I'm so sorry," gushed the concerned neighbor. "It was foolish of me to leave King George Gnome blocking your path. Oh dear, you're bleeding!"

It's okay, Mrs. McChesney," said Hawk, dabbing his bloody beak with his sleeve. "I should have been paying attention."

"Why didn't you stop?" asked Nestor as he helped his brother to his feet. "I yelled: *Look out!*"

"I thought you were just shouting the name of the street," explained Hawk.

Mrs. McChesney gently grabbed Hawk's elbow and pointed him in the direction of her house. "Come inside the house with me, dear boy, and I'll bandage that nasty scrape on your nose."

"Thank you, Mrs. McChesney, but I'm fine," insisted Hawk. "I'll just go home and clean up."

"Yeah, Mrs. McChesney. Hawk's fine. He does this sort of thing almost every day," agreed Nestor. "Besides, our Mom wouldn't want him bleeding all over your house."

Mrs. McChesney fretted and fussed a few minutes longer before finally waddling away from the scene of the accident. She dragged the toppled King Gnome with her and settled him beside the Queen Gnome on the front lawn chessboard.

With his shirt sleeve pressed on the bridge of his nose to stop the bleeding, Hawk walked with his head pointed at the sky while Nestor guided him home.

On the way up their porch steps, they met little Billy DelSesto coming down.

"Hi, guys!" greeted Billy cheerfully. "I just got done with my piano lesson. You wanna go dig for buried treasure at Portage Park with me?"

"Sorry, Billy. We're busy," said Hawk, his beak still pointed up.

Billy, noticing Hawk's head was tilted toward the sky, looked up at the clouds. "What's up there?"

"Aliens," said Nestor, guiding Hawk in the direction of the door.

"Aliens? Out of my way!" shouted Billy as he pushed his way past the Nestor and Hawk. "I gotta find that treasure before they do!"

Billy ran off as the brothers disappeared inside the house.

In the living room, Audrey was gathering her lesson plans when she heard the front door open and close. "What did you forget, Billy?"

"Better come here, Mom," called Nestor from the foyer. "Hawk had a little accident."

Audrey rushed out of the living room to see Hawk pressing his bloody sleeve against his nose.

"How did this happen? Nestor, did you hit him with your tennis racket again?"

"It was my fault, Mom," said Hawk as he lifted his wrist off his nose so Audrey could assess the damage. "Nestor and I were racing and when I wasn't looking, I tripped over the king."

"Well you scraped the top of your nose pretty good, young man," sighed Audrey. "Let's go upstairs and put hydrogen peroxide on it."

Hawk trudged up the stairs into the bathroom followed by Audrey. Opening the medicine cabinet over the sink, Audrey pulled out her first aid kit and a bottle of hydrogen peroxide.

"Now what do you mean you tripped over the king?" asked Audrey as she dabbed Hawk's beak with a cotton ball.

"Well, he was in the middle of the sidewalk," explained Hawk as he watched the hydrogen peroxide bubble up on his nose in the bathroom mirror. "Mrs. McChesney said she was sorry."

With a confused look on her face, Audrey began putting gauze and a big piece of white medical tape across the bridge of Hawk's nose when the phone in the foyer rang.

"I got it," shouted Nestor from downstairs.

Hawk stared in the mirror at the big bandage on his face as Audrey put the first aid kit back in the cabinet.

"How long do I have to keep this on?" moaned Hawk, tugging at tape running across his nose.

"A few days," answered Audrey. "Why don't you go lay down for a few minutes until dinner?"

"A few days!" protested Hawk. "But Mom…"

Nestor ran up the stairs as Hawk and Audrey were walking out of the bathroom. "It's Killer on the phone," blurted Nestor. "She wants to stop by to talk about the list we dropped off."

"She wants to come over? I can't see her! Look at me!" shouted Hawk in desperation.

"Killer?" asked Audrey, putting her hands on Hawk's shoulders to calm him down. "Is she the nice girl from your football team?"

"She's kind of bossy, Mom," clarified Nestor.

"Nestor, tell her she can't come over! We're gonna have dinner in a little while," insisted Hawk.

"Can't come over? Sure she can," smiled Audrey. "In fact, let's invite her to eat with us. It will be nice to have another woman at the table for a change."

"Okay, Mom," yelled Nestor as he ran back down the stairs.

"But, Mom," sighed Hawk sadly. Then suddenly a glimmer of hope flashed through his head. "Maybe she can't come," he whispered to himself.

"She said okay!" shouted Nestor hanging up the phone.

"Wonderful!" answered Audrey cheerfully.

"Rats!" mumbled Hawk.

"I guess I'd better get downstairs and start getting ready," sang Audrey. Then turning back to Hawk before leaving, "…and remember I want you to lie down for a few minutes and rest. And when our guest arrives, I want you to be nice to her. Don't call her Killer. Call her… what's her first name?"

"Kathy," answered Hawk in defeat.

"Yes, Kathy. Such a pretty name." smiled Audrey as she passed Nestor on the stairs.

At the top of the stairs, Nestor gave his brother a shove toward their bedroom.

"What's the matter, Hawk?" asked Nestor. "I thought you wanted to see Killer."

"Yeah, I guess," sighed Hawk. "But I don't want her to see me with my face all messed up."

Suddenly, Nestor's jaw dropped and his eyes opened wide as he stopped outside the bedroom door and stared at his brother.

Hawk heaved an even heavier sigh. "Promise you won't tell anybody..."

Mouth still open, Nestor nodded.

Hawk swallowed hard and continued. "Well, I think I sort of like her."

Nestor wrinkled his nose in confusion. "Like? You mean like-like? Like you've got a crush on our quarterback?"

"Shhhhhhush! Not so loud! Michael will hear you!" warned Hawk covering Nestor's mouth with his hand. "Now you know why I don't want to see her?"

"What? Because of that bandage on your head?" answered Nestor. "Don't worry about that. It doesn't look that bad."

As they entered the bedroom, Michael glanced up from his Sports Illustrated magazine and blurted out, "Whoa! What happened to your face? Looks like you tried running through a brick wall!"

"Nestor! I thought you said it doesn't look so bad," crabbed Hawk, flopping down on his bed.

"I didn't say you looked bad," laughed Michael. "In fact, with most of your face covered up, you sort of look better."

"So what's with the mummy head?" he asked, still wondering what happened.

"We were racing back from Killer's house, he tripped over the King Gnome and landed on his face on the sidewalk," explained Nestor.

"Killer's? Oh yeah! What did she say about switching out the raisins for chili dogs?" asked Michael with his mouth-watering.

"We didn't see Killer," groaned Hawk. "She was shopping. Now she's coming over for dinner tonight."

Just as soon as Hawk said the words, the doorbell rang. Nestor looked out the window at the front porch below.

"She's here."

"She's early!" complained Hawk.

"Great!" chirped Michael.

"What's so great about it?" questioned Hawk, keeping his crab on.

"What's so great? I'll tell you what's so great, you mummy-head bird-brain," laughed Michael pointing his index finger at his brother's bandaged nose. "Now I can tell her about the chili dog myself. With a chili dog waiting for me in the end zone, I would be amazing."

"C'mon, we gotta go," said Nestor. "Mom will want us downstairs."

Hawk shook his head. "I'm gonna stay up here."

"What are we supposed to tell Killer?" whined Nestor.

"Tell her anything," answered Hawk. "I feel like staying up here a while."

....

Out on the Hapburn front porch, Killer was waiting in her new pink dress, holding her Port Clinton Braves playbook. She was about to ring the bell a second time when Audrey opened the front door.

"Hello, Kathy! Come in! We're so glad you could join us for dinner tonight!"

"Thank you, Ms. Hapburn. It was nice of you to invite me," replied Killer. "I hope you don't mind I came early. Nestor, Michael, Hawk and I need to talk about the game plan for Sunday."

"That's just fine," smiled Audrey. "I'll call the boys down so you can have your meeting and I'll get back to work in the kitchen. Oh, and let me compliment you on your dress! It's such a pretty color on you!"

"That's very nice of you to say Ms. Hapburn. I like black better, but my Mom said pink is more cheery and ladylike. It's for the trip to the

Hall of Fame, but I'm wearing now to get used to it," explained the Port Clinton Braves' quarterback politely.

Smiling, Audrey led the Hapburns' dinner guest to the living room. Shouting up to her boys, she excused herself and disappeared back into the kitchen.

Seconds later, Nestor and Michael came storming down the stairs.

"Hi, Killer!" greeted the brothers in unison.

"Hi, guys," said Killer, smiling for the first time since she arrived. "I came early so we could talk about what snacks we need for the game on Sunday."

"Good idea," said Nestor. "I'll run upstairs and get my playbook."

"Where's Hawk?" asked Killer.

Nestor and Michael looked at each other in silence for a second, each one waiting for the other to answer. Finally, Michael spoke up.

"Hawk? Um .... he's upstairs in the bathroom."

After another moment of awkward quiet, Michael spoke up again.

"You know how it goes. When nature calls."

"Okay!" blurted out Nestor a little too loudly, "I'll get my playbook and be right back!"

Nestor bolted out of the living room, ran up the stairs and burst into the brothers' bedroom.

"Nestor! Why are you back here?" asked Hawk. "What's going on?"

"She came early to have a meeting," answered Nestor, grabbing his playbook off the desk and turning back toward the door.

"Did she ask about me? Did she want to know where I was? What did you say?"

Nestor paused a second and then sighed. "Michael told her you were in the bathroom. He sorta made it sound like you were pooping."

"NO!" yelled Hawk, horrified.

Nestor shrugged his shoulders, "Sorry, Hawk, but you said we could tell her anything."

"Yeah, I know!" groaned Hawk in disbelief. "But why did he say *that*!"

"Well you know, people gotta go," shrugged Nestor as he turned to leave.

"Wait for me," insisted Hawk. "I don't want to go down alone."

Seconds later, Nestor was back into the living room, followed by the nose-bandaged Hawk.

Killer, having a serious conversation with Michael, didn't even notice the brothers as they plopped down on the sofa.

"I'm sorry, Michael, but chili dogs on the football field? It's too messy. It's not a good idea," explained Killer.

"Okay then, how about a chili dog with light sauce, light mustard?" argued Michael. "That wouldn't be bad!"

"Hey, if we win, I'll buy you TWO chili dogs after the game," offered Nestor, jumping into the conversation.

"Good idea!" whooped Killer, her head snapping over to where Nestor and Hawk were sitting. "Oh wow! What happened? Does that hurt? You look super bad!"

"Super bad?" winced Hawk.

"Bad's not bad. Bad is good. You look tough. Like a kid you don't want to mess with," smiled Killer, moving over to the sofa to get a closer look. "Cool! There's blood oozing through the gauze. This is perfect...the players on the other team are gonna be so scared of you!"

Killer sat next to Hawk and gently touched his cheek, turning his head toward her so she could inspect the big bandage wrapped around his face. Hawk's heart started beating faster.

"You like the way I look?" asked Hawk, flashing a surprised smile.

"I told you it was an improvement," laughed Michael. "But forget about Hawk, what about the chili dogs?"

"Yeah, right. Back to business," agreed Killer.

Reaching down to pick up her playbook, she pulled out the list of top secret trick-treat plays and held it up so the Hapburn brothers could see.

"We've got two Snickers sweeps. I think we should get rid of one and replace it with this," suggested the Brave's QB as she pulled a small, green bag out of her pocket and tossed it. "Here...catch!"

Michael reached up and snatched it out of the air. Flipping it around, he held it up and read the label.

"Mango Tango Almond Snack Mix? Blah! Sounds awful!" frowned Michael.

"How do you know unless you taste it?" argued Nestor.

"That's right," agreed Hawk, squawking through the bloody gauze wrapped around his head. "Besides Michael, you'll eat anything."

"That's true," agreed Michael with a nod.

"Open the bag and try it," encouraged Killer. "One serving has 160 calories, three grams of dietary fiber, four grams of protein and no cholesterol. Plus, it has vitamin C, calcium and iron."

Michael took a deep breath and studied the green Mango Tango Almond Mix snack sack suspiciously. Shaking his head, he tossed it to Nestor across the room.

"I don't think so. Something that healthy can't be any good."

"C'mon, Michael! Do it for the team," urged Hawk.

"Hey, listen to what it says here on the bag," said Nestor excitedly. "Mango Tango Almond Mix. Enjoy this satisfying salty-spicy combo of whole almonds and peanuts with the sweet, tart chewiness of lime-infused mango, punctuated by the subtle kick of chipotle chili for a burst of flavorful energy."

Inspired by infused mango and the kick of chipotle, Nestor ripped open the sack and popped a handful in his mouth.

"Crunchy, chewy, spicy...it's great," proclaimed Nestor. "Here guys, try it." He got up and shook some Mango Tango Almond Mix out of the bag and into everyone's hand.

"It does taste good!" agreed Hawk.

"And," chimed in Killer. "I forgot to mention, it's gluten-free."

Then in unison, Nestor, Hawk and Killer turned toward the Port Clinton Braves star running back and they waited.

Fidgeting, Michael looked at the almonds, peanuts and mango in his hand. Finally, he sighed and after a few, long seconds, he pinched his nose like he was about to swallow bad-tasting medicine and he tossed the mix in his mouth.

Almost immediately, Michael was smacking his lips and making yummy noises.

"So, what do you think?" questioned Killer.

With his mouth watering, Michael stuck his hand out in front of Nestor's nose.

"More, please. I haven't decided yet."

"Ha! You like it!" laughed Nestor, shaking more into Michael's outstretched hand.

"Yeah, okay. That sweet, salty-spicy thing is pretty tasty," admitted Michael munching on the Mango Tango. "Still a chili dog is better."

"Great!" exclaimed Killer. "Well change Snickers Sweep Left to a Mango Tango Sweep and we can give the list to Coach Yak at practice tomorrow."

While the Port Clinton Brave QB went to work changing the play list, the three Hapburns fought over the last bit of Mango Tango Almond Mix in the bag.

"Give me more," yelled Michael, chasing Nestor around the sofa.

"You've already had two handfuls," complained Hawk, chasing Michael. "I want what's left!"

"Why should you get it?" argued Nestor, doing his best to play keep-away. "I'm the one who had the guts to try it first!"

Just then Audrey walked into the room and held up her stainless-steel kitchen tongs.

"Stop!" ordered Audrey in a no-nonsense tone. "Is this any way to behave in front of your guest?"

The brothers, slamming on the brakes, slammed into each other and tumbled to the floor.

"But she's not a guest, Mom. She's our quarterback," said Nestor from the bottom of the pileup.

Michael, spotting the bag of Mango Tango Mix unguarded on the floor, made a desperate lunge to grab it. But before he could secure the snack, Audrey snatched it up with her kitchen tongs.

"No more of this until after dinner! Which, by the way, is ready in the dining room," she announced happily.

"What are we having?" asked Nestor, pulling himself off the floor.

"On the menu tonight is a crisp garden salad, sweet potato fries..."

Audrey paused momentarily to step away from the path leading to the dining room, then she continued. "And chili dogs."

Jumping to his feet, Michael jet-propelled himself from the living room to the dinner table and actually provided a nice breeze for everyone as he blew past.

As Audrey and Nestor headed out of the room, Hawk gently reached out and touched Killer's wrist to keep her from following.

"I need to tell you something," said Hawk softly.

Killer smiled and waited.

Hawk leaned close and whispered in the cute quarterback's ear...

"When I was upstairs a few minutes ago..." Hawk paused and Killer leaned in closer. "I wasn't pooping."

....

Einstein Wozniak rose from the dinner table, patting his full belly.

Sticking his head into the kitchen where Henrietta was busy doing dishes, he thanked his mom in Polish. "Dziekuje Ci matko!"

And then he turned and trudged up the stairs to his bedroom. He had important phone calls to make.

Lifting the corner of his mattress, Einstein found the Pasteurized Brotherhood of Limburger Heads Top Secret folder and flipped it open to his list of telephone numbers and began dialing. Seconds later, he was greeted by Floyd Dowler yodeling hello.

"Hello-eo-eo-eo-eo! Floyd Packer-backer speaking."

"Floyd. Could you ever maintain some decorum for one minute?" complained Einstein.

"I don't know, Albert. A minute is a long time," replied Floyd in all seriousness.

"Floyd, time is of the essence," said Einstein trying not to be irritated.

"Operation Georgie Porgie will commence when we board the bus exactly 39-hours, 48-minutes, 27-seconds from now. Dairy Dan has requested all Limburger Heads convene in Baumgartner's basement tomorrow night at 20-hundred hours for a final walk-through to ensure there are no blunders on our mission."

"Stinkin' Bishop! A meeting tomorrow night?" exclaimed the voice on the other end of the phone. "I'm busy packing tomorrow night!"

"I suggest you re-evaluate your strategy," fired back Einstein. "If I were you, I'd manage to achieve a methodology redefining your packing priority as one of your obligatory activities for this evening instead."

"I guess I better pack for the Packer trip tonight," sighed Floyd.

"That is what I just articulated," grumbled the frustrated Einstein.

"No, it isn't," argued Floyd. "But no matter, you can count on me. I'll be Baumgartner's tomorrow at 20-hundred hours sharp."

"Excellent," replied Einstein.

"Oh, Albert. Just one more thing. What time *is* 20-hundred hours?"

"8pm," answered Einstein, heaving a heavy sigh. "And don't call me Albert."

Hanging up the phone Einstein ran his finger down the list of Limburger Heads. He still had four calls to make before he could begin his own packing.

Looking at his watch, he noted Operation Georgie Porgie was now exactly 39-hours, 39-minutes and 57-seconds from the launch pad.

CHAPTER 5

August 22 – 7:57 am EDT | Port Clinton, Ohio
2 Days to Hall of Fame Game | 11 Days to Kickoff at Lambeau Field

By the time Nestor, Michael and Hawk (with his bandaged nose) were jogging onto the turf at True Lay Stadium for the Braves' 8 am practice, most of the team had already arrived and were tossing footballs and banging shoulder pads.

On the sideline, Nestor spotted Killer talking to Coach Yak.

"Look over there," said Nestor pointing at the huge 400-pound coach standing next to the 4-foot, 6-inch tall quarterback. "Killer's giving Coach the play list."

"Snack list," corrected Michael. "I bet Coach thinks chili dogs should be on it. Maybe I better go over and get in on that conversation."

"Not a good idea, Michael," said Hawk grabbing his brother by the back of his number 99 jersey.

"Horse collar tackle," yelled Michael. "Fifteen-yard penalty! "TWEEEEEEEEEEEEEEEEEEEEEEET!"

The sound of the whistle sent Michael, Hawk and Nestor spinning around to see where it came from. At the far end of the field, Coaches Jekyll and Hyde stood waving.

Eight o'clock. It was time for practice to start. Quickly, the players trotted down and gathered around them.

Within a few seconds, Coach Yak joined his two skinny assistants under the goalpost where a series of plays were drawn on a portable dry erase board.

The three coaches bunched together and had a short talk. Then nodding to each other, Coach Yakunshenko turned to face the team.

"We've only got two days before Sunday's game with the Bulldogs," announced Yak holding up his meaty right hand. "Everyone! Pay close attention."

"We'll get to banging pads in a second, but first, Coach Jekyll will go over our game plan and Coach Hyde will announce the starting lineup."

Hearing the words "*starting lineup*" sent a buzz through the 25 players.

"This is exciting," murmured Nestor.

"Where's Killer?" whispered Hawk.

"I'm hungry," grumbled Michael.

Coach Jekyll stepped forward and pointed to the diagrams drawn on the dry erase board.

"Here are the first six plays we are going to run on offense against Olmsted Falls on Sunday."

Nestor, Michael and Hawk quickly studied the board and their jaws dropped.

"Oh no," sighed Nestor.

"No way," whined Hawk.

"No snacks," groaned Michael.

"We'll surprise them with two pass plays to start, followed by four running plays," explained Coach Jekyll.

Instantly, Killer's voice came out of the group gathered around the coaches. "What about our trick plays?"

"We'll keep those in our back pocket. Depending on how it goes, we might not need them."

Hearing that the secret plays were not part of the game plan immediately took the air out of the football. All twenty-five players hung their heads and kicked at the ground in disappointment.

Clapping his hands to re-energize his team, Coach Yak walked to the dry erase board. "Okay, now Coach Hyde will go over our starting lineups," shouted Yakunshenko, flipping the board around to reveal three columns of jersey numbers and names.

OFFENSE *Coach Jekyll*		**DEFENSE** *Coach Hyde*		**SPECIAL TEAMS** *Coach Yak*	
#1 Nestor Hapburn	WR	#4 Bobby Kargosian	DB	#1 Nestor Hapburn	
#8 Tommy O'Connor	WR	#23 Horace Hapburn	FS	#5 Apollo Vargas	QB/Punter
#9 Kathy Kopecky	QB	#34 Auggie Sommers	LB	#17 Jack Oropallo	WR/Kicker
#20 Tim Mathews	WR	#36 Jimbo Banks	SS	#19 Theo Nichols	DB/Holder
#53 Frankie Fitzwater	C	#37 Teddy Hyland	LB	#23 Horace Hapburn	
#59 Don Wujciak	OL	#43 Moses Kupperman	LB	#25 Stinky Smothers' brother	
#66 Diego Sauceda	OL	#44 Hayes Herman	DB	#36 Jimbo Banks	
#77 Dave Francisco	OL	#59 Don Wujciak	LB	#50 Fremont Bellywampus	
#78 Stinky Smothers	OL	#66 Diego Sauceda	DL	#88 JJ Kennelly	TE
#89 Ray Ray McKay	TE	#78 Stinky Smothers	DL	#89 Ray Ray McKay	
#99 Michael Hapburn	RB	#99 Michael Hapburn	NT	#93 Jerry Ball	NT

"This is the starting line-up for Sunday only," Coach Hyde stated. "We'll assess how everyone plays. So I advise you to give a hundred and ten percent effort whenever you're on the field!"

Clapping his hands again still trying to get everyone excited, Coach Yak stepped forward.

"We've only got two more practices to get ready to play in front of 23,000 football fans, so let's get to work!"

"Warm-up drills!" instructed Coach Hyde, "Over to the goal line!"

Heads down, the Port Clinton Braves shuffled into place and faced their taskmaster.

"Let's start with fifty jumping jacks!"

"50?" groaned Hawk a little too loudly.

"Oh, would you rather do 100?" sneered Coach Hyde cheerfully. "Good idea, Hapburn! Do 100 jumping jacks."

Immediately the whole team let out a groan. Moses Kupperman, who was standing next to Hawk, reached out and gave his teammate's bandaged beak a little tweak.

"Thanks a lot, HORACE," complained Moses.

"Hey! Easy on the nose, MOSE!" snapped Hawk.

Coach Hyde let gave three sharp blasts of his whistle and, all at once, 100 arms and legs starting moving as the team begrudgingly began their count to 100.

August 22 – 8:32 am CDT | Monroe, Wisconsin

Holding the steering wheel of his Ford pickup with one hand and a toasted bagel smeared with cream cheese in the other, Dairy Dan pulled into the parking lot of the Chalet Cheese Co-op.

His To-Do List for that night's Limburger Heads' meeting was long and the first thing on it was to pick up the stink bombs from Cheese Master Helmut Lunquist.

Jumping out of his truck, Dairy Dan wiped the cream cheese from his fingers onto his #66 Ray Nitschke jersey as he ran around to the back entrance. *Ray Nitschke #66 Green Bay Packer Linebacker 1958-1972. Inducted into Pro Football Hall of Fame 1978.*

The head Limburger Head was in such a hurry, he didn't notice the bold sign posted on the door.

DANGER! NO ADMITTANCE! EXPERIMENT IN PROGRESS!

The instant he opened the door, Dairy Dan was blasted by the smell of 10,000 stinky socks times ten. Staggered by the blow of the world's most pungent cheeses hitting him full force in the face, the rugged farmer fell to the floor with a thud.

Dressed in a white lab coat and with his back to the door, Cheese Master Helmut Lunquist was in deep concentration, carefully pouring his emerald and gold ooze creation from a beaker into a mason jar. Upon hearing the thud, he jumped and bumped the jar, spilling some of the syrupy goop on the laboratory table.

Turning around he saw what he thought was Dairy Dan dead on the floor.

"Oh, for the love of Lombardi!" squawked Helmut who was wearing his protective clothespin on his nose. "What have I done?!" *Vince Lombardi was the Green Bay Packer Head Coach from 1957-1967. Inducted into the Pro Football Hall of Fame 1971.*

Quickly, Helmut grabbed his friend by the ankles and dragged his lifeless body outside into the fresh air, slamming the door to his workshop shut.

Shaking with fear, the cheese master knocked the clothespin off his nose and bent over, putting his ear on Dairy Dan's chest.

"Thank goodness!" sighed Helmut hearing the strong, steady thump, thump, thumping heartbeat. "He's alive!"

Helmut spent the next few minutes frantically fanning the air with his hand to drive fresh oxygen into nostrils of the knocked-out Limburger Head. Finally, Dairy Dan's eyelids fluttered and his eyes opened to a beautiful blue and billowy cloud-filled sky.

"Am I in heaven? I wanna meet Curly Lambeau," coughed Dairy Dan with eyes blinking. *Curly Lambeau was the founder, a player and the first coach of the Green Bay Packers. Inducted into the Pro Football Hall of Fame 1963.*

Then, seeing the cheese master's face hovering over him, he cried, "Helmut! You're in heaven, too?!"

"No, we're right out here…outside the cheese co-op," answered Helmut, pointing toward the building. "I was pouring the last stink bomb when you walked in."

"Stink bomb? Oh yeah, that's right," said Dairy Dan as his brain slowly began working again. "That's why I'm here, to pick up the stink bombs."

"You wait here and take some deep breaths," Helmut instructed. Then, locating the clothespin on the ground, he picked it up and clipped it on his nose.

"I'll pack up the stink bombs and load them on your truck."

Dairy Dan nodded his approval and watched as the cheese master disappeared inside his workshop.

Struggling to get up on his feet, the groggy dairy farmer pounded on the side of his head to get the cobwebs out. By the time Helmut came back outside with a wooden box filled with stink bombs, Dairy Dan was back to normal.

"Wow! Those things really work!" he laughed, slapping Helmut on the back.

"Maybe you better get extra clothespins in case of emergencies," suggested Helmut, reaching up to remove the one from his nose. "Hey!

Since I'm not going with you guys, ya want me to say something about stink bomb safety at our meeting tonight?"

"Good idea!" smiled Dairy Dan. "You know what they say, stink bomb safety first!

"I wish I was getting on that bus with you guys tomorrow," sighed the cheese master. "If our little Maddie Rose wasn't getting baptized Sunday, you know I would be."

"We wish you could be with us, too," sympathized Dairy Dan. "Operation Georgie Porgie is going to be history-making."

Strapping the box of stink bombs down in the bed of his pickup, Dairy Dan gave his fellow Limburger Head a wave and sped out of the Chalet Cheese Co-op parking lot, kicking up gravel. His long To-Do List was now one item shorter.

....

The Port Clinton Braves were walking off the field of True Lay Stadium with their heads down. It had been a terrible practice.

After the coaches told the players their special trick plays were not part of the Sunday game plan, everyone's enthusiasm vanished.

As bad as they had performed earlier in the week, the team looked even worse now. Offensive and defensive players kept lining up on the wrong side of the ball. Half the time there were too many players on the field and the other half, not enough.

Frankie Fitzwater kept hiking the ball on the wrong snap count, Michael ran like he was wearing cement boots and, to top it all off, Ray Ray McKay's mouth guard popped out and a crow swooped down and flew away with it.

Coach Yak stood at midfield scratching his head as he watched his twenty-five players shuffle off like zombies toward their homes.

Reaching into his back pocket, he pulled out a crumpled piece of paper and gave it a long, hard look. It was the list Killer Kopecky had given him a couple of hours earlier.

A minute later, Coach Yak attached the shopping list to his clipboard and, with a beefy hand, he smoothed out the wrinkles.

"Maybe I better go buy a few things on this list, just in case," said Coach Yak, a little worried because he was talking out loud to himself.

....

Nestor stood in front of Mrs. McChesney's house on the corner of Grant Street and Look Out Drive waving at his brothers who were lagging behind.

"C'mon, guys! I'll play you in a game of chess!" shouted Nestor. He grabbed the King gnome Hawk had tripped over the day before and put it in its place on the checkerboard patterned lawn.

"Not in the mood," said Hawk.

"I'm too hungry. No snacks at practice this morning," said Michael, rounding the corner and heading toward home and the Hapburns' 25.2 cubic foot refrigerator filled with food.

"I'll play without either of my bishops," offered Nestor, trying to cheer up his brothers a bit. "You might even beat me this time!"

"Sorry! Hungry!" apologized Michael as he walked past.

Hawk stopped and studied the King gnome.

"Look," said Hawk pointing at a chipped spot on the King gnome's nose. "He got hurt in the big crash yesterday, too."

"You wanna play a quick game?" asked Nestor, patting the King gnome on the head.

"I'm not in the mood. All I can think about is how crummy we looked at practice."

"We were pretty crummy," agreed Nestor. "But look at the bright side...in a couple of days, we're going to the Pro Football Hall of Fame! Plus, we get to play on the Hall of Fame football field in front of 23,000 people!"

"Yeah, well, the way we looked, I don't even want to play in front of 23 people. It's embarrassing! If we don't use our secret plays, those Olmsted Falls Bulldogs are going to rip us apart!"

Nestor, Hawk and the King gnome stood together in silence, staring at each other. After a few seconds, Hawk pulled the bandage off his nose and stuck it over the chipped spot on the King gnome's nose.

"C'mon…let's get home before Michael eats everything in the house," said Nestor giving Hawk a nudge to get him started. "And stop worrying. It's gonna get better."

"Get better? How could it get any worse?" moaned Hawk as he turned and slowly headed toward the Hapburn front porch.

"How could it get worse?" repeated Nestor, laughing just a little. "Well, if the team finds out you've got a crush on our quarterback… that might be worse."

Hawk moaned again and kept shuffling toward home. Out of the corner of his eye, he thought he saw the King gnome nodding his bandaged head.

....

Down to the last item on his To-Do List before the big meeting that night, Dairy Dan turned off County Road K onto 18th Street. Cruising past the gravestones in Greenwood Cemetery, he pulled into the driveway with a mailbox shaped like a Green Bay Packer helmet. Slamming on the brakes of his pickup, he skidded to a stop next to Demetri Papadopoulos' front porch.

As Dairy Dan jumped out of the truck, he could hear a banging sound coming from the direction of Papa's run-down airplane hangar. Following the noise around to the big hangar door, he saw Papa bent down with a hammer, pounding on the landing gear of his old C-47 Sky Train.

"Hey, Papa!" shouted Dairy Dan, trying to be heard above the loud banging. "Stop that hammering for a minute! I need to talk to you."

Unable to hear anything above the racket he was making, the old Greek Aviation Officer continued working on his plane, unaware that his friend was standing in the doorway of the hangar.

After shouting a couple more times without any luck, Dairy Dan finally walked up behind the hard-of-hearing pilot and tapped him on the shoulder.

Startled, Papa whipped around and brought his hammer down hard on Dairy Dan's foot.

"Owwwwww!" bellowed Dairy Dan, hopping up and down.

"Squadron Leader Dan! Sorry for hammer foot!" apologized Papa. "Big mistake. I thought danger, enemy attack."

"Nope, it's just me, your Packer backer comrade," answered the head Limburger Head, as he tried rubbing the hurt out of his toes.

Hearing the name of his favorite football team Papa immediately jumped up and put his hand over his heart. "Yes! Go Pack Go!"

"I see you're still working on that old plane of yours. How long has it been since you last flew that junk heap? Fifty years?"

"Before they put me in the dirt across my street," smiled Papa, pointing in the direction of Greenwood Cemetery. "Someday I fly her again. Some day my Aphrodite, she touch the clouds one time more." *Aphrodite is the Greek goddess of love and beauty.*

Dairy Dan, still rubbing his foot, stood in ancient Greek's airplane hangar and looked around as Papa gave his C-47 an affectionate pat.

"Papa, after we steal those Bear Hall of Fame heads, we need a place to hide 'em...and I was thinking..."

"Okay, okay, sure-sure...hide Bears here," offered Papa, realizing what Dairy Dan was about to ask. Then, the old man wobbled over to a stack of burlap potato sacks piled up in the corner and stuck his head inside.

"Mm mmm mmm mmmm mm Bears mmm mmmm mm."

With his sore foot, Dairy Dan wobbled over to where Papa stood and lifted the potato sack off the 82-year-old's noggin.

"Say again, Papa. I can't understand you with that sack on your head."

"Okay, okay, sure-sure," coughed Papa, spitting out the dust from inside the bag. "I say: We put bags on Bears and hide in corner here."

"Perfect," said Dairy Dan as he threw the potato sack back on the stack. "See you at the meeting tonight. Eight o'clock sharp!"

"Okay, okay, sure-sure," said Papa, still coughing and trying to clear his throat. "You see 'em, eight sharp!"

Dairy Dan limped outside to his truck, then turned and looked back at the ramshackle airplane hangar, rubbing his chin in thought. It was the perfect hiding spot. Those Hall of Fame George Bear busts in burlap sacks shoved in a dark corner with all of Papa's junk, they would be impossible to find.

The very instant Dairy Dan put his hand on the door of his pickup, the banging sound from inside the hangar started up again.

Rubbing his foot and shaking his head, Dairy Dan mumbled to himself, "Crazy old coot. Fly that plane again? Never! It's a death trap."

....

Einstein Wozniak looked at his Packer wristwatch as Floyd Dowler came crashing down the stairs to Baumgartner's basement. 7:59 pm CDT.

The rest of the Pasteurized Brotherhood of Limburger Heads were standing around (except for Dairy Dan, who was soaking his sore foot in a dishpan of warm water and Epsom Salt) and they were trying to remember in how many games the Packers had won the coin toss the season before.

"When I said our meeting was scheduled for 8 o'clock, I assumed you knew that it was Lombardi Time," snarled Einstein. *Hall of Fame Packers Coach Vince Lombardi always operated 15 minutes ahead of schedule.*

"We have dawdled away 15 minutes waiting to commence this last briefing of Operation Georgie Porgie before we embark on our mission," Einstein spouted.

"Sorry, everybody. I got running behind, getting ready for our trip tomorrow," apologized Floyd, out of breath and holding up two green and gold tee-shirts on hangers. "I couldn't decide which one of these to pack, so I brought 'em over so you guys could help me pick."

"Sit down, Floyd. I did not accommodate time for your personal fashion demonstration," complained Einstein.

"Easy, Albert. This is really important," said Floyd with conviction.

"If it makes him happy, let him do it, Einstein," sighed Dairy Dan, sprinkling more Epsom salt from the box into his tub of water. "It'll only take a few seconds."

Groaning, Einstein threw up his hands and sat down.

"Thanks, guys!" gurgled Floyd. He held up the first tee-shirt that said: *Roses are Red, Violets are Blue…the Bears Suck and the Vikings Do, Too.* "Okay, do you think I should pack this one for the trip…?"

Then he lifted the other shirt. "Or…this one that says, *Education is Important, but Green Bay Football is Importanter…?*"

"Boy, I don't know Floyd," said the youngest Limburger Head, Rick Monroe, scratching his chin thoughtfully. "They're both good."

"I think the one about football and education has a better message," chimed in Rick's dad, Nick.

"Let me propose this revolutionary concept: Why not pack both garments?" offered Einstein sarcastically.

"What a great idea! Thank you, Albert!" exclaimed Floyd. "No wonder you finished 29th in our class at Monroe High!"

The solution to Floyd's problem was met with cheerful shouts from the assembled Limburger Heads. Smiling, he took his seat between Helmut and Papa.

Pacing nervously back and forth in front of the group, one hand rubbing his shiny bald head and the other holding a wooden pointer, Einstein began the final briefing.

"Tomorrow…we depart on a history-making journey, a crusade to put Packer football in its rightful place, on the highest pedestal in the land. However, if we fail and fall short of accomplishing our goal, it would most certainly spell the end of the Pasteurized Brotherhood of Limburger Heads.

"It would mean humiliation, shame, and ridicule. It would mean…"

"For the love of Lombardi, Einstein…TRY to keep your briefing brief!" interrupted Dairy Dan. "You're talking to a bunch of guys who have the attention spans of goldfish!"

"Actually, mine might even be shorter," admitted Floyd with an embarrassed chuckle.

Einstein, head bent down staring at the cement floor, took a deep breath and started over.

"My apologies, let me attempt to be more succinct."

"Great! If that means you're going to try and keep it short, we're all for it," grumbled Dairy Dan, his sore foot causing crabbiness.

"Operation Georgie Porgie...Our mission: Remove all the Chicago Bears named George from the NFL Hall of Fame so our beloved Green Bay Packers can claim the most players enshrined than any other team in the league."

A loud cheer sprang up from the Limburger Heads as they chanted, "Go Pack Go! Go Pack Go!"

Einstein, smiling because his opening remarks were so well received, paused for a few moments and waited for the room to quiet down.

"We board the Packer tour bus in the morning in Green Bay at 11:45 am and we arrive at the Ramada Hall of Fame Hotel 11:00 tomorrow night."

Then, taking two steps toward a card table piled high with green and gold Packer backpacks, Einstein continued.

"Each one of you will be issued a Packer backpack which you will use to transport your stink bombs..."

"Stinkin' Bishop, you say," blurted out Floyd, "we get to have one of those? To keep?"

"Sweet!" shouted Rick Monroe excitedly. "Swag for the Rickster!"

Disregarding the spontaneous outburst, Einstein moved onto the most important part of the meeting.

"Now to instruct us on the safety issues associated with stink bomb transport and detonation is our own and the world's foremost authority on the subject, Cheese Master Helmut Lundquist."

Once again, the Limburger Heads roared their approval with whoops and whistles as the slightly-embarrassed stink bomb expert took his place in front of the group.

"Well, there's really not much to it," admitted Helmut modestly, holding up a mason jar of his sparkling yellow-green oozy creation and a wooden clothespin.

"The most important thing to remember is BEFORE you unscrew the lid on your stink bomb, you need to put one of these..." Helmut paused and clipped on the clothespin "...<u>on your nose.</u>"

"Oh, that's hilarious!" giggled Floyd.

"<u>No, it's not funny, Floyd,</u>" insisted the cheese master, shaking a serious finger at his friend. "If you forget to put the clothespin on first, you'll drop flat on the floor, completely helpless!"

"Sorry, Helmut," apologized Floyd, giggling harder than ever. "But you sound so funny with that thing on your nose! You're killing me!"

Rick and his dad, Nick, sitting behind Floyd, covered their mouths and stared at the floor, trying hard not to laugh, too.

Realizing the problem, Einstein reached up and removed the clothespin from Helmut's nose, instructing him to continue. Taking a deep breath, Helmut resumed his briefing.

"Remember, safety first. Clip the clothespin on your nose before you do anything else. Then, open the lid to your stink bomb and carefully place it on the floor without spilling it. It will only take a few seconds for everyone in that area to be out like a light.

"Once you get all of the Bears named George out the building… go back to your stink bomb…screw the lid back on and put it in your backpack," explained the cheese master speaking slowly to make sure everyone was understanding the words coming out of his mouth.

"Do not…I repeat, DO NOT remove your clothespin until you are out in the fresh air. After a few minutes, all those knocked out from the stink bombs will wake up like nothing has happened and all will be back to normal."

"Except we'll have MORE Green Bay Packers in the National Football League Hall of Fame than stinking Chicago Bears!" yelled Dairy Dan. He splashed out of his foot bath and grabbed Helmut and Einstein's arms, raising them up triumphantly over their heads.

Immediately, the basement filled with Limburger Heads roaring their approval.

"Go Pack Go! Go Pack Go! Go Pack Go! Go Pack Go!"

After a few minutes, Einstein started waving his hands downward, indicating he wanted everyone to sit back in their seats.

"Does anyone have any interrogatories?" asked Einstein once quiet was restored.

Floyd sprang up. "I have a question."

"Let's hear it, Floyd," replied Dairy Dan as he eased down in his chair and slipped his aching foot back in the dishpan of Epsom Salts.

"What's an interrogatory?"

Before Einstein could answer, Nick Monroe popped up with a question of his own. "How will we know which George we take?"

"How we know where we put stink bomb?" added Papa, pulling himself up out of his chair and leaning on his walker.

"Excellent inquiries," replied Einstein as he unrolled a map of the Pro Football Hall of Fame. Reaching up as high as his short arms would allow, he taped the map to the basement wall and continued.

"Papa, you place your stink bomb here at the main entrance," said Einstein as he slapped an X on the map. "Then, you take the elevator near the First Century exhibit up to the Hall of Fame Gallery on the second floor and remove Papa Bear George Halas.

"Inducted in 1963, he will located right at the beginning of the Gallery. Approximately here," continued Einstein tapping his pointer on the map. "Here's a photograph, so you can be assured you have absconded with your assigned statuette."

"Good! Papa get Papa Bear. Got it up here!" smiled Papa, tapping the side of his head with his index finger.

After finishing with Papa, Einstein handed out photos to the rest of the Limburger Heads and showed them on the map where to find their assigned Bear George and the strategic placement of each stink bomb.

"Okay, that's it for tonight. Go home, get some rest. We've got a big day ahead of us," said Dairy Dan as he carefully pulled a sock over his swollen foot and squeezed it into an untied tennis shoe. Wobbling to his feet, the head Limburger Head continued.

"Everybody meet in the courthouse parking lot across the street at 6:45 in the morning…Helmut is going to drive us up to Green Bay. I thought we could get there early and spend some time in the Packer Pro Shop. Then we'll board the bus and be on our way to becoming heroes!"

Once again the excited group let out a cheer and began chanting "Go Pack Go! Go Pack Go! Go Pack Go! Go Pack Go!"

Einstein moved toward Dairy Dan and instructed everyone to huddle up. Quickly, a tight circle formed with a stack of seven Limburger Head hands piled on top of each other in the center.

"Operation Georgie Porgie on three," shouted Dairy Dan. "One... two...three..."

"Operation Georgie Porgie!" yelled everyone except Floyd.

"I still don't know what an interrogatory is," sighed Floyd.

....

Pushing three grocery carts piled high with mountainous stacks of snacks, Coach Yakunshenko lumbered toward the front of the store to check out.

Sick from worrying all day about how bad his football team looked in practice, the troubled leader of the Port Clinton Braves decided to make an emergency late-night run to Bassett's Market and pick up a few things on the list Kathy Kopecky had given him.

Huffing and puffing as he arrived at the registers, Coach Yak was scanning the long lines when he noticed the tall, thin clerk working the express lane excitedly waving him over.

"Hey, Coach! Mr. Yakunshenko! Check out over here!"

"But your sign says 15 items or less. I've got about 1500," said Coach Yak, swinging his arm over the three overflowing grocery carts.

Jumping from behind the counter, he steered one of the carts crammed full of snacks into his checkout lane. "Don't pay attention to that," laughed the clerk. "It's not like you're breaking a law or anything."

"Thanks a lot," said Coach Yak. "I had no idea it would be so busy at 10:15 pm."

"Oh, yeah, Coach. Second shift at the screw machine factory lets out at ten. It's always crazy at this time," chirped the clerk as he scanned boxes of Twinkies.

Yakunshenko stopped loading snacks on the conveyor and scratched his chin, "Did you call me Coach? Do I know you?"

"Oh, yeah, Coach. About eleven years ago...I played for you. Well, I didn't play much," the cheerful clerk paused for a second and pointed to the name tag pinned to his green Bassette's smock. "Jim Clark. I was your 57-pound third-string middle linebacker. You called me Slim Jim."

Coach Yak studied the skinny kid in front of him, then went back to unloading his grocery cart. "Well, Slim Jim, that was a while ago. Did we have a good team?"

"Not really. We didn't win a game. We almost beat Oak Harbor though," recalled Slim Jim with a smile, as he continued ringing up snacks on his register. "Whaddya doing…buying treats for the team?"

"For a player," grunted Yakunshenko as he dropped a case of Mango Tango Almond Mix on the check-out conveyor with a thud.

Slim Jim shook his head. "One player? Three grocery carts full?"

"Yeah, well, I'd buy four grocery carts full of stuff if I thought it would get me a championship," sighed Coach Yak. "After all these years…if we could just get to the state finals and win it all. Just once, that's all I want."

"Well, who knows Coach," sang Slim Jim cheerfully. "Maybe this is the year!"

"Maybe it is," mumbled the massive man thoughtfully.

Scanning the last box of Snickers snack-size candy bars, Slim Jim punched the total button on the cash register.

"That'll be $253.57."

Holding up a beefy index finger, Coach Yak turned and walked back toward the snack aisle.

"I'll just be a minute. I think I should get a couple more boxes of Twinkies."

CHAPTER 6

August 23 – 7:57 am EDT | Port Clinton, Ohio
1 Day to Hall of Fame Game | 10 Days to Kickoff at Lambeau Field

"Achoooo!"

It was the tenth time Michael sneezed during the brothers' ten minute walk to practice.

"COVER YOUR MOUTH!" complained Hawk. "I don't want your germs flying around my head!"

Feeling another sneeze coming on, Michael jerked Hawk's football helmet out of his hand and, holding it over his face, he let loose again.

"Ah-Ah-ACHOOOO!"

Wiping his nose with his sleeve, Michael handed the headgear back to Hawk.

"Eewww!" exclaimed Hawk. "You slimed my helmet! Gross!"

"Stop goofing off, you guys," ordered Nestor as he pushed his brothers through the gate at True Lay Stadium and onto the football field. "The whistle is going to blow any second now."

On the sideline, Coaches Yak, Jekyll and Hyde were huddled up talking and scribbling on their clipboards. A few feet away, Killer Kopecky was practicing taking snaps with Frankie Fitzwater.

Seeing the Hapburn brothers walking onto the field, Killer flipped the ball back to Frankie and ran over to meet them.

"Oh, you did scrape your nose up good," winced Killer as she got her first close-up look at Hawk's unbandaged beak. "You should probably cover that."

"Yeah! That's exactly what I was telling Michael," answered Hawk, his heart beating faster just standing next to the little quarterback. "Then he sneezed in my helmet!"

"I've got a cold," moaned Michael. "Hey! Aren't you supposed to feed a cold?"

"I don't know, but I do have good news," hummed Killer as she pulled them all closer to share her information.

"It's either 'Feed a fever and STARVE a cold' or 'Feed a cold and starve a fever'. I can't remember," offered Nestor.

"I heard the coaches talking," said Killer, trying hard to contain her excitement. "And they're putting the special plays BACK into the game plan!"

"Look there," she said smiling as she pointed to a scarlet Suburban in the parking lot. "Coach's Chevy is loaded with snacks!"

"That's great!" exclaimed Nestor. "Wonder why they changed their minds..."

"Probably how crummy we played in practice yesterday," cheered Hawk happily.

"That's exactly why," agreed Killer. "More than anything Coach Yak wants to win a championship, and he thinks with Michael, this is his chance!"

"So, the snack plays are back in! Woo hoo!" shouted Hawk. "What do you say about that Michael?"

Lifting his head and taking a deep breath, Michael paused.

"Everybody down!" screamed Nestor at the top of his lungs.

Immediately, twenty-four players and three coaches hit the ground as Michael let loose a mighty one-hundred mile per hour sneeze.

"Ah-Ah-Ah-ACHOOOO!"

....

Helmut Lundquist tapped the brakes and exited the expressway onto Lombardi Avenue. The three-hour ride from Monroe to Green Bay in the Chalet Cheese Co-op delivery truck was almost over.

"Look!" shouted Floyd, excitedly bouncing up and down in his seat.

"Do you see the stadium?" asked Dairy Dan, looking out his window.

"No, a Red Lobster restaurant!" hollered Floyd.

Everybody groaned as the delivery truck continued sputtering down the street. Minutes later, as they approached a traffic light, they saw it rising up majestically out of an all-American neighborhood filled with all-American, working class homes.

Holding his breath, Helmut executed a sharp turn onto Lombardi Avenue, followed by a quick left into the parking lot. Then, slamming on the brakes, the delivery truck screeched to a stop.

There, before them stood Lambeau Field, the legendary stadium of the Green Bay Packers.

"Wow!" shouted Rick Monroe.

"She's beautiful!" added Nick Monroe.

"Not since I visit the Temple of Athena have I owned such joy," exulted Demetri Papadopoulos. The old cargo plane pilot was crying happy tears.

"Chcialbym zeby go usciskac," squealed Henrietta Wozniak, who was just waking up from a snooze in the back next to her cooler filled with cabbage rolls.

Dairy Dan gave Einstein a poke in the ribs with his elbow.

"What's your ma saying?"

"She said she would like to hug it," smiled Einstein.

"Me, too, Mrs. Wozniak!" roared Dairy Dan, laughing loudly. "ME, TOO!"

"There's the Packer bus," announced Floyd. "Let's get on and get a good seat!"

"Easy, Floyd. We're two hours early," noted Dairy Dan. "Helmut, drive around the stadium. We've got time to visit the pro shop."

"Sure thing, DD!" said Helmut, shifting into *Drive*.

The Limburger Heads chattered non-stop as they circled the hallowed grounds. A chorus of "ooohs" and "aaahs" filled the van.

"Hey! There's Vince Lombardi and Curly Lambeau," shouted Rick.

"What?" exclaimed Floyd with a horrified look. "I thought they were dead!"

"Compose yourself, Floyd," ordered Einstein. "Those are statues."

"Stinkin' Bishop!" sighed Floyd. "I guess that means no autographs, huh?"

His heart beating fast, Helmut pulled into a parking space in front of the Lambeau Field Atrium and shut off the engine.

"Helmut! This is Suite Parking," warned Nick Monroe, pointing at a sign in front of them.

"I'll say it's sweet!" gushed Helmut happily. "Look! We're just fifty feet from the Packer Pro Shop."

"Okay, everybody. It's quarter to ten. Look around, have a good time," urged Dairy Dan. "Be back here at 11 and then we'll go over and get on the bus. Leave your backpacks here with me."

"You won't accompany us?" asked Einstein with concern.

"My foot's a little sore. I thought I'd sit here and rest it, so I'll be good to go tomorrow," answered the big dairy farmer, reassuring his friend. "Besides, somebody's got to keep an eye on those stink bombs! Now, scram! Go! That's Lambeau Field right there!"

Excited, the Limburger Heads tumbled out of the delivery truck headed toward the stadium and the Packer Pro Shop singing...

> *"Go, you Packers, go and get 'em,*
> *Go, you fighting fools upset 'em,*
> *Smash their line with all your might,*
> *A touchdown, Packers, Fight, Fight, Fight!*
> *On, you Blue and Gold, to glory,*
> *Win this game the same old story,*
> *Fight, you Packers, Fight,*
> *and bring the bacon home to*
> *Oooooolllld Greeeeeeen Baaaaaaaaay!"*

....

"TWEEEEEEEEEEEEEEEEEEEEET!"

Coach Yak spit his whistle out of his mouth and let it dangle on its cord around his thick neck as he waved everyone over to where he stood near the goal line at the north end of the stadium.

"Everyone! Huddle up over here," he shouted, clapping his hands. With the special snack plays back in the game plan, the team had looked sharp. Despite his sneezing and feeling a little sluggish from his cold, Michael was a runaway freight train. As long as there was a treat waiting when he rolled into the end zone, there was no way he would let himself be tackled.

In the parking lot, Coach Jekyll was wrestling out a case of Mango Tango Almond Mix from Yak's SUV jam-packed with snacks. Finally pulling it free, he started walking back toward the field, holding the prize package up over his head.

Clearing his throat with a cough, followed by a big gulp of air, Coach Yak began talking.

"Tomorrow we face our first test of the season. Even though it's a scrimmage, to me it's the Super Bowl!"

Joining the team gathered at the goal line, Coach Jekyll handed off the box of Mango Tango Almond Mix to Coach Hyde as Coach Yak continued.

"Those Olmsted Falls Bull Dogs were league champions last year. They are good! They're big…they're mean…and they're tough!"

Now in charge of the cardboard box, Coach Hyde slipped in front of the bellowing big head coach and placed it at his feet.

"So, THIS IS OUR CHALLENGE…" Coach Yak paused to suck in another huge swallow of oxygen. "If we can play BIGGER…if we can play TOUGHER…AND, if we can play MEANER, I promise you that *THIS* WILL BE THE YEAR the Port Clinton Braves win it all!"

Worked up into a foaming frenzy, Coach Yak ripped open the box at his feet and started tossing snack-sized bags of Mango Tango Almond Mix to the team.

All twenty-five Port Clinton Braves bounced up and roared their approval as they scrambled to snatch salty-spicy, lime-infused deliciousness out of the air. Joyously, the team exchanged high fives, fist bumps and hugs.

Nestor hugged Michael. Michael, still sneezing, hugged Hawk. Hawk, his scraped-up nose oozing a little blood, looked around to hug Killer, but she was already hugging Stinky Smothers.

Stinky Smothers' brother's head was spinning in search of a brick wall to run through. Spotting the goalpost, he took off at full-speed to knock it down. Halfway to his target, he got tangled up in the empty Mango Tango box and immediately crashed on the True Lay Stadium turf.

"That's it for today," bellowed Coach Yak as he surveyed the joyous snack party. "Be here tomorrow at 9am to board the bus."

The Port Clinton Braves let out another loud cheer and headed off in different directions, happily munching Mango Tango Almond Mix.

Hawk, hoping to walk home with Killer, turned to locate her in the departing crowd when he heard his name called out.

"Hold on, Hapburn!"

Immediately the three Hapburn heads whipped around toward Coach Yak.

"Yes, sir?" answered the brothers at the same time.

Realizing what had happened, the big man pointed a beefy finger at Hawk. "You...the Hapburn with the bloody beak...stick around for a few minutes so Coach Hyde can bandage you up. Can't have you bleeding all over Canton, Ohio tomorrow."

"I'm okay, coach," groaned Hawk.

"Over here, Hapburn," hissed Coach Hyde as he opened the team's first aid kit. "On the bench."

Hawk gave the turf a kick and shuffled over to the sideline.

"See ya later, Hawk," said Michael with a sneeze and a wave.

"You want me to wait for you?" asked Nestor.

Before Hawk could answer, a shout came from the parking lot.

"Hey, Hawk! Nestor! Michael! My dad wants to know if you want a ride home?"

Standing by a white van, Killer Kopecky was waving them over.

"Sure!" shouted Michael immediately, jogging off toward the parking lot. "C'mon, Nestor! We got a ride!"

"Yeah, okay!" answered Nestor. "Sorry, Hawk! Gotta go!"

"Rats!" grumbled Hawk as he watched his brothers high-five Killer and jump into Big John Kopecky's mini-van. Seconds later, the van started up and drove off down 6th street.

On the bench, Coach Hyde was preparing his field hospital, setting out medical tape, gauze, sterile adhesive strips, ointment and scissors.

Satisfied with his temporary operating room, Coach Hyde pulled on a pair of latex disposable gloves and inspected his patient. "Okay, let's clean up that beak of yours. Like Coach said, can't have you bleeding all over Canton."

After a good ten minutes of dabbing, wiping, cutting and taping, Hawk's nose was completely covered. Tape and gauze stretched from ear to ear.

"Coach Hyde, I don't mean to complain, but the bandage feels a little tight. I can't breathe through my nose," said Hawk, sounding pinched.

"Can't breathe through your nose?" repeated Coach Hyde, scratching his chin. "Well, that's okay. Breathe through your mouth until after the game tomorrow."

Packing up his first aid kit, Coach Hyde gave Hawk a pat on the back and walked off the field. "Go Braves!"

Suddenly inspired, Hawk reached down and grabbed his helmet by the face mask and thrust it up over his head, shouting, "That's right! Go Braves!"

His voice echoed in the empty True Lay Stadium.

Still sitting on the bench, his nose bandaged up, he thought about the next day. Touring the Pro Football Hall of Fame. Playing in the Hall of Fame stadium. Watching a real pro football game!

"Maybe I'll get to sit next to Killer on the bus," sighed Hawk, thinking out loud.

Shoving his stuff in his duffle bag, Hawk shuffled off toward home with a smile.

....

"What's taking them so long," grumbled Dairy Dan, looking at his Packer wristwatch. "I told them to get back to the truck at 11!"

After stewing a few more minutes, Dairy Dan spotted the smooth bowling ball head of Einstein Wozniak. He and the rest of the Limburger Heads were strolling away from Lambeau Field, loaded down with souvenirs, smiling and still singing the fight song.

> *"On, you Blue and Gold, to glory,*
> *Win this game the same old story,*
> *Fight, you Packers, Fight..."*

Dairy Dan leaned to the driver's side of the Chalet Cheese Co-op delivery truck and pressed the horn. *HONNNNNNNNNNNK!*

"Hurry up!" shouted Dairy Dan, sticking his head out the window. "It's time to board the bus!"

Hearing the horn, the Limburger Heads broke into a trot as they continued to jabber with excitement.

Rick Monroe, the youngest and most physically fit Limburger Head, was the first to arrive back at the truck.

"You should have seen it, DD!" gushed Rick. "There was green and gold everywhere!"

"That's just great," growled Dairy Dan sarcastically. "Now get in! We gotta go!"

Next, Floyd Dowler appeared on the scene shouting, "Dairy Dan! Look at this!"

Shoving up the sleeve of his *Education is Important, but Green Bay Football is Importanter* t-shirt Floyd revealed an **I ♥ Packers** tattoo. "Isn't it a beauty!"

Seconds later, the rest of the Limburger Heads were pushing their way onto the truck while Cheese Master Helmut Lundquist started the engine.

"Hey, watch it! Don't step on my foot!" complained Dairy Dan as Demetri Papadopoulos tromped past with his walker.

"No you worry. Your foot I no kaboom again," reassured Papa, taking his seat in the back of the truck. "I buy Dan a Packer ham in can. A gift to you. Here."

Papa reached into his sack of souvenirs and pulled out a two-pound canned ham decorated with the Packer logo. Then, with a nod toward the front seat, he passed it to Henrietta Wozniak, who passed it Nick Monroe, who passed to Floyd who then stretched out his arm to hand the ham to Dairy Dan.

"Oh, ah, thanks, Papa," sighed Dairy Dan, suddenly feeling bad for being so cranky. "That was nice of..."

But before he could finish his sentence, Floyd let loose of the ham a split-second before Dan was ready to receive it and the two-pound can crashed down hard on the big dairy farmer's sore foot.

"OWWW!" cried Dairy Dan as a bolt of pain shot to his brain.

"Oops! Sorry, DD!" apologized Floyd, reaching down to pick up the fumbled ham. "How about I just I'll set it over here on the seat beside you?"

"Good idea," moaned Dairy Dan as he took off his shoe and tried rubbing the pain away.

"Stinkin' Bishop! Look at that foot swell up!" exclaimed Floyd. "Those tootsies of yours are twice their normal size!"

Einstein Wozniak, worried about Dairy Dan's foot, got up from his seat to inspect the damage.

Shaking his bald head, Einstein heaved a sigh. "I don't know, Dairy Dan. It is my perception your injury has put the successful completion of our mission in serious jeopardy. Perhaps we should postpone Operation Georgie Porgie until you are fully recovered from your debilitating injury."

"Poke me in the eye and chew on my ear! There's no way I can do that!" barked the leader of the Limburger Heads. "We've got a ten-hour drive ahead of us. By the time we get to Canton, the swelling will be down and I'll be fine!"

Dairy Dan directed Helmut to drive around to the other side of the Lambeau Atrium and, seconds later, the gleaming green and gold deluxe 55-passenger motorcoach came into view.

A long line of Packer fans, all wearing big yellow foam cheese wedge hats, were waiting to board.

"Helmut! Maneuver into close proximity of the motorcoach," instructed Einstein. "We need to minimize the amount of pressure

DD is required to apply to his injured phalanges."

"Yes, sir," replied Helmut with a salute.

The green and gold bus in his sights, Helmut stepped on the gas and honked his horn to warn the people in line. Cheeseheads, in a frenzied panic, scrambled out of the way, angrily shouting and waving their fists as the Chalet Cheese Co-op delivery truck skidded to a stop just two feet from the door of the bus.

"Do you want me to get closer?" asked Helmut.

Dairy Dan shook his head, "No, no, no…this is fine. Good job."

"Excellent!" exclaimed Einstein. "Now listen. Please refrain from any discourse regarding the objective of our quest. We all must be mindful not to arouse suspicion. Understand?"

"No," confessed Floyd.

"When you get on the bus, don't talk to anybody about why you're going to the Hall of Fame," explained Helmut to his friend.

"Why *are* we going?" asked Floyd, scratching his head.

"You know!" answered Helmut. "To steal the Bears' statues, so the Packers have more guys in the Hall!"

"Oh, that! Yeah, okay. You don't need to worry, Albert!" assured Floyd giving Einstein a slap on the back. "Secret's safe with me!"

Einstein buried his bald head in his hands and moaned.

With a pained expression on his face, Dairy Dan carefully squeezed his swollen foot into his shoe and turned to say a final few words to his team.

"Okay, everybody! Time to make history! Put on your cheese hats and blend in. Operation Georgie Porgie starts now!"

Grabbing their bags and belongings, the Limburger Heads stepped out of the delivery truck and tried to mix in with the agitated group of Packer fans. But shouts from the crowd and dirty looks came from every direction.

"What's the matter with you guys! You coulda run somebody over!"

"You need to be reported…that's reckless driving!"

"Are you people nuts?"

Hearing that question, Floyd immediately raised his hand and yelled, "Yes, we are! And don't ask us what we're doing here because it's a secret!"

Nick Monroe, who was standing beside his fellow Limburger Head, leaned over and mumbled in his ear, "Good job blending in, Floyd."

Quickly, Nick and Rick surrounded their clueless comrade and led him away from all the commotion before he could think of anything else to say.

"Our apologies," shouted Einstein, taking his cheese hat off and holding it over his heart to demonstrate his sincerity. "We have an injured Packer fan on board and our driver was endeavoring to place him in the closest proximity to the motorcoach as possible."

Hearing this, the angry mob softened a little as they watched 82-year old Demetri Papadopoulos step off the delivery truck with his walker.

"Go Pack Go!" cried out Papa, letting loose of his walker with one hand and raising a fist into the air.

Instantly, the pack of Packer lovers was united and the assembled Cheeseheads roared back…

"GO PACK GO! GO PACK GO!"

The agitated atmosphere was defused by the old cargo pilot's cheer and suddenly, it was smiles, handshakes and fist bumps. A bolt of excitement buzzed through the crowd with the anticipation of a road trip to watch the Packers play at the NFL's Hall of Fame Stadium.

Finally, Dairy Dan, struggling and in pain, hobbled out of the Chalet Cheese Co-op delivery truck and joined his crew of conspirators.

Disturbed by the difficulty Dairy Dan was having, Einstein opened his mouth to speak, but the Limburger Head leader threw up his hand to stop him.

"I'm okay," he grimaced. "It's now or never, so it's got to be now!"

"Here. I'll carry your canned ham for you," offered Nick. "Rick, you grab his duffle and we'll go save everybody a place in line."

"Sure thing, Pop!" chirped Rick cheerfully.

Nick and Rick Monroe scooped up Dairy Dan's belongings and

hustled over to get in the line that was re-forming to board the bus.

"Thanks, guys," sighed Dairy Dan as Papa scooted toward him with his walker.

"Squadron Leader Dan, you take her, Papa's walker," offered the ancient Greek proudly. "She is good friend."

"No, Papa, I can't do that," protested Dairy Dan.

"Yes, yes! It is fine. Today you need her more than me."

Smiling, Papa slid the walker to Dairy Dan.

"Try her. She work good."

Dairy Dan, nodding his appreciation, took hold of the walker and started rolling. Seeing their leader slowly on the move, the rest of the Limburger Heads fell in line behind him moving inch-by-painful-inch toward the front of the bus where people were boarding.

"I hope the bus doesn't decide to leave before we get there," fretted Floyd, looking at his Packer wristwatch.

Finally, the slow-marching Limburger Head parade arrived at the entrance to the motorcoach, where they were greeted by a smiling, toothless bus driver wearing thick eyeglasses and a green jacket. Embroidered above the pocket in yellow script was his name: *Sharky.*

"Tickets, please," said Sharky pleasantly, his toothless pink gums on full display.

Reaching into the pocket of his Packer pullover hoodie, Dairy Dan pulled out an envelope and handed it to the bus driver.

Opening the envelope, Sharky squinted through his glasses and counted the tickets. Then looking at the line of Limburger Heads, he silently counted heads.

"There are 13 tickets here, but I only count eight people," slobbered Sharky. "Where's the rest of your group?"

"Well, really, we're going to use only seven tickets now. Cheese Master Lundquist is here to see us off," answered Dairy Dan, leaning heavily on Papa's walker.

"I can't go," explained Helmut, identifying himself with a little wave to the bus driver. "Our Maddie Rose is getting baptized at Saint Victor's tomorrow and grandma and me gotta be there,"

"You're a cheese master?" slurred Sharky, reaching around Dairy Dan to shake Helmut's hand. "Bless you, sir!"

Turning back to the Leader of the Limburger Heads, Sharky continued his talk. "You're only using seven? What about the rest of 'em? It's too late for a refund."

"No-no-no…we don't need a refund," said Dairy Dan shaking his head. "We're …um… picking up six more guys at the Hall of Fame. They're already in Canton. They just need a ride here to Green Bay."

"Okay. I see," said Sharky, satisfied with the explanation. "So, I'll punch these seven tickets now and you hold on to the rest until you hook up with your buddies for the return trip. How's that?"

"Yeah, good," agreed Dairy Dan, shoving the extra six tickets back in the envelope and into the pocket of his Packer hoodie.

"Hey, but let me just say," added Sharky, spit flying. "If something like this ever happens again…"

"Yeah?" nodded Dairy Dan, holding his hand in front of his face to block some of the airborne drool.

"Think about one-way tickets…save ya some dough!"

"Good idea. Thank you," replied the slightly damp dairy farmer.

One by one, the Limburger Heads said goodbye to Helmut and boarded the bus. Henrietta, the last in line and lugging a heavy cooler, stopped in front of the cheese master and gave him a hug. Then, lifting the lid to the cooler, she handed Helmut a cabbage roll.

"Daj Maddie Ro'za." *Give to Maddie Rose.*

"Thank you, Mrs. Wozniak," acknowledged Helmut politely. "I am sure she will be thrilled with it."

Inside the bus, the line of Limburger Heads slowly made their way down the aisle to the available seats at the back.

"This is ideal," said Einstein softly, leaning forward to whisper to Dairy Dan. "We will have a modicum of privacy on our expedition."

"Right," agreed Dairy Dan. "Plus, we're back here by ourselves."

Stopping at the first empty seat, Dairy Dan handed the walker to Einstein, who pushed it to the end of the aisle. Then, taking off his backpack containing a toothbrush, clean underwear and two stink bombs, he reached up and stashed it in the overhead luggage rack.

"Papa, how about a window seat?" offered Dan with a wave of his hand. "I'd like to sit on the end here, so I can stretch out my leg."

"Window is good," agreed Papa, sliding past Dairy Dan.

Nick and Rick Monroe chose the seats across from Dairy Dan and Papa. Floyd and Einstein sat in the row behind Nick and Rick and across the aisle from them plopped Henrietta with her cooler full of cabbage rolls.

Dairy Dan turned his head to make sure his team was in place. Then, giving a glance at the empty bench seat at the very back, he smiled. "Tomorrow night, that seat would be packed ear-to-ear with Chicago Bears named George."

At the front of the bus, Sharky settled in behind the steering wheel and pulled the lever to shut the door. The sound of the engine starting was followed by the hiss of the air brakes. Seconds later, the Packer tour bus pulled away from its parking spot.

Taking off his Cheesehead hat, Floyd pressed his nose against the window to see his friend, Helmut, trotting alongside the green and gold deluxe 55-passenger motorcoach. He was waving and shouting.

"Good luck! Remember…put your clothespin on your nose before you take the lid off your stink bomb!"

....

Nestor was looking at a diagram of the Pro Football Hall of Fame on the computer when Hawk came running up the stairs and crashed through the bedroom door with excitement.

"Look what came in the mail!"

"Is it something to eat?" sniffled Michael, sitting on his bottom bunk and wiping his nose with a tissue.

With outstretched arms in front of his bandaged beak, Hawk held up a postcard featuring the Green Bay Packers' logo.

"We made it!" squawked Hawk. "We're on the Green Bay Packer Waiting List for season tickets! Our number is 109,550!"

"Let me see that!" exclaimed Nestor, taking the postcard from

Hawk. "This is cool! So, this means there are only 109,449 people ahead of us?"

"I guess so," said Hawk, breathing heavily through his mouth, thanks to his bandaged nose.

"*Only* 109,000 people," chuckled Michael. "Not bad…if the list goes down a thousand people a year, you're up in 109 years!"

"Yeah, but if it goes down TWO thousand a year, it'll be half that!" smiled Hawk.

"Oh yeah," scoffed Michael, coughing and wiping his nose again. "Fifty-five years…that's a LOT better."

Downstairs in the dining room, Audrey was just finishing setting the table. On each plate was a grilled cheese sandwich and next to that, a steaming bowl of tomato soup.

Disappearing back into the kitchen, Audrey returned with three glasses of milk. "Now, all I need is to add the surprise," she said to herself, "and then I'll call them down for dinner."

Up in the brothers' room, Hawk laid flat on his back on the floor and studied his postcard from the Packers.

Nestor went back to looking at the Hall of Fame diagram on the computer while Michael kept blowing his stuffy nose.

"Hey! It says here that they will email me when single-game tickets are available!" announced Hawk. "So maybe we won't have to wait a hundred years. Something like that could happen anytime! Maybe even this season!"

"What if it did?" laughed Michael. "How are you gonna get there? I guess if you were a real hawk, you could fly there."

"Sure…maybe!" argued Hawk defiantly. "Nestor, google how much it costs to fly to Green Bay."

"Not right now," said Nestor logging off the computer. "It's time for dinner. Mom's gonna be calling us down any second now."

"How do you know that?" challenged Hawk.

"Because I can smell it…It smells like-like…"

Struggling to identify the scent that was drifting up from downstairs, Nestor finally gave up and called on the expert.

"Michael, tell him what Mom's cooking for dinner."

"I can't smell anything," sniffed Michael. "I'm all stuffed up."

"Me, either," admitted Hawk. "My nose is taped shut."

Just then their mom's voice rang out from the bottom of the stairs. "Boys! Wash your hands! It's dinner time!"

"See, I told you!" gloated Nestor as he headed to the bathroom.

"Okay," said Hawk following his brother out the door. "After we eat, we can find out what it costs to fly to Green Bay. It would be way cool to see Lambeau Field."

"Keep dreaming bird-brain," chuckled Michael, pushing his way to the bathroom sink first.

Seconds later, the brothers came roaring down the stairs and into the dining room to discover - next to each soup and sandwich - sat a large, gold-colored, wedge-shaped piece of foam.

"Cheesehead hats!" shouted Nestor.

"No way," yelled Hawk.

"Looks pretty tasty," marveled Michael in complete awe.

Immediately, Nestor and Hawk tried on theirs, but instead of putting it on his head, Michael took a bite of his Cheesehead hat.

"Blech!" objected Michael, spitting out gold foam. "That's awful!"

"Thanks, Mom! These are great," declared Nestor as he adjusted the wedge on his head.

"Yeah! Thanks, Mom," chirped Hawk.

"Yeah, Mom! Even though it doesn't taste good, thanks anyway," chimed in Michael, blowing his nose with the napkin on the table.

"Since you're going to see the Packers play, I thought you should look like you belonged there," smiled Audrey, pleased with herself. "But no wearing them at the dinner table, okay?"

The brothers took off the foam hats and placed them by their chairs.

"Are you gonna come watch us play tomorrow, Mom?" Hawk asked while blowing on the hot tomato soup.

"Of course! I wouldn't miss it!" answered Audrey cheerfully. "I'm planning to get to Canton sometime during the first half, so I'll be in the stadium in plenty of time to watch you play. I'll probably leave right after your game. That way I can have bedtime snacks waiting for you when you get home and you can tell me all about your day at the Hall of Fame!"

"But what about the Packers and Broncos? You don't want to see that game?" asked Nestor, between bites of grilled cheese.

"All I care about is watching you three," smiled Audrey. "What time does your bus leave in the morning?"

"Ni…ni…ni…" Feeling another sneeze coming on, Michael made a desperate grab for his napkin. "Ah-Ah-Achoo!"

The sneeze sent the napkin flying off the table, so Michael wiped his nose on his sleeve and finished his answer.

"Nine o'clock, Mom."

"Not on your shirt," objected Audrey handing Michael another napkin. "Do you feel all right? Maybe you should sit out tomorrow. There'll be plenty more games this season."

"He's gotta play, Mom!" whined Hawk. "Michael is our star running back!"

"We'll take care of him, Mom," reassured Nestor. "You know, make sure he drinks fluids and stuff."

"I'm good Mom. It's just a cold," sniffed Michael. "All I need is some cheese nachos with jalapeno peppers."

Audrey, Nestor and Hawk all stopped eating and stared in confusion.

"You know, spicy food to unstuff my nose," explained Michael. "They cost $5.50 at Hall of Fame Stadium. I looked it up online."

"I want you all in bed early tonight. Lights out by 8:30," ordered Audrey.

"But Mom, I'm not sick," argued Hawk.

"You could use some extra rest, too. It'll give your scraped-up nose time to heal," explained Audrey, tenderly touching the bandage on his face. "Besides, you all have a big day ahead of you."

Knowing better than to argue, the brothers spent the rest of dinner talking about touring the Hall of Fame, playing in Tom Benson Stadium and watching the Packers and Broncos from the stands.

Nestor, the first to finish, asked to be excused so he could pack his duffle bag for the next day's adventure. Michael tossed the last bite of grilled cheese in his mouth and Hawk slurped up the little bit of soup left in his bowl. Putting on their Cheesehead hats, they soon followed their brother upstairs.

By the time Michael and Hawk tromped into the bedroom, Nestor was shoving his red football jersey into his duffle and zipping it up.

"Done!" proclaimed Nestor, placing his bag by the door so he could grab it on his way out in the morning. Then he made a mad dash to the desk before anyone else could beat him to the computer. "Hawk, you still want to know how much it costs to fly to Green Bay?"

"Look it up! Give him the bad news," laughed Michael looking over Nestor's shoulder at the monitor. Then, feeling a funny sensation in his nose, Michael turned his head and let loose.

"Ah-Ah-Ah-ACHOOOO!!!"

Michael's sneeze was so powerful, it catapulted the cheese hat off his head, knocking over his life-size cardboard cutout of Hot Dog Eating Champ Joey 'Jaws' Chestnut, which was standing five feet away.

"C'mon, Michael! Put a lid on it," warned Hawk. "Keep sneezin' like that and Mom's gonna make you stay home tomorrow."

"Sorry, Joey," apologized Michael as he stood up his cardboard cutout idol before crashing on his bottom bunk.

"$324 round trip," announced Nestor, pointing at the computer screen. "That's if you fly tomorrow. They say you can get better deals if you plan your trip a couple months ahead of time."

"That's a lot," sighed Hawk. "How much is a one-way ticket?"

"One-way ticket?" sniffed Michael. "What? You gonna just stay in Green Bay?"

Hawk drifted to the closet and pulled his duffle bag off the shelf as his brain shifted into mumble-talk.

"I sure would like to see Lambeau Field. The Frozen Tundra. Titletown USA. Maybe I could get a job at McDonald's. Stinky Smothers told me his big brother makes $8 an hour putting Happy Meals in a box. $8 an hour! I'd be rich. Movies. Killer. Yeah, I could take Killer to a movie."

"What am I sayin'?" stammered Hawk quite loudly.

"What?" asked Nestor, now studying the map of the Hall of Fame.

"Oh, nothing. I was just thinking out loud," said Hawk, shaking his head hard in order to empty it.

"Hey, look," gulped Nestor, pointing at the computer screen. "The Hall of Fame has a Time Tunnel!"

Michael rolled off the bottom bunk and took a couple of steps to where Nestor was sitting. "Whaddya mean, a Time Tunnel?"

"Could you actually go back in time?" asked Nestor, a little puzzled.

Michael leaned in and studied the diagram. Suddenly, his face brightened. "There it is! That's what I'm talkin' about!"

"What are you talking about?" asked Nestor, annoyed with his stuffed-up brother sniffling in his ear.

"The Hall of Fame Cafe! You go to the Time Tunnel....I'll be happy hanging out over here," smiled Michael, pointing to the cafeteria area on the map.

Just then, Audrey's voice rang out from downstairs.

"Time to brush your teeth! I will be up in five minutes!"

Shutting off the computer screen, the brothers headed down the hall to the bathroom. A couple of minutes later, they all shuffled back and slid under their covers, as Audrey arrived to kiss them good night.

"Big day tomorrow. Try and get some rest," she said softly. Flipping off the light, she quietly closed the bedroom door behind her.

Hawk yawned and drifted off to sleep, thinking about riding the same bus as Killer Kopecky during the two-hour drive to Canton.

Michael blew his nose and closed his eyes, thinking about scoring a 90-yard touchdown against the Bulldogs and getting a Twinkie.

And Nestor, excited and a bit nervous, stared at the ceiling from his top bunk and thought about walking through the Time Tunnel.

"I wonder what will happen in there," he whispered to himself.

....

Except for a short dinner break at a Steak 'n Shake in South Bend,

Indiana, Sharky kept the gleaming green and gold deluxe 55-passenger motorcoach moving toward Canton at a constant 65-miles per hour.

Boarding the bus again after they ate, Einstein asked Rick if he'd switch places because Floyd was talking so much. Now, with their bellies full of burgers and fries, the Limburger Heads all nodded off to sleep, except for Dairy Dan whose aching foot was keeping him awake, and Papa, who was looking out the window at the brightly moon-lit countryside.

Groaning a little as he shifted in his seat, Dairy Dan reached for his backpack and pulled out a map of the Hall of Fame.

"I might as well study my assignment," the Limburger Head leader mumbled to himself. On the diagram, he found the circled S where he was supposed to activate his stink bomb.

"Okay. I open my stink bomb here…in the middle of the Time Tunnel," he said continuing to think out loud.

"Then I go up the stairs to the Hall of Fame Gallery, grab my statue, which should be right about here. Carry the statue down the stairs and load it on the bus."

Papa turned away from the window and looked over at Dairy Dan looking at the map of the Hall of Fame.

"Stairs?" Papa shook his head. "Squadron Leader Dan, with bad foot, you ride elevator." The ancient Greek tapped his finger on the map where the elevator was located. "Which Bear George you go for?"

Dairy Dan reached into his backpack and pulled out a photograph.

"George Trafton," answered Dairy Dan, identifying the leather-helmeted man in the photo. "He played for the Bears from 1923 to 1932. I googled him and found out he was the first guy to hike the ball with one hand. He got inducted to the Hall in 1964."

"64? He sits by my Papa Bear George," said Papa.

"Yeah, that's right," agreed Dairy Dan. "We should probably stick with each other. That way I can help you if you need it."

"Yes, stick together is good plan," nodded Papa. "I help you if you need it."

Papa turned his head to look out the window again, so he didn't see

Dairy Dan frown at the idea of needing help from an 82-year old.

Stuffing the map of the Hall of Fame and the photo of George Trafton back in his Packer backpack, Dairy Dan closed his eyes and tried to ignore the throbbing pain in his foot.

Except for the sound of Sharky slurping up the last little bit of his chocolate milkshake through a straw, the deluxe 55-passenger motorcoach was completely quiet.

Papa gazed up at a beautiful full moon and thought about cheese. Then, following the moonlight down to a grassy field, he saw a cow holding up a sign: **Don't dO it!**

Immediately, Dairy Dan, who had just that moment dozed off, received a sharp jab in his side from Papa's bony elbow.

"You see 'im?"

"See what?" yawned Dairy Dan, struggling to open his heavy eyelids.

"Cow holding sign in field! Don't do it, cow tells me!" cried Papa.

"A cow holding a sign?" Dairy Dan heaved a heavy sigh and chuckled. "You were dreaming, Papa. Go back to sleep and tell me what happens next."

"Maybe cow with sign is sign. Do not steal Bears. Maybe the Operation Georgie Porgie is bad idea," fretted Papa.

"You're tired. Close your eyes and get some rest," said Dairy Dan. "Tomorrow night at this time, the Packers will have the most players in the Hall of Fame and the Limburger Heads will all go down as the greatest fans in Green Bay history."

Papa looked back out the window wondering. Had he been sleeping? Was it a dream? Or did he really see that cow? Was it a warning?

Every time he tried closing his eyes, the image of the black and white Holstein and the words **Don't dO it!** flashed in his head.

At the front of the bus, Sharky touched the menu button on his Magellan GPS system and glanced at his watch. In another ninety minutes, he would be pulling the motorcoach into the parking lot of the Ramada Hall of Fame Hotel.

Papa spent the entire time wide awake and worried.

CHAPTER 7

August 24 – 8:29 am EDT | Port Clinton, Ohio
Day of the Hall of Fame Game

"Should I be worried about you?" asked Audrey, standing at the front door, holding a hankie and ordering her stuffed-up son to blow.

Michael blew into the hankie and shook his head.

"I'm okay, Mom," insisted Michael.

"Yeah, he's okay, Mom," chimed in Hawk. "C'mon, guys. We gotta go. I wanna make sure I get a good seat on the bus."

"And what about you? Are you okay?" asked Audrey, tenderly touching Hawk's bandaged nose.

"I'm fine, Mom," insisted Hawk. "Coach wants me to keep the bandage on until after the game, so I don't bleed on everybody."

Giving Audrey a quick hug, Hawk put on his Cheesehead hat, picked up his duffle bag and started walking. Michael did the same and followed.

Nestor, still standing on the porch, stretched up to give his Mom a peck on the cheek and then whispered in her ear, "Don't tell Hawk I told you, but he's in a hurry because he wants to sit by Killer...er, I mean, Kathy...on the bus."

"Oh, really," smiled Audrey. "Well, don't worry. Your secret's safe with me."

"Thanks, Mom," chirped Nestor. Inspecting his Cheesehead hat before putting it on, he noticed it had a bite out of it.

"Hey, Michael! You've got my hat!" Picking up his duffle, he raced to catch up with his brothers.

"See you at the game tonight," shouted Audrey.

The boys gave their Mom a quick wave and headed down Look Out Drive past the lawn gnomes in Mrs. McChesney's front yard.

"Here's your hat, Michael," barked Nestor. "Now give me mine."

"What's the difference? They're all the same size," griped Michael.

Nestor held up the Cheesehead hat and pointed at the teeth marks. "Yours is chewed up."

Ignoring his brother, Michael turned the corner at Taft Street a few steps behind Hawk, who was leading the way.

"C'mon, Michael! Hand it over!" demanded Nestor as he shoved the wedge-shaped piece of foam into Michael's gut.

Michael made a mad-face and stopped walking. He took off Nestor's Cheesehead hat and was about to hand it off to his brother when he exploded again.

"ACHOOOO!" The spray from Michael's sneeze sparkled on Nestor's Cheesehead hat.

"Here! Take it!" said Michael, holding out the moist foam hat.

Nestor sighed and took possession of his sparkly Cheesehead hat. "Gee, thanks for getting it all germy," he groaned with sarcasm.

With a shrug of his shoulders, Michael put on the Cheesehead hat with the bite out of it and grabbed his duffle bag off of the sidewalk.

Up ahead, Hawk was frantically jumping up and down, yelling at his brothers to hurry.

"C'mon, guys! All the good bus seats will be gone!"

Picking up the pace, Nestor and Michael caught up with Hawk as he was turning the corner at 6th Street. In the distance, they could see some of their teammates milling around a yellow school bus parked in front of True Lay Stadium.

"Relax, Hawk," grumbled Michael. "Nobody's on the bus yet."

Just then, Stinky Smothers and Stinky Smothers' brother appeared from Clinton Street and joined the Hapburn boys hustling down 6th.

"Way cool!" shouted Stinky Smothers' brother. "Michael! Can I wear your Cheesehead hat tonight when you're in the game?"

"Sure, I don't mind," sniffed Michael. "Just don't eat it."

"Looks like somebody already tried," laughed Stinky Smothers.

"Yeah! That was Michael," said Nestor. "First thing he did when we got 'em was taste it."

"Yours is wet...what did you do? Run through a sprinkler?" asked Stinky, inspecting the Cheesehead hat on Nestor.

Nestor shook his head in disgust. "That was Michael, too. He sneezed all over it."

"Yeah, blame everything on me," muttered Michael.

Hawk, leading the pack and anxious to get there, broke into a trot. Stinky Smothers' brother took off after him. "Wait up, Hawk! Hey! Can I sit with you on the bus?"

"No!" shouted Hawk over his shoulder.

Hawk jogged into the parking lot ahead of both Smothers and both his brothers and dived into a group of teammates gathered around the bus. His head spinning, he finally spotted Killer in her new pink dress talking with Assistant Coach Jekyll.

Coach Jekyll was checking things off his clipboard and handing snacks to Killer. Killer would then stuff the treats into her pink duffle bag and make notes on her armband.

A few feet away, Frankie Flat-Nosed Fitzwater was practicing snapping the football to Apollo Vargas.

"What's up, Frankie?" asked Hawk, wondering why Frankie was working out with the Braves backup quarterback.

"Coach wants AV ready just in case Killer gets hurt," answered Frankie, pounding the ball back in Apollo's hand with a loud smack. "He told me that the Bulldogs have three guys on their D-Line who weigh over 200 pounds!"

"Wow! That's bigger than Michael," said Hawk with a worried look toward Killer. Trying not to think about it, Hawk changed the subject.

"Did you find anything at Portage Park?"

"I didn't," admitted Frankie. "But Billy Del Sesto dug up some bones. We thought we found the pirate grave, but Mr. Kopecky said they were just chicken bones. I'm gonna dig again tomorrow. You wanna go?"

"Naw, I don't think so," answered Hawk. "Thanks, anyway."

Then, noticing that Coach Jekyll and Killer were finishing up their meeting, Hawk drifted off in that direction.

Zipping up her bag, Killer looked up to see Hawk headed her way.

"Hey, Hawk! I like your hat!" she said cheerfully. "How's your nose?"

Hawk's stomach fluttered, happy the cute quarterback was talking to him. "The bandage is super tight, but Coach says I can take it off after the game. He just doesn't want me getting the field and everybody all bloody."

Killer leaned closed to Hawk and gently touched his beak. "Do you think it will pop back up or will it stay flat like Frankie's nose?"

With her touch, Hawk's stomach turned a complete somersault. "What?" he gurgled, completely lightheaded.

"Nothing," laughed Killer as she grabbed a baseball cap out of her bag and put it on over her short, dark hair. "I'm just joking."

"Joking? How can you joke right now? What about the game? Didn't Coach warn you about those 200-pound guys on the Bulldogs? Aren't you worried about getting hurt?"

Kathy Kopecky laughed again. "They'd have to catch me first. And there's no way I'm going to let some boy catch me!"

"No way?" sighed Hawk.

Killer leaned in close to Hawk and looked in his eyes. "I'm going to tell you this, but you can't tell anybody else. Okay?"

Hawk, unable to move his lips, nodded weakly.

Killer looked around to make sure no one else was close enough to hear what she was going to say. Satisfied, she put her hand up to Hawk's ear and whispered.

"We're running Twinkie Off Tackle first play!"

Struggling to speak, Hawk managed to dribble out, "Twinkie."

"Exactly!" laughed Killer. "Coaches want us to get ahead in the game right away, so we're going to try and catch the Bulldogs by surprise. Great, right?"

Waiting a moment to think of what he wanted to say, Hawk took a deep breath, kicked at a stone in the parking lot and started stammering away, "Kathy. I mean Killer, ah, well, I was wondering if maybe we could…if you wanted to…you know…when we get on the bus…as long as you don't have other plans…possibly we could sit togeth…"

"TWEEEEEEEEEEEEEEEEEEEEET!"

Coach Yak, at the front of the bus, spit his whistle out and waved his arms in the air to get everyone's attention.

"Today's the big day! I want you to have fun at the Hall of Fame, but I also want you thinking about the game. THE GAME! THE GAME! THE GAME!"

"ACHOOOO!" Michael wiped his nose with his sleeve as he, Nestor and the Smother's brothers moved alongside Hawk and Killer.

"Which game?" asked Stinky Smothers' brother, tugging on Nestor's arm. "I used to like Candyland. Now, I like Monopoly better."

Nestor patted Stinky Smothers' brother on the top of his head and kept his eyes glued on the big man talking.

"So, when we get on the bus," continued Yak. "I want the starters on Offense to sit up front with Coach Jekyll. The starters on Defense, you guys sit in the back with Coach Hyde. And everybody else, special team players and backups, you're in the middle of the bus with me."

Then, looking around to find the faces of the starters on both the offense and defense, Coach Yak pointed at Dave Francisco, Diego 'Hot Sauce' Sauceda, Stinky Smothers and Michael.

"You…you…you and you…you four sit up front. I want the entire offense together. And Hapburn, Michael…eat a light lunch, I want you hungry when we call our special plays."

"I'm always hungry, Coach," sniffed Michael.

"Well, eat a light lunch anyway…and if we win, I'll buy you a cheeseburger after the game," promised Yak, pausing a moment to scratch his chin. "In fact, win or lose, I'll buy the whole team cheese-burgers. Just go out and play your best and it'll all work out. Pick up your gear, get with your coach and let's get going!"

The Port Clinton Braves let out a loud cheer and started separating into groups outside the bus.

"This is going to be fun," announced Killer as she picked up her duffle bag. Then, suddenly remembering she turned to Hawk, "What were you asking me before the whistle blew?"

Hawk tugged at the bandage on his nose and sighed. "Oh, uh, nothing important."

Killer reached up and pressed Hawk's hand away from his bandage. "Don't pull at that. Your Mom wouldn't like it," she said with a smile.

The pint-sized quarterback started off toward the players gathered around Coach Jekyll, calling over her shoulder to Hawk, "See ya later!"

"Yeah, great...see ya later," repeated Hawk, trying to hide his disappointment. "Maybe we can hang out at the Hall of..."

"Hey, Nestor!" shouted Killer, interrupting Hawk mid-sentence. "You wanna sit with me on the bus? We can go over the plays."

"SURE!" answered Nestor as the excited group of Braves buzzed around pairing up for the bus ride.

By the time Hawk caught up with his group outside the bus, Moses Kupperman and the rest of his teammates on defense had already found partners, leaving him to spend the two-hour trip sitting next to the no-nonsense Coach Hyde.

"Sorry, Hapburn. I guess you're stuck with me," apologized Hyde, giving Hawk a pat on the back. "And I know that bandage on your nose is a little uncomfortable, but right after the game, I'll get you unwrapped."

"Thanks, Coach," said Hawk, trying not to be sad.

Coach Hyde pointed his finger at the players around him and counted. Satisfied everyone was there, he herded his unit on the bus.

Walking down the aisle, Hawk passed Nestor and Killer with their heads together going over the playbook. With a sigh, Hawk shuffled slowly to the back of the bus to the last available pair of seats.

"You want the window seat, Hapburn?" asked Coach Hyde as he threw his gear in the overhead luggage rack.

"Okay. I like the window," nodded Hawk, somewhat surprised that the hard Hyde was showing a soft side.

"Here...I'll throw your stuff up here," offered Coach Hyde, grabbing Hawk's duffle bag and Cheesehead hat and stowing it above.

Hawk slid across the bench seat and looked out at the True Lay Stadium parking lot. There, right outside his window, was the trash can into which Coach Hyde had dumped the red folder containing Nestor's secret plays a few days back.

Turning away from the window, Hawk watched as the skinny defensive coordinator sat down beside him and cracked open a book called *Coaching Football for Dummies*. On the cover, there was a picture of a youth football team in red uniforms.

Hawk dipped his head in the book's direction. "Sort of looks like our team," he said smiling.

Coach Hyde lifted his nose out of the book and looked at the photo on the cover.

"Yeah, it does. And look, this kid here is wearing your number 23," observed the suddenly-agreeable coach. "Are you excited about the game today?"

"Yeah. But mostly, I'm nervous," admitted Hawk.

"You're one of my best guys," confided Coach Hyde with a smile. "In fact, I think you're going to make a big play to help us win. No need to worry. You'll do fine."

"Thanks, Coach," replied Hawk, managing a grin.

"Have you ever been to the Hall of Fame before?" asked Coach Hyde, changing the subject to help take some pressure off his player.

"No, this is my first time," answered Hawk.

"You'll like it. It's a cool place. It's got some hands-on stuff, a Time Tunnel, huge gift shop," said Hyde, poking his nose back in the book. "Relax, hang out with your friends and have a good time."

Hawk turned and looked out the window and again his eyes were drawn to the trash can in the parking lot and he remembered how mad he was when he fished out the red folder. Coach Hyde seemed a lot different to him now. He was…nice.

The engine roared to life and then, with a jerk, the bus lurched forward. The excited voices got louder over the sound of the motor.

As they pulled onto 6th Street, an explosion from up front rocked the bus.

"ACHOOOO!"

"Excuse me," sniffed Michael, pulling out a tissue and wiping his nose. It was his biggest sneeze yet.

....

The drive to Canton ended the same way it began, with an explosive, Michael Hapburn, bus-rattling sneeze.

"Are you sure you're okay?" asked Coach Jekyll for the tenth time during the two-hour trip.

"I feel great," assured Michael for the tenth time. He was glued to the window as the bus moved slowly through traffic, passing a George Halas Drive street sign.

Then suddenly, there it was: the Pro Football Hall of Fame. Behind it, the Braves could see Tom Benson Hall of Fame Stadium where Green Bay and Denver would play later that night. And where they would play Olmsted Falls at halftime.

"There's a Packer bus!" shouted Ray Ray McKay, pointing at the gleaming green and gold motorcoach in the parking lot. "Do you think the Packers are on it?"

"No," answered Nestor shaking his head. "It's a bunch of old people getting off. See the guy with the walker? I don't think he's a player."

"Maybe they used to be players," said Frankie Fitzwater, shrugging his shoulders.

The Port Clinton team bus buzzed with excitement as they watched what they thought might be old Packers shuffling toward the entrance of the Hall of Fame.

"I bet the guy with the walker is Brett Favre!" declared Stinky Smothers. *Brett Favre Green Bay Packer Quarterback 1992-2007. Inducted into Pro Football Hall of Fame 2016.*

"I'm gonna get an autograph," shouted Braves wide receiver Tommy O'Connor.

"Me, too!" exclaimed linebacker Teddy Hyland.

Finally, their bus came to a stop and the Braves immediately jumped up.

"Hold it hold it hold it!" yelled Coach Yak, moving his 400-pound body into the aisle and blocking anyone's escape. "A couple of things before we go in..."

As Coach Yak began, Hawk glanced back out the window to see the last few people from the Packer bus break away from the rest of the group and gather by some benches in front of the entrance. They all had matching green and gold Packer backpacks and were wearing Cheesehead hats. One of them was the guy with the walker.

There was an old woman with them and she was dragging a cooler. Hawk watched as she opened the cooler and handed out plates. "Oh, look," he thought to himself. "Brett Favre is having lunch."

....

"Thank you, Ms. Wozniak," said Nick Monroe, taking a plastic plate, knife and fork from the short and sturdy Polish woman.

"Prosze!" she nodded. *You're welcome!*

She continued to hand out eating utensils to the row of Limburger Heads sitting on bench in front of the building.

"After we eat, we'll hang out here for a while," announced Dairy Dan, leaning on the walker and trying to ignore the throbbing pain in his foot. "Then, an hour before closing, we'll go in and find all the Bears we're going to nab. We gotta be sure we know the layout so when we activate our stink bombs we get in and out lickety-split. You follow?"

Everyone but Papa nodded in agreement as Henrietta Wozniak passed by a second-time, plopping cabbage rolls on their plates.

Without hesitation, they all hungrily attacked the delicious mixture of ground beef, pork sausage, onion, garlic and parsley wrapped in cabbage leaves.

"Floyd, I asked Mama to prepare enough cabbage rolls to feed the armed forces of the Republic of Poland, so consume your heart out," urged Einstein.

"Gee, thanks, Albert," said Floyd with his mouth full. "But I got to watch it. If I eat too much, I'll want to take a nap."

Einstein smiled, thinking to himself, "That is precisely what I want to occur."

In between bites, Dairy Dan looked down the row of Limburger Heads and noticed the ancient Greek cargo pilot staring at his plate. "Papa! What's the matter? You okay?"

"No. Not sure. Cow said do not do it," sighed Papa. "And you see sign on street?

"Sign?" repeated Dairy Dan, confused.

"George Halas Drive. Street named for MY George. Important guy, no?"

"Well, maybe. But let's face it, Papa, he's no Vince Lombardi," laughed Floyd, chewing non-stop.

"That's right, Floyd," agreed Dairy Dan. "Remember, Papa. MORE PACKERS in the Hall of Fame. That's what matters."

Papa looked down at his plate and stuck his fork in a cabbage roll. "Okay, okay. I do my duty," he promised, choking on the words.

....

"I wonder if they are old Packer players," daydreamed Hawk as he stared at the old guys eating. "I've heard of Brett Favre. I wonder if that's him." Turning away from the window, he tuned back into Coach Yak, who was just finishing his instructions to the team.

"...it's almost noon," bellowed the big coach, looking at his watch. "I want everybody back here by 4:45. That gives you plenty of time to explore.

"Leave your gear on the bus. We'll pick it up on our way to the practice field for our pre-game warm-up. You got it?"

Twenty-five excited Port Clinton Braves jumped up and cheered, ready for the events of the day to unfold.

"OKAY!" shouted Coach Yak. "TEAM on three! Ready? One... two... THREE..."

"TEAM!" they all yelled in unison. Even Stinky Smothers' brother.

Satisfied, Coach Yak moved out of the aisle and the mad rush to get off the bus began.

Hawk, stuck in the back, was one of the last to step down onto the sidewalk leading to the entrance of the Hall of Fame. Squinting into the bright light reflecting off the football-shaped dome jutting out of the building, Hawk put on his Cheesehead hat to block the sun.

Up ahead, he saw Nestor and Michael wearing their Cheesehead hats, waiting for him. Taking a quick look around, he spotted Killer and Apollo Vargas near the front of the bus. Next to them, Coach Yak and Coach Jekyll were talking to each other with their heads bent over their clipboards.

Hawk took a step in Killer's direction and waved to get her attention. "C'mon, you wanna hang out with Michael, Nestor and me?"

"Yeah! Sure!" she yelled back with a nod. "Coaches want to talk to us a minute, I'll catch up with you inside!"

Hawk nodded to her, his heart pounding in his chest.

"She said, 'Yeah! Sure!'" he thought happily to himself. With his head in the clouds, he looked to where his brothers were waiting.

"Speed it up, Hawk," called Nestor. "I wanna go inside!"

Hawk yelled back. "I'm coming! Keep your Cheesehead hat on!"

Joining his brothers, Hawk grabbed their shirt sleeves and pulled them close. "Before we go in, I wanna see if those guys over there are old Packers."

"They're old for sure, but I don't want to bother 'em. They're having lunch," pointed out Nestor.

"Lunch? Let's go see," said Michael, licking his chops.

Not wasting another second, Hawk and Michael took off toward the benches in front of the Hall of Fame with Nestor dragging behind.

Looking up from his plate, Einstein Wozniak was the first to spot the three boys heading in the Limburger Heads' direction. Wiping his mouth with his sleeve, he eyed them suspiciously and shouted.

"Halt! Identify yourselves! Friends or foes?"

"Fa-fa-fa-friends," stammered Hawk nervously, as the brothers stopped dead in their tracks.

Dairy Dan, sitting next to Einstein, gave him an elbow to the gut. "Cool it, Wozniak. They're just kids! And they got Cheeseheads on!"

"Correction. Greetings and salutations, fellow Packer backers! Oh, what a beautiful afternoon it is in Canton, Ohio," babbled Einstein, embarrassed at overreacting.

Confused at the mixed messages, Hawk swallowed hard and tried to remember what he wanted to say.

"Sorry to interrupt your lunch," apologized Hawk, a bit flustered. "But my brothers and I were wondering if you used to be Packer players."

"Packer players?" repeated Dairy Dan as the group of Limburger Heads chuckled and shook their heads.

"No, none of us actually played for the Packers," admitted Floyd. "But that guy there..." he said, pointing at Dairy Dan, "He tried out for the Packers during the NFL Players' strike."

Disappointed, Hawk looked at the big dairy farmer leaning on the walker. "Tried out? So you're not Brett Favre?"

"Brett Favre?" laughed Dairy Dan, pleased he was being mistaken for the all-time great Packer quarterback. Then, rubbing his sore foot he let out a long, sad sigh. "No, I'm afraid not. Got a tryout is all. But I was too slow. Bad wheels. Got cut the first day."

Sitting on the cooler, Henrietta Wozniak waved her serving spoon at Nestor, Michael and Hawk. "Czy chciałbyś się zwinąć w kostkę?"

"My mother is inquiring as to whether you would like to partake in a cabbage roll," translated Einstein.

"Yeah, sit down here. We'll get you kids some plates," offered Floyd scooting over to make room. "Best cabbage rolls you'll ever taste!"

"No, thank you," said Hawk, politely.

"Yeah. That's nice of you, but no thanks," chimed in Nestor.

"Sure, I'll have one!" beamed Michael happily, taking a seat among the group of Limburger Heads.

"More for me, too, Ms. Wozniak, please," hollered Floyd, holding up his plate.

Delighted to have another mouth to feed, Henrietta grabbed her baking dish and served up more cabbage rolls.

"Cieszyć się!" she beamed as she handed a fork and a loaded plate to Michael. *Enjoy!*

Seconds later, the always-hungry Hapburn was attacking the food and making yummy noises.

"See? What'd I tell you?" laughed Floyd, giving Michael a gentle jab with his elbow. "Great, right?"

"Don't eat too much, Michael," warned Nestor. "Remember we're playing in the game tonight."

"Playing in the game? Are you guys Packers?" joked Floyd.

Nestor laughed and shook his head. "No, our game is at halftime. We play for the Port Clinton Braves."

"But we are on the waiting list for Packer season tickets!" offered Hawk proudly. "Our number is 109,550!"

"That's cool," said Rick Monroe, wiping his mouth and looking around for a trash can to dump his paper plate. "We're on the waiting list, too. Have been ever since I was born. What number are we, Pop?"

"I don't remember exactly," answered Nick Monroe, as he pulled out his wallet to check the postcard from the Packer Ticket Office. "We're number 47,122."

"Wow!" exclaimed Hawk.

"Yep!" agreed Rick. "Another fifty or sixty years, we'll be at the top!"

Michael, in the process of licking his plate clean, pulled a tissue out of his pocket and blew his nose. "Those cabbage things are the best things ever!" He sighed, patting his belly.

"More for our hungry cheesehead here!" laughed Dairy Dan.

Immediately, Henrietta scooped two more cabbage rolls for his plate. Without hesitation, Michael plowed into his second helping.

"Michael..." whined Nestor, grabbing his eating hand. "I don't think you should."

"Let go of my hand," responded Michael, shaking free of his grip.

"Never come between a man and his cabbage rolls, I always say," laughed Floyd. "I usually eat nine or ten and then curl up in a corner to sleep."

Einstein smiled again. But Nestor had the opposite reaction, shoving his hands into his pockets as he moaned, "That's what I'm afraid of."

Hawk looked over toward the Braves' bus to see Killer, Apollo Vargas and the coaches all still in a huddle. Not in any hurry to go into the Hall of Fame without the Brave's cute quarterback, he decided he'd make some time-killing conversation instead.

"So, you guys from Wisconsin? How long you been Cheeseheads? Do you like cheese?"

"We LOVE cheese! We're from Monroe, Wisconsin. It's the Swiss Cheese Capital of the USA. And we're more than just Cheeseheads," declared Floyd proudly. "We're Limburger Heads and we're on a secret mish..."

Hearing the word secret, Einstein jumped up and covered Floyd's mouth with his hand. All that came out was a mumbled-up mess of sounds.

"Sio taputt ma acker hallof fumbn."

Einstein coughed and chuckled nervously. "What my loquacious brother Limburger Head is intimating is that we are Cheeseheads of a high and secret order. We have a calling to uphold Packer ideals and live a hallowed green and gold existence."

"I'm not sure I understand what you're saying," confessed Hawk, fidgeting with his bandaged nose.

"Nobody does," admitted Dairy Dan.

Hawk and Nestor laughed and Michael kept eating cabbage rolls.

"See what it is, we Limburger Heads are the most devoted of all fans," explained the big dairy farmer, struggling to his feet and putting his hand over his heart. "We eat, sleep and breathe Packer football. We are committed to do whatever necessary to ensure Green Bay's rightful place as the greatest team in the NFL."

"Right! I do my duty and forget what cow says," vowed Papa, speaking up for the first time since the Hapburn brothers joined them.

Nestor scrunched up his face. "A talking cow?"

"Not talk," corrected Papa. "From bus, I see cow by road next to sign with words saying 'don't do it!' "

"Hey! I know that cow," cried Hawk.

Immediately, everyone except Hawk and Papa burst out laughing.

"That's a good one, kid," howled Floyd, slapping his knee.

"No, really! I do know that cow. The sign I saw said 'Have fun in Chicago', only the cow spelled Chicago with a K in the middle," insisted Hawk, which made everyone laugh harder.

Just then, Nestor saw Kathy Kopecky standing by the entrance to the Hall of Fame waving them over.

Nestor tapped on Hawk's shoulder and whispered in his ear. Hawk's head immediately snapped around to locate Killer waiting by the door. His heartbeat doubled, pounding hard in his chest.

"It was nice meeting all of you," Hawk said quickly, dropping the cow. He took off in Killer's direction, leaving the Limburger Heads chuckling and shouting their good-byes.

"C'mon, Michael, we're wasting time," nagged Nestor as he tugged on Michael's arm. "Put down the fork and let's go inside."

"You go. I'm not finished," instructed Michael between bites. "I think I'll hang out here with these guys for a while longer…if it's okay with them."

"Sure! Hang out with us. Who knows? You might even want to become a Limburger Head yourself," said Dairy Dan. "Mrs. Wozniak, I think our new friend here is ready for a third helping!"

Henrietta waddled over to Michael with her dish and plopped two more cabbage rolls on his plate. "Dobrze! Jeść, jeść!" *Good! Eat, eat!*

"Thank you! These are delicious!" said Michael politely, stopping to blow his runny nose with his napkin.

"Michael, remember what the coach said. You gotta be hungry for the game," nagged Nestor.

"Don't worry…I'll be hungry," insisted Michael. "Take off! Go in with Hawk and Killer."

"Ka-Ka-Killer?" stammered Floyd nervously. "Who's Killer?"

"That's Killer over there, talking to my brother. She's our quarterback," answered Nestor, pointing toward the door. Frustrated, Nestor kicked at the pavement and turned to leave. "See ya later."

The Limburger Heads all gave Nestor a happy wave, while Michael kept his head down, totally focused.

Floyd, watching Hawk, Nestor and Killer walk toward the entrance of the Hall of Fame, scratched his chin and revealed what was banging around inside his head.

"Killer's your quarterback? But she's a girl."

....

"Should we wait for Michael?" asked Killer, looking back to the benches where Limburger Heads were finishing their lunch.

"No, he's too busy eating," moaned Nestor. "He's at six cabbage rolls and counting. If he's not hungry at game time, we're in trouble."

"What game?" asked Hawk, unable to think about anything except hanging out with Killer for a little while.

"Don't worry, Nestor. You know that Michael's always hungry, " reassured Killer. "Besides, our game is still hours away. The secret snack plays will work great."

Then, throwing her arms around her teammates' shoulders, she led them into the NFL Hall of Fame. "C'mon! Let's see what this place is all about!

....

The NFL Hall of Fame is located in Canton, Ohio where the National Football League was founded in 1920. The original building, built in 1963, contained just two rooms.

Those two rooms have undergone many expansions, with the latest completed in October 1995. The Hall of Fame now has 82,307 square feet of interior space, making it more than four times its original size.

In addition to Hall of Fame Gallery, the building features an event center, gift shop, café, interactive exhibits, a research library as well as the Super Bowl Theater featuring NFL Film productions on a 20x42 foot Cinemascope screen.

There are more than 300 former players, coaches and administrators enshrined in the NFL Hall of Fame. The Chicago Bears, founded in Decatur, Illinois in 1919 and then moved to Chicago in 1921, have the most players in the Hall with 28.

....

"ZZZzzzZZZZzzZZZZ…"

Floyd, after eating 11 cabbage rolls, was snoring loudly as he slept sitting up on the bench outside the Hall of Fame.

"zzz-ACHOOOO-zzZZz!"

Michael, asleep with 14 cabbage rolls in his belly, was laying down on the bench next to Floyd, snoring *and* sneezing.

The rest of the Limburger Heads were getting restless. Would their Operation Georgie Porgie be a success and make them heroes? Or, what would happen if they failed and got caught?

Nervously, they studied the visitor maps Einstein had passed out and watched the steady stream of tour groups and families enter and exit the Hall of Fame.

Rubbing his aching foot, Dairy Dan groaned and looked at his Packer wristwatch. It was 3:30. Time for final instructions.

"Okay, everyone. Huddle up!" he announced firmly.

The Limburger Heads gathered around their leader, all except for Floyd who was still catching some ZZZs alongside Michael, who was catching ZZZs and sneezing.

"What about Floyd?" asked Rick. "Want me to wake him up?"

"Absolutely not! Although it appears Floyd is asleep, he is actually in deep meditation," explained Einstein.

Rick frowned. "Floyd? Deep meditation?"

Dairy Dan nodded. "Yes. You may not be aware of this but…uh… Floyd…Floyd is a…a…"

"Zen Master," injected Einstein, helping Dairy Dan find the words.

"Floyd?" chuckled Nick.

"Yes," insisted Einstein. "If he has told me once, he has told me one thousand times: When you have an assigned task, you should perform with your whole body and mind. You must shut out whatever is going on around you and your entire being must be concentrated on what you need to accomplish."

"You may think he's sleeping," added Dairy Dan, "but no…Floyd's getting himself totally focused and…uh…what Einstein said. He's shutting everything out."

At that moment, Floyd let loose a loud, thunder-rumbling snore. "zzzzZZZZzzZZZZ...ZZZZ!"

"Okay, then. Better let the Zen Master focus," said Nick.

"Yeah, right," nodded Rick.

The next ten minutes were spent with Dairy Dan quizzing the Limburger Heads to make sure everyone knew every detail of the plan. After he was satisfied, he instructed everyone to open their backpacks to check their equipment.

With his backpack laid open in front of him, Dairy Dan starting calling out items on the checklist.

"Stink bomb..."

"CHECK," replied the Limburger Heads in unison.

"...clothespin..." "CHECK!" "... potato sack..." "CHECK!" "...Packer wristwatch..." "CHECK!" "...Hershey bar..." "CHECK!"

"Hershey bar?" questioned Nick Monroe, holding up the great American chocolate bar in its distinctive brown wrapper. "What's that for?"

"Floyd wanted to include it, in case anybody got hungry," explained Dairy Dan.

Nick's head turned to where Floyd was napping next to Michael and sighed. "Are you sure we shouldn't wake up the Zen Master? He should be hearing this."

"Do not concern yourself with Floyd," insisted Einstein. "Just carry out your assignment."

"Right," chimed in Dairy Dan. "You'll see in a minute that Floyd is dialed in.

"Remember, we are a team. If we all do our jobs, we'll be fine. Okay, the last thing on my list...tell me which Bear you're bringing out and the year he got inducted.

"If you know the year your Bear got into the hall, he's gonna be easier to find. Wozniak...you first."

Einstein jumped up off the bench and snapped to attention. "George McAfee. Inducted into the Hall of Fame in 1966."

Dairy Dan nodded and continued his roll call. "Nick..."

"George Connor. 1975," replied Nick.

"Correct," said Dairy Dan. Putting a check next to Nick's name, he continued down his list. "Rick..."

"George Musso. He got in the Hall of Fame in 1982," answered Rick confidently.

"That's right Rick. Very good."

"Booyah!" shouted Rick, thrusting his fist in the air.

"Okay, Papa. You're next," announced Dairy Dan.

Demetri Papadopoulos slowly stood and placed his hand over his heart. "I take Papa Bear. George Halas. He is in Hall of Fame first class of 1963."

Wiping a tear from his cheek, Papa sighed and sat back down on the bench.

Dairy Dan looked down the list. There were check marks next to everyone's name except for his and Floyd's.

Leaning on the walker, the head Limburger Head struggled to his feet with a pained expression. "George Trafton. Inducted 1964."

Then, looking at his wrist, Dairy Dan took a deep breath and continued. "Okay, everybody. Synchronize your watches. It is exactly four-O-one in the PM. In exactly 29 minutes, go to your designated area in the building and take the lid off your stink bomb. You follow?"

Adjusting the time on their wristwatches, the Limburger Heads all nodded.

"Don't forget: Put your clothespin on your nose first! Find your George, throw your sack over him and get back here. Floyd's gonna lead the way."

Nick Monroe looked at Floyd snoring next to Michael and shook his head in disbelief. "Floyd? Lead the way? You're kidding..."

Dairy Dan put up his hand for silence. Then, throwing his backpack over his shoulders, he pointed at Einstein.

Nodding, Einstein walked over to where Floyd was sawing logs on the bench. Bending down, he whispered in Floyd's ear. Immediately, the sleeping Limburger Head snapped to attention. Although his eyes were wide open, his face had a blank expression.

"George Blanda. Inducted into the Pro Football Hall of Fame. 1981," hummed Floyd in a steady robotic tone.

Then, without another word, Floyd fidgeted with his Packer wristwatch, put on his backpack and his Cheesehead hat and marched toward the building.

With their jaws dropped in amazement, Nick and Rick Monroe fell in line behind Floyd, followed by Einstein and Papa with Dairy Dan, supported by the walker, bringing up the rear.

One by one, the six Limburger Heads, wearing Packer backpacks and Cheesehead hats, passed through the front door of the Hall of Fame.

Operation Georgie Porgie had begun.

....

"That was fun," smiled Hawk as he walked out of the Hall of Fame Store in between Killer and Nestor.

"What are you going to do with all those little NFL helmets you bought?" asked Killer waving her hand toward the bag containing Hawk's purchases.

"I don't know," shrugged Hawk. "Maybe I'll get some hamsters and teach them how to play football."

"I wonder where Michael is," sighed Nestor. "It's almost time to get ready for our game."

"Hey, look," chirped Hawk, pointing to a Cheesehead walking toward the Time Tunnel. "Isn't that one of the guys we met outside?"

"Yeah. I think his name is Floyd," added Nestor. "Let's go talk to him. Maybe he knows where Michael is."

Hawk, Nestor and Killer headed in Floyd's direction, while outside on the bench in front of Hall of Fame, Michael was waking up from his snoring/sneezing nap.

Wiping the sleep from his eyes, he discovered he was alone except for Henrietta Wozniak. She stood a few feet away with her back to him, washing dishes in a small tub of soapy water.

"Excuse me," said Michael, tapping the short, stocky woman on her shoulder. "Where did everybody go?"

Smiling, Henrietta dried her hands on her apron and waddled over to her baking dish to scoop out another cabbage roll.

"Oh, no more. Thank you THEY WERE REALLY GOOD," said Michael loudly and patting his tummy. "But I need to find my friends. DO YOU KNOW WHERE THEY WENT?"

Henrietta stood there for a few seconds with a puzzled look, then her face brightened.

"Moi chłopcy weszli do środka, aby kraść niedźwiedzie," she proclaimed proudly, waving in the direction of the Pro Football Hall of Fame. *My boys went inside to steal the bears.*

Michael pointed at the doors of the building and Henrietta nodded her head and smiled. After thanking her again for the cabbage rolls, Michael turned and took off toward the entrance.

He wasn't sure how long he had been sleeping and he felt a little discombobulated. Stopping in front of the door, Michael gave himself a couple of raps on the side of his head to clear the cobwebs.

Satisfied he was seeing things more clearly, he stepped inside.

The place was packed. There were hundreds of people everywhere, and like himself, most of them were wearing Cheesehead hats. Standing in the Grand Lobby, Michael spun around in a circle looking for a familiar face.

Finally, on the far side of the lobby, he spotted Nestor, Hawk and Killer walking into the hallway leading to the Time Tunnel. Wiping his stuffy, runny nose on his sleeve, Michael took off after them.

....

On the Upper Level, Dairy Dan was standing with the walker in his spot by Elevator 1. He looked at his watch and heaved a heavy sigh. It was 4:27. Three minutes to go before it was time for the Limburger Heads to activate the stink bombs.

Down the hallway, by the entrance to the Hall of Fame Gallery, Papa worried about what the cow had said. Rocking from side-to-side, he watched as throngs of football fans were pulled in like magnets to view the bronze busts of their gridiron heroes. Slipping his Packer backpack off his shoulders, he set it carefully on the floor at his feet.

Stationed at the exit of the Hall of Fame Gallery, near the stairs and Elevator 2, Einstein glanced at his Packer wristwatch with nervous excitement. Unzipping his backpack, he reached inside and wrapped his hand firmly around the two-quart mason jar.

At the bottom of the stairs, between the Grand Lobby and the Hall of Fame Store, Rick Monroe was carefully lifting his stink bomb out of his backpack. Out in the light, the glass container of yellow-green ooze suddenly sparkled. Surprised, Rick quickly slid the glimmering emerald jar in the pouch of his Packer hoodie so no one would notice.

Also on the Lower Lever, Nick Monroe was hiding in the shadows of the First Century Exhibit by Elevator 1, directly below Dairy Dan. He looked around to make sure no one was watching him. Satisfied, he pulled his clothespin from his pocket and placed it on his nose, pinching both of his nostrils completely closed.

And in between Rick and Nick, right in the middle of the Time Tunnel, Floyd stood silently and motionless. His eyes were glazed over, staring eerily straight ahead. He had his clothespin on his nose and a stink bomb in his hand. He was in his proper position in front of the wall with a life-size illustration of Don Hutson. *Don Hutson Green Bay Packer receiver 1935-1945. Inducted into Pro Football Hall of Fame 1963.*

....

On the lookout, Nestor, Hawk and Killer entered the Time Tunnel.

"There he is!" shouted Nestor as the three of them approached Floyd standing frozen by the image of the immortal Don Hutson.

"Hi, Floyd! How ya doing?" chirped Hawk with a happy wave.

Floyd didn't move a muscle.

"Why does he have that on his nose? And what's that jar of green stuff he's holding?" frowned Killer. She waved her hand in front of Floyd's face. "He doesn't even blink!"

"That's strange," said Hawk, rubbing an itch on his bandaged nose. "Outside, he was talk-talk-talk. He didn't stop blabbering."

"Maybe he's hypnotized," offered Nestor. "It's like how Michael acts when he sleepwalks."

Just then they heard a sneeze from behind them.

"ACHOOOO!"

Nestor, Hawk and Killer turned around to see their star running back walking toward them, wiping his nose with a tissue.

"Michael!" they all cheered in unison. Killer gave him a happy hug, which caused Hawk to make a frowny face.

"Sorry, I'm late," apologized Michael.

"Late? Look at the clock" laughed Hawk, pointing to a clock on the wall of the hall. "It's more than late! It's almost time to go."

"I guess I fell asleep after my snack," sniffled Michael.

"You call what you had a snack?" grumbled Nestor. "How many cabbage rolls did you eat?"

"Not that many. Maybe 14 or so," sniffled Michael again. Then, pointing at Floyd, he said, "He ate at least 11 or 12! Whoa! Weird! What's with the thing on his nose?"

"Don't know," answered Hawk. "He doesn't talk. He doesn't even blink. It's like he's frozen."

"Where are his friends?" asked Michael.

Hawk shrugged his shoulders. "Haven't seen 'em."

"You're right, Michael," said Nestor. "His friends. We need to find those...those..."

"Limburger Heads," Hawk offered.

"Right! We gotta find those Limburger guys and let them know about this, then hustle back to the bus to get ready for our game. C'mon, Michael! Let's go!"

"What should we do?" asked Hawk.

"Keep an eye on this guy and make sure he stays put."

Hawk and Killer nodded their heads as Nestor and Michael took off toward the elevator to the second floor. Hawk was secretly happy to be sharing watchdog duty with Killer and took advantage of the opportunity to throw his arm around the quarterback's shoulder.

"Don't be scared," gurgled Hawk gently. "It'll be okay."

"Scared? I'm not scared!" laughed Killer, ducking out from under his arm. "This is fun!"

His efforts to stand close to Killer thwarted, Hawk heaved a heavy sigh. "Yeah…lots of fun."

At that moment, Floyd twitched.

"Look! Did you see that?" gasped Killer.

Slowly and without blinking, Floyd robotically moved his watch directly in front of his face.

It was 4:29.

....

The elevator bell chimed, the doors slid open and Nestor and Michael bolted out onto the second floor. Their heads spinning, they found a familiar face.

"Over there! The guy with the walker!" shouted Nestor.

Seconds later, Nestor and Michael were telling Dairy Dan about Floyd in his strange trance in the Time Tunnel, holding a jar of green stuff with a clothespin on his nose.

"Something's wrong with him and he needs your help," cried Nestor. "He's right below us! C'mon, we'll take you to him!"

"Wait-wait-wait…calm down," insisted Dairy Dan, shifting his weight off his aching foot. "Say that again."

"Your Limburger friend, Floyd, he doesn't move. Doesn't talk. He doesn't even blink," exclaimed Michael.

"It's like he's asleep standing up…with a clothespin ON HIS NOSE!" added Nestor. "Come see for yourself!"

"Let me get this straight," said Dairy Dan calmly. "You're telling me he was holding a jar like this one?"

Nestor and Michael watched and nodded their heads as Dairy Dan pulled his stink bomb from his backpack.

"And he had THIS…" the head Limburger Head held up a clothespin and clipped it on his nose. "On his nose?"

Nestor and Michael's jaws dropped.

"Yeah! Just like that!" shouted Nestor.

Dairy Dan scratched his chin thoughtfully and looked at his Packer wristwatch. It was 4:30.

"Excuse me a second," said Dairy Dan, holding up his index finger. "I have to take the lid off this jar."

At that exact moment, all the Limburger Heads, Rick, Nick and Floyd on the first floor and Papa, Einstein and Dairy Dan on the second floor, unscrewed the top of their stink bombs, letting the powerful odor of Helmut Lundquist's combination of the most foul, rank, reeking, horrible smelling cheeses escape and explode inside the Hall of Fame.

The noxious fumes roared through the building, knocking football fans flat as if they had just been run over by 300-pound defensive linemen. In the Super Bowl Theater, people were slumped over in their seats. In the Hall of Fame Store, people were piled on the floor up and down every aisle.

The Hall of Fame, a bustling, buzzing hive of activity a few seconds prior, was now frighteningly still and completely silent.

Dads with sons walking through the Hall of Fame Gallery, Moms with strollers headed toward restrooms, kids pushing buttons at hands-on exhibits...they all dropped on the spot after one sniff of the cheese master's putrid and festering creation.

Everybody in the building without a clothespin clipped on their nose...BAM...all knocked out cold.

Everybody except Michael and Hawk.

....

Floyd, expressionless with his eyes glazed, placed his stink bomb at his feet. Turning slowly, he moved like a robot down the Time Tunnel toward the elevator leaving Hawk standing alone and horrified among hundreds of bodies, including Killer's, lying all around the Hall of Fame floor.

"Wait! What happened? Where are you going? I need your help!" shrieked Hawk, as he watched Floyd disappear around the corner.

Quickly, Hawk bent down to check if Killer was still breathing. Putting his hand in front of her mouth, he could feel air moving in and out. Relieved she wasn't dead, Hawk pulled her to the wall and propped her up.

"Killer! Killer!! Wake up!" pleaded Hawk, patting her hand to try and revive her.

Just then, Rick Monroe came running into the Time Tunnel with an empty potato sack slung over his shoulder. Desperate, Hawk jumped up and grabbed him before he could fly by.

"Hey! What happened to everyone?" cried Hawk, wild-eyed.

"Oh! Hi!" huffed Rick, out of breath, in part because he was in a hurry and also because he had a clothespin on his nose. "Sorry can't talk now. Operation Georgie Porgie. Gotta go!"

"Wait, you gotta help me with her! She's knocked out," howled Hawk, waving an arm in Killer's direction.

"Everybody's knocked out! We exploded stink bombs!" explained Rick, pulling away. "Get her outside. She'll be okay!"

Hawk watched as Rick flew out of sight around the corner. Then looking back at Killer, he stood there wringing his hands and tried to think. Suddenly, the *fireman's carry* Coach Yak had taught them in gym class flashed in his head.

Bending down, Hawk grabbed Killer's right hand with his left and draped it over his shoulder. Then squatting, he took a hold of her knee and pulled the lightweight quarterback onto his back.

After taking a second to balance himself, Hawk with Killer on his back was weaving his way through the body-strewn lobby to the exit.

As he weaved, he puzzled about what Rick said.

"Stink bombs? Why did they explode stink bombs? And why didn't the stink bombs knock ME out?"

Slow and steady, trying to balance Killer and also avoid the fallen fans, he was nearly to the front door when it struck him.

"The bandage on my nose! I can't smell anything!"

....

And because of his cold, Michael couldn't smell anything either. So, when Nestor dropped but Michael didn't, Dairy Dan was very confused.

Dairy Dan, looked down at Nestor on the floor and up to Michael still on his feet and woefully exclaimed, "What the…? Something's wrong here!"

"I'll say! Nestor's fainted!" yelled Michael. Then, looking around, he yelled even louder, "HEY! EVERYBODY'S FAINTED!"

"Here, take a whiff of this," urged the perplexed dairy farmer as he waved his stink bomb under Michael's nose.

Michael took a couple of sniffs and shrugged his shoulders.

"I don't understand it. This stink bomb should've knocked you out like everybody else," declared Dairy Dan, fanning the rancid stench in Michael's direction.

Suddenly, Michael's stuffy head was swimming with questions. "Stink bomb? What's up with that? Why do you want me knocked out? Are all these people…*ACHOOOO!*…okay?"

"Take it easy! Take it easy," instructed Dairy Dan, patting Michael on the top of his Cheesehead hat to calm him down. "Everything's fine…"

"Fine? How can you say that?" interrupted Michael. "My brother… that family over there…that security guard against the wall…they're all…all…"

"Resting!" explained Dairy Dan, finishing Michael's sentence. "Yeah, that's it…they're all resting while we collect some…uh-uh-uh…SOUVENIRS. For a special ceremony at Lambeau Field. To start the NFL season."

"Souvenirs? Special ceremony?" repeated Michael, baffled.

Dairy Dan nodded. "Yeah, but it was supposed to be a surprise. That's why we had to knock everybody out temporarily. Except now the surprise is sorta spoiled 'cuz you know about it."

"I don't know anything," said Michael, shrugging his shoulders. "And if I did, I don't have to tell anybody. I mean, I wouldn't want to ruin your … *whatever*."

Just then, the elevator doors opened and Nick and Rick ran out, heading in a hurry to the Hall of Fame Gallery to collect their Bear busts. A few steps behind the father and son was Floyd, moving in a robotic way with a blank expression on his face.

"There he is!" yelled Michael, pointing at Floyd. "See? Like we said! He's like in a trance or something!"

"Don't worry. He's in a somnambulistic state," explained Dairy Dan as he wobbled away with his walker down the hall behind the other Limburger Heads.

"No, he's not. He's in Ohio," corrected Michael. "Hey, where are you going? What should I do about my brother?"

"I gotta go collect those…uh…you know…souvenirs," shouted Dairy Dan over his shoulder. "Stay with your brother. He might be a little confused and groggy when he wakes up."

Michael heaved a heavy sigh and blew his stuffy nose as he watched Dairy Dan shuffle off behind Floyd down the hallway. As he sat down on the floor beside his knocked-out brother, his stomach rumbled. He was getting hungry again.

....

Outside the Hall of Fame, in the sunshine and fresh air, Hawk was frantically fanning his Cheesehead hat over Kathy Kopecky's face. After a few seconds, the little, dark-haired quarterback's eyes blinked open to see Hawk's bandaged beak in front of her.

"Hooray! You're okay!" shouted Hawk happily.

"Hey! What happened? How did we get out here?" asked Killer, shaking her head to get the cobwebs out. "Last thing I remember that…that guy was taking the top off that jar of….gooey green junk."

"I think it was a stink bomb!"

"Stink bomb?" questioned Killer, scrunching her face.

"Yeah," answered Hawk with a nod. "And when Floyd took the top off, you and everybody else in the building passed out."

"How come YOU didn't?"

Hawk shrugged his shoulders and pointed at his bandaged nose. "I guess 'cuz of this. I can't smell a thing."

"How'd I get out here?"

"I carried you," said Hawk. "No way I was leaving you in there."

"You carried me out? Wow! You're amazing!" declared Killer, causing the parts of Hawk's face that weren't covered in white surgical tape to turn bright red.

Taking a deep breath, Killer looked toward the doors to the Hall of Fame and frowned. "Something strange is going on in there. Where are Nestor and Michael? You think they're okay?"

At that instant, Hawk felt a tap on his shoulder which made him jump, spin in midair and land on his backside.

There in front of him stood Stinky Smothers' brother, already wearing his number 25 football jersey.

"Coach is looking for you guys. It's time to get ready for the game."

"We'll be right there. We're just waiting for Nestor and Michael to come out," explained Killer.

"Yeah! We're waiting for Nestor and Michael," agreed Hawk, as he and Killer got up off the ground.

Stinky Smothers' brother gave a worried look back toward the team bus parked by the practice field. "Coach is gonna be mad. I better go in and get 'em."

He started toward the door, but before the backup running back could take a step, Hawk reached out and grabbed his jersey.

"Hey! Don't go in there!" hollered Hawk.

"Why not?" squealed Stinky Smothers' brother, struggling to escape.

"I don't know, it's um…sorta hard to explain," sputtered Hawk.

"Just go back and tell Coach Yak you found us and we're on our way," instructed Killer clearly.

"Go back without you guys?" Stinky Smothers' brother stood there with a worried look on his face. "I'd rather run through a brick wall."

Spinning Stinky Smothers' brother around, Hawk gave him a shove toward the practice field. "Go! We'll be right behind you."

Killer and Hawk watched as Stinky Smothers' brother moped slowly away. With a sick feeling in his stomach, Hawk wondered what they should do next.

He did not have to wonder long because little Kathy Kopecky tapped him on the shoulder and pointed toward the building.

"Hawk! You need to go back inside!"

....

Inside the Hall of Fame, Einstein had already thrown his potato sack over the head of Chicago Bear Halfback George McAfee and he was lugging his heavy load down the hallway leading to Elevator 1.

Rick Monroe, carrying George Musso, was right behind, followed by Nick Monroe with his burlap bag containing the bust of Bear's Linebacker George Connor.

Floyd, still trying to locate his George, was sleepwalking his way down the long row of bronzed football legends in robot-like fashion. Stopping in front of each year, his head moved from left to right to check the names and dates.

Class of '79...Dick Butkus...Yale Lary...Ron Mix...Johnny Unitas

Class of '80...Herb Adderly...Deacon Jones...Bob Lily

Class of '81...Red Badgro...George Blanda...Willie Davis...Jim Ringo

Floyd's head stopped, paused for a second, then with machine-like precision, his noggin clicked back two spaces. Bending over, he looked more closely at the name again. George Blanda. His Bear George.

Without blinking, he put his sack over the bronzed bust of the old Chicago Bear quarterback and kicker and he lifted it off the pedestal with a grunt. Exiting in the direction of Elevator 1, Floyd left Dairy Dan and Papa alone in the Hall of Fame Gallery.

Dairy Dan, standing in front of the Hall of Fame Class of 1964, was working up a sweat trying to throw his sack over Chicago Bear George Trafton without putting any weight on his painful foot.

Next to Dairy Dan, in front of the Class of 1963 and the smiling bronzed bust of George Papa Bear Halas, stood Papa with teary eyes.

"What's the matter Papa?" asked Dairy Dan, after finally bagging and wrestling his Bear George off its pedestal and struggling to lower it to the floor.

"Look!" answered Papa, pointing at the founding father of the National Football League. "He is so much happy. How can I take him away from his home? Remember what cow said."

"More Packers than Bears in the Hall of Fame, Papa. That's all that matters," reminded Dairy Dan. "Throw your potato sack over his head and take a peek in the bag later. Believe me, he'll still be smiling."

Wiping a tear away with his sleeve, Papa opened his burlap bag and threw it over Papa Bear's head. Grunting as he grappled with the heavy sack, the old cargo pilot finally managed to place it on the floor next to Dairy Dan's.

Struggling with the heavy sacks, Dairy Dan with his sore, swollen foot, and the rickety ancient Greek slowly dragged their loads away from the Hall of Fame Gallery. After they'd been huffing and puffing a while, they looked back to see they had moved only a few feet.

At this rate, getting their Bears out of the building would take until midnight.

....

"Go back inside?" questioned Hawk, giving Killer a frown. "Why?"

"Because one, we gotta get back with the team. Two, Nestor and Michael are stuck inside because of the stink bomb and they need to be rescued. And three, it's gotta be you because, with that bandage on your nose, you can't smell anything!"

"I don't know. I might be able to carry Nestor out, but there's no way I can budge Michael. He's too heavy," complained Hawk.

"He's not heavy. He's your brother," argued Killer, peeking through the large plate glass window at the front of the Hall of Fame. "Look! There's a wheelchair right there by the front door. Grab that and go get Nestor and Michael. Then load 'em up and wheel 'em out! Easy!"

"Yeah sure," answered Hawk saying yes, but shaking his head no.

"Great! You saved me …now go save your brothers!" cheered the Braves quarterback. "I'll go tell Coach what's happening. Good Luck!"

With an encouraging nod and a smile, Killer sprinted off in the direction of the practice field, leaving her teammate to tackle another fearsome rescue mission.

Turning back to face the Hall of Fame, he looked at his reflection in the glass door. Hawk studied the bandage on his nose to make sure it was tight. Satisfied, he was stink-bomb-proof, he walked in.

Seeing bodies lying everywhere sent a shiver down his spine. It was spooky, but Hawk tried not to think about it. Grabbing the wheelchair, he went looking for his brothers.

Maneuvering the wheelchair around the crowded floor was a difficult process. Sometimes bodies completely blocked his path, so Hawk had to grit his teeth, grab a hold of a limp arm or leg and drag a body out of the way.

Hawk started and stopped and pushed and squeezed the wheelchair through the Time Tunnel until he found himself standing in front of Elevator 1.

Everything inside him wanted to give up the search and run out of the building. But he hated the thought of disappointing Killer, so he pushed the elevator button to go up instead.

When the doors opened on the second floor, what was staring him in the face made Hawk let loose a blood-curdling scream.

"AHHHHHHHHHHHHHHHHHH!"

"AHHHHHHHHHHH! ACHOOOOO!" screamed (and sneezed) Michael, just as terrified.

"Michael! You scared me!" cried Hawk. "Stink bombs! How come you're not knocked out?"

"My cold. I can't smell anything," answered Michael with a sniff. "How come you're still walking around?"

Hawk pointed to the bandage covering his nose. "I can't smell anything either! Where's Nestor?"

"I propped him up over here by the wall," answered Michael, leading Hawk to the spot Nestor occupied on the floor. "As soon as that Limburger Head guy took the top off that jar of green stuff, Nestor went down!"

Michael pointed at the glowing green-gold stink bomb in the corner. "I'd cover it up except he put the lid in his pocket."

"It looks dangerous. Don't touch it," said Hawk shaking his head. "C'mon, help me get Nestor in the wheelchair. We gotta get outta here!"

Hawk pushed the wheelchair to where Nestor was propped on the floor. Applying the brake so the chair wouldn't move, they lifted their brother on board.

Suddenly, a loud crash came echoing down the hall, followed by a loud cry of someone in pain.

"Whoa! Go! Go! Go!" yelled Hawk as he released the brake and zoomed the wheelchair to the elevator doors. Terrified, he kept poking the *down* button, hoping to make the elevator show up faster.

Within seconds, the elevator dinged, the doors opened and Hawk raced the wheelchair and Nestor inside.

"Michael! Come on!" shouted Hawk frantically.

"You get Nestor out of the building! I'm going to see what that crash is about. Someone might need help!"

"No, Michael! Coach wants us on the practice field! Let's go!" pleaded Hawk.

"Go! Don't worry! Tell Coach I'll be right there!" cried Michael. He took off running down the hall toward the loud moaning and groaning as the elevator doors closed with his brothers inside.

Just outside the Hall of Fame Gallery, Michael spotted Dairy Dan and Papa on the floor, tangled up with the walker and two burlap sacks.

"Thank the Greek Gods!" shouted Papa, thrilled to see Michael in his Cheesehead hat at the scene of the accident. "A Packer backer has come to save us!"

Waving his arms frantically, Papa tried to explain what happened.

"We are dragging our heavy sacks. I stop to catch breath when BOOM! Squadron Leader Dan, his bad foot bump OUCH into Papa Bear. We crash up and fall down. Now we are mixed up together like this."

"Here, let me help you!" offered Michael, reaching down to grab Dairy Dan's arm.

"No, no. I think I'd better sit here on the floor a while," moaned Dairy Dan. "But we do need your help with an important matter of life or death."

153

Michael swallowed hard, "Life or death?"

"You're a sturdy kid," said Dairy Dan, gritting his teeth in pain and pointing at the burlap sack next to him. "Do you think you can lift this bag of...ah...souvenirs? It's kind of heavy..."

Michael reached down and hoisted the bag containing the bust of George Trafton easily over his shoulder.

"Sure, no problem. I can probably lift them both."

Repeating the motion, Michael slung the bag with Papa Bear George Halas over his other shoulder.

"Hercules! He is Hercules!" marveled Papa, clapping his hands.

"Take those souvenirs to our bus. It's Packer colors...green and gold. You follow?" instructed Dairy Dan.

Michael nodded, "Yeah, we saw your bus when we pulled in the lot outside."

"Right!" wheezed Dairy Dan, all the time applying pressure to his throbbing foot. "Give the sacks to Einstein..."

Michael scrunched up his face, "Einstein?"

"Short guy. No hair. Uses big words. His mom cooked us cabbage rolls," explained Dairy Dan, trying to describe his friend.

"Cabbage rolls, oh yeah-yeah," sniffled Michael, licking his lips. "Those cabbage rolls? Do you think there are any left?"

"Oh, sure! Sure! Do this and Ms. Wozniak will give you all the cabbage rolls you want," answered Dairy Dan, nodding his head and looking at his watch. "Hurry! Go now and take the bags to our bus. Tell Einstein it's time to deactivate. Say that word: *deactivate...*"

"Deactivate," repeated Michael.

"Right! Then tell him to come get me here outside of the Hall of Fame Gallery and bring a wheelchair. I think my foot's broke. You follow?"

"Yup! Got it!" replied Michael. Without another word, he took off to find Einstein, lugging the two Bears in bags and thinking about cabbage rolls.

....

On the Lower Level of the Hall of Fame, Hawk was rolling Nestor out the front door into the fresh air. A few seconds later, Nestor's eyes blinked open and he was spouting questions.

"I'm confused. How'd I get out here? Where's Michael?"

"The Limburger Heads exploded stink bombs. You fainted and I went in and wheeled you out. Michael's still inside," reported Hawk with rapid-fire answers.

A little unsteady, Nestor wobbled up out of the wheelchair. "I don't get what's going on."

"Me, either, but we don't have time to find out. Coach sent Stinky Smothers' brother to come get us. We're late!" hollered Hawk.

"But what about Michael?" protested Nestor.

"He said he's coming," added Hawk, pulling on Nestor's arm. "C'mon! Take some deep breaths and let's go!"

Nestor, still in a fog, filled his lungs with the crisp early evening air and took off jogging with Hawk. Along the way, Hawk told him about the Limburger Heads wearing clothespins and why he and Michael probably didn't pass out. Hawk explained about carrying Killer outside and how she sent him back in with the wheelchair to get his brothers.

Hawk told Nestor everything that had happened, hoping his brainy brother could solve the mystery of what was going on.

"So, whaddya think?" huffed Hawk, out of breath from jogging and talking at the same time.

"I have no clue," admitted Nestor. "It's really strange and spooky."

Spotting their teammates doing warm-ups on the practice field, the brothers sprinted the last 50 yards.

On the sidelines, they quickly located their gear, tossed their Cheesehead hats aside and pulled on their jerseys. Trying not to be noticed, they slipped in behind Frankie Fitzwater and started doing jumping jacks with everybody else.

Coaches Jekyll and Hyde were in front leading the warm-ups, while Coach Yak, walking between the rows of players, was taking attendance. When he came to Nestor and Hawk, he stopped, grabbed the pencil from behind his ear with his thick, meaty fingers and put check marks by the names of two of the three Hapburns listed on the Braves roster.

"Nestor…Hawk…it's so good you could join us," growled the big coach, looking at his watch. "Where is your brother?"

....

Michael, exiting the Hall of Fame, spotted the Limburger Heads waiting outside the parked Packer bus, each one with a burlap bag like the ones he was carrying.

Floyd was sitting on the curb, slumped over and snoring again. Nick and Rick were both massaging their snouts where the clothespins had been. Henrietta was sitting on her cooler, rinsing dishes in a bucket of soapy water. And the short, squatty Einstein was nervously pacing back and forth, looking at his watch.

Seeing Michael walking toward them with sacks slung over both shoulders, Einstein knew something was wrong.

"What fate has befallen my fellow Limburger Heads?" exclaimed Einstein, grabbing one of the sacks from Michael.

"I'm not sure, but I think your friends have befallen into each other and now one of them has a busted foot," answered Michael, lifting the second sack off his shoulder. "He just told me to take the bags to you and that it was time to DEE...DEE…"

"DEACTIVATE?" broke in Einstein, blurting out the word Michael was fishing for.

"Yeah, that's it…dee-activate," nodded Michael.

"Is that everything he said in its entirety?" asked Einstein, rubbing his chin.

"Yep! Nope! Ah, there was one more thing…no-no…two more things," nodded Michael.

Einstein waited to hear what those two more things were, but after a few frustrating seconds of silence, he started waving his hands impatiently at Michael to try and coax the rest of the story out of him.

"Welllll?" spouted the Limburger Head.

"Well, what?" shrugged Michael.

"What are the two other items?" asked Einstein sharply.

Suddenly, a light bulb flashed in Michael's brain, "Oh, yeah! He wants you to bring a wheelchair because he doesn't think he can walk on his broke foot."

Then, pointing at the cooler that Henrietta Wozniak was using as seating, he added, "And he said I could have more of those delicious cabbage rolls, if there are any left."

"Certainly! I am positive we can accommodate that request," said Einstein, looking at his watch again. "But we are woefully behind schedule. If you would just take a moment to assist us in transferring these…these…sacks from their current location on the concrete to the relative safety of this motorcoach, I will alert my mother to your dietary needs."

Michael paused for a moment to allow his brain to translate what Einstein had said.

"Sure, I'll help," agreed Michael, thinking of food instead of football.

"Excellent," declared Einstein.

Then, walking to where Floyd was snoring on the curb, Einstein whispered in his ear. Just as before, the sleepwalking Limburger Head snapped to attention and picked up the burlap bag in front of him.

Einstein, Nick and Rick each picked up a sack and the muscular Michael picked up two.

"Proceed to the motorcoach," ordered Einstein.

As they all marched with Bears to the bus, Einstein turned and called to Henrietta over his shoulder.

"Mama! Nasz młody przyjaciel chciałby więcej kiełbasek po naszym powrocie." *Our young friend would like more cabbage rolls upon our return.*

....

Coach Yak stood in front of Nestor and Hawk and waited for them to finish their 50 jumping jacks.

Coach Hyde, at the front of the entire group, was shouting the count.

"47…48…49…50! Twenty-second break and then 50 knee hugs!"

Bent over with their hands on their hips, Nestor and Hawk were breathing hard as Yak tugged at the bill of his red Ohio State cap and asked the question again.

"Where is your brother?"

"Not sure, Coach. Hawk saw him last," confessed Nestor, nodding toward his brother.

Hawk swallowed hard and started stammering, "When…ah…I yelled at him to get in the elevator…he told me to go and he'd be right behind me."

Peeking around Hawk, Coach Yak shook his head.

"I don't see him right behind you. I thought I told you to keep an eye on him."

"Sorry, Coach. We tried," apologized Nestor. "You want us to go look for him?"

Coach Yak shook his head, "No, you stay here and keep warming up. I'll send Coach Jekyll to find him."

"TWEEEEEEEEEEEEEEEEEEEEET!" With that, 24 heads turned to Coach Hyde. "Okay, team…50 knee hugs! Take a deep breath! Ready … EXERCISE! One…two…three…"

....

Michael, following the Limburger Heads, walked along the aisle of the motorcoach and placed his two burlap sacks next to the others on the bench seat at the very back.

Turning around, he followed Floyd, who was following Rick, who was following Nick, who was following Einstein back out of the Packer tour bus. Waiting for Michael as soon as his feet hit the pavement was Henrietta Wozniak holding a plate loaded with cabbage rolls.

"Jeść, jeść … cieszyć się!" *Eat, eat…enjoy!*

Giving Henrietta a big hug, Michael plopped down on the spot and began devouring the yummy pile of deliciousness while Einstein and the Limburger Heads hurried to the entrance of the Hall of Fame.

Before entering, Einstein stopped to give instructions.

"Time is of the essence. Locate and deactivate your stink bomb, then exit the edifice immediately. Rick, once we have returned and the first phase of Operation Georgie Porgie is complete, collect and secure the evidence in the large metal receptacle located at 8:00."

"You mean, you want me to throw the stink bombs in the dumpster over there?" asked Rick, pointing at the Packer green and gold Waste Management container in the far corner of the parking lot.

"That's an affirmative," nodded Einstein.

"What about getting Dairy Dan out of the building?" asked Nick.

"I will commission Floyd to deactivate my stink bomb as well as his, while I perform a search and rescue for our injured comrade," answered Einstein with authority.

Then, pulling his clothespin from his pocket, he placed it on his nose and shouted, "LET'S GO!"

Putting their own clothespins in place, the Limburger Heads raced into the Hall of Fame to remove the smelly stink bombs.

Once inside, the rebel Cheeseheads took off in different directions. Almost immediately, Einstein discovered the wheelchair Hawk had ditched by the door a few minutes before and was maneuvering his way around all the bodies scattered on the floor.

Finding no trace of Dairy Dan in the Lobby or the Hall of Fame Store, Einstein rolled through the Time Tunnel and into the elevator.

As soon as the doors slid open on the second floor and he pushed the wheelchair out, he heard the low groaning of the head Limburger Head disrupting the eerie silence.

Following the sound down the hall, he found the old Greek cargo pilot slowly dragging the groaning Dairy Dan by his arms.

Papa caught sight of the approaching wheelchair and waved Einstein over. "Help! Squadron Leader Dan down on battlefield!"

Without a word, Einstein positioned the wheelchair directly behind Dairy Dan and put on the brakes. With Einstein on one side and Papa on the other, the two Limburger Heads grabbed their injured friend by the shoulders and hoisted him into the wheelchair.

"We need to evacuate without delay!" declared Einstein. "The deactivation process has been launched!"

"Good!" replied Dairy Dan in spite of the throbbing pain in his foot. "Papa, put the lid on your stink bomb, grab your walker and get outta here before all these people start waking up!"

Demetri Papadopoulos snapped to attention, gave a quick salute and marched down the hallway with his walker, while Einstein rolled Dairy Dan in the opposite direction.

Stopping by the elevator, Dairy Dan reached over the arm of the wheelchair and picked up the stink bomb he'd placed on the floor. Careful not to spill any of the glowing green and gold ooze, he screwed the lid back on the jar and shoved it in his backpack. A minute later, they were downstairs and rolling out of the building, leaving the door propped open to let in some fresh air.

Headed toward the Packer tour bus, they both reached up and removed the clothespins from their noses. Taking deep breaths, they filled their lungs with unpolluted oxygen. Then, as he pushed the wheelchair, Einstein leaned forward and whispered into Dairy Dan's ear. "Phase One of our mission is complete! At this moment, there are more Green Bay Packers in the Hall of Fame than Chicago Bears!"

....

With all the stink bombs removed, football fans inside the Hall of Fame were waking up woozy and wondering how - suddenly - it was 5:05, five minutes *past* closing time.

Confused, security guards hurriedly rounded up visitors and rushed them to the exits.

Coach Jekyll stood outside the entrance doors as the groggy visitors poured out, searching the crowd for Michael. After ten minutes, the flood of humanity had slowed to a trickle and still no sign of him.

Knowing he could not go back without the team's star player, Coach Jekyll walked up to the Hall and rapped on the locked door to get the attention of the security guard directly on the other side.

"We're closed!" shouted the guard without opening the door.

"I need to come in and look for someone," shouted the skinny coach.

"You'll have to wait out there," came the muffled reply. "We're still rounding up a few stragglers."

Coach Jekyll took off his ball cap, scratched his head and heaved a sigh. Looking at his watch, he began pacing in front of the door.

Inside the Hall of Fame Gallery on the second floor, Papa was pacing, too, with his walker in front of the empty space Papa Bear George Halas had occupied since his induction in 1963.

A security guard escorting a half dozen slowpoke Packer fans to the elevator spotted Papa shuffling back and forth. Ignoring the fact that the old man in front of him had a clothespin on his nose, he politely told him it was time leave. Placing his hand on Papa's shoulder, he gently guided him into his herd of Cheeseheads.

Completely focused on getting them out of the building, the guard didn't even notice the bronze bust of the legendary Chicago Bear's coach was missing.

Too upset to talk, the troubled old Greek Cargo Pilot joined the pack of Packer fans without protest. A few minutes later, he drifted out the front entrance where he immediately bumped into Coach Jekyll. The minor collision sent the clothespin on Papa's nose flying.

"Oh! Sorry," apologized Coach Jekyll as he bent down and picked up the clothespin. "Here is your...ah...ah...nose clip?"

"Oh, cow is right," babbled Papa, shaking his head at the ground. "Cow says don't."

Not really listening to the old man, Coach Jekyll blurted out what he had on his mind.

"I'm looking for one of our football players. Michael Hapburn. He's our star running back, solid kid, all muscle, black, about five-foot. Did you see him? Do you know if he's still inside?"

Suddenly realizing someone was talking to him, Papa looked up.

"His brothers said he was right behind them, but he hasn't shown up yet and we've got a game to play," continued Coach Jekyll with desperation in his voice.

Papa's eyes blinked and brightened. Raising his index finger in front of his face, he began to speak. "Oh, yes! Hercules! Very strong! Carried Papa Bear to bus for me. Wanted more cabbage rolls."

"He wanted something to eat? Sounds like Michael!" said the coach.

"Come…come…I take you to bus. Maybe Hercules is having snack," offered Papa, pointing in the direction of the motorcoach.

"That's your bus there?" questioned Coach Jekyll, anxious to locate the missing Brave and get back with the team. "Do you mind if I run up ahead and check?"

"Go! Run!" urged Papa with a wave of his hand.

"Thank you!" shouted Coach Jekyll as he sprinted away leaving the troubled Papa to stew about stealing the legendary Papa Bear.

Nick and Rick Monroe were the first ones to spot the skinny Braves' assistant coach running toward their bus.

"Oh-oh! Could be trouble headed this way," groaned Nick.

"Ya think he saw what we did?" gulped Rick, a lump in his throat.

"We better tell Dairy Dan," blurted Nick. "C'mon!"

Seeing the two Limburger Heads turn and start walking away, Coach Jekyll waved his hands and yelled. "Hey! Wait! I need to talk to you two!"

"Go get Dan," instructed Nick. "I'll try and slow this guy down."

The younger Monroe quickly disappeared around the back of the motorcoach as Coach Jekyll dashed up to Nick out of breath.

"Whoa-Whoa-Whoa!" demanded Nick, blocking Coach Jekyll from getting any closer to the bus. "Can I help you?"

"Yes! Yes!" gasped the skinny coach. "I was told you might have some information about a missing…missing…"

As Coach Jekyll paused a second to swallow a big chunk of air, Dairy Dan rolled onto the scene in the wheelchair pushed by Einstein.

"Missing? Something's missing? Sorry! We have no information whatsoever about anything missing!" he insisted from his wheelchair. "We're here to see the Packers play in the Hall of Fame Game… whatever missing thing you're looking for, we definitely don't have it."

"But I just bumped into an older gentleman, he had like…ah… I don't know…a clothespin on his nose," babbled Coach Jekyll. "And he said that on your bus, I might find…"

"Oh, no! No, no, no! No! Absolutely not!" protested Dairy Dan, holding up his hands. "There's nothing to find on our bus. Thanks and have a good day."

"You don't understand. I just want a quick look around," pleaded the desperate coach as he tried to get past the group of assembled Limburger Heads.

"Look! You can't look here. This is a no-look zone," growled Dairy Dan.

"All looking is strictly prohibited," chimed in Einstein forcefully, pushing the wheelchair to block Coach Jekyll's path.

"ACHOOOOOO!" The loud sneeze came roaring around the bus, followed by Michael, wiping his nose and chewing on cabbage rolls.

"Hey, Coach!" sang Michael as he strolled into the scene. "I thought I heard you!"

"Michael!" shouted Coach Jekyll with joy. "I've been looking for you! We've got a football game to play!"

"Is this what…I mean, who you're looking for?" asked Dairy Dan, heaving a sigh of relief. "Oh, I thought you were snooping around to find…"

The Limburger Head leader stopped himself mid-sentence and coughed. "Well, never mind what I thought," he said quietly.

"Yeah! He's Port Clinton Braves' star running back," answered Coach Jekyll as he took the plate of cabbage rolls from Michael and set it down on the pavement. "We're playing the Olmsted Falls Bulldogs at halftime."

"Let us not detain you a moment longer," replied Einstein, anxious to get rid of the coach and his player.

"Yeah! Right! You better get going!" chimed in Dairy Dan with a wave. "Thanks for helping us, kid…good luck in the game."

Coach Jekyll and Michael waved back and hurried off toward the practice field and the rest of the team. The assembled Limburger Heads watched the two of them dash past Papa, who was still plugging along in the parking lot headed back to the bus.

Papa stopped long enough to give coach and player a salute as they flew by.

"How come that old Cheesehead thinks your name is Hercules?" asked Coach Jekyll, slowing down to a jog so he could catch his breath to speak.

"I don't know," huffed Michael. "He called me that when I helped those guys carry some stuff out the Hall of Fame back to their bus."

"Stuff?"

"A couple of big brown bags. The bags were kind of heavy, so I helped the old guys carry 'em out."

"They were really jumpy," said Coach Jekyll, scratching his head. "I wonder what was in those bags..."

"Souvenirs, I guess. That's what they told me," answered Michael.

The puzzled coach stopped altogether and looked back at the bus. "Heavy souvenirs?"

Michael stopped jogging and looked back as well.

The two of them watched as Papa, finally completing his trek across the parking lot, was greeted by his friends with happy hugs and high-fives.

"If you want, I can go back and look in the bags," offered Michael. "Besides, I wouldn't mind having another cabbage roll. I'll even grab one for you!"

Coach Jekyll shook his head. "No. We gotta get back. We're late and you need to warm up. Whatever's in those bags is none of our business anyway."

The curious coach gave his player a nudge and the two of them jogged off, passing throngs of football fans hurrying in the opposite direction toward the Hall of Fame Stadium. Kickoff between the Denver Broncos and the Green Bay Packers was just minutes away.

....

Back at the gleaming green and gold deluxe motorcoach, the Limburger Heads were quietly celebrating the successful first phase of Operation Georgie Porgie.

"So far, so good! Right, Pop?" crowed Rick Monroe, giving his dad a slap on the back.

"Yeah, I guess," agreed Nick Monroe. "But it isn't over yet."

As he looked around nervously to see if the police were closing in on them, he noticed Floyd, still asleep and snoring next to the bus.

"Hey! Shouldn't we wake up Floyd? It's time to go to the game."

Dairy Dan, looked at his watch and nodded toward Einstein. "Yeah, he's had a productive two-hour nap. Wake him up."

Einstein put his right hand up to his bald head and saluted his commander. Then, walking over to the front bus bumper, he grabbed Floyd's shoulder and gave it a gentle shake. Floyd brushed Einstein's hand away and continued snoring.

"You gotta shake him harder than that," winced Dairy Dan, rubbing his sore foot.

Einstein nodded and tried shaking Floyd again, this time with a little more force. Floyd frowned, but his eyes stayed glued shut.

"HARDER!" instructed Dairy Dan loudly.

Einstein took a deep breath, spit in his hands and rubbed them together and then, with a firm grip on both shoulders, he shook the slumbering Limburger Head with all the strength he had and yelled, "SEIZE THE CHEESE!"

Immediately, Floyd sprang to his feet with his eyes wide open, shouting, "Whoa! Whoa! Whoa! Is it time? I'm ready to go! Albert, have you seen my stink bomb?"

"Calm yourself, Floyd," insisted Einstein. "For your information, the initial phase of Operation Georgie Porgie has reached a successful conclusion."

"Say that again. In English this time, please," said Floyd, shaking his head to get the sleep out.

"We did it already. You led us in and back out again. The Bears are on the bus," explained young Rick Monroe, waving his thumb toward the motorcoach. "You are our Limburger Head MVP!"

Floyd raised his eyebrows. "Bears are on the bus?"

"That's right!" smiled Rick.

"I'm the MVP?" added Floyd with surprise.

"You executed your assignment with perfection," smiled Einstein.

"Stinkin' Bishop," beamed Floyd, throwing his shoulders back proudly. "Could you guys fill me in? I'm a little fuzzy on the details."

"Not now," growled Dairy Dan as he spun around in his wheelchair and looked at his wristwatch. "If you guys wanna see the kickoff, you gotta go!"

"Stinkin' Bishop! Where did ya get the wheels, DD?"

"I'll tell you about it later...now go!" repeated Dairy Dan, his face pinched in pain.

"Does everyone have their authorization for ingress?" asked Einstein, holding up his ticket.

The Limburger Heads looked at Einstein with blank expressions while they tried to process what he said.

After a two-second delay, the lights flashed in their brains and they all responded at once.

"Yeah! I got mine!"

"Me, too!"

"Got it in my pocket!"

"M'oj bilet w mojej torebce," declared Henrietta Wozniak, holding up her purse. *My ticket is in my purse.*

"All right then, take off!" yelled Dairy Dan, pointing toward the stadium.

Struggling to get on his feet, the big dairy farmer rolled the wheel-chair to Nick Monroe and hopped on one foot to the door of the bus.

"Do me a favor, Nick. When you go by the Hall of Fame, dump the chair at the door. I don't want anybody thinking I stole it."

"For the love of Lombardi, you're not going with us," cried Floyd.

"My foot is killing me," winced Dairy Dan. "Besides, someone has got to stay on the bus, so nothing happens to those Bears."

"But it's our Packers! The sacred green and gold! Playing in the Hall of Fame Game," argued Rick Monroe. "We'll carry you in!"

"Good idea, Rick," nodded Floyd. "C'mon, let's lift him up."

Rick and Floyd moved in toward their fearless leader to try to muscle him up on their shoulders, but the big dairy farmer knocked them away with a powerful forearm.

"I'm staying here and guarding the Bears," insisted Dairy Dan, leaning on the bus. "You guys go! I'll watch the game on my phone."

Einstein rounded up the Limburger Heads and herded them toward the stadium. But instead of moving with the group, Papa tromped with his walker toward Dairy Dan.

"Georgie Porgie Operation make me tired. I watch game on phone with Squadron Leader Dan," he declared.

"No-no! Go see the Packers play!" urged Dairy Dan.

"Yeah Papa…you've been looking forward to this all week. You gotta come with us," begged Rick Monroe.

Henrietta tugged on Papa's arm and pointed to the stadium. "Przyjdź i obejrzyj grę z nami." *Come watch the game with us.*

"I stay to keep Squadron Leader Dan and Papa Bear company," argued the old Greek cargo pilot.

Dairy Dan shook his head and waved them all away. "I'll be fine. Go! Have a great time!"

Scratching his chin, Papa looked back at the bus. "But what about Papa Bear?"

"Don't worry. I'll keep him company," promised Dairy Dan. "Now you all get out of here. Go Pack Go!"

Einstein, Floyd, Nick, Rick, Papa and Henrietta shouted the cheer in unison and hurried off. The pack of Packer backers had barely moved ten feet away when Dairy Dan called out to them.

"Bring me back a bratwurst and a root beer."

"You want onions on that brat?" shouted Floyd over his shoulder.

"Peppers and onions!" yelled Dairy Dan.

....

By the time Coach Jekyll and Michael arrived at the practice field, the Port Clinton Braves had finished warming up and they were now watching the Olmsted Falls Bulldogs, dressed in all-black uniforms, go through their pre-game routine.

Announcing his return with a powerful sneeze, Michael grabbed his duffle bag and joined Hawk, Nestor and Killer along the sidelines.

"It's about time!" yelled Nestor, both crabby and relieved to see his brother.

"Anybody got a snack?" asked Michael, strapping on his shoulder pads.

"Michael! Look at how BIG those guys are!" gulped Hawk.

"Check out #60…he's twice Michael's size," added Killer calmly.

"He's big all right," agreed Nestor. "But I bet he's slow as a turtle."

"They're lining up to do sprints," announced Hawk.

The Braves watched as the Olmsted Falls' coach blew his whistle to start the Bulldogs charging down the field. Big #60 finished the 40-yard dash a good three feet ahead of the rest of his teammates.

"I guess he's a fast turtle," laughed Killer.

Suddenly, a loud roar erupted from inside George Benson Stadium. The game between the Packers and the Broncos had started.

Hearing the crowd cheer, Coach Yak let loose a blast on his whistle.

"TWEEEEEEEEEEEEEEEEEEEEET!"

"To the bus," bellowed the coach. "Time for final instructions!"

The Braves turned and followed their three coaches. Nestor, Hawk and Killer lagged behind as they waited for Michael to pull on his jersey.

"C'mon, Michael! Hurry up!" ordered Nestor. "Coach is already mad at us because of you!"

"Yelling at your brother is snot nice," chuckled Michael as he blew his nose and stuffed the tissue in the ear hole of Nestor's helmet.

Nestor gently removed the snotty tissue with his thumb and index finger and chased Michael with it until they caught up with the rest of the team just as Coach Yak was clearing his throat.

"Change in plans! We'll run a Go Route our first play," announced Coach Yak. "Nestor Hapburn and Tommy O'Connor go deep and Kopecky will heave it to whichever one gets open. Got it?"

"But what about Twinkie Off Tackle?" asked Killer.

"And what about my snack?" grumbled Michael, under his breath.

"No trick plays. Michael missed warm-ups…he's gonna be on the sidelines stretching. Where's Stinky Smothers' brother?" hollered Coach Yak.

Stinky Smothers' brother threw his arm up, "Right here, Coach!"

"Once we get on the field, I want you to go to the end of the bench and take Number 99 through all our stretches. Full routine. Walking knee hugs, lateral lunges, backward ninjas...everything!"

"Okay, Coach!" nodded Stinky Smothers' brother, happy Coach Yak had chosen him for the special assignment.

"How about you, Hapburn? Got it?"

Michael kicked at the pavement and sighed, "Got it, Coach. But what about the snacks? I mean, the game? Do I get to play?"

"Once you're warmed up, we'll see," growled Yak. "Better to miss one game than miss the whole season with a pulled hammy. Right?"

Bummed out, Michael sniffed, sneezed and heaved another sigh before finally muttering, "Right, Coach."

Satisfied he was understood, Coach Yak made a couple of check marks on his clipboard and then pointed to Coach Hyde.

Coach Hyde spoke loudly, as he tossed a football from one hand to another. "We met with the Olmsted Falls' coaches this afternoon. We'll play this scrimmage as if it were a regular game. Instead of four 15-minute quarters, it'll be two 10-minute halves. We'll have punts, but no kickoffs. Drives at the beginning of each half and after a touch-down will start on the 25-yard-line. We won the coin toss and will get the ball first. Any questions?"

Immediately Stinky Smothers' brother's hand shot up, "What's your favorite color?"

A few players clucked and chuckled as Stinky Smothers' brother shrugged his shoulders. "Don't you guys want to know?"

"What about the clock? Is it going to be running the whole time?" asked Killer.

"Good question, Kopecky," acknowledged Coach Hyde. "The only time the clock stops will be after a score or an incomplete pass. So, it's important we hustle back to huddle so we can get in as many plays as possible."

Coach Hyde lateralled the ball to Coach Yak and Stinky Smothers' brother frowned. "How come he didn't say MY question was good?"

Again, a few players chuckled while the big coach lumbered back and forth with excitement.

"It's prime time and bright lights for the Braves!" shouted Coach Yak, clapping his massive hands together. "After we break the huddle, I want the Offense to line up behind Coach Jekyll. Defense over there behind Coach Hyde and all the special teamers follow me. Okay, let's go run through some brick walls!"

Then, with a nod, Yak tossed the football to Kathy Kopecky.

The players crowded around their little quarterback and team leader as she raised the football over her head and shouted strong and clear, "Ready? TEAM on three! One...two...THREE..."

"TEAM!" yelled the Port Clinton Braves with nervous excitement.

Lining up behind their coaches, the team started their march toward Tom Benson Hall of Fame Stadium and 23,000 screaming football fans.

7:30 pm EDT | Inside Tom Benson Hall of Fame Stadium
HALL OF FAME GAME

"Wow! Look at all the people!" marveled Little John Kopecky, blinking in the bright stadium lights. "Where are we sitting?"

"Section 122...row 20. Seats 9, 10 and 11," yelled Big John Kopecky over the crowd noise. "Mrs. Hapburn and Stinky Smothers' mother have 12 and 13."

"Are you excited to see your big sister play?" asked Audrey as they walked down the steps toward their seats.

"She's not so big. I'm almost as tall as she is!" boasted Little John.

"Here's row 20," informed Big John. "Let Mrs. Hapburn and Stinky Smothers' mother go first. You sit between your mom and me."

"50-yard line? Behind the Green Bay bench? This is great!" shouted Little John.

Big John Kopecky scooted his son aside to let Audrey and Stinky Smothers' mother slide down the aisle first. Moving down the row, Audrey found that her seat 13 was occupied by a man wearing a

Cheesehead hat and a t-shirt that said, *Education is Important, but Green Bay Football is Importanter.*

"Excuse me, sir. I believe you are in my seat," said Audrey politely, showing the Packer fan her ticket stub.

"Stinkin' Bishop! I'm sorry," apologized the man. Then turning his head toward his friends, he shouted out, "Everybody, move down one! I'm in the wrong seat."

Without taking their eyes off the action on the field, the group of cheeseheads popped up, moved over and settled back down.

"Stinkin' Bishop, you've missed a heck of a game so far. Packers are playing good," gushed the man giving his new neighbor a friendly nod. "Let me introduce myself. I'm Floyd. Floyd Dowler."

"Pleased to meet you, Mr. Dowler," smiled the Port Clinton piano teacher, shaking Floyd's hand. "My name is Audrey Hapburn."

"How come you're getting here so late? The first half is almost over…you get stuck in traffic?"

"We came to watch the Port Clinton Braves play at halftime. Our kids are on the team" explained Audrey. "I've got three boys playing."

Pointing down the row, she continued with informal introductions. "That's Stinky Smothers' mother and she has two boys on the team. And down at the end, the Kopeckys' daughter is our quarterback."

Floyd scratched his head and tried to think. Then, snapping his fingers, he blurted out, "Is her name Killer?"

"Yes. Well, no. Actually, her name is Kathy, but my son calls her Killer, even though I've told him not to," answered Audrey, giving her new acquaintance a perplexed look. "How did you know that?"

"For the love of Lombardi, we met some of your kids this afternoon at the Hall of Fame!" laughed Floyd. "One of the boys hung out with us almost the whole day. The kid could eat, too. He probably put down 15 cabbage rolls."

"Fifteen cabbage rolls?" repeated Audrey, rolling her eyes. "That had to be my son, Michael."

"Yeah, Michael! That was his name. He's your boy? Great kid!" crowed Floyd.

Floyd turned to the Limburger Heads with excitement. "Hey, guys! Y'know our new friend who helped us out today? This is his mom!"

The Limburger Heads turned their attention away from the game for a second to greet Audrey with happy waves and smiles.

Papa bowed deeply and leaned past Floyd to shake Audrey's hand. "Much pleasure to meet mother of Hercules."

Audrey sat there with a puzzled look on her face. "What do you mean helped you? And why did he call Michael *Hercules*?"

The action on the field pulled Floyd's attention away before he could answer Audrey's questions. Green Bay quarterback Aaron Rodgers had just taken the snap, rolled to his right and launched a Hail Mary pass into orbit.

The football hung high in the air for what seemed an eternity. On its way back into the earth's atmosphere, the ball landed in the arms of a Packer receiver for a touchdown just as the last seconds of the first half rolled off the stadium clock.

Cheeseheads throughout the stadium exploded in joyous celebration. Hugs, high-fives and happiness flooded the stands.

The Packers trotted toward the locker room leading the Broncos 24-10, passing the Olmsted Falls Bulldogs and Port Clinton Braves running on the field.

....

"Are you nervous?" gulped Hawk as he jogged onto the stadium turf alongside Braves' linebacker Moses Kupperman.

"No. I'm too scared to be nervous," confessed Moses.

Hawk nodded and looked up at the stands as he jogged. "I just don't want to look stupid in front of 23,000 people."

Directly in front of Hawk, Strong Safety Jimbo Banks stopped suddenly to tie his shoe. Hawk, still gazing at the crowd, crashed into his teammate, flipping up and over Jimbo and landing on his bandaged beak.

Hoping no one noticed his tumble, Hawk scrambled to his feet, got turned around and started running in the wrong direction, straight into the path of Coach Yak, who was leading the special team squad onto the field.

Unable to put on the brakes, the 400-pound steamroller bowled over the lightweight Hapburn, sending him head over heels a second time.

"You okay, 23?" asked Coach Yak as he helped his player to his feet and brushed him off.

Dazed and confused, Hawk nodded and wobbled to the sidelines where the Braves welcomed him with cheers and howls of laughter.

"That was great!" shouted Ray Ray McKay.

Frankie Flat-Nose Fitzwater gave Hawk a friendly pat on the back, "You sure are funny, Hawk!"

"Way to go, Hawk!" smiled Kathy Kopecky, giving him a high-five.

"Whaddya mean?" asked Hawk, shaking his head to clear it.

"I mean, way to get the team relaxed and ready to play. A minute ago, everybody was uptight and tense. Like we were going to the dentist," explained the Braves' quarterback. "Now, look! You got us all smiling and laughing! Way to go!"

Hawk blushed, but before he could say anything, Coach Jekyll's voice rang out over the crowd. "OFFENSE...TAKE THE FIELD!"

"Gotta go!" chirped Killer with a wave.

Hawk watched as Killer, Nestor and the rest of the offense ran out to the 25-yard line. Down past the end of the bench, Stinky Smothers' brother and Michael were going through their warm-up exercises.

On the opposite sideline, the Olmsted Falls' defense strutted out elbow-to-elbow chanting, "DESTROY! DESTROY! DESTROY!"

The very first play was a disaster for the Braves.

The ball slipped out of Frankie Fitzwater's hand on the snap and he kicked it straight to the Bulldogs' Big #60, who scooped it up and ran 25 yards for a touchdown.

After the extra point, Port Clinton was already behind 7-0 just seven seconds into the game.

On the Braves' next possession, they lost five yards on first down and six yards on second down. Then on third down, with a reverse to

Nestor, they only lost one yard. Coach Yak sent out the punting unit. Hawk ran out and jammed into the huddle next to Nestor.

"It looks bad!" grunted Hawk, giving his brother a nudge.

"Yeah? Well, it feels worse," groaned Nestor. "These guys are really big, really fast and REALLY mean."

Breaking the huddle, Hawk nervously ran to the line of scrimmage. Across from him was the menacing #60, kicking the dirt like a bull ready to charge.

The snap from Freemont Bellywampus was low, allowing time for Big #60 to trample Hawk and smother the punter Apollo Vargas in the end zone for a safety. The scoreboard at the end of the field glowed Olmsted Falls 9...Port Clinton 0.

From there, things got worse. After two more quick scores, the Bulldogs were ahead by 22 points. Faced with another third down and long - and with only 29-seconds left in the half - Coach Yak called a time out and waved Killer over to the sideline.

"Is Michael ready to play?" asked the little quarterback hopefully.

"Quick kick," growled the big coach. "Pooch it deep in their end. Maybe we can run out the clock and stop them from scoring again."

Then, spotting Hawk on the sideline, he shouted, "Hapburn! 23!"

Hawk sprinted over and waited for instructions.

"Go in for Stinky! We need more speed," ordered Yak.

Hawk nodded and ran onto the field with Killer. When they reached the huddle, Hawk nudged the bruised and bloody Stinky.

"You're out," informed Hawk.

"Thank you, Jesus," muttered Stinky as he jogged away.

Killer knelt down in the middle of the huddle. "Okay...Coach called for a quick kick. We need to get the ball out of our end."

"Kick?" But it's only third down," objected Nestor.

"Coach doesn't want them scoring again before the half," explained Killer. "If we can kick it deep, they might play it safe and take a knee."

Ten red helmets bobbed up and down at the same time. Breaking the huddle, the Braves trotted to the line of scrimmage.

Killer, standing seven yards behind Frankie Fitzwater, barked out the signals. On the third HUT, the football came spiraling back from the center. With the ball in her hands, Killer rolled right to make it look like a pass play.

Sidestepping a ferocious rush from #60, Killer planted herself on the Brave's 15-yard line, and, with all her power, she punted the ball.

It was a line-drive kick that rolled forever. The surprised Bulldogs scrambled down the field, chasing the low kick.

Two Bulldogs caught up with the football at the Olmsted Falls 30-yard line and tried to pounce on it. But instead of securing the ball, the slippery pigskin squirted loose and players from both teams bobbled it deeper into Bulldog territory.

With players tripping and diving all over the place, a Bulldog lineman grabbed the ball with his heavily-taped hands. Just as he was pulling the football safely into his gut, Nestor appeared out of nowhere and punched it free.

Hawk, who was rushing up to help, snatched the ball in midair and dropped to his knees on the two-yard-line.

"Time out! Time out!" yelled Killer, immediately signally the ref.

Jumping up and down, a happy bunch of Braves ran to the sidelines and Coach Yak. The stadium clock had stopped with one second left in the half.

"Field goal!" shouted Yak. "Let's get on the scoreboard!"

Hawk, Nestor and the rest of the special teams unit rushed out for the field goal attempt. Across the line from Nestor was Big #60, foaming at the mouth, waiting for his chance to bust through the line and block the kick.

After Killer and Stinky Smothers' brother, Nestor was definitely the smallest player on either team. Instead of hopelessly trying to block the super-sized #60 and getting buried in the Hall of Fame Stadium turf, Nestor came up with Plan B.

"Look! Your shoe's untied!" Nestor shouted to the freight train in front of him.

Surprised and momentarily distracted, the 260-pound #60 looked down at his feet just as Freemont Bellywampus snapped the ball to

holder Theo Nichols, who placed it in the perfect position for Braves'
kicker Jack Oropallo to boot it straight through the uprights.

The referee signaled the kick was good and the Braves ran to the
sideline with no time left on the clock. The scoreboard read: Olmsted
Falls 22...Port Clinton 3.

Hawk slapped his brother on the back.

"Wow, Nestor! That big guy never moved!" laughed Hawk. "How'd
you think of that?"

Nestor smiled. "His shoe really was untied."

As the brothers reached the sideline, they looked back at the goal
line to see Big #60 still kneeling down on the field, tying his shoe.

....

Dairy Dan, after watching the first half of the Hall of Fame game
on his phone, was busy limping around putting disguises on the six
Bear busts lined up on the back bench of the empty tour bus.

He put Cheesehead hats on a couple of them. On another, he put
Floyd's *Roses are Red, Violets are Blue, the Bears Stink and the Vikings
Stink, Too* t-shirt.

Half-finished, Dairy Dan stood there scratching his chin. Then he
grabbed his duffle from the overhead rack. Rummaging through, he
pulled out a Packer hoodie, a Chalet Cheese Co-op baseball cap, his
light-up Green Bay Packer stadium sweater and a pair of sunglasses.

After thinking it through, Dairy Dan put the hoodie on George
Blanda. He dressed George Connor in the light-up stadium sweater
and he gave Papa Bear the Chalet Cheese cap and the sunglasses.

Satisfied with the disguises, Dairy Dan gathered up the travel
pillows and blankets scattered around on the bus and used them to
tuck around the Bears. They looked like they were hibernating.
Happily, he hobbled back to his seat to watch the second half of the
Hall of Fame game on his phone.

Rubbing his swollen foot, he surveyed the Bears at the back of the bus
and nodded. "Look like Packer fans to me."

....

The Limburger Heads seated in the stands were in a good mood. The Bears were on the bus and the Packers now had the most players in the Hall of Fame. Green Bay was winning the game. Plus, they were thoroughly enjoying the scrimmage between Olmsted Falls and Port Clinton.

Sitting next to them, Audrey Hapburn, the Kopeckys and Stinky Smothers' mother were not as jolly, worrying about their kids getting hurt playing against the bigger, stronger Bulldog team.

"I wonder why your Michael isn't playing," sighed Stinky Smothers' mother.

"I don't know," said Audrey. "He just keeps doing warm-ups."

"For the love of Lombardi," chimed in Floyd Dowler, overhearing the parents' talk. "Your coach needs to put him in! He's the biggest kid on your team!"

"Yes!" agreed Demetri Papadopoulos, leaning past Floyd to join the discussion. "Coach should put Hercules on field of battle."

"He does have a cold. Maybe Coach is keeping him out because of that," reasoned Audrey. "I think I'll go down and check."

Walking down the steps to the railing, she waved at her boys who were standing with Kathy Kopecky, waiting for the second half of their game to start.

"Hey, your mom's waving at us," said Killer, waving back. Nestor, Michael and Hawk turned and waved at their mom, too, but Audrey just waved harder in return.

"You better go see what she wants," urged Killer.

The brothers trotted over to the stands and shouted "Hi, Mom!" in unison.

Audrey started rattling off questions. "Is everything okay? Are those boys from Olmsted Falls your age? They're so much bigger! Michael, why haven't you played? Is it because of your cold?"

"Coach didn't want me to pull a muscle," said Michael.

"He missed the team warm-ups, Mom," blurted Nestor.

"How'd that happen?" asked Audrey, concerned.

"It's been a crazy day, Mom," said Nestor. "A lot of stuff happened."

"Yeah, Mom. A lot of stuff!" agreed Hawk. "There were stink bombs and everything."

"Stink bombs? replied Audrey, her face scrunched up.

At that moment, Coach Yak let loose a blast on his whistle. "TWEEEEEEEEEEEEEEEEEEEEEET!"

"Gotta go, Mom. Second half's starting!" shouted Nestor as they sprinted back toward the team.

"Wait! I'm not done," cried Audrey. "Don't get hurt. Be careful. How do you feel?"

"I'm fine, Mom," yelled Nestor over his shoulder.

Hawk gave his mom a smile and a thumb's up.

And Michael sneezed and shouted, "I'm hungry!"

Audrey watched as her boys joined the rest of the team huddled around their coaches. More confused than before, she went back up the steps and settled in her seat.

"Why isn't Michael playing?" asked Stinky Smothers' mother.

"He missed team warm-ups," answered Audrey, perplexed. "And then they said he missed because of stink bombs..."

"Stink bombs?" repeated Stinky Smothers' mother.

"Yes...I'm sure they said stink bombs," insisted Audrey.

Hearing the words stink bombs, Floyd nudged Papa and whispered in his ear. Then Papa nudged Einstein and whispered in his ear.

After Papa finished, Einstein looked down the row at the parents. Clearing his throat, he interrupted their conversation.

"Excuse me, ladies, but I believe I can shed some light on a very minor incident occurring this afternoon inside the Hall of Fame," stated the Limburger Head with a reassuring smile on his face.

"You know about this?" asked Audrey anxious for the information. "Were there really stink bombs?"

Einstein shook his head and forced himself to give a fake chuckle.

"Well, I wouldn't classify it as a bomb. You know how children can embellish a story. There was a report regarding a foul-smelling odor causing some people to be momentarily incapacitated. But I can assure you no one was hurt."

"You mean people passed out? Fainted?" said Audrey, trying to understand what Einstein was saying to her.

"Precisely," nodded Einstein. "But let me reiterate, no one suffered an injury of any significance. The episode more than likely will not even be chronicled in the local newspaper."

"A foul-smelling odor?" asked Audrey, still perplexed.

"Yeah! We're thinking maybe one of the bathrooms broke," chimed in Floyd, trying to help explain things. "I'm tellin' ya...when one of them sewer pipes explodes...PU! You don't want to be there!"

"Audrey! It looks like they're putting Michael in!" reported Stinky Smothers' mother, pointing toward the Port Clinton sideline.

This news abruptly ended the stink bomb discussion as everyone immediately turned their attention to the field, where Coach Yak and Coach Jekyll were giving Killer and Michael last-minute instructions.

Coach Yak was down on one knee so he could talk directly into Michael's face mask.

"Are you warmed up? Are you ready to play?"

"ACHOOOO!" sneezed Michael, while nodding his head yes and wiping his nose with the sleeve of his jersey. "I'm ready, Coach!"

At the same time, Coach Yak was talking to Michael, a couple of yards away, Coach Jekyll was quietly giving instructions to Killer.

"We're gonna run Twinkie Off Tackle," whispered Coach Jekyll, slipping the treat to the quarterback so Michael didn't see.

"Once you break the huddle, check where #60 is lined up," added Jekyll. "When you locate him, run the play to the opposite side."

Finished with their talks, the coaches sent Killer and Michael out on the field to join the rest of the offense. The team's spirits soared at seeing their star running back join them in the huddle.

"Quiet!" ordered Killer, taking charge of the situation. The chatter stopped immediately as all eyes fixed on the Braves' little quarterback.

"We're running Twinkie Off Tackle," Killer said firmly. "Michael. The third number I call? That's who has the Twinkie."

"Can't you just give me the Twinkie now?" whined Michael.

Killer shot him a look that could kill and Michael backed down.

"Okay, okay! Third number you call. I got it!"

"Good!" huffed Killer. "Snap count on two! Ready..."

"BREAK!" shouted the Braves with a clap of their hands.

The offense trotted up to the line where the menacing Bulldog defense was making ugly faces and foaming around their mouths. Killer, with the Twinkie hidden up her sleeve, immediately found Big #60 on her left side across from Ray Ray McKay. Nestor, the Braves' #1, was on her right.

Getting into shotgun formation, Killer barked out the signals. "Kingman! Barstow! San Bernardino!"

Nodding her head at Nestor to start him in motion and the Braves' receiver ran from right to left. As he passed, she slipped him the Twinkie.

"Kingman! Barstow! San Bernardino!" she repeated once more, then she started shouting the sequence of numbers to the secret code.

"EIGHT..."

Michael's head swiveled and he found #8, Tommy O'Connor, flanked out far to the left, "He doesn't have the Twinkie," he noted.

"EIGHTY-NINE..."

Michael looked around and found #89, Ray Ray McKay, lined up at tight end, "Ray Ray doesn't have the Twinkie either."

Finally, Killer yelled the third number. "ONE!"

Michael's eyes rolled down the line of players in front of him. Split to the right was #1, his own brother. "Of course! Nestor has it," grinned Michael, licking his chops.

Clapping, Killer finished the snap count. "HUT... HUT..."

On the second hut, Frankie Fitzwater sent the football flying in between his legs straight to Killer five yards behind the line, who caught it waist-high. Turning to her right, she shoved the ball firmly into Michael's middle as he zoomed forward.

But before he could take another step, Big #60, with steam pouring out of his ears, broke through the line and was in position to blow up the play.

Killer tried throwing a block at the charging Bulldog, but with his powerful forearm, #60 swatted the lightweight QB ten yards away.

Arms spread wide for the grab, Big #60 pounced at the same time Michael did a magical 360-degree spin. It was a beautiful move that sent the monster-sized steam engine crashing to the ground, grabbing nothing but air.

After escaping a couple more tacklers using a shake-n-bake and a stiff arm, Michael spotted Nestor sprinting toward the Bulldogs' end zone, holding the Twinkie high over his head.

His stomach let out a loud growl as he took off in pursuit of his brother, leaving opposing players scattered on the field along the way.

Dashing over the fifty into enemy territory, Michael could see two Bulldog defensive backs coming up from either side of him, ready to dive at his legs.

Michael stopped suddenly - dead in his tracks - and the two Bulldogs crashed into each other, rolling on the grass in a tangled mess. With no one left between him and his Twinkie, Michael sailed into the end zone.

"Hand it over!" ordered Michael, tossing the football to his brother. Nestor tossed the Twinkie to Michael and gave him a happy slap on the side of his helmet.

The Braves' sideline erupted in celebration and the Port Clinton fans in the stands roared their approval.

Audrey and the Limburger Heads were dancing in the aisle and high-fiving each other.

"What a run!" yelled Big John Kopecky.

"Get him a Packer uniform!" roared Floyd.

After kicking the extra point, the scoreboard flashed Olmsted Falls 22...Port Clinton 10.

A minute later, the Braves were on offense again, thanks to Moses Kupperman, who broke into the Bulldog backfield with arms up to block a pass. But instead of knocking it down, the football hit him in his face mask and got stuck there.

Once the officiating crew managed to pull the ball free, they ruled it an interception and an excited Port Clinton team took possession on their own 45.

On first down, Killer completed a pass to Nestor. The next play, Coach Jekyll sent Stinky Smothers' brother into the game with a Snickers tucked in his sock.

Pulling Killer aside, Stinky Smothers' brother whispered in her ear, slipping her the candy bar.

"Huddle up!" commanded Killer confidently.

"We're running Snickers-Halfback-Sweep-Right. Michael…it's the first number I call this time. Got it?"

"I love Snickers," confessed Michael, his mouth watering.

"Snap count on one," informed Killer. "Ready…"

"…Break!" shouted the offense in unison.

As the players trotted up to the line of scrimmage Killer secretly handed off the bite-size snack bar to the Braves' tight end, Number 89 Ray Ray McKay.

Then, getting behind Frankie Fitzwater at center, Killer shouted out the signals.

"ALVIN…SIMON…THEODORE. ALVIN… SIMON… THEODORE. 89…8…88…HUT!"

Taking a quick step to her left, Killer whirled back to the right and lateralled the ball to Michael, who was sweeping around the end, while Ray Ray was barreling toward the end zone with the Snickers.

As Michael charged over midfield, Big #60 was waiting for him, but this time, it was Michael who had steam coming out of his ears.

Instead of dodging to his right or left, Michael plowed straight into the super-sized #60, bowling him over along with a half-dozen other hapless Bulldogs.

Turning on the jets, Michael flew the remaining 49 yards, stepping across the goal line at the very same time as Ray Ray. After a quick exchange of football for Snickers, some high-fives, a sneeze and an extra point, the scoreboard glowed Bulldogs 22…Braves 17.

Once again, the fans in the stands were jumping for joy!

"Hercules! Hercules! Mighty hero and son of the gods!" shouted Papa, thrusting his fist to the heavens.

Back on the Port Clinton sidelines, Coach Yak took a quick glance at the clock and shouted for the team to gather around him.

"All those times you worked your butts off in practice…it was for this moment!"

Immediately, Stinky Smothers' brother raised his hand and blurted out, "My mom doesn't like us to use the word 'butt'. Say 'bottom'."

Coach Yak coughed, cleared his throat and started over, "All right, yeah, you guys worked your…ah…bottoms off! And because of that… now at the end of the game, you've each got plenty left in your tank!

"There's over a minute on the clock. We've got two time-outs. If we stop 'em from getting a first down, we get the ball with enough time to run ONE play! DEFENSE, put up a brick wall…DON'T let 'em through! TEAM on three! Ready! One…two…THREE…"

"TEAM!" shouted all 25 fired-up players.

As the Port Clinton defense ran out on the field, Coach Hyde pulled Hawk aside to give him some last-minute instructions.

"Be prepared. They might put #60 in to power through for a first down," warned Hyde. "If he gets the ball, you show him what #23 is all about."

Hawk, his bandaged beak smudged and muddied, smiled and ran onto the field.

"Okay, guys!" shouted Hawk clapping his hands to energize his teammates. "You heard what Coach Yak said! We're a brick wall!"

The defense responded with shouts of encouragement to each other as they lined up to stop the Bulldogs' massive offensive machine.

On first down, Olmsted Falls gained four yards up the middle. As the whistle ended the play, Coach Yak immediately called a time-out from the sideline.

On the next play, the Bulldogs' quarterback ran around the right end to pick up five more yards. Again, Coach Yak quickly signaled for a time-out.

On third down and, with just one yard needed to a first down to win the game, onto the field came big, hulking, triple-beef-burger-sized #60. As he trotted out to the Bulldog huddle, the ground seemed to shake.

Hawk glanced over at the Braves' sideline where he saw Coach Hyde nodding and giving him a thumbs up.

With a lump in his throat, Hawk pulled up tight to the line from his safety position and prepared himself for what he was convinced was going to be a running play to the unstoppable, BIG star player.

The Bulldog quarterback, called out the signals, took the snap and pitched the ball to #60. Starting five yards behind the line, Big #60 powered his way around the left side. The Bulldogs' blocking was solid. The only Brave in a position to make a play was Hawk.

He flashed back to all the times in practice he couldn't bring down his brother, Michael, by trying to wrap him up high on his shoulders. Hawk knew his only hope was to throw himself at the pounding, tree-trunk-sized legs of #60.

With knees pumping and cleats tearing up the turf, the burly Bulldog plowed forward toward a certain first down and maybe more. Suddenly, from out of nowhere, Hawk came flying in low, knocking Big #60's legs out from under him, slamming the behemoth down for an earthquaking one-yard loss.

Jumping back up with his nose bleeding through the bandage, Hawk was swarmed by his teammates as he happily trotted to the sideline, where his defensive coach was waiting for him with a towel.

"Let me take care of that nose," said a concerned Coach Hyde.

"No, Coach! It doesn't hurt a bit!" laughed Hawk.

"I knew you were going to make a big play," said the Coach with a smile. "Now, take a break on the bench. We still have a chance to win this thing!"

After the Bulldog punt rolled dead on the Port Clinton four, only nine seconds remained on the stadium clock.

Coach Jekyll gathered his offense around him, clapping his hands, hoping to convince his battered players they could pull off one more miracle play.

"We can do this," encouraged Coach Jekyll. "We're only 96-yards away from a touchdown. That's better than being 99-yards away, right?"

Nodding their heads, the nervous bunch of Braves chuckled.

"Whatever happens, I am proud of you guys. You got behind, but you never gave up," the coach continued. "Go out there and do your best, but most important... have fun!"

With his hand on Killer's shoulder to hold her back, Coach Jekyll sent the rest of his offensive unit tearing out onto the field.

"Killer, which play should we run?" asked Jekyll, kneeling in front of his fearless little quarterback. "Mango-Tango-Almond-Mix-Half-back-Sweep?"

"I like that one," admitted Killer, looking down at her pink duffle bag. "But I think we should call an audible."

"An audible?" asked Jekyll, scratching his head.

Kathy Kopecky dug around in her duffle for a few seconds and pulled out an oblong object wrapped in red-checkered wax paper. Carefully unwrapping it, she showed her coach what was inside.

Jekyll let out a surprised gasp. "Where did you get that?"

"No time to explain," answered Killer as she quickly re-wrapped the edible audible and slipped it into the kangaroo pouch of her jersey.

"Okay, go do it!" agreed Jekyll.

With her coach's approval, Killer ran out to join her team in the Braves' end zone. Everyone was silent as they waited for her to speak.

"We're trying something different," began Killer.

All at once, objections were coming from every direction.

"You're kidding!"

"Do you really think this is the time for that?"

"Whoa, whoa, whoa! Can we talk about this?"

"Different? Whaddya mean different?"

"I think I'm going to cry!"

Ignoring the chatter, Killer pointed at her center. "Frankie! The count is on three...on the third hut, you do a direct snap to Michael."

"Direct snap? We never practiced that!" Frankie whined.

"It's the same as a shotgun, only snap it to Michael instead of me," Killer said sharply. "Michael, the fourth number I shout ...the fourth number...that's who's got your snack."

"But what is the snack?" asked Michael, wiping his nose with his sleeve. "I need to know if it's worth running 96 yards for."

"C'mon, Michael! Don't you want to win this game?" scolded Nestor, giving his brother a sharp jab to the gut.

"Sure, that would be good, too," grinned Michael. "Especially if it means something yummy for my tummy."

Killer raised her hands and the huddle immediately fell silent.

"Like I said, I'll call the play at the line. Michael, listen for the fourth number." Then pausing a second to look into the faces of her teammates, she hollered out, "Let's do it! Ready...."

...BREAK!" shouted the offense in one loud voice.

Up in the stands, Audrey, Stinky Smothers' mother, the Kopeckys and the Limburger Heads, along with 23,000 other cheering fans, watched anxiously as the Braves and Bulldogs lined up head-to-head for one last play.

"Go, Braves!" shouted Audrey Hapburn.

"Hercules! Hercules! Hercules!" yelled old Demetri Papadopoulos.

"Dad! I have to go to the bathroom!" cried Little John Kopecky.

Their half-time break over, Packers and Broncos came pouring out of the tunnel, stopping along the sidelines to witness the end of the epic Braves-Bulldog battle.

All eyes were glued on the pint-sized Port Clinton quarterback as she walked confidently to the line of scrimmage. But as Killer settled in behind Frankie Flat-Nosed Fitzwater, the shouts coming from the other side of the line told her that something was terribly wrong.

"Don't let anyone break loose down the field!" shouted one Bulldog linebacker.

"Watch the quarterback! She's the one who hands off the snack," sneered a Bulldog defensive back.

"Grab the snack and we win the game!" bellowed #60.

The Bulldogs, seeing the end zone exchanges after each Braves' touchdown, had figured out the secret to the special plays was the snack. The only way to stop Michael from scoring was to snatch the snack.

Killer paused to study the defense, then started calling the signals.

"MUSTARD...CHILI...EXTRA ONIONS. MUSTARD... CHILI...EXTRA ONIONS."

Michael's eyes flashed fire. "My snack! It's a chili dog!"

Suddenly Killer began darting from one end of the line to the other, faking hand-offs and whispering the names of candy to her teammates as she flew by.

"Gummy Bears...Skittles...M & M's..."

On the other side of the line, the Bulldogs were screaming as their heads were spinning in circles trying to catch sight of who was getting the snack.

"Watch her! Watch her!" yelled a Bulldog.

"I heard her say Gummy Bears!" shouted another.

"No-no-no, she handed off M & M's to #20!"

In the middle of all the confusion, Killer dashed back behind Frankie to finish calling the signals.

"ONE..."

"First number..." grunted Michael under his breath.

"FIVE..."

"Second number..." whispered Michael.

"EIGHT..."

"Third number..." hummed Michael.

Pausing to look down the line, Killer shouted the final number.

"NINE!!"

"Nine? She called her own number! Killer has my chili dog!" drooled Michael, dizzy with excitement.

"HUT-HUT.......HUT!" shouted Killer.

On the third hut, she took a quick step to the left just as Frankie Fitzwater sent a direct snap to Michael.

Quickly, Michael did the math: football + 96 yards = chili dog!

What happened next had the 23,000 fans in the stands dropping their jaws.

Instead of the Bulldogs trying to tackle Michael with the football, they were charging after the other Braves on the field, desperate to find who had the snack.

A hefty Bulldog defensive lineman grabbed Tommy O'Connor in a headlock growling, "You got candy? Give it up!"

"Candy?" cried Tommy, struggling to get free. "What are you talking about?"

Another Bulldog shoved Nestor down and was frisking him.

"Cut it out," giggled Nestor, rolling around on the ground. "You're tickling me!"

In the middle of all the commotion, Killer slipped through untouched and was ten yards out when she slid her hand into her pouch and pulled out the chili dog for Michael to see.

Michael saw it. But so did Big #60! The race was on!

Tucking her head, Killer dashed toward the end zone.

Michael, with visions of mustard and chili and extra onions dancing in his head, was tearing up the turf in hot pursuit.

Despite the head starts of Killer and Michael, Big #60 had turned on his own jets and he was gaining on them.

Hawk, knowing #60 was the fastest player during warm-up, jumped from the bench and ran down the sideline alongside them shouting.

"RUN, KILLER! RUN! He's catching up!"

Tearing over midfield, Killer took a quick glance over her shoulder. Michael was a couple of steps behind her and Big #60 was just a step behind Michael.

Realizing she wasn't going to be able to outrun him, Killer began evasive techniques and started zig-zagging her way down the field. Big #60, determined to catch the Braves' quarterback before she crossed the goal line, was locked in on his target. He blew past Michael and was right on Killer's heels.

"Hey, Big Foot!" yelled Michael. "I'm the one with the football!"

"Yeah! But she's the one with the chili dog!" shouted Big #60 over his shoulder.

Michael was horrified. "He's after my chili dog!"

Frantic, Michael kicked it up another gear.

The time on the stadium clock registered all zeroes, as the mad dash continued.

Past the point of exhaustion, Killer's spirit rose as the goalposts loomed closer with every step. Just when she thought she was going to make it, a massive hand grabbed her by the shoulder and she tumbled down on the four yard-line, fumbling the chili dog.

Killer immediately sprang to her feet and made a last-gasp scramble to grab it. But Big #60 swooped in and scooped it up, holding the prize over his head out of Killer's reach.

A second later, Michael arrived at the scene, screeching to a stop five yards short of the goal line.

"Michael! Michael! Run! Score the touchdown" pleaded Killer as she shoved him toward the end zone.

"Don't do it!" snarled Big #60. "Give me the football and I'll give you the chili dog."

Michael, his mouth watering, stood still.

"Michael! Just five more yards and we win the game!" cried Killer.

Unwrapping the chili dog, Big #60 put the prize up to his open mouth. "Give me the football or else I'll eat it! I swear I'll eat it!"

Michael's mouth was watering but so were his eyes. Still, he didn't move.

As the standoff continued, the rest of the Olmsted Falls' players started arriving on the scene. One after another they piled on, trying to bring Michael down.

One Bulldog jumped on Michael's shoulders. One player grabbed an arm and was trying to pry the ball loose. Two more were tugging at a leg, while another had his hands wrapped around an ankle.

On the other side, the Brave players were all shouting at their star running back, urging him to trudge on into the end zone.

"C'mon, Michael…five more yards!" hollered Nestor.

"Michael! I'll give you half of any buried treasure I find for the rest of my life! JUST CROSS THE GOAL LINE!" exclaimed Frankie Flat-Nosed Fitzwater.

From the sideline, Hawk was shouting, "MICHAEL! IT'S ONLY A CHILI DOG! SCORE THE TOUCHDOWN!"

Coach Yak was yelling and jumping up and down waving his hands toward the goal line. Coaches Jekyll and Hyde were on their knees praying Michael would plow ahead five more yards for the victory.

The Packer and Bronco players, scattered along the sidelines, were mesmerized as they witnessed something they had never seen in all their years of playing football.

The entire stadium was going wild.

"I'll tell you what!" yelled #60. "Don't give me the football. Just go to the ground and I'll give you the chili dog! If you don't, I'll swallow it whole!" Big #60 held the chili dog an inch from his open mouth, threatening to devour it.

Michael - his teammates all around him begging, Bulldogs hanging all over him, 23,000 fans in the stands all screaming - took one last, loving look at the chili dog with extra onions and closed his eyes.

Summoning every ounce of inner strength, Michael broke loose from all the would-be tacklers and busted into the end zone for the touchdown. Then he sneezed.

Tom Benson Hall of Fame Stadium exploded! The scoreboard flashed Port Clinton 23...Olmsted Falls 22. Audrey, Stinky Smothers' Mother and the Kopeckys were hugging and cheering. The Limburger Heads were dancing on top of their seats.

On the field, the Braves piled on top of Michael in celebration.

"Way to go, Michael!" shouted Killer.

"You did it, Michael! We won!" cheered Hawk.

"All for one and one for all!" hollered Nestor.

Still standing on the five-yard line, Big #60 threw the chili dog down and walked off the field with the rest of the Bulldogs, his head down in defeat.

"Hey, look!" cried Michael. "There's the chili dog!" He bent down, picked it up and brushed it off.

"Eew. You're not going to eat that," winced Nestor in disgust. "It's got pebbles and dirt all over it."

When the two teams met on the sideline for the traditional post-game handshake, Michael still had a little dirt and mustard stuck at the corner of his mouth.

8:08 pm Inside the Pro Football Hall of Fame

Hot, sweaty and running behind schedule, security guard Elliot Ness punched the time clock a few minutes late for his 8pm shift.

Sprinting into the cafeteria, Elliot shoved his lunch sack into the refrigerator and rushed to the front desk where his boss was watching a row of video monitors.

"Officer Ness...you're late," growled the Pro Football Hall of Fame night-shift security supervisor without looking up.

"Sa-Sa-Sorry," stammered Elliot, wiping sweat from his forehead with his sleeve. "Flat tire."

"Your first week on the job. Seems like you'd want to make a better impression," barked the security chief.

"Yes sir," agreed Elliot, starring down at his shiny black shoes.

Elliot's boss shook his head and handed him a flashlight. "Well, don't just stand here...get going! Make your rounds!"

Flicking the flashlight on, Elliot gave his supervisor a quick salute and took off on his patrol into the darkened shrine.

Starting on the Lower Level, the rookie security guard took a look around the gift shop, then looped through Madden NFL. Elliot wanted to stop and play, but on the ceiling was a camera pointed right at the game. He knew if his supervisor caught him, his first week on the job would be his last.

Elliot looked up at the camera, smiled and gave a little wave.

Then he walked through the Time Tunnel, shining his flashlight into the shadowy corners as he passed. Seeing nothing out of the ordinary on the first floor (although his nose did detect a faint musty, socky, cheesy kind of smelly odor), Elliot took the stairs up and circled around the Upper Level's First Century display, then strolled in the direction of the Hall of Fame Gallery.

Turning the corner, he pointed his flashlight at the first class of Hall of Fame inductees.

"1963..." mumbled Elliot, barely moving his lips. "That's a long-long-long time ago..."

Shining his light on the plaque below each bust, he whispered each name and then moved his flashlight up to look at each ancient football god cast in bronze.

"Sammy Baugh......Bert Bell......Joe Carr......Earl (Dutch) Clark......Harold (Red) Grange......George Halas......Mel...Mel... *WHAT THE?!...*"

Suddenly frightened, Elliot jerked his flashlight back to George Halas...except there was NO GEORGE HALAS there!

His heart pounding fast, Elliot moved deeper into the Hall of Fame Gallery and in the Class of 1964, he made another dreadful discovery.

"Oh no! George Trafton is gone, too!" groaned Elliot.

Shining his flashlight down the row, he saw another empty spot above George McAfee's plaque.

Shaking and upset, Elliot ran to the Upper Level security box, broke the glass over the scarlet panic button and sounded the alarm.

Breathing hard, he pulled his walkie talkie from the clip on his belt and stammered into the mic, "Code Red! Hall of Fame Gallery! I repeat...CODE RED! HALL OF FAME GALLERY!"

....

On the field, the Packers and Broncos were midway through the third quarter of their exhibition game, with Green Bay leading 31-13.

The Limburger Heads were happy, laughing and singing about the Packers playing in the Super Bowl. All of them except Henrietta, who was asleep in her seat, smiling and snoring in Polish.

Audrey, Stinky Smothers' mother and the Kopeckys were happy, too. They had witnessed their Port Clinton Braves' astounding come-from-behind victory and were now basking in the magical afterglow.

And Killer, Hawk, Nestor, Michael and the Smothers brothers, bruised and beaming, were working their way up from the field to join their families in the stands. As they moved through the crowd, Michael, wearing his Cheesehead hat, was getting stopped every few steps by fans asking for his autograph.

After watching Michael scribble his name and number on a few programs, Killer made a suggestion. "C'mon, Michael! You gotta put some personality into it. Name and number. BORING."

"Yeah, Michael. Don't be boring," laughed Hawk.

A few seconds later, still pushing their way through the swarm of people, a stadium usher handed Michael a pen and a pizza box to sign. Michael, noticing the usher's name tag, paused for a moment. Then, inspired, he started writing.

To Marvin!
There's no better feeling in the world
than a warm pizza box on your lap.
Michael Hapburn - Port Clinton Braves #99

Handing Marvin back his pizza box and pen, Michael sneezed. "ACHOOOO!"

Cheesehead hat, pen and pizza box all toppled to the concrete steps. Bending down, the stadium usher picked up the cheese wedge as Michael scrambled around and retrieved the pen and pizza box.

"Looks like you tried to eat this!" chuckled Marvin, as he handed Michael his hat.

"I did try," admitted Michael, delivering the usher his belongings with a grin, "But it didn't taste very good."

At that moment, Nestor noticed Audrey waving at them in the next section. "There they are! Section 122," he said. "C'mon, let's go!"

The Braves hurried through the throng and skipped down the steps to row 20 where they were greeted with smiles, handshakes and hugs.

"Kathy! You played a wonderful game! Those Olmsted Falls' boys were so large, but you stood right up to them! I'm really impressed!" smiled Audrey.

"Thank you, Ms. Hapburn," said Killer politely. "And just think if Michael had played the whole time instead of only one half."

Down the row, the Limburger Heads congratulated Michael with high-fives and slaps on the back.

"That was an amazing performance, young man," smiled Einstein. "By my calculations, you gained 220 yards in three attempts. That's

73.333333333333 yards per carry. Truly spectacular!"

"For the love of Lombardi! The Packers need to get up here and sign you to a contract now," laughed Floyd.

"Hercules! Hercules! Hercules!" sang Papa.

"Great game, kid," complimented Nick Monroe.

"Here! Sit down next to us," chimed in Rick Monroe.

Michael, embarrassed by all the attention, smiled and pointed at Henrietta Wozniak snoring in her seat.

"Do you know if she brought any of those cabbage rolls with her?" asked Michael, punctuating his question with a sneeze. The Limburger Heads roared with laughter and started slapping Michael on the back all over again.

At the end of the third quarter, Big John Kopecky gathered up Little John Kopecky in his arms. "Well, this is about all the excitement we can stand for one night. Time to get this little one home," he said. "Kathy...you want to go with us?"

"I'd really like to ride the bus back with the team," said Killer.

"Michael, you ride home with us," ordered Audrey.

"But Mom! Can't I ride the bus, too?" begged Michael.

"You're fighting that cold," explained Audrey. "Nestor, tell Coach Yak we took Michael home to get some rest. He'll understand."

"Sure, Mom! I'll let him know," nodded Nestor.

There was another flurry of handshakes and hugs as Audrey and her bunch said goodbye and headed up the steps and out of the stadium.

Happy that their big adventure was not quite over, Nestor, Hawk, Killer, Stinky Smothers and Stinky Smothers' brother settled back down in their seats among the Limburger Heads to watch the end of the Packer-Bronco game.

Floyd, in between Nestor and Hawk, talked non-stop about Packer Legends Curly Lambeau, Vince Lombardi, Bart Starr, Brett Favre and why the Green Bay Packers are the best franchise in football history.

"And here's another reason the Packers are above all others," crowed Floyd. "They have the most players of any team in the Pro Football Hall of Fame!"

"I thought the Bears had the most," said Nestor, puzzled.

"Not anymore!" laughed Floyd.

Coughing, Einstein jumped out of his seat with a shriek, "Floyd! I propose we make a sojourn to concessions and procure popcorn for this fine group."

Grabbing Floyd by the arm, Einstein pulled his fellow Limburger Head out of his seat and gave him a shove toward the aisle.

"Guess I'm making a sojourn to procure popcorn," laughed Floyd.

As the two of them headed up the stairs to the concession stand, Einstein gave Floyd an earful. "In the name of Jerry Kramer, show some restraint, Floyd! You practically announced to the entire stadium the purpose of our secret mission."

"Stinkin' Bishop, Albert! I was just making conversation and showing some Packer Pride," explained Floyd.

"Cease and desist with all dialogue endangering the successful completion of Operation Georgie Porgie. Do you understand?" ordered Einstein, shaking a finger in Floyd's face. "I do not want to arouse any suspicion."

"Okay! Okay," sighed Floyd. "I'll talk about the weather in Green Bay or maybe the time I watched an entire Packer-Lions' game standing on my head."

"That would be acceptable material for discussion," nodded Einstein in frustration.

"You know, Albert, the world record for standing on your head is 3 hours, 37 minutes and fifty seconds," informed Floyd. "If that game had gone into overtime, I think I could have broke it."

Stepping up to the concession stand, Einstein rolled his eyes and placed his order. "Ten bags of your very best buttered popcorn, please."

....

On the bus, Dairy Dan had his nose pressed up against the dark window, counting police cars as they screeched to a stop outside the Hall of Fame, all with their red and blue lights flashing.

"Nine. Ten. Eleven…twelve…" mumbled Dairy Dan.

With a nervous sigh, he glanced at the Bears in the back row.

"Well, boys, it looks like they've discovered you've gone missing."

Police were swarming the place. Some were blocking the front doors with barricades and crime scene tape. Others were pulling out boxes of equipment from mobile command post vans and rolling them into the building on steel dollies.

In the middle of the mass confusion, Dairy Dan spotted the bus driver, Sharky, strolling through the parking lot toward the motor-coach. As Sharky reached the gleaming green and gold tour bus, he paused for a few moments to watch the uproar and slurp soda from the plastic souvenir cup he was holding.

Not wanting Sharky to get too close to the Bears in the back, Dairy Dan limped to the front and greeted him as he turned to step inside.

"You're back early," said Dairy Dan, pretending to be watching the Packer-Bronco game on his phone.

"Yup," answered Sharky making sucking sounds with the straw as he slurped up the last of his soda. "Packers are killing 'em, so I figured I get back to the bus and warm up the engine for the drive home. How long you been here?"

"A little while, I guess. We had a big day. Some of us are pretty tired," explained Dairy Dan. "Oh, and here are the other six tickets for the guys we...um...picked up here."

Sharky shoved the tickets in his shirt pocket and adjusted his thick glasses. Peeking around the big dairy farmer, he squinted at the Bears, disguised as Packer fans, sitting in the last row.

"Are them your buddies back there?" asked Sharky, spitting droplets of soda through his toothless mouth. "I think I'll go say hello."

"No, no," objected Dairy Dan, holding up his hands to block the bus driver from walking down the aisle. "Like I said, they're tired."

"It'll it be okay," assured Sharky. "I'll just chat with 'em a while and then fire up the bus."

"No, really. They're sleeping," explained Dairy Dan. "And they're, they're Bears..."

"They're bears?" repeated Sharky with a puzzled look.

"I-I-I mean, they're LIKE bears. Bears sleeping," stammered Dairy Dan. "And you know how grumpy a bear is when you wake him. Like when they're hibernating and stuff."

Wanting to change the subject, Diary Dan pointed out the windshield of the bus. "I wonder what's going on with all the police cars..."

"Maybe somebody drew a mustache on one of those Hall of Fame statues," laughed Sharky as he slipped behind the steering wheel. "Wouldn't that be funny!"

"Yeah, hilarious," nodded the Limburger Head, grimacing in pain from his throbbing foot.

Sharky shoved the key into the ignition and gave it a turn. The engine started and a low, soothing vibration gently shook the bus.

"Why don't you try and catch a few winks before we hit the road?" suggested Dairy Dan, turning to hobble down the aisle.

"Good idea," agreed Sharky, reaching down to grab the pillow stashed under the driver's seat. "I think I will take a quick nap."

Sharky fluffed up the pillow, placed it behind his head and closed his eyes just as Dairy Dan slid into his seat in the row in front of the Bears' bench.

His heart beating fast, Dairy Dan stared out his window as a stream of police cars with lights flashing continued to pull up in front of the Hall of Fame.

"The sooner we get out of here, the better," he mumbled to himself.

....

With the Packers way ahead and all the backups and rookies in the game, the crowd was paying little attention to what was happening down on the field.

Stinky Smothers' brother was counting Cheeseheads in the stadium.

Demetri Papadopoulos and Nestor were exchanging cell numbers so that the old Greek cargo pilot could get texts from his young friend to find out how Team Hercules was doing during the season.

And Hawk and Killer were reliving the stunning and unbelievable finish to their game with Olmsted Falls.

"And where did that chili dog come from?" said Hawk, baffled.

"When I left you to go tell Coach Yak you guys were on your way, I passed a hot dog stand. So, I bought one...extra onions, of course..."

"Of course," laughed Hawk.

"...and I stashed it in my duffle in case Michael needed some extra motivation."

"That sure was smart," gushed Hawk, happy to have some time alone with Killer in a stadium filled with 23,000 people.

"Here you go!" shouted Floyd as he and Einstein returned from the concession stand. "Popcorn!"

The two Limburger Heads passed out the bags of popcorn and the group of new friends munched their way through the last five minutes of the game. Final score, Green Bay 38...Denver 16.

"We better get back to our bus," announced Nestor, rolling the top of his popcorn bag down to save what was left for the ride to Port Clinton. "Are you guys going all the way to Green Bay tonight?"

"Yep! Got a long ride ahead of us, but we gotta get back to complete the operation," informed Floyd.

"Operation?" repeated Hawk, his forehead wrinkled in confusion.

Coughing and spitting out popcorn, Einstein Wozniak slapped his hand over Floyd's mouth to keep his loose-lipped Limburger Head from spilling more beans.

"Yes! Yes! Operation! Our friend, Daniel, was forced to remain on our motorcoach, foregoing his opportunity to attend tonight's contest because of a possible fracture of the medial malleolus, which may require surgery to repair," explained Einstein.

"Say that again," requested Nestor.

"I bang Squadron Leader Dan with hammer," confessed Papa sadly. "Broke bone on accident."

"That's too bad, we hope the...ah...operation goes okay," blurted Killer, jumping into the conversation while dragging Hawk and Nestor toward the exit. "It was nice meeting you all! Have a safe drive home."

Hawk, Nestor, Killer, Stinky Smothers and Stinky Smothers' brother waved goodbye to the Limburger Heads and walked up the stairs and out of the stadium.

"They're sure nice guys," said Hawk as the five Port Clinton Braves moved slowly with the departing crowd.

"They bought us popcorn!" agreed Stinky Smothers' brother.

"Yeah, they're nice…but I don't know. There was something strange about them," said Killer, trying to put her finger on it. "Like they were up to something."

"Look!" shouted Nestor, pointing at the Hall of Fame as they spilled out of the stadium. "Something's happening over there! Look at all the police cars!"

"Let's go see what it is!" shouted Hawk.

"No!" objected Killer. "C'mon! There's our bus over there."

Killer took off running and Nestor, Hawk and the Smothers brothers followed. A minute later, the five of them were standing in line with their teammates, waiting to board the bus.

Standing at the bus door holding his clipboard, Coach Yak was checking off player names. Looking over his shoulder were Coaches Jekyll and Hyde with their clipboards, double and triple-checking.

Tired from their day-long adventure, each player slowly stepped up.

"Stinky Smothers…#78," blurted out Stinky when it was his turn.

"Check," said Coach Yak, without looking up from his clipboard. "Take your seat."

"Stinky Smothers' brother…#25. You want some popcorn, Coach?" he asked, holding the bag out in front of him.

Coach Yak tried reaching in the bag, but his hand was too big.

"Take the whole bag," offered Stinky Smothers' brother. "I'm done."

"Thanks," said Yak as he held the bag above his mouth and dumped some in. "Take your seat!" he added.

As Nestor and Killer reported in, Hawk turned back to survey all the flashing lights around the Hall of Fame. He was concentrating so hard on all the commotion, he didn't realize the coaches were trying to get his attention.

"Horace! Hawk!" yelled Coach Hyde, tapping him on the shoulder.

"Oh, sorry," apologized Hawk, as he turned forward.

"You can board. We got ya," smiled Coach Hyde, pointing to the bus.

Still keeping his eyes on all the activity outside, Hawk stumbled as he stepped onboard. As he walked down the aisle looking for a seat, Kathy Kopecky tugged on his sleeve and pulled him into the row where she was sitting with Nestor.

"C'mon, Hawk," said Killer softly, as she scooted over on the seat cushion. "Squeeze in here with us."

Without a word, Hawk sat down next to Braves' quarterback. Nestor, noticing the blank expression on his brother's face, leaned past Killer and snapped his fingers in front of Hawk's bandaged nose.

"Hey! Hawk! Are you okay?"

Hawk cleared his throat and heaved a sigh. "I'm thinking about what Killer said about those guys being up to something," answered Hawk with a worried look. "I mean, what about those stink bombs? What were they doing?"

"Don't know," shrugged Nestor.

"Now all those police cars are out there," he added.

"Whatever it is, it doesn't concern us," concluded Killer. "We visited the Hall of Fame. We won the game. Now, we're going home. End of story."

At the front of the bus, Coach Yak gave a short double burst on his whistle. "TWEET-TWEET."

Suddenly the noisy bus fell silent.

"Everyone's checked off our list except Hapburn, Michael, #99," barked Yak. "Why is *he* always the one…"

"Sorry, Coach!" interrupted Nestor, jumping up from his seat. "I forgot to tell you our Mom took Michael home to get some rest 'cuz of his cold. She said you'd understand."

Immediately, the three coaches' heads snapped down to the clipboards they were holding and put check marks by Michael's name.

"Okay, we're good to go," said Coach Yak, giving the bus driver a thumb's up. As the engine started, he turned back to the team and gave another quick tweet on his whistle.

"Let me just say, *that* was a good team you beat tonight and we are real proud of the way you played hard the whole game," boomed the big coach. "We got behind but you never gave up."

"Way to go, everybody!" chimed in Coaches Jekyll and Hyde.

"As a reward, there'll be no practice for a few days," announced Coach Yak. "Rest up, give your bumps and bruises a chance to heal, and we'll see you on the field Thursday at three o'clock."

The team let out a loud cheer.

"Anybody wanna dig for buried treasure at Portage Park tomorrow?" shouted Frankie Fitzwater.

"No way!" groaned Stinky Smothers. "I'm gonna sleep all day."

Coaches Yak and Jekyll chuckled and settled into their seats. Coach Hyde dug around in his duffle bag. Pulling out his first aid kit, he walked down the aisle toward Hawk.

"Why don't we get that bandage off and clean you up," offered Hyde, as he knelt down by the seat.

Carefully removing the tape, Coach Hyde dabbed Hawk's beak with a wipe and inspected the scrape.

"How does that feel?" asked the coach.

"Better...I can breathe again," sniffed Hawk.

"We'll leave it uncovered now, so the air can get to it," explained Coach Hyde as he packed up and stood up smiling at the three Braves.

"You all had a great game. I think it's going to be a fun season."

"Thanks, Coach," chirped Hawk, Killer and Nestor.

Coach Hyde walked back to his seat as the bus lurched forward.

Hawk took a deep breath and filled his nose with the buttery smell of popcorn. Leaning past Killer, he reached into the bag Nestor was holding and pulled out a handful.

Slowly, the Braves' bus pulled out of the parking lot, past all the flashing lights, police cars and people buzzing like bees around a Hall of Fame hive.

....

"Stinkin' Bishop! Look at all the cop cars!" gasped Floyd Dowler, as he and his fellow Limburger Heads trudged past the Pro Football

Hall of Fame after the game. "I wonder what happened?"

"What happened?" mocked Nick Monroe. "C'mon, Floyd. Think about it!"

"Big trouble," lamented Demetri Papadopoulos. "Big, **BIG** trouble. Police looking for missing bears."

"What? For the love of Lombardi! All of this brouhaha over a few Bears gone missing?" squealed Floyd.

"Defcon Two!" declared Einstein, alarmed by all the activity. "Proceed to our means of transportation post-haste!"

Stepping up to triple speed, the Limburger Heads sped through the parking lot, arriving at the gleaming green and gold Packer motorcoach huffing and puffing. Everyone except Papa, who fell behind the rest of the group after a wheel popped off his walker.

As they boarded the bus, Henrietta Wozniak, tapped Sharky on the shoulder and pointed at Papa pushing his crippled walker across the parking lot.

"Nie idź jeszcze...Stary człowiek nadchodzi," directed Henrietta. *Do not go yet ... the old man is coming.*

"Yep! It's starry are out," slurred the toothless bus driver squinting up at the sky through his thick glasses. "Well, let's get rollin'!"

Adjusting himself in the driver's seat, Sharky released the brakes, filling the air with a loud hissing sound and shifted the bus into *Drive*.

"Czekac!" cried Henrietta, clubbing Sharky with her purse. *Wait!*

"Whoa! What's wrong?" cried Sharky, covering his head.

"I think she's saying we can't go yet," said Floyd, wrapping his arms around Henrietta to stop the flogging. "We gotta wait for Papa."

"Oh, oh! Sorry, lady! I thought we had everybody on board," apologized Sharky. "Don't you worry...we'll wait for daddy."

Floyd escorted Henrietta, who was still annoyed and cackling in Polish, down the aisle to her seat.

A full five minutes later, Papa climbed onboard and screeched his way down the aisle with his one-wheeled walker. Sitting down in the row behind Dairy Dan and Einstein, he leaned forward and listened in on the emergency meeting in progress.

"I think once we're away from all these flashing lights and on the highway, we'll be okay," murmured Dairy Dan. "Only thing that bugs me is how to get dem Bears off this bus without anyone seeing us."

"Not to worry," whispered Einstein confidently. "I've poured over every possible scenario on how to successfully accomplish Phase Two of our operation and the solution is simple…a stink bomb."

Once again, a loud hissing sound filled the bus as Sharky took his foot off the brake and the motorcoach gently jerked forward.

"Stink bomb? But we used them all," argued Dairy Dan.

"I believe I have come up with a solution to that predicament," replied Einstein, smiling ever so slightly.

The two Limburger heads paused to look out the window as Sharky maneuvered his way through the maze of police cars.

Popping up and down in their seats as the bus rolled over a speed bump, they pulled onto George Halas Drive, leaving the flashing lights and confusion behind.

"Okay, give me the details. Where-how can we get a stink bomb?" asked Dairy Dan, a little more relaxed now that they were on their way home.

Einstein stood up and looked around at all the other passengers before continuing their conversation. Satisfied no one was paying any attention, he pulled a map out of his back pocket and sat back down.

"Well, I have done a thorough analysis of our nine-hour, twenty-six-minute journey from Canton, Ohio to Green Bay," explained Einstein, running his finger along the map.

"I have scrutinized the three stops we are scheduled to make on our return trip and I have come to the conclusion our optimal opportunity for extracting the bears will happen right here," whispered Einstein, pointing at a spot in Wisconsin just north of the Illinois border.

"Pleasant Prairie Premium Outlets? You want to take the Bears to a mall?" asked Dairy Dan.

"Correct!" said Einstein. "Drive time from Monroe to Pleasant Prairie Premium Outlets is exactly one-hour-fifty-four minutes."

"Yeah, so?" growled Dairy Dan.

"So, you text the cheese master, give him the exact coordinates of our intended rendezvous location. Inform him of our estimated time of arrival, which I have computed to be at 6:02 in the AM, factoring in a ten-minute margin of error."

"You want me to text Helmut to meet us at the mall at 6am?"

"Precisely!" nodded Einstein. "Inform him to depart Monroe in his Chalet Cheese Co-op delivery truck no later than 4:07 AM. Tell him to bring a half dozen nose clips and...a stink bomb."

Suddenly, the light flashed on in Dairy Dan's head and he smiled. Pulling his phone out of the duffle bag, he gave his friend an admiring pat on his bald head.

"Einstein...you ARE a genius."

....

In the two hours following Elliot Ness' Code Red distress call, the Hall of Fame had exploded with activity.

A SWAT Team (Special Weapons And Tactics) was preforming a methodical inch-by-inch search of the entire building inside and out. Dozens of fingerprint experts were elbow-to-elbow gathering clues in the Hall of Fame Gallery where the six Bears had gone missing.

In the Conference and Meeting Room, detectives were questioning gift shop clerks, building custodians, cafeteria cooks, stadium staff and ushers and anybody else that might have seen something suspicious.

At the front desk, the night shift security supervisor and Elliot Ness were examining hours and hours of video from the security cameras within the building.

Pushing the eject button on his remote, Elliot pulled a DVD from the machine and replaced it with one marked *Upper Level Elevator – Current Class Gallery*. Grabbing the disc by its edge, he plopped it into the player and pushed another button. The monitor lit up showing visitors to the Hall of Fame getting on and off the elevator and touring football's sacred shrine. In the bottom corner of the screen, there were numbers indicating the date and time of day.

"So far, all I've seen on these tapes are a bunch of Cheeseheads," muttered Elliot, rubbing his bleary eyes.

The security supervisor glanced up from his screen and looked at the one Elliot was monitoring. "Don't watch it at regular speed! Fast forward! Or we'll be here 'til Christmas," complained the crabby boss. "But don't miss anything either."

"Aye-aye, sir," answered Elliot with a salute and a sigh. Pushing the FWD button, he watched as the people on the monitor comically whizzed around at high speed.

Just then, a tall, square-jawed man in a dark blue suit surrounded by a dozen men and women in navy blue windbreakers burst through the front door and rushed to where Elliot and his boss were studying video. On their jackets in large yellow type were the letters FBI/FD.

"Who's in charge?" demanded the square-jawed man.

"Who wants to know?" the security supervisor barked back.

The square-jawed man pulled his wallet out of his back pocket and flipped it open to reveal a shiny, metal badge, announcing his presence with authority.

"Senior Special Agent Roman Noodle, Federal Bureau of Investigation Football Division. We're taking over this case."

"Fine with me," sneered the security supervisor. "I'm going on lunch break in a few minutes anyway."

"No breaks until you brief me on exactly what you've found out so far," hissed Noodle.

"Six Hall of Fame busts are gone. All of the statues were Chicago Bears. And all of them named George. That's it. That's what we've found out so far."

With that, the security supervisor closed a folder on his desk, stood up and handed it to Special Agent Roman Noodle.

Then he opened a file drawer behind him, pulled out his lunch sack and walked away.

"I said, no breaks!" shouted Noodle as he watched the security chief head off toward the cafeteria. "This will go on my report!"

His face red, the new Noodle in charge opened the folder, jotted something down, then turned to shout out instructions to the dozen

FBI/FD agents who charged in with him.

"Listen up! We are going to solve this crime and put those responsible behind bars, but first I want to say three things. Number one! I don't want this leaking out to the newspapers and TV stations! Understand? No leakers! I hate leakers!"

"No leakers!" repeated the bunch in blue jackets.

"Number two…the Hall of Fame is off-limits to the general public until further notice. Issue an announcement that the building is closed for emergency repairs…or spraying for bugs…or something."

"Spraying for bugs!" shouted the agents.

"And number three…"

At that moment, Elliot Ness nervously interrupted his new boss. "Excuse me…ah, Officer Noodle. I-I-I think I have something here you should see," stuttered Elliot, pointing at his monitor.

Walking around the front desk, Senior Special Agent Roman Noodle bent over and stuck his nose in front of the computer screen.

"Time code here is 4:29 pm" said Elliot, reversing his DVD and then pushing play. "Everything is normal. Then, here at 4:30, look what happens."

"WHAT THE…!" exclaimed Noodle. "Run that back again!"

Following orders, Elliot reversed the DVD and hit play again as Special Agent Noodle pulled up a chair and sat down.

"At exactly 4:30, everybody drops like they got hit," noted Noodle. "Visitors, employees, security guards …all on the floor motionless!"

He grabbed the remote out of Elliot's hand and, punched the fast-forward button. Noodle and his crew kept their eyes glued to the monitor. Suddenly, a blurry image flashed past the screen.

"What was that?" shouted one of the agents.

Noodle hit the stop button, reversed the DVD and paused it on a shadowy figure.

"Can you make this picture any bigger?" asked Noodle handing the remote back to Elliot.

Without a word, Elliot picked up the mouse and clicked on the image. Typing some instructions on his keyboard, he zoomed in.

"Look! He's carrying two brown sacks," announced Noodle.

"And whatever's in them looks heavy," added Elliot.

"I tell you what's in them…it's the stolen Bears! But I can't see his face because of that blasted Cheesehead hat!" grumbled Noodle.

"Cheesehead hat," murmured Elliot as he zoomed in on the headgear. "That's it, sir!"

"That's what?" demanded the puzzled chief investigator. "Almost everybody has a Cheesehead on."

"Yes," agreed Elliot. "But see there?" He pointed to the corner of the cheese wedge. "This one has a bite out of it!

CHAPTER 8

August 25 - 12:01 am EDT | Somewhere on I-80 in Ohio
8 Days to Kickoff at Lambeau Field

Unable to sleep, Demetri Papadopoulos looked out the window and listened to the sounds of passengers snoring, accompanied by Sharky quietly humming the Packer's fight song as he drove the gleaming green and gold motorcoach westward through the dark Ohio night.

It was just a minute past midnight when the sound of a text coming in on Dairy Dan's phone interrupted the sleepy calm, causing everyone around him to jump.

Blinking, Dairy Dan glanced at the touchscreen on his phone and then handed it to Einstein. Putting on his glasses, the Operation Georgie Porgie mastermind read the text from Helmut.

will meet u at mall 6am. bringing 2 sbs.

"Excellent!" nodded Einstein, handing the phone back to Dairy Dan. "I suggest we strive for a degree of quiescence, to better cope with pending events."

"Fine. You do that," yawned Dairy Dan. "Me...I'm going back to my little catnap."

The two Limburger Heads leaned back in their seats and closed their eyes. In the row behind them, Papa was still looking out the window, wide awake and worried.

With his help, his beloved Packers now had more players in the Hall of Fame than the Bears. But instead of being happy, he had a sick feeling in his stomach.

Papa gazed up at the full moon and sighed. Trying hard to think about something else, his eyes followed a surprisingly bright moonbeam down to a pasture. And there, in the moonbeam, stood that cow again! And again, he was holding up a sign!

Warning! Protek PAPA!

Papa let out a gasp! He rubbed his eyes and looked out the window again, but the cow with the sign in the moonlight was gone.

Papa shot up from his seat and looked around the bus to see if anyone else was shocked by the sight of a sign-holding cow.

But no. Up front, Sharky was still driving and humming. Behind Sharky, the passengers were still sleeping and snoring. And in the very back, the six Bear Georges, disguised as Packer fans, were bouncing gently along on their bench.

His stomach was really turning somersaults now. Not knowing what else to do except follow the cow's instructions, Papa hobbled down the aisle and squeezed in the back seat of the motorcoach between George Halas, wearing the Chalet Cheese Co-op cap and sunglasses, and George Blanda, dressed in the Packer hoodie.

After riding in troubled silence with the Bears in the back row for a few minutes, Demetri Papadopoulos put his arm around Papa Bear and whispered in his ear.

"You no worry. I protect you."

3:13 am Inside the Pro Football Hall of Fame

Marvin Gardens was sitting outside the Conference and Meeting Room along with dozens of other ushers and stadium employees all waiting to be questioned by FBI/FD investigators.

Although the game between the Packers and the Broncos had ended hours ago, the police showed up just as the stadium staff was ready to punch the time clock and leave. Sadly, instead of getting to go home, they were pushed and shoved and herded next door to the Hall of Fame.

One by one, the employees were grilled about what they were doing and what they observed before, during and after the game.

Marvin, sitting with a pizza box on his lap and eating cold pizza, was next in line.

"Hey, you. Pizzaman," snarled a bleary-eyed woman, wearing a navy FBI/FD jacket. "You're up...follow me."

"Yes sir, I-I-I mean, ma'am" stuttered Marvin as he stood up and trotted toward the conference room door.

Inside the room, there were five desks with numbers on them. At each desk was an FBI/FD agent with a computer, firing questions at Hall of Fame and stadium worker bees seated on the other side.

The agent pointed at an empty seat in front of one of the desks.

"Take a seat at Station #4," barked the angry agent, giving Marvin a shove in that direction.

Nervous, Marvin hurried to the desk, brushed some pizza crust crumbs off his face and sat down.

"State your name," instructed the FBI/FD agent, without looking up from his computer screen.

"Marvin Gardens."

"How long have you been employed as a vendor, Mr. Gardens?"

"This September, it will be five years."

"What time did you arrive for work today, Mr. Gardens?"

"My shift started at 4:30."

"I didn't ask you what time your shift started," snapped the FBI/FD agent, peering over his computer and giving Marvin a cold stare. "I want to know exactly what time you reported for work."

"Oh, sorry," apologized Marvin. "I think I punched in about 4:25."

"I have your time card here, Mr. Gardens. It shows you punched in at 4:24. See?" The unfriendly agent flashed the card at Marvin, showing the time-stamped in blue ink. "What are you trying to pull Mr. Gardens? Are you hiding something? What's in that pizza box?"

"Pa-pa-pa-pizza," stammered Marvin, opening the box to show the agent his last piece of pepperoni pizza.

"Pep...per....oni piz...za" mumbled the agent as he typed.

"Excuse me, sir. Can you tell me what's going on? Am I in some sort of trouble?" asked Marvin, trying to be as polite as possible.

"Question #1: I can't tell you what's going on... it's classified," the agent answered. "The answer to Question #2: Maybe."

Marvin sat quietly while the FBI/FD agent typed on his keyboard and shuffled some folders. After his organizing effort, he continued.

"We are trying to locate a certain person of interest. We have photographic evidence that this somebody was in *this* general area this afternoon and we believe he...or she...might be able to provide us with important information on a particular incident that occurred."

Not sure what to say, Marvin shrugged his shoulders.

"The person we are looking for was wearing a Cheesehead hat today," added the agent.

"I saw a lot of people wearing Cheeseheads today," said Marvin with another shrug of his shoulders.

Reaching into one of the folders beside his keyboard the agent pulled out a blurry photograph and handed it to Marvin.

"This is who you're looking for?" asked Marvin, studying the photo. "I can't see the face,"

"Correct. But you'll note the Cheesehead hat this particular person is wearing has a chunk missing out of one corner," answered the FBI/FD agent pointing at the hat.

Marvin looked at the photo again, squirmed in his seat and then swallowed hard. "I-I know who this is," announced Marvin. "Look! I got his autograph!"

Marvin slid his box across the desk and pointed to the signature.

To Marvin!
There's no better feeling in the world
than a warm pizza box on your lap.
Michael Hapburn - Port Clinton Braves #99

"This was written by the person in the picture?" asked the agent. "Are you sure? Why would you want his autograph?"

"He was the hero of the kids' football game. He scored three touchdowns," explained Marvin. "He walked through my section and everyone was stopping him to shake his hand and take selfies with him."

Marvin continued. "After he signed the autograph for me, he dropped the pen. When he bent over to pick it up, his Cheesehead hat fell off. That's when I noticed the hunk missing."

Holding the pizza box in one hand and punching numbers on his cell phone with the other, the FBI/FD agent tried to remain calm.

Putting the phone to his ear and hearing a voice on the other end, he blurted out "This is Agent Sanders, Interrogation Station Four. Tell Senior Special Agent Noodle to come quickly!"

Seconds later, the square-jawed Noodle burst into the interrogation room and charged over to where Marvin was sitting.

"You got something, Agent Sanders?" boomed Noodle.

"Yes, sir! The identity of the suspect in the photograph!" answered Sanders. "It's Michael Hapburn. He's a player on a youth football team called the Port Clinton Braves. He signed this pizza box."

"Signed a pizza box? That's crazy! Are you okay, Sanders?" asked Noodle.

"Look here!" said Sanders, handing his superior the pizza box and pointing to the signature.

"The suspect in the photograph signed this? How do you know?" snarled Noodle, still not convinced.

Sanders gave Marvin a nod.

"Well, see, he scored three touchdowns," began Marvin, "and let me just say they were all pretty amazing plays. In fact, I never saw anything like it before and…

"Get to the point," barked Noodle impatiently.

"Oh, okay…sorry," apologized Marvin. "He signed my pizza box and dropped my pen. When he picked it up, his Cheesehead fell off. That's when I saw it had a bite out of it."

"Did he say anything to you?" asked Noodle.

"I said, *'It looks like you tried to eat it'*," explained Marvin, thinking back. "Then he said, *'Yeah, I did, but it didn't taste very good.'*"

Senior Special Agent Roman Noodle stood there, studying the signature on the pizza box thinking about what the vendor had said. Finally, he handed the box back to his now-smiling subordinate.

"Send this to the lab and have it analyzed. Cross-check with dental records, DNA, the whole nine yards," ordered Noodle, as he turned to leave. "Oh, and fine work, Sanders. This is quite a breakthrough. With this information, we shouldn't have any trouble locating this Hapburn character."

With that, the square-jawed Noodle was gone, busting out of the room as fast as he charged in.

Sanders, still smiling, dug around in the briefcase at his feet and pulled out a fairly large clear plastic bag. With a Sharpie, he wrote on the label: *Evidence - Case #21315295357 NFL Football Hall of Fame.*

Just as he was about to slide the pizza box in the bag, Marvin hollered out to him. "Hey! That's my box! That's *my* pizza!"

Agent Sanders looked at Marvin. Then, opening the pizza box, he dumped out the pizza, closed the box and slipped it in the plastic bag.

Buttoning up his navy FBI/FD jacket, Sanders grabbed his briefcase and the plastic bag and walked out of the room, leaving Marvin sitting there alone with his last slice of pepperoni pizza face down on the desk.

5:59 am CDT | Pleasant Prairie, Wisconsin

Cheese Master Helmut Lundquist didn't want to miss meeting up with his fellow Limburger Heads, so he arrived at the outlet mall 30 minutes early. To make sure he would spot the green and gold motorcoach as soon as it turned on the Pleasant Prairie exit, Helmut parked his Chalet Cheese Co-op delivery truck facing the expressway.

On the floor beside him were two stink bombs wrapped carefully in Packer beach towels along with six wooden clothespins.

Helmut took his eyes off the highway exit ramp for a moment to inspect his two jars of sparkling yellow-green ooze. Satisfied the lids were on tight and the stink bombs had survived the drive, Helmut wrapped them up again and carefully put them back on the floor.

At that very moment, he heard a text come in.

we r here. r u? meet us @ culvers. dd

Just as Helmut read the text, he saw the Packer tour bus whiz past him, heading toward the glowing Culver's sign a short distance away.

Quickly, Helmut punched in a reply, adjusted himself in the driver's seat, pushed the gas pedal and took off following the bus.

"Here we go," mumbled Helmut as he pulled in behind his friends. Shutting off the engine, Helmut waited and watched.

Sharky was first off the bus. He stretched, did some not-so-deep knee bends and ambled off to get a cup of coffee. Behind Sharky, a couple dozen Cheeseheads spilled into the parking lot. Stiff from the long ride, they did some stretches as well and then drifted off in groups, following the bus driver into the restaurant.

Finally, Helmut saw his friends stepping off the bus. First, it was Nick and Rick Monroe. Then Floyd hopped off, followed by Einstein, Henrietta, Papa and the leader of the Limburger Heads, Dairy Dan, limped off last.

Happy to see the conquering heroes, Helmut got out of his delivery truck and ran over to the bus.

"Welcome to delicious," shouted Floyd, giving the cheese master a hug. "We did it! We got the Bears!"

"Floyd! Zip it up!" ordered Dairy Dan. "Somebody will hear ya!"

"Sorry, DD!" apologized Floyd. "I thought it was okay to yell now that we're back in Wisconsin."

Slipping in between Floyd and Dairy Dan, Einstein pulled the cheese master aside and whispered in his hear.

"It is of the utmost importance that we remove the Bears without arousing any suspicion. Do you have the secret weapons?"

"You mean the stink bombs?" asked Helmut.

"Precisely," nodded Einstein.

"Yes, they're in the truck. But why don't we just take the Bears off the bus now while everyone is in the restaurant?" suggested Helmut.

"Nu-uh. Can't do it now," mumbled Dairy Dan, getting in on the conversation. "There are still some people on the bus."

"So, what's the plan?" asked Helmut.

"We wait until all passengers and the driver have re-established themselves on the motorcoach," explained Einstein. "Then just prior to departure, we place our clothespins in position, detonate the stink bombs and transport the Bears from the motorcoach to the delivery truck while everyone is incapacitated."

"After that, we'll send Nick and Rick back in the bus to pick up the stink bombs. By the time everybody wakes up, we'll be long gone down the road in your cheese truck," added Dairy Dan.

"Yeah, that'll probably work," agreed Helmut.

"Of course, it'll work," laughed Dairy Dan, throwing his arm around Einstein. "He's a genius!"

"I suggest we limit this idle chatter in order to cover more pressing matters. According to the itinerary, this respite is only a quarter of an hour," pointed out Einstein. "We need to proceed with the utmost efficiency to accomplish Phase Two of Operation Georgie Porgie."

"Can you say that again?" Helmut inquired.

"I think he wants ME to stop talking and YOU to go get the stink bombs," said Dairy Dan.

Helmut sprinted off and Dairy Dan huddled with the rest of the Limburger Heads, quickly explaining the plan. Satisfied everyone knew what to do, Dairy Dan broke the huddle just as Helmut returned with stink bombs in each hand and clothespins in his pocket.

"Here you go," said Helmut, carefully handing one of the stink bombs to Dan and the other to Einstein.

"Good. Perfect," smiled Dairy Dan. "All right, I'll set off my stink bomb in the front of the bus and Einstein will put his near the back."

All the Limburger Heads nodded, except for Henrietta who was standing up snoring in the Culver's parking lot.

"Helmut, take Mrs. Wozniak with you back to your truck and wait for my signal," instructed Dairy Dan. "When you see me wave, drive right over here by the bus so we can get the Bears in there faster."

"Got it, DD!" confirmed Helmut as he gently guided the sleep-standing woman away. "I almost forgot! You need the clothespins!"

The cheese master reached into his pocket and handed them over. "Remember, put them on your noses before you take the lids off."

"Don't worry, good buddy. We're old pros at this danger business now," declared Floyd as he passed out the clothespins. "In fact, Danger is my middle name."

Rich Monroe laughed and slapped Floyd on the back. "That's funny, Floyd."

"It's not a joke. My full name is Floyd Danger Dowler. Oh-oh, look!" cried Floyd, pointing at the restaurant. "The bus driver is paying the cashier."

"Okay, everybody! Back on the bus," ordered Dairy Dan. "Sharky's coming out."

The Limburger Heads headed back to the motorcoach. Hobbling on his bad foot, Dairy Dan was bringing up the rear.

Suddenly, he heard some juicy breathing and felt a tap on his shoulder. It was Sharky.

"I saw you gabbing with your buddies," slurred Sharky, flashing his toothless grin. "Whazup? You guys planning on blowin' up the place?"

Sharky slapped Dairy Dan on the back and laughed. Dairy Dan tried to laugh, too.

"Blowin' up the place. That's funny!" coughed Dairy Dan. "Yep! That's what we were talking about."

"How come your friends in the back aren't out here stretching their legs?" inquired Sharky, taking a sloppy sip of his coffee. "Come to think of it, I didn't see them up and around once on the way back."

"Yeah, well, those guys are really tired," explained Dairy Dan.

"Heavy sleepers, huh?" said the bus driver, spraying coffee as he enunciated the *S* in *sleepers*.

Dairy Dan wiped his cheek with his sleeve. "Yeah, they're heavy all right. I-I mean, heavy sleepers," he stammered, correcting himself. "It was a long day."

"That's for ssuurre," slurred Sharky, spraying more coffee. "But, it's only a couple more hours back home to Mrs. Sharky and my bed in Green Bay."

Sharky got on the bus and squeezed behind the steering wheel, while Dairy Dan waited outside, allowing the other passengers to board ahead of him.

As the last Packer fan found his seat, Dairy Dan limped up the steps and stood beside Sharky. Pulling the jar of sparkling green-gold goo out of his pocket, he nodded at Einstein at the back of the bus.

"Whatcha got in the jar?" snickered Sharky.

Dairy Dan held up his clothespin, like a flight attendant giving a pre-flight safety demonstration, and he clipped it on his nose. Seeing this, the Limburger Heads all clipped their clothespins on their noses.

"Ho-ho!" laughed Sharky, taking another sip from his coffee cup. "Whatcha doin'? You gonna put on a show?"

"Yeah, that's it! I'm putting on a show!" nodded Dairy Dan with a slow smile.

Sharky, choking and laughing, sprayed coffee all over the bus windshield. "Whoa, ho! Say something else! You sure sound funny with that clothes-thingy on your snout!"

"Watch carefully as I take the lid off this jar. Presto-chango..." hissed Dairy Dan, giving a thumb's up to Einstein.

Timing it perfectly, they unscrewed the covers to the stink bombs at the very same moment.

"And **BOOM!**" shouted Dairy Dan. "Look what happens!"

Immediately, an explosion of the most powerful and foul odor filled the bus, causing everyone, except the Limburger Heads, to pass out instantly.

Dairy Dan waved with both arms over his head and Helmut raced up in the Chalet Cheese Co-op delivery truck, right next to the stink-filled motorcoach.

In the very back, Floyd grabbed George Connor dressed in the light-up stadium sweater and, with a grunt, carried him off the bus and into the delivery truck.

Einstein went to grab George Halas, wearing the sunglasses and Chalet Cheese Co-op cap, but Papa pushed him out of the way.

"You get Bear in Packer hoodie," instructed the old cargo pilot, pointing at George Blanda. "I protect Papa."

With a burst of energy, Papa grabbed Papa and loaded him into the delivery truck, took the clothespin off and sat down beside him.

With machine-like efficiency, the Limburger heads moved the remaining Bears from bus to truck. With the transfer complete, Dairy Dan sent Nick and Rick back on the bus to put the lids on the stink bombs and drop them in the trash can outside the restaurant.

Dairy Dan limped onto the truck, quickly followed by Nick and Rick. "All set, DD!" crowed Rick Monroe, giving his leader a salute.

"Did you crack open a few windows to let some fresh air in?" asked Helmut. Nick and Rick nodded happily.

"All right, Helmut, let's get out of here before those Cheeseheads on the bus wake up," ordered Dairy Dan, smiling from ear-to-ear.

With that, Helmut strapped on his seat belt, started the engine and pulled out onto Wisconsin State Highway 50, headed west to Monroe.

A few minutes later, back on the gleaming green and gold motor-coach, the fresh air floating was starting to cause a stir.

Sharky, who had been slumped over the steering wheel, suddenly popped back up and yawned as if nothing had happened. Without even noticing the Limburger Heads and the Bears were no longer on board, he started the engine and drove out of the parking lot.

Then, grabbing his coffee from the cup holder, he gave it a couple of sniffs and mumbled to himself. "This coffee smells funny."

With a shrug of his shoulders, he took a sip, put his blinker on and turned onto Interstate 43 headed north to Green Bay.

7:37 am CDT | Monroe, Wisconsin

The Limburger Heads passed the Monroe City Limits sign on 18th Street just as the sun was about to rise in the eastern sky. Helmut gave a big yawn, flipped on his blinker and made a right-hand turn into the driveway of Demetri Papadopoulos.

"Back 'er up close to the door," said Dairy Dan, pointing at Papa's old, run-down airplane hangar.

Following instructions, Helmut threw his delivery truck in reverse and parked it a few feet from the large metal doors.

Shutting off the engine, groans came rolling from the cargo area as the Limburger Heads blinked their eyes and woke up to find themselves at Papa's hangar with a ghostly fog lifting across the street in Greenwood Cemetery. Disturbing the early morning quiet was a dog howling sadly by one of the gravestones.

Out of the truck, Papa, shivering from the chill, undid the padlock and slid open the hangar doors. Flipping on the light switch, a bright flash reflected off the silver Douglas C-47 Sky Train, causing Papa to cover his eyes.

Blinking, Papa kissed his fingertips and touched the nose of his old plane. "Good morning, Aphrodite," he cooed, his voice full of affection.

Behind Papa, Dairy Dan limped into the hangar followed by the Limburger Heads, carrying the Bears in their Green Bay disguises.

"Take all that stuff off 'em! Then haul them over there and throw a sack on their heads," ordered Dairy Dan, pointing to a dark corner of the metal barn.

"And make it snappy! The quicker you get this done, the quicker you'll be in your beds getting shut-eye."

Moving as fast as their tired bodies could go, the exhausted group pulled the Packer shirts, hoodies, sweaters and caps off all the Bears. Then, for a few seconds, they all just stood there in stunned silence, staring at the six Hall of Fame busts lined up on the cement floor of the airplane hangar.

"They sort of look out of place here," said Nick Monroe, his hands stuffed deep in his pockets.

"That's right," agreed Dairy Dan, forcing a smile and trying to lighten the mood. "They are out of place! Stick 'em over in that corner and throw a sack over 'em!"

Again, the worn-out Limburger Heads groaned and shuffled into action. Einstein bent over and picked up George McAfee. Rick spit on his hands and hoisted George Musso. Nick, wanting to speed things up, put George Trafton under one arm and George Connor under the other and lugged them both into the dark and dusty corner.

"Okay, Mr. Blanda. Your turn," muttered Floyd as he lugged the

Hall of Fame placekicker and quarterback over to join the others.

"I'll drag this last one over," said Helmut, reaching down to grab Papa Bear George Halas.

"No, no, no," objected Papa. "I do my job."

"But Papa, you're tired and he's heavy," explained Helmut.

"Cow told Papa to protect Papa. Not you to protect."

"Cow?" repeated Helmut, his face scrunched.

Dairy Dan shrugged his shoulders and waved Helmut away. "If it makes him happy, let him do it."

"Okay..." sighed Helmut as he watched Papa walk over to his workbench and return pushing his shop stool on wheels.

With a grunt, Papa lifted Papa Bear and gently placed him on the stool. Then, strapping the bust down with bungee cords, the old cargo pilot wheeled the Founder of the NFL over in the corner to join his Bear buddies.

Reaching down to pick up a burlap sack, Papa heaved a huge sigh and threw it over the bald, bronzed head of George Halas.

"Excellent job, everyone," congratulated Einstein, clapping his hands. "Thanks to impeccable planning and execution, Phase Two of Operation Georgie Porgie has come to a successful conclusion."

"Yeah, good job!" added Dairy Dan. "Go home and get some rest. We'll let the dust settle and meet at Baumgartner's on Thursday at 6."

"That's in exactly 81-hours, 29-minutes-and...ah, 37-seconds," announced Einstein, looking at his watch. "Is that an affirmative?"

Bleary-eyed and yawning, the Limburger Heads nodded, patted each other on the back and trudged outside to their cars parked in Papa's driveway.

Papa, leaning on his walker, waved good-bye to his friends and walked to the front door of his house. Just as he was about to turn the doorknob, he stopped.

Looking back at his airplane hangar, he stood there scratching his stubbled chin.

He returned to the hangar and disappeared inside. A couple of minutes later, Papa came back out, wheeling his shop stool with the big bulge on top, covered with a burlap sack and bungee cords.

Pushing the stool through his front door, he stopped by the living room sofa, unhooked the bungees and removed the sack to reveal the smiling face of Papa Bear George Halas.

With a wave of his arm, Demetri Papadopoulos smiled back. "Welcome to my home!"

....

Hawk rolled out of bed and rubbed the sleep out of his eyes. Looking around, he saw his brothers' beds were both empty. Turning his head in the other way, he saw Nestor staring at the computer.

"Where's Michael?" yawned Hawk.

Hawk waited for a couple of seconds for an answer and when he didn't get one, he asked another question.

"How long you been up?"

Once more, Hawk waited for an answer that never came. Determined to get a response, he tried once more with volume.

"WANNA GO DOWN AND GET SOME BREAKFAST?"

And again...no answer. Finally, Hawk walked over to the desk and whispered in his brother's ear. "Nestor."

Immediately, Nestor bolted up out of his chair, did a backward somersault and crashed to the floor.

"What's the matter with you, sneaking up on me like that?" Nestor shouted, rubbing his elbow.

"I didn't sneak up on you! I've been yelling at you for a hundred years!" howled Hawk. "But you've just been staring at that computer."

"Well, yeah! Look at this!" cried Nestor, pointing to a headline on *espn.com*.

NFL FOOTBALL HALL OF FAME CLOSED
UNTIL FURTHER NOTICE

"Wow! I'm glad that didn't happen yesterday," said Hawk. "Why is it closed?"

"It says they're spraying for bugs," said Nestor. "It says it'll be a couple of weeks before it opens up again."

"Wonder if it has anything to do with those guys and their stink bombs..." mumbled Hawk, scratching his head.

"Probably never know..." said Nestor, still scanning ESPN's top headlines. He clicked on a story about the Hall of Fame game.

"See if they say anything about our game," directed Hawk.

Nestor scrolled down the article. "Hey, it does!" laughed Nestor. "Here at the bottom!"

While the outcome of the Packer-Bronco game was never in doubt, the 23,000 fans were treated to an entertaining halftime exhibition by two local youth football teams.

A smaller, but tough Port Clinton squad, spearheaded by an outstanding performance from running back Michael Hapburn, scored three second half touchdowns to overcome a 19-point deficit and defeat Olmsted Falls 23-22.

"ESPN wrote about our team! We're famous!" crowed Hawk. "Where's Michael? He needs to see this!"

"Mom took him to see Dr. Bartlett 'cuz of his cold. Then they're going to McDonald's," said Nestor.

"How come he gets to go to McDonald's?" moaned Hawk.

"He didn't want to go the doctor so Mom bribed him with an Egg McMuffin," said Nestor.

Just then, they heard the back door open and a cheerful voice called from downstairs. "Hey, guys! We're home! Egg McMuffins!"

Nestor and Hawk knocked each other over as they bolted from the bedroom and down the stairs. Flying into the kitchen, they zoomed past Michael, who had his head in the refrigerator, and bumped into Audrey as she was setting out napkins on the table.

"Sandwiches are in the bag, juice is in the fridge!" sang Audrey, giving each of her boys a peck on the forehead.

"Mom! ESPN wrote about our team!" crowed Nestor as he wedged in between Michael and the fridge in search of the orange juice.

"I know! Isn't that exciting!" laughed Audrey. "Dr. Bartlett already had the article printed out and on his bulletin board. He underlined Michael's name!"

Hawk, in the middle of unwrapping his breakfast sandwich, shouted, "Way to go, Michael! Hey! My Egg McMuffin has a bite out of it!"

Nestor immediately tore the wrapper off his and then held it up for all to see. "Mine does, too!"

"Yeah, but let me explain," said Michael. "First, I took a bite out of one. Then, I figured I'd better take a bite out of the other. To be fair."

"But you already ate two!" said Audrey.

"Yeah, but I was two bites short of being full," shrugged Michael.

"I can't eat this now. It's all germy," complained Hawk.

"It's not all germy. Dr. Bartlett said Michael isn't contagious and he hasn't sneezed once today."

"If you don't want it, give it to me," said Michael.

Hawk was about to reject Michael's offer when the doorbell rang.

"Gotta go…Billy DelSesto's here for his 10 o'clock lesson," sang Audrey as she breezed out of the kitchen. "Have fun today. Maybe go dig for that buried treasure at Portage Park!"

Hawk studied his Egg McMuffin as his Mom's footsteps echoed down the hall. Finally, he flipped the sandwich around and took a bite as far away as possible from Michael's mouth print.

"You guys want to go dig in the park?" asked Nestor, sitting down next to Hawk at the table.

"No. Not in the park…not in the dark…not on a cart. All I want to do is eat and sleep," Michael chimed. He grabbed a banana and headed out of the kitchen. "Wake me up in time for lunch."

Michael disappeared, leaving Nestor and Hawk in the kitchen.

"I don't want to dig either. It's a waste of time. There's no treasure there," snickered Hawk, wiping crumbs off his mouth with his sleeve. "Besides, I've got more important things on my mind."

"Like what? Killer?" teased Nestor.

"Like stink bombs," replied Hawk.

"C'mon. Can't you just forget about stink bombs?" urged Nestor.

"No, I can't! It's strange what happened yesterday. You, Killer, all those other people passed out on the floor at the Hall of Fame. And now it's closed to spray for bugs!" said Hawk with a huff. "I think I'll go see Killer and see what she thinks."

"I told ya!" laughed Nestor. "You're looking for an excuse to see her!"

"Am not!" argued Hawk.

"Are, too!" teased Nestor.

The back and forth bickering continued for three or four more *am nots* and *are, toos* when the brothers heard a knock on the back door.

Nestor gulped down the last bit of orange juice in his glass and stood up to look out the window.

"Hey! It's Killer!" announced Nestor as he wiped his mouth.

Hawk popped up from the kitchen table, stumbled over a chair and scrambled to the window. There, on the back porch stood the adorably tough, little Kathy Kopecky, her short, dark hair peeking out beneath a Cleveland Indian baseball cap. She held a shovel.

"What's *she* doing here?" gasped Hawk nervously.

"Why don't you answer the door and find out?" chuckled Nestor.

Hearing another knock, Hawk brushed off his shirt and ran his tongue along his teeth to make sure there weren't any chunks of Egg McMuffin stuck in his smile. Satisfied, he opened the back door.

"I heard the piano and I figured your mom was giving lessons, so I came around back," said Killer softly. "Hey, you got a little egg or something right there," she added, pointing at the edge of Hawk's mouth.

As Hawk reached up to knock away the egg, he burped. "Oops... excuse me. I guess I ate breakfast too fast," apologized Hawk quietly.

"Don't worry about it. My little brother burps all the time," said Killer. "Since we don't have practice, I thought we could dig for the buried treasure in Portage Park."

"Sure! Great!" chirped Hawk with a silly smile.

"A minute ago you told me it was a waste of time," argued Nestor.

"Did not!" growled Hawk, giving his brother a shove.

"Did, too!" responded Nestor, pushing back.

Before the shoving match rocketed into an all-out war on the back porch, Killer stepped in between the brothers and changed the subject.

"Did you guys see they closed the Hall of Fame to spray for bugs?"

"I think it's got something to do with those stink bombs and those Limburger Cheeseheads," exclaimed Hawk, giving his brother a last little hip check.

"Me, too," agreed Killer, leaning on her shovel. "I mean, they were nice and all that, but they seemed like they were up to no good."

"That's what I was saying to Nestor," added Hawk. "And those police cars! That doesn't sound like a bug problem."

"I've got a creepy feeling something else is going to happen," sighed Killer. "Something crazy."

"I don't like thinking about it," said Nestor as he walked out the back door and down the steps.

"Hey! Where you going?" shouted Hawk.

"To the shed to get a shovel," yelled Nestor over his shoulder.

"Get me one too," ordered Hawk.

"Say, please," insisted Killer.

"Please, Nestor," hollered Hawk with a grin.

A few minutes later, with shovels on their shoulders, Hawk, Nestor and Killer paraded down Lookout Drive, past the garden gnomes in Mrs. McChesney's yard, and straight to Portage Park, thinking more about the Limburger Heads than buried treasure.

3:10 pm CDT | Monroe, Wisconsin

Still wearing his *Education is Important, but Green Bay Football is Importanter* t-shirt from the day before, Floyd Dowler turned off 18th Street into Demetri Papadopoulos' driveway, hopped out of his Chevy and skipped up the sidewalk to Papa's front door.

Inside the house, the sound of the television was blaring through the wooden screen door.

After knocking a couple of times without an answer, Floyd walked in the house to find Papa sitting on the sofa next to Papa Bear George Halas watching ESPN Sports Center.

"Hey, Papa! How's it going?" yelled Floyd, shouting so he could be heard above the TV. "HEY! PAPA!"

"Too loud! Too loud!" scolded Papa, as he put his index finger to his lips. "Papa Bear and me, we watch TV. Big news about Green Bay-Chicago game coming soon! Sit down. Listen."

"Stinkin' Bishop, Papa! Whaddya doing being friendly with the enemy?" howled Floyd, motioning to Papa Bear on the couch.

"Enemy? Oh, no! Papa Bear is okay guy. Sit down by him. You see," declared Papa, pointing to the empty sofa cushion next to the NFL legend.

"Okay, but I can't stay long," said Floyd, sitting down on the couch beside George Halas. "I got orders from Dairy Dan to stop by and check on things and make sure you'll be at the meeting on Thursday,"

"Things all good. Papa Bear and me having fine time. See how happy he is?" smiled Papa, throwing his arm around his new bronzed buddy.

"Yeah, he looks happy now," admitted Floyd. "But just you wait until the Packers beat up those Bears to start the season!"

"Oh no, good sportsman Papa George. Victory...losing...same score. He always still smile," insisted Papa.

Floyd leaned forward stared into the face of the Hall of Fame statue for a few seconds and then settled back into the sofa and yawned.

"Yeah, I see what you mean. He's a nice enough guy."

"Yeah, nice guy," agreed Papa with a yawn of his own.

Tired from their wild adventure at the Hall of Fame the day before, Papa and Floyd both yawned a couple more times and settled into the comfy sofa. With heavy eyelids, they both drifted off to sleep with their heads leaning against Papa Bear, who remained in the middle, still with a big smile on his face and eyes wide open watching ESPN.

4:33 pm EDT | Port Clinton, Ohio

"There sure is a lot of dirt in the world," moaned Hawk as he walked toward home with Nestor and Killer, dragging his shovel behind him.

"Yeah," agreed Killer, "And a lot of it is on you."

"Everywhere you dig, there's dirt! No treasure. Just dirt and dirt," continued Hawk.

"What about that old bottle you found?" laughed Nestor. "That might be worth a dime."

Tired and caked in mud, the three Port Clinton Braves trudged down the sidewalk in silence until they stopped for a second in front of Mrs. McChesney's yard to let Nestor tie his tennis shoe.

Spotting the chess garden gnomes, Killer perked up.

"Hey! You guys want to play a game of chess?"

"I'm wiped out. Maybe tomorrow," muttered Hawk. "Besides Nestor always wins."

"Okay, tomorrow. I like chess," admitted Killer. Then, she noticed the king with the bandage on his nose and she blurted out, "Hey what happened to that one?"

"Hawk tackled him," explained Nestor.

"You know, they kind of remind me of those statues we saw at the Hall of Fame yesterday," said Killer. "Same size."

"Yeah, kind of," nodded Nestor.

The three of them stood there staring at the gnomes a little while longer. Then, picking up their shovels, they continued their slow march home for dinner.

CHAPTER 9

August 28 - 2:33 pm EDT | Port Clinton, Ohio
5 Days to Kickoff at Lambeau Field

"Checkmate," announced Killer as she moved the queen gnome two squares forward to trap Nestor's king.

Nestor stood there in silence for a few seconds. When he saw he had no escape, he nodded his head and smiled.

"Good game," congratulated Nestor, giving his adversary a fist bump.

Instead of digging for buried treasure in the park, Nestor, Michael, Hawk and Killer had spent the past couple of days playing chess in Mrs. McChesney's front yard.

Only taking breaks for lunch and dinner, the four Port Clinton Braves had played nearly 100 games, with Nestor winning 47, Killer winning 47 and Michael and Hawk, playing as a team, winning one. The one game was won by forfeit when they claimed Nestor showed up a minute late.

"C'mon, let's go. Time for practice," cried Hawk, grabbing his football helmet off the sidewalk.

"One more game," begged Killer as she moved the gnomes back into position. "I'll play you and Michael with my eyes closed."

"I'm tired of chess," complained Michael. "I want to go to practice."

"That's something I never tought I'd hear you say," laughed Nestor.

"Hey, Killer, I've been thinking," smiled Michael as he picked up Kathy Kopecky's pink duffle bag and tossed it to her. "There's one play that needs some work."

"Yeah, which one?" asked Killer, sipping from her water bottle.

"Twinkie-Off-Tackle. You should call it three or four times to make sure we're running it right," suggested the always-hungry Hapburn.

Killer, Nestor and Hawk all laughed and started walking down Grant Street toward True Lay Stadium carrying their football gear.

"No, I'm serious," crabbed Michael, calling out to his teammates. "That play is our bread and butter. We should practice it! A lot!"

Michael stood there on the sidewalk for a minute, thinking about bread and butter. When he finally started in the direction of football practice, Killer and his brothers were a good fifty feet ahead.

At the very moment he began to walk, three black sedans and a windowless black cargo van parked in a single line further down the street started their engines. Killer, Nestor and Hawk didn't notice they were being followed. Neither did Michael.

....

When Nestor, Michael, Hawk and Killer stepped on the field at True Lay stadium for practice, the rest of the team greeted them like conquering heroes with cheers and high-fives.

"Did you see the ESPN story about our game?" roared Ray Ray McKay.

"We're going to the Super Bowl," yelled Frankie Fitzwater.

"I like jellybeans," shouted Stinky Smothers' brother.

Out on the football field, Coach Yak gave a long, shrill blast of his whistle interrupting the celebration.

"TWEEEEEEET!"

"Let's go," shouted Yak, waving his huge hand to where he was standing with the assistant coaches. "We've got work to do today!"

All twenty-five players picked up their helmets and duffle bags and trotted out to midfield to join Coach Yak as he began taking attendance.

Coach Yakunshenko began calling names in alphabetical order and no one noticed the three sedans and the windowless cargo van as the bone-chilling black convoy slowly crept into the stadium parking lot.

Suddenly, a SWAT (Special Weapons And Tactics) Team dressed in navy blue windbreakers and wearing bulletproof helmets with reflective visors (so you couldn't see their faces) rushed the field and surrounded the startled and surprised youth football team.

"Whoa, whoa, **WHOA!** Who invited you guys?" yelled Coach Yak, stretching out his massive arms to shield his players from danger.

Before anyone could answer Yak's question, a loud roar filled the air. Everyone looked up to see a black helicopter hovering above the end zone near the parking lot. As the chopper touched the ground, the whirring blades stirred up a mini-tornado of trash, leaves and dust.

Out of the thick cloud of debris appeared a tall, menacing blue jacketed man. He quickly approached the terrified Port Clinton team and flipped up his reflective face guard.

"I'm Senior Special Agent Roman Noodle, Federal Bureau of Investigation Football Division," announced the serious, square-jawed man flashing open his wallet to reveal a shiny, metal badge. "You are **all** under arrest!"

"Under arrest? What for? Practicing football?" protested the super-sized head coach.

Standing stunned and completely still with his teammates, Nestor swallowed hard and mumbled, "Did you guys know the FBI had a *football* division?"

"Agent Sanders, read the charges," barked Special Agent Noodle.

Immediately, a man in a navy blue windbreaker marched up beside Noodle with a thick, blue folder in his hand. Pulling out a sheet of paper, he began to read.

"In violation of the Department of Justice Model Penal Code 2295753, grand theft of historical artifacts, Michael Hapburn and the Port Clinton Braves' Youth Football Team are sought in connection with the disappearance of six National Football League Hall of Fame busts."

"What?! That's ridiculous! No one on this team would do a thing like that," shouted Yak.

"You **all** have the right to remain silent," continued Agent Sanders, still reading from his crime sheet. "If you DO say anything, what you say can be used against you in a court of law."

When Sanders was done, he shoved the paper back into his thick, blue folder and took a brisk step back behind his supervisor.

"Court of law?" howled Yak, his face turning red. "You listen here, Special Agent Spaghetti, Macaroni or whatever your name is...."

"My name is Senior Special Agent Roman Noodle, Federal Bureau of Investigation Football Division...badge number 318-1018-424. And NO, big man! YOU will listen to *ME!*" Noodle shouted back. "A serious crime has been committed and we have photographic evidence that this...this Michael Hapburn is involved. Which means YOU and your entire team are all suspects. Someone's gotta go to prison!"

Hearing the word prison, the players and coaches gasped in disbelief.

"Hope you like jail food, Michael," whispered Hawk, staring down at the ground.

"First! Which one of you is this Michael Hapburn?" snarled Noodle, as he surveyed the frightened faces of Port Clinton Braves.

After five torturous seconds without a sound from the team, Michael took a deep breath and was about to step forward when a shout broke the terrifying silence.

"I am Michael Hapburn!" yelled Killer, her hand straight up.

A second later, Nestor raised his hand and shouted, "I am Michael Hapburn!"

After that, Hawk, Frankie Flat-nosed Fitzwater, Ray Ray McKay, Moses Kupperman and Stinky Smothers stepped forward and shouted: "I am Michael Hapburn!"

Suddenly, the whole team including the coaches, had their hands raised and were proclaiming..."**I am Michael Hapburn!**"

Everyone except Stinky Smothers' brother who was yelling, "I am Stinky Smothers' brother!"

Frustrated, Special Agent Noodle began waving his arms downward to quiet the symphony of shouts.

"Look! We need some cooperation here," announced Noodle once the yelling stopped. Then, he quickly turned to Agent Sanders and stuck out his hand, "Sanders...the photograph."

Once again, Sanders stepped up beside his boss, opened his blue

FBI/FD folder, pulled out a glossy 8"x10" photo and gave it to Noodle.

Holding it up for everyone could see, Noodle continued.

"Here we have the suspect, whom we have identified as one Michael Hapburn, running back for the Port Clinton Youth football team, who has been caught on video with two large burlap sacks, each containing a Chicago Bear Hall of Fame bust."

Coach Yak took a step forward and squinted at the picture.

"You can't tell who that is! The photo's all fuzzy. You can't even see the person's face with that Cheesehead hat on!"

"If you will notice, this Cheesehead hat has a bite out of the corner. Bite marks which - and we have confirmed this, sir - match the dental records of our suspect, Michael Hapburn," explained Noodle.

"I don't believe it!" roared Yak.

"Believe it, Coach," confessed Michael, stepping out of the crowd of teammates. "That's me in that picture."

Again, players and coaches let out a gasp, this time louder.

"But honest, I didn't know what was in those bags," said Michael, pleading his case. "I was just helping some guys we met. And...you know, those cabbage rolls."

"What guys?" barked Noodle, pulling out a pair of handcuffs.

Seeing the handcuffs, skinny Coach Jekyll bolted forward and stood in front of his star running back. "Wait a minute! Are those really necessary?"

"Priceless, historical artifacts have been stolen. Someone's gotta go to prison!" repeated Noodle.

"Maybe we can help you get the statues back," offered Nestor, nervously.

"Yeah! Maybe we could help!" chimed in Hawk.

"Help? How? Do you have the stolen Hall of Fame busts?" snapped Noodle.

Hawk shook his head. "No, but we kinda might know the guys who took 'em."

"Again with the guys! What *guys* are you talking about?" grumbled the FBI/FD Special Agent.

"You know...ah, kinda, well...*strange guys.* They're Packer fans from Wisconsin," stammered Hawk.

"They're Limburger Heads," added Nestor. "They had stink bombs."

"Limburger heads? Stink bombs? I've heard enough of this nonsense! Slap on the handcuffs! We'll take that one, that one and that one in for questioning," ordered Noodle, pointing at Nestor, Michael and Hawk.

"Wait a minute!" shouted Killer, charging forward to join her friends. "What Nestor and Hawk said is true! There *were* a bunch of guys. They did call themselves *Limburger Heads* and they had jars filled with green-yellow goop. I don't know, stink bombs, I guess. And when they took the lids off the jars everybody in the Hall of Fame... including me...*fainted.*"

"So what happened then?" questioned Noodle.

"He carried me outside the building," explained Killer, pointing at Hawk. "And when I got outside, I woke up."

"Then he came back in and got me out," added Nestor.

"And that's when two of the guys asked me to help carry out the bags," blurted Michael. "They were old and couldn't walk very good and the bags were heavy."

"How come the stink bomb didn't knock you out?" asked Noodle, staring at Hawk.

"I had a bandage on my nose, sir," answered Hawk politely. "I couldn't smell anything."

"What about you?" grumbled Noodle, nodding at Michael.

"I had a cold," explained Michael.

"And these old guys...Limburger Heads, you call 'em...how come the stink bombs didn't make them fall on the floor?" inquired the now-curious FBI/FD agent.

"**They had clothespins on their noses!**" answered Michael and Hawk at the same time.

Agent Noodle stood there silently for a moment, scratching his chin. Then, turning around, he called over Sanders and three other blue-jacketed agents and they talked quietly in a tight circle.

"Stink bombs. Clothespins. Noses! That's funny!" laughed Stinky

Smothers' brother, slapping Michael on the back.

Finally, after a few minutes of top-secret talk and heads bobbing up and down, the group of blue-jacketed FBI/FD agents broke the huddle and Roman Noodle stepped forward with another sheet of paper in his hand.

"We've checked the Federal Bureau of Investigation Football Division Rules and Regulations," stated Noodle, glancing down to read from the paper. "And a rarely-employed statue statute #418-828-317-119 does allow for a person or persons wanted for aiding and abetting in the burglary of statues to assist government officials in the recovery of said missing or stolen property in order to receive special consideration of reduced sentences for cooperation."

Hearing this, Nestor raised his hand. "Does that mean if we help, we don't have to go to prison?"

"How many times do I have to tell ya, kid?...SOMEBODY'S GOTTA GO TO PRISON!" barked Noodle.

Hearing this, Agent Sanders stepped forward and whispered in Noodle's ear, then stepped back behind his boss.

"Ahem...but..." added Noodle, clearing his throat. "As Agent Sanders here has pointed out to me, in special consideration of your cooperation in the apprehension of the true perpetrators of this crime, you and the rest of your team...ah...*could* possibly avoid going to jail."

"TWEEEEEEEEEEEEET!"

Coach Yak, after letting loose a sharp blast on his whistle, stepped forward and got nose-to-nose with Noodle. "So! If we help you catch these-these..."

"Limburger Heads," interjected Nestor.

"...these Limburger Heads," continued Yak. "We get back the Hall of Fame Bears statues and make everything okay. If we do that, you guys will go away, leave us alone and let us play football. No prison for these kids, right?"

"Well, I didn't exactly say that," answered Noodle.

"Sure you did! Give us a week and we'll find the guys and get back those Bears. Deal?" offered Coach Yak, sticking out his meaty hand.

Senior Special Agent Roman Noodle took a deep breath and looked back at his blue-jacketed SWAT team.

Agent Sanders shrugged and nodded. "Sure, why not?"

Turning back to Coach Yak, Noodle reached out and shook the coach's sizable paw.

"Okay...deal! But all you've got is ONE WEEK!" barked Noodle.

Reaching into the pocket, Noodle pulled out a business card and handed it to Coach Yak.

"Text if you need to contact us," instructed Noodle. "And don't think you can fly to China and escape the long arm of the law because we will be watching you!"

The FBI/FD boss made a V with two fingers, put them up to his eyes and then pointed them at Coach Yak and at the rest of the Braves to illustrate his point. Then, looking down the field in the direction of the goalposts, he raised his right arm over his head and moved his hand in a circular motion.

Instantly, the helicopter engine roared back to life, chopper blades spinning. The army of blue-jacketed agents dashed toward the parking lot and disappeared into the swirling cloud of dust and debris. Poof! The helicopter, the black cars, the black van, Noodle and all the agents were all gone.

Coach Yak, having a hard time believing what he just saw, rubbed his eyes.

"Somebody pinch me. I gotta be dreaming. And hey! Did you even know the FBI had a football division?"

"My mom says you learn something new every day," chirped Hawk.

"I never knew my brother's name was Richard," chimed in Stinky Smothers' brother.

Frankie Fitzwater's head snapped around to Stinky Smothers standing next to him and blurted out, "Your name is Richard?"

"Well, uh...okay. Turns out we have some detective work to do," snorted Yak. "Anybody know where to find these Limburger Heads?"

"They were from Wisconsin," said Michael.

"Did they tell you their names?" asked Yak.

"The oldest guy, Papa was his name. He gave me his cell number so we could text him the scores of our games," said Nestor. "He was nice."

"All of them were nice!" added Hawk.

"They were! They shared their cabbage rolls with me," said Michael.

"Our parents sat with them," chimed in Killer.

Coach Yak heaved a heavy sigh and then turned to consult with his assistants, Jekyll and Hyde. After a couple of minutes, Yak flipped his Ohio State ball cap around backward and waved his arms, instructing his team to huddle up.

Kneeling down so he was at eye level with his players, the huge coach laid out the game plan.

"We've got a good team here. *I* think we have a chance to win a championship."

Hearing that, Stinky Smothers' brother's hand shot up. "There is no *I* in *team*."

"That's right," agreed Coach Yak with a nod. "But…we can't win a championship if we're all in prison."

"We could maybe win the prison league championship," cheered Stinky Smothers' brother, interrupting a second time.

Quickly, Coach Yak reached into the equipment bag, pulled out a roll of athletic tape and tossed it to Stinky Smothers.

"If he opens his yap again, use this to tape it shut," instructed Yak.

Smiling, Stinky Smothers nodded.

"Like I was saying, if we go to jail, we can't play for a championship. So, in order to save our season, we're going Bear hunting in Wisconsin."

Immediately, the 25 braves let out a loud cheer.

"Sorry. Most of you will have to stay here with Coach Jekyll and Coach Hyde and keep practicing. We've got our first regular-season game coming up a week from this Saturday," said Coach Yak.

Hearing this, the happy cheer quickly became a disappointed groan.

"Besides me, I've got room in my Suburban for you, you, you, you, you and you," explained Yak, pointing at Michael, Nestor, Hawk, Killer, Frankie Fitzwater and Stinky Smothers.

"And don't worry...I'll explain the situation to your parents. If these Limburgers are as nice as you say, we won't have any trouble. I'm guessing they just wanted to borrow the statues for a few days."

"Yeah, like for a science project or something and make bubbles come out of their ears," explained Stinky Smothers' brother.

Holding up the tape, Stinky Smothers looked at Yak. "Should I do it, Coach?" he asked.

"No, I'm done talking," said Yak. "If we're gonna win a championship, we need to practice."

Hearing this, Michael's hand shot up in the air, "Twinkie-Off-Tackle. I think we need to call it three or four times to make sure we're running it right."

"Good idea," agreed Coach Yak. "Twinkie-Off-Tackle it is. Let's go! And with that, twenty-five Braves charged onto the field.

5:45 pm CDT | Monroe, Wisconsin

Speeding past Greenwood Cemetery on 18th Street, Floyd Dowler barely slowed down to make his right turn into Demetri Papadopoulos' driveway. Screeching to a stop, he jumped out of his Chevy Cavalier humming the *Flying Car Polka* and ran to Papa's front door.

He was just about ready to knock on the wooden screen door when he heard banging coming from Papa's run-down airplane hangar outback.

Following the noise around to the big hangar door, he found Papa bent down with a hammer, pounding on the landing gear of his Douglas C-47 Sky Train, surrounded by Papa Bear George Halas and the other five Bears busts.

"**Papa!**" shouted Floyd, tapping the pilot's shoulder.

Looking down and startled to see a foot on the floor beside him, Papa instantly brought his hammer down hard on Floyd's toe.

"Hey! Watch it, Papa," laughed Floyd, dusting off the dirt of his boot. "You could hurt someone that way!"

"Oh! Oh! Sorry, Packer friend Floyd," apologized Papa. "I think enemy attack. I break foot?"

"Nope! Didn't hurt a bit! Steel-toe boots. Safety first, I always say," answered Floyd. "C'mon! We gotta go or we'll be late for the meeting."

"No-no...you go, I stay," said Papa, shaking his head. "After I fix Aphrodite, we all go in house, have snack and play card game."

"Play cards? With them?" laughed Floyd, pointing at the six bronzed Bear busts. "They can't play cards."

"Oh, sure-sure! I help. They play good!" insisted Papa.

"But, Papa!" whined Floyd. "Dairy Dan's gonna want you to report on how everything's going."

"Tell Squadron Leader Dan all good here. Bears happy. Everybody smiling."

"Okay, but I don't think Squadron Leader Dan's gonna be happy," sighed Floyd.

"Believe my words...all will be a-okay, okay?" said Papa, adding "Go Pack Go!" as he gave Floyd a nudge toward the airplane hangar's sliding metal door.

"Go Pack Go," repeated Floyd sadly, walking out into the evening air. Checking his Packer watch, he discovered he had one-minute to make the two-minute drive to Baumgartner's.

Floyd ran to his car. He didn't want to show up at the meeting without Papa *and* be late.

....

Upstairs, Nestor, Michael and Hawk had been sitting on the edges of their beds for almost an hour. Downstairs, Coach Yak was asking for Audrey Hapburn's permission to drive to Wisconsin with her boys to rescue the missing Hall of Fame Bears.

Unable to sit still any longer, Hawk jumped up and started pacing back and forth.

"I wonder what's taking so long. Do you think Mom will let us go?"

"Sure, she'll let us go," replied Nestor. "She won't let Michael be a jailbird!"

"I wonder if prison food is good," muttered Michael.

"It doesn't look good in the movies," said Hawk, shaking his head.

"I can't believe you helped those Limburger Heads steal those Bears," exclaimed Nestor. "What were you thinking?"

"Cabbage rolls," answered Michael immediately. "Besides, I didn't know what was in those bags."

Suddenly, they heard the sound of the front door closing. Nestor and Hawk scooted over to the window to see Coach Yak with his head down, lumbering toward his Suburban.

Then came a gentle knock and Audrey appeared in the doorway. "Well, pack your bags. You're going to Wisconsin," said Audrey softly.

"You're not mad at me?" asked Michael.

"No. How could I be upset with you? You were just trying to help those...ah...strange men," admitted Audrey, struggling to find the right words.

"You're not worried?" questioned Hawk.

"Of course, I'm worried," admitted Audrey, blinking back the tears. "But Coach Yakunshenko explained it all to me and I believe him when he says it will all be fine and that none of you will have to go to-to-to..."

"Prison?" interjected Nestor, filling in the blank.

"Yes, P-P-P-PRISON!" she blurted out, sobbing.

Feeling terrible, Michael, Nestor and Hawk gave their mother a hug together.

"Don't cry, Mom. We'll get those Bears back. It'll be okay," said Nestor.

"Yeah, Mom. It'll be okay. And we might even get some cabbage rolls, too," added Michael.

"And if we do go to prison, they have visiting hours and stuff, so you can come and see us!" chirped Hawk.

"Thanks...that makes me feel better. And I can bring a cake with a saw in it," joked Audrey, wiping away the tears.

"German Chocolate?" asked Michael in a serious voice because food was never to be joked about.

"Sure," smiled Audrey, giving her son a hug.

"When are we leaving? How long we will be gone?" asked Nestor, reaching under his bunk to grab his duffle.

"Coach is picking you up Monday morning. He said you'd only be gone two or three days. And I want you to text me, so I know what's going on," added Audrey, giving each of her boys a firm look.

"We will, Mom," agreed Nestor. "Promise."

"How come we're not leaving until Monday?" asked Hawk, looking at the calendar on the wall. "That's one...two...*three* days away."

"Your friend, Kathy Kopecky, has a dance recital Sunday night," explained Audrey. "Coach Yakunshenko said she's an important part of the team. A real leader. So he delayed the trip so she could go."

"Yeah, she's kind of smart," nodded Michael. "I just wish she'd call the chili dog play more often."

"Anyway, Monday is soon enough," said Audrey, her voice full of concern. "It gives me time to make sure you have enough clean socks."

Giving her boys each a kiss on the forehead, Audrey walked out of the bedroom and back downstairs.

Taking a deep breath, Hawk kicked off his shoes and flopped down on his bed. Michael sighed and started bouncing his squishy football off the wall. And Nestor, kneeling down on the floor, zipped open his duffle. He still hadn't unpacked since the Canton trip.

Reaching into the bag, he pulled out the program from the Hall of Fame Game. Right on the front, under the Green Bay Packer helmet, was where Demetri Papadopoulos had scribbled his name and number.

"Hey, look," said Nestor, pointing at Papa's handwriting.

"Call him. Tell him we're coming and we need cabbage rolls," begged Michael.

"Now? Tonight?" asked Nestor.

"It's not late," argued Michael.

"I wonder what time it is," sighed Hawk.

"Well, it's 7:15 here," said Nestor, looking at the Cub's clock on their wall. "So that makes it 6:15 in Wisconsin."

"No. I wonder what time Killer's recital is on Sunday," clarified Hawk.

"Recital? We're talking cabbage rolls!" grumbled Michael. "Okay, don't call him. Text him."

Nestor shook his head. "I don't think we should. Coach might not want those guys to know we're coming."

Frustrated, Michael bounced his squishy football off the back of Nestor's head and flopped down on his bunk. "I can't believe you won't text him."

"I can't believe you're not worried about going to prison," replied Nestor.

And Hawk, lying on his back, staring at the ceiling, murmured under his breath so no one could hear, "I can't believe I'm going to Wisconsin. With Killer!"

....

Floyd burst through Baumgartner's basement door and plopped down in the empty chair between Nick and Rick Monroe.

Einstein looked at his watch. "You're one minute, twelve-seconds late."

"And where's Papa?" added Dairy Dan, hobbling to the door to look out at the alley.

"He's not coming," announced Floyd. Then pointing at the walking boot on Dairy Dan's fractured foot, he asked, "Hey! Where did you get the fancy shoe?"

"Doc says I have to wear it for 8 weeks," huffed Dairy Dan, hobbling back to his seat and throwing his bad foot up on a milk crate.

"Stinkin' Bishop! Eight whole weeks?" gushed Floyd.

"Never mind that, Floyd. Where's Papa?" repeated Dairy Dan in a crabby voice.

"He was working on his plane," answered Floyd. "He told me to tell Squadron Leader Dan it's all good. The Bears are happy and smiling."

"Sometimes I worry the old man's getting soft," grumbled Dairy Dan. "Guess it doesn't matter. We can tell him about the plan later."

"Let's get this party started. The sooner we get done, the sooner I can go home and soak my foot in some hot water," snarled Dairy Dan. "Einstein!"

Hearing his name, Einstein Wozniak snapped to attention, gave Dairy Dan a salute and marched to the front of the room. Then, as he did ten days ago when Operation Georgie Porgie began, Einstein reached up and pulled a white sheet off the wall to reveal the chalkboard, now scribbled with these words:

OPERATION GEORGIE PORGIE
THE FINAL PHASE: SMASH AND BURY THE BEARS!

Everybody, except Einstein, Dairy Dan and Henrietta Wozniak, who was already sound asleep and snoring in Polish, let out a gasp.

"Smash the statues?" shouted Cheese Master Helmut Lundquist.

"And ba-ba-ba-bury 'em?" stuttered Rick Monroe.

"WAIT A DARN MINUTE!" exploded Nick Monroe. "The deal was to *steal* the Bears. You never said anything about smashin' 'em!"

Dairy Dan threw up his arms and bellowed back, "What did you think we were going to do with them? Have them over to dinner and watch TV with 'em?"

"That's what Papa's doing," shrugged Floyd.

"I am telling ya, Dan…if that's the plan, I'm out," threatened Nick.

"I'm sorry, DD. I love the Packers as much as anyone, but destroying those Bears and all that history…I don't know," moaned Helmut.

"For the love of Lombardi, what's going on here?" yelled Dairy Dan. "You don't want to do it? After we've gone this far? Are you all getting soft?"

"C'mon Rick, Helmut, let's go," urged Nick, making a move toward the door.

"STOP! Please! You must appreciate *our situation* now," Einstein said firmly.

"That's right! You gotta appreciate our situation" complained Dairy Dan. Kicking the milk crate out from under his foot, he hobbled to the chalkboard and pounded it with his fist.

Then turning toward Einstein, he asked, "What situation is that?"

"I am convinced that if we return the stolen property now, it would still - in all probability - mean incarceration," explained Einstein.

"What?" shouted Floyd. "You mean, even if we gave the Bears back, we'd end up in the state prison?"

"Federal penitentiary," corrected Einstein. "Transporting stolen property across state lines is a federal offense. Our best and only option is to continue as planned to avoid getting caught."

"That's right," growled Dairy Dan. "We need to smash and bury the Bears in Greenwood Cemetery. Even if it means jail...the Packers having the most players in the Hall of Fame is all that matters."

Nick Monroe shook his head. "Smash and bury those statues? I don't think so."

"But Pop, we've come this far...we might as well finish it now," said Rick, shrugging his shoulders.

Helmut sighed, "I guess I vote for that, too."

Einstein, taking advantage of the Limburger Heads' change in attitude, stood and shouted, "All those in favor of smashing and burying the Bears in Greenwood Cemetery, say *aye!*"

"AYE!" hollered Dairy Dan, raising his hand.

Then, Floyd and Rick raised their hand and said, "Aye," followed by the cheese master.

"All those opposed..."

Nick Monroe raised his hand. Henrietta, who was still sleeping, didn't vote.

"The majority declares we continue as planned," announced Einstein.

"Good! Now that we have that nonsense out of the way, what's next?" asked Dairy Dan, looking at his bald-headed buddy.

"Monday, we dig the graves. We will convene at the cemetery at midnight," instructed Einstein.

"Good! It'll be dark. No one will see us," added Dairy Dan.

"Correct," agreed Einstein. "Then, on Tuesday, precisely two hours before game time, we'll converge at the Papadopoulos residence for cabbage rolls. After, we'll transport the Bears across the street, place the statues at the gravesites and bust them up with sledge hammers. At that point, we can deposit the pieces in the graves and cover them thoroughly. Done and done. Any questions?"

Einstein paused for a moment and his bald head swiveled from one side of his audience to the other.

"Excellent! Monday at midnight at Greenwood Cemetery," he concluded. "See you then."

Silently, the Limburger Heads, with mixed feelings, headed out the basement door and up the steps.

Dairy Dan, limping along with them in his walking boot, tried to lighten everyone's mood.

"Hey, it's all going to be okay! After we bust up and bury those stinkin' Bears, we'll just skedaddle back here to Baumgartner's for the game, have a root beer and watch the Packers bury the Bears again!"

"I'm still not convinced," grumbled Nick Monroe.

"STC! Seize the cheese!" roared Dairy Dan happily. "Oh, and Floyd. You need to stop by Papa's and fill him in on the plan."

"Will do, DD," said Floyd with a nod. "But I don't think he's going to like it."

CHAPTER 10

August 31 - 6:44 pm EDT | Port Clinton, Ohio
2 Days to Kickoff at Lambeau Field

"C'mon Mom! We're going to be late to the dance recital," howled Hawk, waiting at the front door.

"A tie? My, don't you look handsome," sang Audrey as she glided down the stairs in a blue chiffon dress.

"It's just a clip-on," confessed Hawk as he tugged uncomfortably at his collar. "Ah...you look nice, too."

"Thank you! I'm tickled you wanted to go to this tonight," admitted Audrey, sneaking a peek at herself in the hallway mirror. "I love you showing an interest in something besides sports."

"C'mon, Mom!" whined Hawk, his hand on the doorknob. "Let's go!"

"Oh! I almost forgot! The flowers!" said Audrey, rushing off into the kitchen.

"Flowers? What do we need flowers for?"

Audrey came back, smiling and carrying a happy bouquet of yellow daisies. She handed them to Hawk, "Okay! All set!"

"What? You want me to give these to Kill...er, I mean, Kathy?" stammered Hawk. "I can't give flowers to our quarterback!!"

"Tonight, she's not your quarterback. She's your girlfriend," Audrey clarified.

"She's not my girlfriend, Mom, She's my friend who happens to be a girl," protested Hawk.

"Fine," laughed Audrey, giving her youngest a nudge out the door. Before walking out, she called up the stairs to her two other sons.

"Nestor! Michael! We're leaving...be back a little after 8! Love you!"

"Love you, Mom!" came Nestor and Michael's shout.

"They're leaving," said Nestor, at the window, watching his brother and mother jump into the blue Malibu.

"I can't believe Hawk's going to a dance recital. The only way I'd go is if they gave out free fried chicken," insisted Michael.

"Michael, look! There're two black cars parked across the street! One just took off following Mom in the Malibu!" announced Nestor, his nose pressed up against the glass.

"It's those FBI football guys! They're watching us!" exclaimed Michael. "Pull the shade!"

"Hey! You're right! The guy riding shotgun looks like that Noodle guy," said Nestor, standing at the window waving hello.

"Why are you waving at them?" howled Michael.

"I'm just being friendly," insisted Nestor.

"Those people want to put me in prison!" protested Michael.

Nestor shook his head. "Nah, they don't really want to put kids in prison. They want those Bears back."

"Nestor! Pull down the shade!" demanded Michael.

"Okay, okay! I'm doing it," grumbled Nestor. Reaching up over his head, Nestor grabbed the shade and pulled it down. Then, peeking his head around the shade, he waved out the window one more time.

....

"Who are you waving at?" asked Special Agent Roman Noodle.

"The kid in the upstairs window. He was waving at us, so I waved back," answered Probationary Agent Elliot Ness. "I think he's the one they call Nestor."

"Rule #1...FBI/FD agents don't get friendly with the individuals under investigation. It muddies the water," stated Noodle. "Remember Ness, you are on probation. Time will tell if you have the stuff to be one of us."

"Yes, sir," nodded Elliot. "And I want to thank you for giving me this opportunity. I'll do my best to prove I'm worthy."

"Don't thank me. I was against the idea," grunted Noodle. "Agent Sanders thought since you were the one who discovered the Bears were missing, you might be a valuable asset on this case."

At that moment, Roman Noodle's FBI/FD-issued shoe phone starting ringing. In a flash, Noodle untied his shoe, took it off and gave the heel a twist to reveal a hidden mouthpiece.

"Noodle here. Report in, Agent Sanders…"

"I have one of the suspects and the mother in view. They're getting out of the blue Malibu and walking toward a large, two-story structure. 604 Sixth Street."

"A building? What kind of building?" asked Noodle, talking into his shoe. "Do you think the Hall of Fame busts are hidden in there?"

"The sign says, *Playmakers Civic Theatre*. There's a large crowd gathering for a performance of some sort. Maybe a dance recital," replied Sanders.

"What! The kid is going to a dance recital and he's wanted by the FBI/FD?" complained Noodle. "This doesn't make sense."

"They just entered the building," announced Sanders. "I'm going in!"

"Be careful! This could be a trick," warned Noodle. "Call if you need back up!"

"10-4! Over and out!" responded Sanders.

Hearing the click on the other end, Agent Noodle slid the heel back in place and put his shoe back on and nervously started cracking his knuckles.

Probationary Agent Elliot Ness looked down at Noodle's shoe and back up at his boss. Then, clearing his throat, he asked, "If I become a real agent, will I get one of those?"

....

Agent Sanders sprinted across 6th Street and scrambled back behind the steering wheel of his shiny, black sedan in a mad dash to report into his boss.

Squealing the tires as he pulled out of the theatre parking lot, he made a left turn onto Taft Street and then another high-speed left onto Look Out Drive. Seconds later, he was slamming on the brakes, stopping just inches from Noodle's black sedan, which was still parked across the street from the Hapburn house.

In a flash, Agent Sanders was out of his car and into the back seat of Noodle's vehicle, talking a mile a minute.

"The suspects are packing up! They're leaving town! Wisconsin! Tomorrow! 8 AM!"

"Whoa! Slow down," barked Noodle. "Take a deep breath and start over. And where are the suspect and the mom? Why aren't you still following them?"

"I left before they did to give you the news," panted Sanders.

"You found the Bears?" asked Special Agent Noodle, his hairs on the back of his neck standing straight up.

"No, but I think *they* have a clue where to find them," explained Sanders. "The Coach is taking some of his players and traveling to Wisconsin tomorrow morning."

Noodle rubbed his square chin thoughtfully, "Tomorrow? How do you know this?"

"There they are," interrupted Elliot Ness, pointing at the blue Malibu as it turned into the Hapburn driveway. The three agents watched Audrey and Hawk get out of the car and disappear into the house.

Noodle noted the time and jotted it down, then repeated his question. "How do you know they're going to Wisconsin tomorrow?"

"I sat a couple rows behind the mother and son. During the intermission, I followed them out to the lobby and I overheard the mother, Ms. Hapburn, conversing with a Mr. Kopecky,"

"Kopecky? Who's that?"

"The night the Bears disappeared...when we found out some of the Braves players were involved...I got a team roster," interjected the eager-to-please Elliot Ness, as he pulled a sheet of paper from his pocket. Quickly scanning the roster, he pointed at a name near the top of the list. "There *is* a Kopecky on the team. Yeah...Kathy Kopecky, #9, quarterback."

"A girl quarterback?" frowned Noodle.

"Good work, Probationary Agent Ness," nodded Sanders, proudly. "I told you he might prove valuable."

"Yeah, yeah, get on with it…so you overheard the mother and this Mr. Kopecky talking. Then what?" grumbled Noodle.

"That's when I found out the Coach, the Hapburn boys, this Kopecky kid and a couple of other players are driving to…," Sanders paused to look down at his notes again, "…to Monroe, Wisconsin to locate someone called Papa. I'm thinking he's one of those Limburger Heads the kids told us about the other day."

"Hmmm," nodded Noodle. "I guess we're going to Wisconsin tomorrow. Anything else, Sanders?"

"I thought it was interesting that after Kopecky's ballet performance to Eine Kleine Nachtmusik…"

"Mozart?" interrupted Noodle.

"Yes," continued Sanders. "After she danced, the Hapburn kid stood and applauded for a full five minutes *after* everybody else sat back down. Finally, an usher asked him to stop. I was a little embarrassed for him."

"I guess so," agreed Noodle.

"After the show, he ran up on stage, gave her some flowers and shook her hand."

....

"You shook Killer's hand?" blurted Michael. "What did she do? Did she laugh?"

"No, she didn't laugh. Anyway, what should I have done?" asked Hawk sheepishly.

"I don't know. Hug her, have her hit the rock…KISS her! Anything but shake hands," scoffed Michael.

"Leave him alone. Let him finish his story," said Nestor.

"You shook her hand in front of all those people. *Now* you have to marry her," laughed Michael.

Laughing, too, Hawk pulled off his tennis shoe and threw it at his funny brother. "I'm gonna finish packing, then go to bed. Mom said Coach Yak is picking us early tomorrow."

"I hate early," sighed Michael, throwing Hawk's sneaker back across the room. "I wonder what time they get out of bed in prison?"

Nestor zipped up his duffle bag and dropped it by the bedroom door. Then he walked to the window and peeked around the shade.

"Now, there're two black cars parked across the street again. You know, one of 'em followed you and Mom when you left for the recital."

"Yeah, we saw him driving behind us," said Hawk. "You think they'll follow us all the way to Wisconsin?"

"Yeah, probably," sighed Nestor. as he climbed the ladder to the top bunk. "What if those Limburger Heads don't even have the Bears?"

"They have 'em. What else could've been in those sacks?" muttered Michael.

"Yeah and remember after our game that one named Floyd said the Packers had the most players in the Hall of Fame," recalled Hawk.

Suddenly, a light flashed on in Nestor's head. "Oh yeah, and when I said the Bears had the most...HE said, *not anymore!*"

"Right!" nodded Hawk.

"I'm going downstairs for a snack," grunted Michael. Then turning to the life-size cardboard cutout of World Hot Dog Eating Champion Joey Chestnut, he asked, "You wanna come with me?"

"In prison, they don't let you go downstairs for snacks," said Hawk.

"I'm not in prison...yet," snorted Michael. Grabbing Joey around the waist, the two of them walked out of the bedroom.

Nestor, slipping under the covers of his bed, stared at the ceiling and started worrying again. "Can we find those Limburger Heads? And if we do...will they let us have the Bears back?"

....

The crowd at Baumgartner's was shuffling toward the exit as the four members of the Taleggio Trio hit the last few notes of Moonlight Polka. Finished for the night, Floyd Dowler hugged his band members, grabbed his tuba and headed for the parking lot.

Looking at his watch, he decided he'd better stop by Papa's on his way home. He'd been putting off telling him about the plan to smash and bury the Bears in Greenwood Cemetery.

Shoving his tuba into the backseat of his compact Chevy, he jumped in and headed down 16th Avenue. Five minutes later, he pulled into Papa's driveway and was walking up to the house. The glow from the living room lamp spilled out onto Papa's front porch.

From the dark, spooky cemetery across the street came a long, sad howl. It was the same dog that had been crying when they stashed the Bears in Papa's airplane hangar. He was howling again by the same gravestone.

It sent a shiver down Floyd's spine as he knocked on Papa's door.

"Open! Coming in!" shouted Papa seated in his favorite recliner in front of the TV.

Hearing the invitation, Floyd opened the door, stepped into the living room and his jaw dropped hard.

"Stinkin' Bishop! What's going on here, Papa?"

"Party!" answered Papa, raising his bottle of orange soda high over his head. "Papa Bear wanted all the Georges inside house to watch Cubs play Brewers!"

Floyd heaved a heavy sigh as he surveyed the scene. Smiling Papa Bear George Halas was plopped down in the middle of the sofa. On one side of him were George Trafton and George McAfee. On the other was side were George Connor and George Musso. Perched on a dining room chair between the sofa and recliner sat George Blanda.

"Bring chair here," chirped Papa, pointing to a chair at the dining room table. "Good game! Two-two…inning seven!"

Floyd shook his head, "No baseball. I just stopped by to tell you about tomorrow."

"Tomorrow?" Papa looked next to him at the baseball schedule taped to the wall. "Brewers play Mets."

"Could ya forget baseball for a minute?" moaned Floyd, anxious to get his unpleasant task over.

Papa took a swig of his orange soda and stood up.

"Where are you going? Sit down! I gotta tell you about the plan!" insisted Floyd.

"Inning seven stretch!" chirped Papa. "I follow rules!"

"Okay. But when I tell you what's gonna happen, you'll probably wanna sit down," responded Floyd, his face scrunched up.

"Why frown face, my Packer friend?" laughed Papa.

"Well…because…ah…at midnight tomorrow, all the Limburger Heads are meeting at the cemetery…

Papa, still standing, waited and listened.

Taking a deep breath, Floyd swallowed hard, then blurted it out. *"We're meeting at the cemetery and digging six graves to bury the Bears in!"*

That instant, another howl from across the street bled through the screen door.

Now, Papa had the frowny face. His knobby knees buckled and he collapsed into his cushy recliner.

"The plan is to dig the holes at midnight tomorrow. Then come back the next day, smash the statues to pieces, bury 'em, then go to Baumgartner's to celebrate," explained Floyd.

"Smashing to pieces?" gulped Papa, blinking away a tear.

Floyd nodded. "Yeah! We voted on it."

"But why? They are not in hall now. They are in Papa's living room. So, more Packers in Hall of Fame, right? Papa Bear and friends not hurting anyone. Why they just can't stay *here*?"

Floyd looked at Papa Bear George Halas smiling from his front row seat as a Brewer belted a home-run to break the 2-2 tie. Then Floyd's eyes moved along the other Georges in the room, giving each a hard stare.

Finally, he shook his head and turned to go. "Sorry, Papa. Dairy Dan and Albert say that's the plan. I'll see you tomorrow."

Floyd let the screen door slam as he walked back out to his car. As he slid behind the steering wheel and before he turned the key, the lonely dog keeping watch at the cemetery across the street let out yet another long, sad howl.

CHAPTER 11

September 1 – 7:27 am EDT | Port Clinton, Ohio
1 Day to Kickoff at Lambeau Field

Nestor climbed from his top bunk and peeked out the window. The black cars were nowhere in sight. Rubbing his eyes, he looked up and down the street mumbling to himself, "Wonder where they went…"

Before he could give that bothersome question any more thought, the problem that had been banging around in his brain last night popped back in his head.

"If we find the Limburger Heads, will they give us the Bears?"

Walking away from the window, he gave both his brothers a poke.

"Get up. Coach will be here soon," Nestor said.

"Morning? Ten more minutes," moaned Michael.

Rolling out of bed, Hawk shuffled to the window. "Those FBI guys are gone!"

"Yeah," nodded Nestor. "I know. I was thinking they'd follow us all the way to Wisconsin."

"Me, too," admitted Hawk, yawning as he took off his pajama top and pulled his red *STAND BACK. I'M GOING TO TRY SCIENCE* t-shirt over his head.

A few minutes later, Michael finally opened his eyes to catch Nestor and Hawk grabbing their duffle bags and heading out the bedroom door.

Heaving a sigh, Michael stumbled out of bed, ambled across the room and bumped into the closet door a couple of times. He was fumbling around for his clothes when the smell of bacon drifted into the bedroom. In a nano-second, he was dressed and sitting at the table as Nestor and Hawk walked into the kitchen.

"Wh-wh-here did you come from? How-how did you beat us downstairs?" stuttered Hawk.

"Bacon," answered Michael, his napkin on his lap.

"I just got a text from your coach," announced Audrey as she scooped a heaping spoonful of scrambled eggs onto Michael's plate. "He's at the Kopeckys' house now and he'll be here in a few minutes."

Hearing this, Hawk turned around and headed to the front door.

"Where are you going, young man?" asked Audrey, plopping a plate of toast on the table.

"To the front porch to wait for Kill…er, ah…Coach Yak and everybody," stammered Hawk.

"Sit down and have some breakfast. You need to eat," insisted Audrey. "I have enough stress right now without worrying about you being hungry."

"More, please," burped Michael.

"What do you say?" reminded Audrey as she loaded Michael's plate with more bacon and eggs.

"I said, please," muttered Michael.

"That was good," admitted Audrey. "But you also burped."

Michael shoved in a forkful of scrambled eggs in his mouth. "Oh, yeah, excuse me."

"And don't talk with your mouth full," added Audrey.

"Eating sure does come with a lot of rules," nodded Nestor as he smeared grape jelly on his toast.

"Someday you might get invited to the White House for dinner and you'll be glad you know those rules," lectured Audrey. "Manners are important."

"What about in jail?" asked Hawk, snapping a crispy piece of bacon in half and shoving it his mouth.

"No one here is going to jail, so let's not talk about that," Audrey stated firmly.

Just then, the *ding* of the doorbell rang and Hawk stood up from the table so fast, he beat the *dong.*

"Kill...er, ah...Coach is here! May I be excused?"

Audrey nodded. "Finish your orange juice first."

Hawk gulped down the rest of the juice in his glass, wiped his mouth with his napkin, grabbed his duffle bag and ran to answer the front door. Audrey and Nestor were a few steps behind him.

Michael, the last to leave the table, grabbed three more pieces of bacon, slid them in the back pocket of his jeans and followed them out.

The doorbell rang again just as Hawk swung open the front door. There, blocking the entire opening, stood the massive coach in his scarlet and gray number 99 Ohio State jersey.

"Hey! You got Michael's number," chirped Hawk.

"I think Michael's got MY number," laughed Yak as he gave Hawk a fist bump on the shoulder. "You ready to go bear hunting?"

"Is Killer in the truck?" asked Hawk.

"Everybody's in there, except you guys," answered Yak. "Killer, Stinky Smothers, Stinky Smothers' brother..."

"No! Stinky Smothers' brother?" whined Michael as he arrived at the front door. "Where's Frankie?"

"Give me your bags and I'll throw 'em in the back of Woody," barked Yak, ignoring Michael's question.

Audrey tilted her head and looked out the front door. "Who?"

Coach Yak threw a thumb over his shoulder, "Woody Hayes. My Suburban."

"Oh! Sure!" exclaimed Audrey, realizing the grown man in front of her had named his Chevy after the legendary Ohio State football coach. Then, kneeling down, she spread out her arms and gathered her three boys around her.

"You know I'm going to worry about you the whole time you're gone, don't you?" Michael, Nestor and Hawk nodded.

"I want you to be careful and listen to Coach."

The brothers nodded again.

"Who has the phone?"

"I do," answered Nestor, holding up the cell phone they all shared.

"Good. I want to know what's going on. Text me. Understand?"

"We will, Mom," promised Nestor as Michael and Hawk nodded one more time.

"Okay," sighed Audrey, blinking back a tear and giving them each a hug. "I love you and I'll see you in a few days."

Shouting "Love you, Mom," the brothers squeezed past Coach Yak and headed to the scarlet and gray truck parked at the curb.

"Hey, Michael! I saved you a window seat back here next to me!" hollered Stinky Smothers' brother from the third row.

"I think I'll sit up in the front," replied Michael.

Stinky Smothers' brother shook his head, "No, I tried sitting there and Coach said that seat's for Nestor so he can help with directions and stuff."

"Cool," cheered Nestor, scrambling past his brother and buckling himself in the front seat.

"Fine, I'll just sit here," huffed Michael as he turned to plant himself in the middle row next to Killer. But just as he was about to settle into the seat, Hawk gave his brother a hip check, knocking him aside.

"Too slow," chirped Hawk, clicking his seat belt.

"Hey, no fair!" complained Michael. "I called it!"

Stinky Smothers' brother held up a small green bag of Mango Tango Almond Mix. "You should sit back here, Michael. It's closer to the snacks!"

Michael's head snapped up. "Are there really snacks? Back there?"

"Yeah!" confirmed Stinky Smothers who was sitting next to his little brother. "A couple big boxes full."

"Yeah. A couple boxes full," repeated Stinky Smothers' brother.

Suddenly, the window seat in the back was pulling at Michael like a powerful magnet. Squeezing past Hawk and Killer, he plopped down next to Stinky Smothers' brother.

"Okay, I'll sit here. But no talking until we get to Wisconsin, deal?"

"Deal! cheered Stinky Smothers' brother. "Hit the rock!"

Michael sighed and held up his fist for Stinky Smothers' brother to smack, muttering, "Where's Frankie? I thought he was going with us."

"He had to go to the dentist, so I got to take his place," beamed Stinky Smothers' brother.

"He doesn't have a dentist appointment," countered Killer. "He just wants to stay home and dig for buried treasure in Portage Park. It's all he ever talks about."

Coach Yak, back at the Suburban, opened the rear hatch of the SUV, tossed in the duffle bags and lumbered around to the driver's side. But, before he could open his door, **WHAM!** He crashed into a man dressed in all-white who suddenly appeared out of nowhere.

The head-on collision sent the man in white tumbling into the street, causing the bottles of milk he was carrying to fly up and smash to the pavement.

"Sorry, buddy! I didn't see you," apologized the super-sized coach as he helped the man out of the puddle of white liquid and glass. "Are you okay?"

"Yeah, yeah, I'm fine," said the man, leaning against the rear fender of Coach Yak's truck trying to steady himself. "I guess I wasn't looking where I was going."

Audrey came running from the house. "Oh my goodness! Is anybody hurt?"

"Nobody's hurt, but we made a big mess in front of your house," admitted Yak pointing to broken glass and all the milk running down to the curb. "Sorry about that. It all happened so fast."

"Oh, don't you worry! I learned a long time ago not to cry over spilled milk. I'll clean that up...you guys get going!" offered Audrey.

As Audrey and Coach looked up from the mess on the pavement, the man in white was gone.

"Where did he go?" asked Coach Yak, rubbing his eyes. Tapping on the window of his truck, he hollered in. "You guys see where he went?"

Kathy Kopecky rolled down the window, "See where who went?"

"The guy I crashed into, the milkman," said Yak.

"What's a milkman?" shouted Stinky Smothers' brother from the back seat.

"You crashed into somebody?" asked Hawk.

"Sorry, Coach. We were all talking," said Kathy. "We didn't see any milk person."

"Strange," mumbled Coach Yak as he jumped into his Suburban. Sliding behind the steering wheel, he twisted his head around. "Everybody buckled in?"

Shouts from the back filled the truck: "Yep!" "Yep!" "Me, too!"

Satisfied, Coach Yak shoved the key in the ignition. "Well then, let's get this bear hunt started!"

Blowing a half dozen kisses good-bye, Audrey disappeared into the house to get her broom. Looking out their windows, everybody in the Suburban waved back and Coach Yak gave a quick, double goodbye tap of the horn.

Then he picked up a folded paper road map and handed it to Nestor. "Here! You're in charge of this."

Nestor took the map but didn't open it. "Coach, have you thought about how we're gonna get the Bears back?"

"You mean, do I have a plan?" replied Yak.

"Yeah, do you have a plan?" asked Nestor. "I've been thinking, since these Limburger Heads *took* the Bears, they probably won't want to give them back."

"Good point," nodded Yak. "Well...why don't you think on that for a little while? And I'll start driving."

Nodding his head, Nestor heaved a big sigh and turned to look out his window.

As they pulled away from the curb, just 3-1/2 seconds into their trip, Nestor shouted at the top of his lungs. "**STOP!**"

Coach Yak slammed on the brakes.

"I've got an idea!" shouted Nestor. He unbuckled his seat belt and bolted out of the truck.

Nestor ran down the sidewalk to Mrs. McChesney's house and rang the doorbell, leaving Coach Yak mumbling, "Well, that was fast."

....

Just a few minutes earlier, Probationary Agent Elliot Ness burst through some bushes at Portage Park and was pounding on the door of a windowless black van.

Instantly, the door opened and Elliot, out of breath, his white uniform wet and muddy, tumbled into the FBI/FD's hi-tech mobile command center.

"What happened to you? How'd you get so dirty?" asked Agent Sanders, slamming the door behind Elliot.

"I crashed into that big coach and spilled milk all over myself. Then I was running through the park and I tripped over a pile of dirt and fell in a hole," wheezed Elliot, still trying to catch his breath.

"A hole?" repeated Sanders.

"Yeah, a hole. The park is just full of holes. I jumped over one and then fell into another one right behind it," explained Elliot as he unbuttoned his dirty white shirt. "You'll probably have to pre-soak this to get it clean."

"Yeah, probably," Agent Sanders nodded. "So, did you plant the GL-300?"

"Affirmative! I attached the tracker to the rear fender, driver's side," reported Elliot, pulling on a clean shirt and a navy blue FBI/FD windbreaker.

"Excellent!" said Sanders as he punched some keys on the command center's supercomputer. The monitor lit up showing a map and a blinking red dot. "Yep! It's working! There they are!"

At that moment, Special Agent Roman Noodle's voice broke in over the radio.

"Noodle to mobile command…Noodle to mobile command…are you there? Over."

Pushing a red button on the control board, Agent Sanders replied. "10-4…we read you loud and clear. Over."

"I need a status report. Have you planted the bird? Over," came Noodle's crackling reply.

"P-FBI/FD Agent Ness made contact with the target and the GL-300 is in place. We are getting a strong signal. We'll be able to monitor their location at all times. Over," informed Sanders proudly.

"Sanders, you lead the convoy in the command center, but keep your distance. Stay at least ten minutes behind. We need to be invisible. I don't want our target waving at us again, understand?"

"Message received," acknowledged Sanders.

"The target's rolling," announced Elliot, watching the blinking red dot move along the computer screen.

"Roger that! Keep me informed," barked Noodle. "The helicopter's waiting, I'm headed back to the Hall of Fame to look for more clues. Over and out!"

As suddenly as the radio had come to life, it went silent again. Agent Sanders quickly turned from the control board to the computer screen just in time to see the blinking red dot come to a stop.

"Stopping? Already? What's that about?"

....

"Everybody grab one and load it in the truck," instructed Nestor, pointing at the chess set of lawn gnomes in Mrs. McChesney's yard.

"Why are we doing this? This is no time for chess," complained Michael.

"I like these two gnomes kissing," chirped Stinky Smothers' brother.

"No, don't take that one…only the chess pieces, the ones with the red and blue hats," clarified Nestor.

"What about Mrs. McChesney?" grunted Hawk as he lifted the King gnome with the blue hat and Band-Aid on his nose. "Doesn't she mind us taking these?

"She said if this keeps Michael from going to prison, she is happy to help.

"Yeah okay, but how can these gnomes help?" asked Coach Yak, adjusting his Buckeye ball cap on his head.

"I'm not sure. I'm still thinking," admitted Nestor. "It's something Killer said."

"What was that?" asked the Braves' quarterback as she hoisted the queen that matched Hawk's King into the back of the Suburban.

"You said that the gnomes are about the same size as the statues at the Hall of Fame. Remember?"

"Yeah, so what?" huffed Michael, sliding a red bishop next to Killer's blue queen.

Nestor moved a couple duffle bags to make room. "Like I said, I'm still thinking."

"Help!" squealed Stinky Smothers' brother, struggling to drag a blue-hatted gnome riding on the back of a squirrel to the truck.

Quickly, Coach Yak swooped in and, with one hand, grabbed the knight by his hat and plopped it down next to the red bishop.

"Thanks, Coach," smiled Stinky Smothers' brother. "I like squirrels, don't you?"

Finally, Stinky Smothers wrestled the red queen gnome into the Suburban with a grunt. "Checkmate!" he chuckled, brushing off his hands.

"Six of 'em. That should do it," said Nestor nervously.

"Okay, everybody back in the truck. Let's see if we can get a little farther down the road this time," laughed Yak. Quickly, everybody piled in a second time and buckled up.

Back behind the steering wheel, the Coach shoved the key in the ignition and gave it a turn. But instead of the sound of the motor turning over, there was only a loud clicking noise.

Taking a deep breath, Coach Yak whispered, "C'mon, Woody." Then he turned the key again. This time the engine roared to life.

"Here we go!" smiled Yak. Shifting the Suburban into *Drive*, the coach and his band of Braves headed out of Port Clinton on Ohio State Route 53, totally unaware they were on the radar of FBI/FD Special Agent Roman Noodle.

....

Dressed in his Packer pajamas, Demetri Papadopoulos was pacing back and forth between the kitchen and dining room worrying.

Every once in awhile, he'd peek into the living room where his guests, the Hall of Fame Bear Georges, were sleeping under blankets.

"Smash to pieces? Dig graves and bury?" Papa whispered to himself. Taking a deep breath, he shook his head. "No. This must not happen. But what to do?"

After pacing for another twenty minutes, he finally sat down in his favorite recliner in front of the TV to watch SportsCenter.

Hitting the mute button so he wouldn't wake up his friends, Papa's eyes drifted from the television to a painting hung on the wall entitled, *Hercules Fighting with the Half-Giant Antaeus.*

Suddenly the old Greek cargo pilot's face brightened. "Hercules!"

Bolting out of his easy chair, Papa rushed to the kitchen table and started digging through a pile of papers. Halfway through the stack, he found it! The program from the Hall of Fame game.

Flipping it over, he saw Nestor's handwriting, listing the three brothers' names and their cell number. Papa smiled, remembering he had crossed out Michael's name and written Hercules above it.

Papa shuffled into the living room and sat down in his recliner. Picking up his phone, he sighed, "Hercules helps me before. Will gods let him help again?"

Before Papa could answer his own question, he saw a flash on his muted TV: **ESPN SPECIAL BULLETIN!**

Papa gasped.

There on the screen were photos of George Halas, George Trafton, George McAfee, George Connor, George Blanda and George Musso. Beneath the pictures in big, bold type, he read:

BEARS REPORTED STOLEN FROM NFL HALL OF FAME!

....

On the other side of town, sitting in his kitchen watching SportsCenter on his tiny 13-inch television, Dairy Dan clapped his hands and cheered. "Ah-ha! Now the whole world knows the Packers have the most players in the Hall of Fame!"

On the TV, standing outside of the famous, football-shaped dome of the Pro Football Hall of Fame was ESPN NFL Insider Adam Schefter with a microphone.

Dairy Dan grabbed the remote and turned up the volume.

"The Pro Football Hall of Fame reported last week that the historic NFL shrine would be closed for a period of time to spray for bugs. However, early this morning, ESPN received an anonymous phone call stating the true reason for the Hall's closure is that six Hall of Fame statues have been stolen.

"According to the caller, the stolen busts were all Chicago Bears and they were all named George, including NFL Founder Papa Bear George Halas.

*"The employee on duty at the ESPN switchboard said the caller refused to identify himself and would not reveal how he came to have this information. It is reported that, before hanging up, he shouted…**Who has more players in the Hall of Fame now?** Then chanted the letters **STC** three times before the line went dead.*

"So far, Hall of Fame officials have refused comment and we've not been allowed in the building. From Canton, Ohio, this is Adam Schefter, ESPN."

Laughing, Dairy Dan shut off the TV and with his fractured foot still in a walking boot, he shuffled off to pour himself some coffee. By the time he got back to the table and dumped two spoonfuls of sugar in his cup, the phone rang.

"Did you see SportsCenter just now?" exploded Einstein's alarmed voice in Dairy Dan's left ear.

"Yeah! I sure did," chuckled Dan.

"An anonymous phone call?" ranted Einstein. "I am positive it was Floyd! Who else would have done something so…so irresponsibly idiotic?"

"Me. I made the phone call," admitted the head Limburger Head.

"YOU! Why would you do that? Why would you endanger the successful completion of Operation Georgie Porgie?" shouted Einstein. "And, I might add, risk spending the rest of your life in a maximum-security federal penitentiary? **Why?**"

"Einstein! Don't overheat that big brain of yours. Calm down and let me explain," snickered Dairy Dan.

"I'm listening!" boomed Einstein.

"So we went to a WHOLE lot of trouble *and* expense, stealing those Bears…would you agree?"

"Yes…that is a true and accurate statement."

"And the goal, or as you would say, our stated objective was so our beloved Packers would have more players in the Hall of Fame than any other team and, as a result, rise to their rightful place as the greatest and most outstanding football franchise of all time."

"Yes, again, I concur."

"Right! So, I say why go to all that effort to steal the Bears if no one knows about it?" concluded Dairy Dan. "This should be headline news and on all the TV networks! Instead, they made up a silly story about spraying for bugs!"

"But Dairy Dan! Exposing us like that! The risks involved!" moaned Einstein.

"What risks? They don't know *who* we are...they don't know *where* we are...they have **no** clues!" added Dairy Dan. "And when we smash the Bears to bits and bury them, there will be no more evidence!"

Then, for what seemed like forever, the telephone line was quiet.

Finally, Dairy Dan broke the silence. "Einstein Wozniak! Wake up! Are you there?"

"I'm thinking," mumbled Einstein.

"Good, good. Keep thinking," laughed Dairy Dan. "Someday, years from now, Packer grandparents will tell this amazing story to their grandkids. People will write songs about it.

"They may even put up statues of *us*! I can see it now! The Limburger Heads, *standing tall* next to Vince Lombardi outside Lambeau Field. And you'll see it, too. Believe me, my Packer pal."

"First, as you are well aware, I am not that tall," came the worried voice on the other end. "Second, I must admit, that would be a dream come true."

"Exactly," sniffled Dan, wiping a sentimental tear from his cheek. "But first things first. Call Floyd and have him meet us at Papa's after lunch. We'll take a look around Greenwood Cemetery and figure out the best place to dig the holes. The quicker we bust up those Bears and bury them, the better!"

"Perhaps you are correct in your assessment," conceded Einstein. "How could they know who we are or where we are?"

"Like I said, they have no clue," repeated Dairy Dan. "See you this afternoon." With that, the two Limburger Heads hung up.

....

In the back of the red Suburban, Stinky Smothers was asleep. Stinky Smothers' brother was pretending he was Taio Cruz, singing *Dynamite* for the seventeenth straight time. And Michael was busy digging through the boxes of snacks, organizing them in the order in which he planned to eat them.

Up front, Coach Yak was pouring his heart out to Nestor, talking about his passion for teaching kids the fundamentals of football and how he believed a person could accomplish amazing things through preparation and hard work.

In the middle row, Hawk was trying to have a conversation with Killer, but instead of paying attention to him, she had her nose in the Port Clinton playbook. The Braves' first regular season game was on Saturday at True Lay Stadium and she wanted to be ready.

"Do you ever think about how in two or three years, we'll be going to school dances and out on dates and stuff?" asked Hawk, trying hard to sound grown-up.

Kathy Kopecky, concentrating on what she was doing, kept flipping through the playbook and Hawk kept talking.

"We'll get driver's licenses...go to the movies...go to parties!"

Reaching down on the floor, the Braves' quarterback grabbed her backpack and pulled out a pen and Hawk kept talking.

"Then probably we'll go to college and...after that, get jobs...get married..."

Killer was jotting notes next to the *Twinkie Off Tackle* play and, at that moment, she looked over at Hawk.

"I'm sorry, Hawk," she offered. "Were you saying something?"

"Yeah," gushed Hawk. "I was talking about getting married."

"Married?" repeated Killer with a chuckle. "You're funny, Hawk."

"What's so funny? Don't you ever think about getting married," asked Hawk.

"No," said Killer, flipping to another page in the playbook.

"Don't you want to get married someday..." Hawk paused and shrugged his shoulders before finally saying "...to someone?"

"I don't know...maybe," answered Killer as she scribbled something next to the diagram of *Mango Tango Halfback Sweep Left*. "I've got a lot of important things to do before I think about things like that."

Then, turning her head, she called to her star running back sitting in the row behind her.

"Michael! I'm thinking instead of calling out numbers, I should use hand signals. Those Olmsted Fall players broke our code pretty fast."

"I think you should keep the chili dog play in," answered Michael, still stacking snacks in the back.

Hawk sighed and turned to look out the window. That's when it happened again. There, in a sunny green pasture, he saw a cow holding a sign: **texT Papa nOw!**

"Killer! Cow! Look!" stammered Hawk.

"A killer cow?" laughed the QB, without looking up from her playbook. "Since when did you become such a comedian?"

Hawk blinked, rubbed his eyes and looked back. The cow was gone.

"No. Not a killer cow...MY cow...the cow that holds up signs! Last time we came by here on the way to Wrigley Field, *that* cow held up a sign and now it happened again," insisted Hawk.

"I've seen cows like that," piped up Stinky Smothers' brother sitting behind Hawk. "In TV commercials. They want people to eat more chicken! I think it's smart."

"I like chicken," said the snack-stacking running back in the back. "Are we stopping for lunch pretty soon?"

"Okay, forget the cow. Pretend it didn't happen," grumbled Hawk.

"Hey! I play pretend sometimes, too," chirped Stinky Smothers' brother happily.

"Hey, Coach. I think we should text that old guy, Papa," said Hawk.

"Why's that?" asked Yak.

"I don't know, it just...sort of hit me all of a sudden," said Hawk, no longer anxious to talk about the sign-holding cow.

Coach Yak sucked in some air and thought about it for a second. "Yeah, okay. That way we'll know going in if there's a problem," said Yak. Then, giving Nestor a nod, he added, "Text the old man. Tell him you guys are taking a trip to Wisconsin and see what he says."

Nestor reached down to his backpack and pulled out the cell phone. Behind him, Stinky Smothers continued to sleep and Stinky Smothers' brother went back to singing.

Michael, sorting snacks, was thinking about lunch. Coach Yak started thinking about lunch, too. Killer stuck her nose back in her playbook and, inside Hawk's head, his thoughts were bouncing back and forth between getting married and sign-painting cows.

"There! Did it! Done!" declared Nestor, stuffing the cell phone back in his backpack and zipping it up.

Keeping his eyes on the highway, Coach Yak adjusted his Buckeye ball cap and asked, "So…what did you say?"

....

After seeing the Bears bulletin on ESPN, Papa, still in his Packer pajamas, stood in front of his television in a trance, frozen with fear.

Then he heard a text come through. He blinked, shook his head and looked down at his cell phone.

remMbR us? My bros & I met u @ Hall of Fame gAm lst wk.
On trip 2 Wisconsin w/ footb coach & thawt of U.
Plz teL yr chez fRnds LO & hOp 2 c U agen sometime.
Nestor Hapburn

His heart pounding fast, Papa quickly pounded a message back, hit the *send* button and held his breath. Less than a minute later, he heard the sweet sound of his text tone. Papa looked down at the phone, then looked up to the sky.

Filled with happiness, he thanked Zeus, Athena, Apollo, Nike and a few other Greek Gods, then hurried off to his bedroom to change into clothes. He had a lot to get done before his friends arrived.

Zeus: God of the Sky; Athena: Goddess of Wisdom; Apollo: God of Music & Poetry; Nike: Goddess of Victory.

....

The ESPN video crew was bustling around setting up equipment in front of the Pro Football Hall of Fame. One of the sound technicians, Orca, slid a tiny microphone up inside Special Agent Roman Noodle's navy blue FBI/FD windbreaker and clipped it to his collar, while the videographer, Flipper, secured his camera to the tripod.

"Hey, Flip!" greeted ESPN NFL Insider Adam Schefter as he walked onto the set. Shaking hands with Noodle, the two of them stood there in the bright lights and waited for the camera to roll.

An important-looking lady, holding a folder with papers, took a peek in the camera. After giving a few detailed instructions to Flipper and Orca, she began to count backward from five. When she got to one, she pointed at Schefter and he began his interview.

"I am in Canton, Ohio with breaking news regarding the shocking report that six Chicago Bear busts, all of them named George, have been stolen. Here with me is Special Agent Roman Noodle from the Federal Bureau of Investigation's Football Division."

"First, Special Agent Noodle...I was not aware the FBI had a football division."

Squinting into the bright lights, Noodle cleared his throat and thought about what to say.

"That's not a question. You said you'd have a few questions."

"That's right, I do," nodded Schefter. "Special Agent Noodle, can you confirm the report of the missing Bears?"

"I can."

"Do you have any leads or ideas about how this happened and who is responsible?

"I do."

"Can you tell us wh…

"No," said Noodle, not waiting for the rest of the question.

The important lady in charge whispered to Orca to cut Noodle's microphone and instructed Flipper to move to a close-up of Adam Schefter, cutting Noodle out of view. Then, making a motion with her hand, she indicated that her announcer should wrap things up.

"Thank you, Special Agent Noodle. So, we can definitely say for sure, there may be Bears missing from the Pro Football Hall Fame. We'll have more on this breaking story soon. We hope. From Canton, Ohio, this Adam Schefter, ESPN."

Immediately the lights went out and Orca rushed in to remove the microphones.

Special Agent Noodle, blinking and rubbing his eyes, impatiently yanked the microphone from under his navy FBI/FD windbreaker, tossed it to Orca and started speed-walking toward the Hall of Fame.

Flustered, Schefter ran to catch up, tapping Noodle on the shoulder just before he reached the entrance.

"Special Agent Noodle...off the record...is there anything else you can tell me?"

Noodle raised his arm, pointed his index finger to the sky and said in a firm and determined voice, "Someone's got to go to prison." And with that, Noodle disappeared into the building.

Immediately, two FBI/FD agents stepped in front of the doors, blocking the ESPN reporter. Defeated, Schefter shuffled back toward the bustling video crew breaking down the set in the Hall of Fame parking lot.

....

Probationary Agent Elliot Ness was in the back of the FBI/FD's mobile command center monitoring the radar screen when he observed the red blip veer off Interstate-80 at Elkhart, Indiana.

Before he could report it to Agent Sanders, Noodle's voice broke in over the two-way police radio.

"Noodle to Mobile Command Center, what's your 10-20?"

Quickly, Agent Sanders slammed his hand down on the red button on the control board and replied, "We're in Indiana on I-80, 30 miles west of the Ohio border. Roughly, 30 minutes behind our target. Over."

"Excellent. Maintain your current separation. The target is not to know we are in the vicinity. We're finishing up here and should be in the air within the hour to join the caravan. Unfortunately, the media has reported the incident, so the pressure is on to act fast."

"Media?" snapped Sanders. "Who leaked it?"

Noodle's voice crackled back over the radio. "ESPN received a call early this morning from some crackpot. We're trying to trace the call right now, but so far, no luck. Do the letters **S-T-C** mean anything to you?"

"S-T-C? No. I have no idea," answered Sanders.

"Excuse me," interrupted Probationary Agent Ness. "The red blip isn't moving."

"Gotta go!" shouted Sanders over the radio. "Our target appears to have stopped."

"Roger that!" said Noodle. "I will contact you again when we're in the chopper. Over and out."

The static from the radio stopped and Sanders crossed over to the other side of the van to where Elliot was pointing at the screen.

"The target exited here, Cassopolis Street. Elkhart."

Agent Sanders looked at the monitor and then looked at his watch. Taking a deep breath, he uttered one word.

"Lunch."

....

"Gangway!" yelled Michael as he unbuckled his seat belt the very instant Coach Yak shifted the vehicle into *Park*.

As always, when food was involved, Michael moved at lightning speed, exploding out of the SUV and into the Steak 'n Shake parking lot.

Coach Yak, almost always hungry himself, cranked the window down and shouted at Michael as he raced toward the restaurant, "Tell 'em we need a table for seven! And order anything you want! It's on me!"

"Are you sure you want to do that, Coach?" asked Nestor, blinking as he stepped out into the noonday sun.

"Do what?"

"Let Michael order anything he wants. He might want one of everything on the menu."

"That's fine with me! I can help him eat it all. I didn't get this good lookin' by eating birdseed," bragged Yak, patting his belly.

Coach Yak adjusted his Ohio State ball cap on his head and led the rest of his bunch of Braves inside the crowded restaurant.

Lagging behind, Stinky Smothers' brother stopped beside the Suburban to tie his shoe. As he bent down, he noticed a small black box with a blinking red light attached under the rear fender.

"Cool! A magnet!" He reached up and pulled it off.

Magnet in hand, Stinky Smothers' brother head spun around looking for someplace to stick it. First, he stuck it on an air conditioning unit next to the building. After that, he attached the magnetic black box to a trash can. Then he spotted a metal sign by the restaurant entrance that read: *I'm not bossy. I just know what you should be doing.* – and he stuck it on that.

Still not satisfied, Stinky Smothers' brother pulled the blinking black magnet off the sign, shoved it in his pocket and walked inside. By the time he got to the table, Nestor, Hawk, Killer and Stinky Smothers had ordered and the waitress was waiting for Michael and Coach Yak to decide.

"This is really hard," moaned Michael.

"I agree," nodded Coach Yak.

"You know, Michael, in prison, they don't give you a choice," said Killer.

"C'mon, Michael! Order!" complained Nestor.

"Okay, okay, I've got it," Michael paused and took a quick peek at the waitresses' name tag and continued. "Courtney. I'd like one yard of the classic footlongs, fries and a Butterfinger milkshake," drooled Michael, licking his lips.

Courtney scratched her head with her pen and said, "I'm sorry. Could you repeat that?"

"A yard of footlongs…"

Wrinkling her nose, the confused Courtney interrupted Michael with an extra helping of drama. "A *YARRRRD?*"

"Yeah! A yard!" confirmed Michael. "You know, three footlongs make one yard, right? Plus, fries and a Butterfinger shake."

Courtney scribbled on her order pad and looked back at Michael, "You want three orders of fries, too?"

"Yes. Thank you," confirmed Michael, handing her his menu.

Courtney did some more scribbling and then turned to Coach Yak.

Coach Yak handed Courtney his menu, tucked his napkin in the collar of his Ohio State jersey and chirped, "I'll have the same."

....

Grabbing one of the bungee cords piled on his front porch, Papa wrapped it around Papa Bear's shoulder and hooked it onto one of the legs of his shop stool with wheels. He repeated the process three more times until he was satisfied his new best friend was firmly strapped down to the stool.

Pushing the stool from the porch to his old airplane hangar out-back, he explained to Papa Bear what was happening.

"You no worry about smashing to pieces. Everything is to be okey-dokey. The gods send Hercules."

Huffing and puffing, Papa rolled the stool back into the same dark corner of the metal pole barn where the Limburger Heads had tucked the Hall of Fame Bears a few nights before.

Taking the bungees off, Papa grabbed Papa and, with a grunt, placed him beside the rest of the Georges he had already moved from the house to the hangar.

Papa stood there for a minute, looking at the group of Hall of Fame Bears and shaking his head, "Big mistake Georgie Porgie Operation."

With a sigh, one by one he started putting burlap bags over their heads. Again, he saved the smiling George Halas for last.

"Sorry for sack on your head, my friend," said Papa sadly as he wrestled to get Papa Bear into the burlap bag. "But when Squadron Leader Dan comes here, he must not know I make a try to change his big plan."

Tying a knot at the top of the bag, he rolled his shop stool back into the light next to Aphrodite.

"How you do today, beautiful?" asked Papa. He kissed the tip of his fingers and pressed them to the nose of his cargo plane. "Someday we fly again. Someday, Aphrodite, we touch the clouds one time more."

Digging around in the toolbox at his feet, Papa pulled out a wrench and walked along the length of his plane, looking for bolts to tighten.

....

Coach Yak shoved the last couple inches of his third footlong into his mouth and waited to swallow before he spoke.

"Okay! We're leaving Elkhart, Indiana! Let's roll!"

Bellies full, the bunch of Braves scooted out of the booth and out of the restaurant. Yak stood there a little longer, taking the time to wipe some mustard off his face and leave Courtney a tip.

Out in the parking lot, Stinky Smothers' brother pulled the blinking black magnet out of his pocket and looked around again for some fun spot to stick it.

"Whaddya got there?" asked Hawk, snatching the magnet from Stinky Smothers' brother's hand.

"Hey, it's mine!" protested Stinky Smothers' brother. "Give it to me."

Hawk started to hand it back, but it was intercepted by Stinky Smothers.

"Where'd you get this?" asked Stinky.

"I found it. Give it back."

"GL-300," mumbled Stinky, reading the lettering on the magnet. "You shouldn't mess with this…it could be radioactive and make your ears fall off."

Stinky Smothers' brother faced dropped and he touched both ears just to be sure they were still attached.

"Don't scare him like that," laughed Killer. "Give it here. I'll get rid of it."

Stinky Smothers handed the magnet to Killer and gave his little brother a shove toward the Suburban.

Looking around the parking lot, Killer spotted an old blue pickup with Iowa license plates and a trailer hitched behind. On the trailer was a brand new green farm tractor. Walking beside the trailer, she shrugged her shoulders and attached the magnet to its metal fender.

Wiping her hands on the pavement just in case it was radioactive, Killer sprinted to the truck to join Yak and her teammates.

Michael, the first one back in the truck, buckled his seat belt and reached around to grab a Twinkie off the top of his pile of snacks.

"Toss me one of those," said Hawk, holding his hand up to catch the throw.

Michael, who had already unwrapped the Twinkie and taken a bite, shouted back with his mouth full, "You're kidding. You just ate lunch."

"C'mon, Michael!" howled Hawk.

With a grumpy face, Michael handed Hawk his Twinkie with the bite out of it and grabbed another snack off the stack for himself.

"Everybody buckled in?" shouted Coach Yak as he settled into the driver's seat. After hearing a "yes", "yeah" and "yup" from everyone, Yak put the key in the ignition and gave it a turn.

Nothing.

Pausing a second, Yak gently patted the dashboard and whispered, "C'mon, Woody" and turned the key a second time.

Still nothing.

"Maybe if we all shout TEAM," suggested Nestor.

"Yeah, okay," agreed Coach Yak. "TEAM on three! Ready? One … two … THREE…"

"TEAM!" shouted everyone at the same time.

Fingers crossed, Yak turned the key and the engine roared to life.

"That did it!" crowed the happy coach as everyone else cheered.

Pulling out of the parking lot, Yak looked at the clock on the dash. "We should get to Monroe around dinner time," he announced.

"Perfect timing," smiled Michael as he ripped open a bag of Mango Tango Almond Mix.

The moment Woody rolled onto Cassopolis Street toward Interstate 80, Mott and Maude Miller walked out of the Steak 'N Shake and headed toward their old blue pickup. Before climbing up into the cab, Mr. Miller put his thumbs behind the straps of his overalls and looked at his brand new John Deere tractor loaded on the trailer.

"Yep. She's a beauty all right!"

Knocking loose a bit of onion wedged between two molars with a toothpick, Mott joined Maude in the truck. He adjusted his rearview mirror to get another look at the tractor, then glanced at his watch and slowly drove off.

"Well, Maude, the way I figure, we should be back at the farm 'bout dinner time."

"Perfect timing," smiled Maude.

....

FBI/FD Agent Sanders was standing outside the mobile command van at a rest stop on I-80, stretching his legs and munching on some carrot sticks when Probationary Agent Ness suddenly stuck his head out of the rear door.

"The red blip...it's moving again!"

Throwing the last two carrot sticks in the grass for a rabbit to find later, Agent Sanders waved his hand over his head in a circular motion to signal the other FBI/FD agents, who were also standing outside their vehicles, getting some fresh air.

Seeing the hand motion, the other agents jumped in their vehicles, started their engines and waited.

Back inside the Mobile Command Center, Sanders joined Elliot at the computer screen.

"How long have they been on the road?" he asked.

"Less than 30 seconds. Radar shows them 15 miles ahead," replied Elliot, watching the red blip move west on his monitor. "Speed: 64 miles per hour."

Sanders turned and called up to the driver, "We're back on the trail, I-80. Set *cruise* at 64 miles per hour."

Moments later, the Hi-tech Mobile Command Center was rolling again, merging onto the expressway followed by a caravan of three SUVs and a half dozen full-size sedans, all of them black.

....

Dairy Dan was driving his Ford pickup south on 23rd Avenue, heading toward Papa's house. With him were Einstein and Floyd, all three crammed in the cab.

"I want to warn you, DD. I don't think Papa's going to be happy to see us. He is pretty upset about the plan to bust up and bury the Bears," fretted Floyd. "He's got those Bears stayin' in the house with him."

"In the house?!" crowed the head Limburger Head.

"Yeah! He's been watching TV with 'em, eating dinner with 'em, playing cards with 'em. They're his buddies...especially that smilin' coach, Papa Bear George."

"Playing cards? How does he do that?" asked Dairy Dan, turning left onto 18th Street.

Floyd shrugged his shoulders, "I don't know, but I'm pretty sure he's the one who has to shuffle every time."

Pulling into Papa's driveway, Dairy Dan slammed on the brakes, mumbling, "I hate shuffling," as he carefully got out of the truck and hobbled in his walking boot toward the house.

The three of them - extra-large, tall and thin, short and round - marched up the sidewalk in perfect formation. Standing on the porch, Dairy Dan knocked on the door and waited.

After a few seconds, Dairy Dan opened the door and peeked in. "He's not there."

"He's usually in his chair and the Bears are sitting on the couch," said Floyd as he took a look over Dairy Dan's shoulder. "Stinkin' Bishop! He's run off! And I bet he's taken his Bear buddies with him!"

"**NO!**" exploded Dairy Dan

"We have a crisis on our hands," moaned Einstein.

"But how could he get outta town? He hasn't even got a car!" crowed Dairy Dan, his head spinning.

"I don't know. Maybe they all got on a bus," guessed Floyd.

At that instant, the sound of metal hammering burst out of Papa's broken-down airplane hangar.

"Relax, everybody," grinned Dairy Dan, taking his finger off the panic button. "The old guy is out back, banging on that junk heap."

Breathing a sigh of relief, the three Limburger Heads trudged toward the noise coming from the building outback. When they slid open the hangar's metal doors, there was Papa, hammering away on his C-47 cargo plane's landing gear.

"Don't get too close. He'll whack ya on the foot," warned Dairy Dan.

Looking around, Einstein saw the light switch on the wall. He flipped it a couple of times to get the old Greek pilot's attention.

"Sound alarm!" shouted Papa. "Air raid!"

"No-no-no, Papa! Everything's okay!" called Dairy Dan, waving his arms.

"Okay-okay, sure-sure!" sighed Papa. "Thanks for the come-over."

"Yeah, sure thing. We're headed across the street to see where to bury the Bears. You wanna come with us?"

"Aw, no, you go. I am very busy fixing Aphrodite," answered Papa, giving a nod toward his airplane. "Someday she touch the clouds one time more."

"Yeah, right," smirked Dairy Dan. "Where are the Bears?"

Papa pointed with his hammer to the burlap sacks stuffed into the dark corner of the metal pole barn. "Bears over there."

Einstein immediately headed off to the dark corner to inspect.

"Why aren't you in the house watching TV with 'em," asked Floyd.

Papa heaved a heavy sigh. "I decide Squadron Leader Dan is right. More Packers in Fame of Hall than Bears. This is what matters."

"That's right! STC! Seize The Cheese and Packer glory," agreed Dairy Dan.

"Six Bears! All present and accounted for," said Einstein, walking back to the group with his thumbs up.

"Okay, Papa. We'll let you get back to your…ah, ah, work," said Dairy Dan, giving a nod toward the cargo plane. "We're going across the street and look around."

Papa pointed toward his workbench. "You need shovels? You see 'em right there."

"We're digging at midnight," answered Dairy Dan. "We'll get the shovels then."

"Good, good. Have nice time in cemetery," said Papa with a wave. Sitting down on his stool on wheels, he picked up his hammer and started banging again.

The three Limburger Heads slid the hangar door shut behind them and walked side-by-side down Papa's driveway toward Greenwood Cemetery.

"See?" said Dairy Dan, giving Floyd a nudge with his elbow. "We don't have any problems here."

Back inside the old airplane hangar, Papa reached down into his toolbox and picked up his cell phone.

....

"Hey look! We're in Wisconsin!" shouted Stinky Smothers' brother, pointing at a *Welcome to Wisconsin The Cheese State* sign along the highway. "It's the first time I've ever been here! How 'bout you guys?"

"First time for me," chirped Killer.

"Me, too!" "Me three!" "Me four." "Me five." Sang out Stinky Smothers, Nestor, Michael and Hawk.

Hawk leaned forward, tapping Yak on the shoulder. "How 'bout you coach?"

"This is my...one-two-three...*fourth time*," said Yak, counting up the visits in his head.

"You've been to Wisconsin four times?" asked Killer.

"Two times in college when Ohio State played Wisconsin. One time when the Browns played an exhibition game at Lambeau Field. And now this time to save our star running back from going to prison."

"Thanks, Coach," yelled Michael from the back.

"You've been to Lambeau Field?" squawked Hawk. "Hey! While we're here, maybe we can go to Lambeau. First game of the season – Packers and Bears - is tomorrow night!"

Coach Yak chuckled. "No time for that. We're on a mission. Get the Bears and get back home. We've got our own game Saturday and you all need to practice.

"That reminds me," muttered the monster-sized coach, looking at

Nestor. "Text Coach Jekyll and ask him how practice went today."

Nestor dug into his backpack, pulled out his phone and started pounding out a text. His thumbs were a blur as they flew across the touchscreen. Hitting the arrow, he sent the message.

"Done," said Nestor.

A text tone sounded immediately.

"Huh? That was fast," said Yak. "What did he say?"

Nestor tapped the icon on his phone and the new text popped up.

Demetri Papadopoulos
with red truck in driveway do not stop go round block
no stop at house til red truck gone i am explain later

Nestor shook his head. "It's not from Coach Jekyll."

....

"Hey look! We're in Iowa!" shouted Probationary Agent Elliot Ness, pointing at a *Welcome to Iowa The Hawkeye State* sign. "It's the first time for me!"

Turning to Agent Sanders, he asked, "Have you ever been to Iowa?"

"Iowa? What are we doing in Iowa?" cried Sanders, taking a look at the red blip moving west along I-80 on the computer screen.

Immediately, he picked up the two-way police radio.

"Mobile Command Center to Noodle…Mobile Command Center to Noodle…come in, Noodle!"

Special Agent Roman Noodle's voice crackled right back. "Noodle to Mobile Command Center…go ahead, Command Center."

"We've just crossed into Iowa…still traveling west approximately 22 minutes behind our target," reported Sanders, trying to remain calm.

"IOWA! What are you doing in Iowa?" shouted Noodle, not at all calm. "You said they were going to Wisconsin!"

"That's what the mom said last night at the recital," maintained Sanders.

"Sounds like they're trying to pull a fast one and make a get-away! Lucky for us we've got 'em cold, thanks to our GL-300 GPS Tracker," sneered Noodle. "Keep me updated. I'm taking off in the chopper in a few minutes. See you in Iowa."

There was a crackle and a click and the police radio went silent. Puzzled, Agent Sanders scratched his chin and studied the red-blip as it blinked slowly west on the computer screen.

"You never answered my question," said Elliot, while keeping his eye on the blinking red-blip as well.

"No," answered Sanders. "This is my first time in Iowa, too."

....

"Hey, guys! There's a good spot to dig the holes," yelled Floyd, pointing at a huge tree away from the other gravestones.

Einstein shook his head. "That location is less than optimal for digging. Judging by the size of the Quercus, which is a member of the Beech family commonly referred to as an Oak, I suspect the root system to be quite extensive. And, as you well know, most Oak roots lie only 18 inches under the soil and can spread seven times the width of the tree's crown."

Floyd heaved a huge sigh. "Yeah, silly me. What was I thinking?"

Einstein lifted his hand to his forehead to shade the sun and surveyed the cemetery. "For maximum excavating ease, I suggest we select a more open area unencumbered by tree roots."

"Right-right...and not so close to these markers either. I'd hate to dig up a skeleton," agreed Floyd, sending a shiver up his spine.

"Look here," called Dairy Dan, pointing at a headstone in the shape of a wedge of cheese a few feet away. "Harvey Havarti. He was the cheese master at the Co-op before Helmut."

Dairy Dan read the dates carved into the monument. "He's been dead almost ten years. People say his dog still comes by every night and howls at his grave."

This time a shiver shot *down* Floyd's spine. "He does! I've heard him! Gives me the creeps."

"This spot looks as good as any," declared Dairy Dan, limping a short distance away from the old cheese master's grave.

"Stinkin' Bishop, DD," gulped Floyd. That's a little too close to Harvey, don't you think?"

"Naw, this is fine," barked Dairy Dan.

Einstein walked over to Harvey Havarti's cheese wedge headstone and counted the steps to where Dairy Dan was standing.

"It is exactly thirteen feet, 7.5 inches between the marker and our proposed excavation site," announced Einstein confidently. "This sector is a suitable distance from any other gravesite. Tree roots are not an issue. We are in a bit of a swale…"

Floyd made a frown, "Swale?"

"Swale…a low or hollow place, a depression between two ridges," explained Einstein.

"Oh sure, of course," nodded Floyd. "And, from the looks of it, I'd say this is one swell swale."

"Most importantly," continued Einstein. "This location is concealed from traffic traveling on 18th Street."

Dairy Dan looked around to make a mental note of the location, then clapped his hands.

"Good! It's settled. We'll get the rest of the Heads and meet back here at midnight with our shovels…thirteen feet from Old Man Havarti."

"Thirteen feet…7.5 inches," corrected Einstein.

A shiver shot up *and* down Floyd's spine at the same time.

"Good, that's settled. Now, for the love of Lombardi, let's get outta this place and back to the truck!"

Immediately, Floyd took off toward 18th Street and Papa's house, followed by Einstein.

Dairy Dan stood there a moment longer. He scratched his chin and muttered, "Looks like you're gonna have some Hall of Fame company out here, Harvey."

Smiling, Dairy Dan limped off to join the others.

....

"There it is! 18th Street…turn here!" cried Nestor.

Coach Yak put on his blinker and turned left from Highway K onto 18th Street. Right away, they saw the city limits sign: Monroe, Wisconsin POP 10,827.

"What's this guy's address again?" asked Coach Yak, slowing down as they entered the town.

Nestor checked the text. "2707 18th Street."

"And hey look, there's a cemetery," said Hawk.

"How many dead people do you think are buried in that cemetery?" asked Stinky Smothers' brother.

"All of them," answered Killer.

"Rats! You heard that joke before," sighed Stinky Smothers' brother.

"Everybody's heard that joke before," groaned Stinky Smothers.

Michael nodded as he ripped open his third bag of Mango Tango Almond Mix since lunch, "Yeah, right. And it's not funny."

Stinky Smothers' brother pointed at three men standing at the edge of the cemetery, waiting to cross the street. "Look! There are people in the cemetery and they're not buried."

"They're not dead either," declared Killer. Then, getting a better look at the faces, she gasped. "Hey! We know those guys!"

Stinky Smothers' brother stuck his arm out of the window and waved.

"2707...there's the house!" exclaimed Nestor.

"And there's the red truck in the driveway!" shouted Hawk.

"Don't wave at those guys!" Michael burst out, trying to grab Stinky Smothers' brother's arm.

"Don't stop! Go around the block!" instructed Killer.

Rattled by the sudden rush of information, Coach Yak hit the gas pedal a little too hard. Tires squealing, the Suburban sped off down the street, with Stinky Smothers' brother waving out the window.

....

"Do we know them?" asked Dairy Dan as he walked across 18th Street to Papa's house. "That kid was waving at us."

Floyd shrugged his shoulders. "Somebody from town just being friendly. I wave at people I don't know all the time. Sometimes I wave at people who aren't even there."

Dairy Dan shook his head as he hobbled to his truck. "I'm not gonna ask you to explain."

"Did you happen to observe as I did that the vehicle that took off with excessive speed had Ohio license plates? I find that extremely odd," declared Einstein, with a troubled look on his face. "Furthermore, I thought I recognized more than one of the passengers."

Floyd, standing beside the Ford truck, opened the passenger door and gave Einstein a nudge.

"C'mon, Albert, get in! I've got a tuba lesson at Scheppele's at 5:30."

Einstein stood there scratching his chin a while longer, forcing Floyd to give his friend another nudge. Only this time, it was more of a shove.

Einstein shook his head, blinked twice, and finally the three piled in the pickup shoulder-to-shoulder and drove off down the street.

"One time I saw a car in town with Hawaii plates," admitted Dairy Dan as he turned left on 23rd Avenue.

"Driving across that big ocean?" Floyd laughed and slapped his knee. "I bet that's one boring drive."

....

"Those were the guys we sat with at the Hall of Fame Game. I'm sure of it," said Killer. "The short, round one and the tall, skinny one bought us popcorn."

"Yeah, right!" agreed Michael. "And the other big, bulky guy…"

"The one wearing the black boot?" asked Hawk.

"Yeah, him. He's the one I helped," continued Michael. "He couldn't walk, so I carried his bag of souvenirs back to the bus."

"You mean his bag of Bears," corrected Nestor.

Coach Yak turned off 28th Avenue back onto 18th Street.

"Look, the red truck's gone," said Coach Yak, pointing toward the driveway. "I guess it's okay to pull in now."

Yak turned in slowly and stopped in front of the house.

"It's painted in Packer colors," said Hawk.

"And the mailbox is a Green Bay helmet," added Stinky Smothers.

"Maybe we should drive around behind the house," suggested Nestor. "If Mr. Papadopoulos didn't want us to stop when that truck was here, he probably doesn't want *anyone* to know that we're here."

"Good thinking," agreed Coach Yak. "We'll park Woody behind that pole barn away from the street." Shifting the Suburban back in *Drive*, they moved slowly around to the back of Papa's airplane hangar.

"This should work," announced Coach Yak as he shut off the engine.

Piling out of the Chevy, they heard banging and followed the sound to the front of the metal pole barn. Waiting a moment for the banging to stop, Coach Yak pounded his meaty fist on the hangar doors.

After several seconds of silence, the metal doors slid open and there in front of them stood the old Greek pilot holding a hammer.

Smiling ear-to-ear, Papa opened his arms wide and shouted, "Hercules!"

....

A mile north of Moscow, Iowa, Mott Miller turned down his gravel driveway and stopped right in front of the family farmhouse. Maude climbed out.

"I'll start supper," called Maude, waving as the truck and trailer continued slowly toward the barn.

Pulling up to the barn doors, Mott got out, hooked his thumbs behind the straps of his bib overalls and looked up at the sky.

Deciding it looked like rain, he spit out his toothpick, opened the barn doors, flipped on the light and drove the truck, trailer and tractor inside. Climbing out of his pickup, he was greeted by a nosy goat, curious to see what was going on.

"How ya doin' there, Doris Day?" chirped Mott, giving his goat's ear a playful tug. "Where's that handsome boyfriend of yours, Rock Hudson?"

"Baaah," bleated Doris, nodding her head toward the tractor.

Mott smiled. "Yeah! We got a new tractor! Beauty, isn't she?"

The farmer stood there a few more seconds with his goat, the two of them admiring the new addition to the family.

"Now Doris, don't go munching on it like you did the old one. Understand?"

"Baaaaah," agreed Doris.

Giving his goat a pat on her furry head, Mott flipped off the light and walked out of the barn toward the house to wash up for supper.

Doris started to follow the farmer out when a flash caught her eye. Unable to resist, the goat walked over to the trailer and looked under the metal fender to see a small black box with a blinking red light.

Giving it a sniff, then a nudge with her nose, Doris licked her lips and wondered what a GL-300 GPS Tracker would taste like.

....

Sitting in the front passenger seat of the parked Hi-Tech Mobile Command Center, FBI/FD Agent Sanders was looking out of the window at a rusted *KW's Nuts & Stuff* sign nailed to an old fence. They were encamped next to a cornfield in Wilton, Iowa and he was getting restless.

"What's the status on the GL-300 Tracker now?" shouted Sanders to Probationary Agent Ness in the back.

"Still not moving," reported Elliot, his eyes glued to the monitor. "Our target is five miles southwest on...let's see...Moscow Road."

"Tell me if anything changes," ordered Sanders. "I'm gonna stretch my legs."

Opening the door, Agent Sanders stepped out onto the shoulder of the deserted gravel road. Seeing their boss outside, the other FBI/FD agents in the long line of black vehicles jumped out of their vehicles to get some fresh air, too.

On one side of the road was the cornfield, stretching as far as the eye could see. On the other side were some trees, the old fence with the rusted sign and a shack.

Listening to the crickets chirping, Agent Sanders was taking some deep breaths and watching the sun starting to set when a woman wearing a beat-up straw hat suddenly popped out of the shack and walked toward him with a pencil and a pad of paper.

"Hi, there," grunted the woman, not in a very friendly way, but not angry either. "What'll ya have?

"Have? I'm sorry. I don't understand what you're asking," apologized Agent Sanders.

The woman scratched her head with the pencil and then pointed at the rusted *KW's Nuts and Stuff* sign nailed to the fence.

"Well, you can order nuts...or else, if you don't want nuts, you can order some stuff," she explained with a hint of frustration.

"Are you KW?" asked Sanders.

The woman nodded, "In the flesh. Who are you?"

"My name is Sanders," answered the FBI/FD agent politely.

"Sanders! Any relation to that Colonel with the cute little white beard?" asked KW, suddenly showing her happy side.

"No. I'm no relation to Colonel Sanders."

"Huh, too bad. I do like his chicken," admitted KW. "So then... what will it be? Nuts or stuff?"

"Nothing for me, thank you. We're going to be back on the road here in a few minutes," explained Sanders.

"Well then, how about the rest of your friends?" asked KW, waving with her pencil at the row of black cars. "Maybe they'd like a snack before you get to that funeral you're heading to."

Before Agent Sanders could explain they weren't going to a funeral, the roar of a helicopter swooping in made them both look up.

Hovering in the sky above them, the black chopper was stirring up a cloud of dust as the aircraft surveyed the landscape before slowly descending across the road.

With her hand on her straw hat to keep it from blowing off her head, KW shouted above the roar of the engine, "Look there! A whirlybird's landing in Lester's cornfield!"

The instant the helicopter's skids touched the ground, the door flew open and Federal Bureau of Investigation Football Division Senior Special Agent Roman Noodle burst out of the chopper. Fighting his way through a few rows of corn, Noodle crossed the road to where Sanders and KW were standing.

With her pencil poised above her pad of paper, KW gave Noodle a nod. "What'll ya have?"

Special Agent Noodle looked at Sanders, confused. "What's she talking about?"

Agent Sanders pointed at the rusted *KW's Nuts & Stuff* sign nailed to the fence.

"She wants to know if you want to order some nuts or some stuff."

"Nonsense!" barked Noodle.

"Sorry. No nonsense. Just nuts and stuff," said KW.

Agent Sanders looked up to the sky and sighed. "Just order something and maybe she'll go away."

"Good idea," agreed Noodle. Then, counting the long line of black vehicles, he turned to the owner/manager/staff of *KW's Nuts & Stuff.*

"We'll have ten orders of nuts, please," Noodle puffed out gruffly.

"Just nuts? No stuff?" asked KW.

"That's right," spouted Noodle as he shooed her away with a wave of his hand.

KW walked off, scribbling on her pad of paper, mumbling as she wrote, "Ten orrr-ders of nuuuts." Then, stopping, she licked the tip of her pencil and looked back at the two men standing by the Mobile Command Center.

"Whose name should I put this order under?"

Noodle groaned and shook his head. "Put the order in my name. Senior Special Agent Roman Noodle. FBI/FD."

KW walked away, scribbling feverishly on the pad of paper. Abruptly she stopped, scratched her head and turned to the agents.

"How do you spell FBI?"

Noodle and Sanders blinked and looked back at her with their mouths slightly open.

"Well, never mind," clucked KW. "I don't need that part anyway." Tucking the pencil beside her ear, she turned and disappeared into the shack by the side of the road.

As soon as KW was gone, Sanders and Noodle hurried into the Mobile Command Center and joined Probationary Agent Ness at the computer.

"Anything to report Ness?" asked Sanders.

"No change," reported Elliot pointing at the blinking red light on the monitor. "Our target is holding steady five miles southwest on Moscow Road."

"It's been that way for over an hour, sir," said Sanders. "Should we move in?"

Roman Noodle scratched his square chin. "Let's wait here. We'll keep our eyes on that monitor. If there continues to be no change, we'll move in after dark."

"10-4," said Sanders, giving his superior a snappy salute. "What should we do about dinner, sir? The guys will be getting hungry."

Just then, they heard solid knocking on the door of the Mobile Command Center. Noodle spun and opened the door to see KW, holding the handles of a rusty red wheelbarrow piled high with peanuts.

"Got 'chur nuts!" crowed KW.

Noodle stood there, scratching his chin again, and then heaved a sigh. "On second thought, we're gonna need to some stuff to go with those nuts."

....

The seven visitors from Port Clinton had just removed the burlap bags from the six Hall of Fame Chicago Bear busts and they stood there looking at them lined up in a row in Papa's airplane hangar.

Hawk blinked and rubbed his eyes. "It's strange to see them here."

"You can say that again," said Michael.

"It's strange to see them here," repeated Hawk.

Nestor walked along the line, touching each Bear on the head and announcing their names. "George Musso, George Blanda, George Connor, George McAfee, George Trafton...George Halas."

"Hey! They're all named George!" hollered Stinky Smothers' brother.

"Yes. We take all Bears called George," said Papa sadly. "Now I am sorry for this."

"If you're sorry, why did you do it?" asked Killer.

"For my Packer heroes to be the most in the famed hall. *Gold to glory. Win this game the same old story.* These words I say, *gold to glory?*

This is Packer song we sing," explained Papa.

"But now I know Bears feel no joy here," Papa hobbled over to the smiling statue of George Halas and gave him a hug. "They feel joy at famed hall of honor with other football gods. Smashed and buried in cemetery is wrong."

"Wrong is right, old-timer," nodded Coach Yak as he bent down and picked up one of the Bears. "But, can't stay here chit-chatting. We need to put these guys in the truck and hit the road."

"C'mon, everybody...grab a statue and load 'em up!"

Stinky Smothers' brother ran over to George Halas and began wrestling with the legendary Bear.

"Sorry, no," said Papa, pulling Stinky Smothers' brother away. "This one is very special. It is my wish Hercules is guardian for getting him safe back home."

Michael gave the old aviation officer a snappy salute and moved in. Giving Papa Bear a bear hug, he lifted him off the ground.

Stinky Smothers' brother raced to the metal door to open it and out went Coach Yak followed by Michael, Nestor, Killer, Hawk and Stinky Smothers each carrying a Bear.

"Line 'em up," instructed Coach Yak, setting his Bear on the ground in front of the airplane hangar. "I'll go get Woody and we can load 'em from here."

As Yak disappeared around the metal pole barn, Michael noticed the old Greek pilot's tears.

"Why are you sad?" asked Michael with concern.

"I will miss my friends. Especially Papa Bear," said Papa, wiping his eyes with the sleeve of his shirt.

Then, pointing at the cemetery across the street, he continued, "But when they stay here, fate waits for them there. Escape with you gives the only hope."

"What will happen to you when the others find out?" asked Killer.

Papa shook his head. "This will make bad time for all. Squadron Leader Dan will be as Lyssa, the Greek spirit of mad rage and frenzy. First, he will be shouting like thunder to the heavens. Lightning bolts will burst from his eyes. From his ears will pour hot, molten lava."

Then he shrugged and added, "But...this is the way cookie makes crumbles."

"You're doing the right thing," encouraged Nestor. "Without you helping us get the Bears back, Michael would be going to prison!"

"No. Absolutely no! Fury from the gods!" insisted Papa. "Prison for me? Okay. Kicked out of *Pasteurized Brotherhood of Limburger Heads?* Oh, sure. But no prison for Hercules."

"I wish I could make lightning bolts come out of my eyes," sighed Stinky Smothers' brother.

Suddenly, Killer's eyes brightened. "Why don't you come with us?"

"Yeah! Come with us!" agreed Hawk.

Just then, Coach Yak appeared from the back corner of the air-plane hangar...walking!

"We're not going anywhere right now," announced the red-faced, super-sized coach. "Woody won't start!"

"Ahhhhgg," groaned everyone at the same time.

Papa scratched his chin. "You could borrow my truck..."

"That would be great!" cheered Hawk.

"One problem," continued Papa. "No truck."

"No truck?" asked Nestor.

"No truck," repeated Papa. "Just Aphrodite."

Nestor wrinkled his nose, "Aphrodite?"

"Yes, Aphrodite, my C-47 Sky Train," Papa nodded toward his cargo plane inside the hangar and smiled proudly. "She is old, but she is beautiful...you agree?"

"Yes, she *is* pretty," agreed Killer.

"You think that, that, that...*antique* can still fly?" asked Coach Yak, struggling to be polite.

"Sure! Sure! She fly good! Load Bears in and we go!" exclaimed Papa, waving his arms excitedly.

Coach Yak took a deep breath and shook his head. "I don't think so, Pops. I'm thinking it's better to keep this rescue mission on solid ground. Let me see if I can fix the truck and maybe we can leave in the morning. So, if it's okay to stay with you tonight…"

Papa gave Yak salute. "Sure-sure, stay here tonight is good. But Bears not to stay outside. We put inside again and cover up."

"What if they come after them tonight?" asked Hawk.

"No-no. Tonight we dig holes at cemetery," explained Papa, motioning across the street. "Tomorrow before Packer-Bear game, smash and bury!

"But!" continued Papa as he paused to look at his Packer wristwatch. "At 6 pm tomorrow, twenty-four hours from this second, Bears must be gone away or terrible-terrible tragedy is striking."

"This is exciting," cheered Stinky Smothers' brother.

"Okay! We got 24 hours to make this happen," announced Coach Yak. Then, with a clap of his hands, he added, "Let's get movin'!"

Immediately, the bunch of Braves bear-hugged the bronzed busts and hauled them inside the airplane hangar. Carefully placing them back in the corner, they covered them with the burlap bags.

"Good-good," nodded Papa. "Same as ever. My Limburger friends have no suspicions."

"All right, I guess I'll get to work on Woody," said Coach Yak, looking around the pole barn. "Can I borrow some of your tools?"

"Sure-sure," answered Papa. "Toolbox sits here. Rest of us come inside for dinner. You eat pizza?"

The Braves all let out a loud cheer and followed Papa to the house while Coach Yak grabbed the toolbox, closed the airplane hangar door and walked off to work on his truck.

Standing between the house and hangar, Stinky Smothers' brother looked at his friends going in the house and then at his coach.

"Save me some pizza," he yelled to the others. "I'm going with Coach Yak. He might need my help."

"Hey, Stinky," teased Killer as they entered the house. "That might be the last time we ever see your brother."

"Wow! Look at all the Green Bay stuff," exclaimed Hawk as he walked in Papa's living room, awed by the Packer posters, pennants and bobbleheads everywhere.

"Yes! I have beautiful home, no?" said Papa with a smile. With his cell phone in hand, he squinted at the number of Vince's Restaurant and Pizzeria he had scribbled on the wall.

"Two outside and one, two, three, four, five more," mumbled Papa, counting the group wandering around in his living room.

Scratching his chin, he looked at Nestor who was standing beside him and asked, "How many pizza to order? Six?"

Nestor pointed at Michael and held up two fingers.

Papa nodded, "Yes-yes, Hercules! You are right. Two-pizza bump. I order eight."

....

Henrietta Wozniak's kitchen was buzzing with activity. The little television on top of the refrigerator was showing Henrietta's favorite program, *Smackdown Live*, on The Wrestling Channel. On the stove, steam was rising from a pot Henrietta was stirring. Einstein Wozniak, working beside his mother at the counter, was laying out cabbage leaves on cookie sheets and putting baking dishes on the table, soon to be filled with scrumptiously-yummy stuffed cabbage rolls.

And, over by the door to the dining room, the old green rotary dial telephone was ringing off the wall.

Wiping his hands on his apron, Einstein walked to the phone and answered it. "Wozniak residence."

Through the earpiece, Dairy Dan's voice came roaring into the kitchen. "**Turn on ESPN!**"

Einstein opened his mouth, but before he could say anything the Limburger Head leader had hung up. Einstein grabbed the remote and flipped the channel.

"Dlaczego zmieniłeś kanał?" shouted Henrietta, waving her spoon. "Samoa Joe i Shinsuke Namamura będą walczyć dalej!" *Why did you change the channel? Samoa Joe and Shinsuke Namamura will wrestle next!*

Hit on his bald head with a clump of rice and ground beef flying from her wooden spoon, Einstein wiped it off with his thumb and patted his mother's shoulder.

"Don't worry, Matka. Dairy Dan insists I view this important announcement. I assure you...I will switch back to The Wrestling Channel in ample time for you to see Samoa Joe perform."

Henrietta huffed and went back to stirring her pot while Einstein, wringing his hands, looked at the TV on top of the refrigerator. He saw ESPN NFL Insider Adam Schefter, once again standing and talking in front of the Hall of Fame, so he turned up the volume.

"...we just received confirmation from an unnamed source that an FBI Football Division SWAT Team is closing in on those responsible for the theft of the six missing Chicago Bears, stolen from the Hall of Fame Gallery last week. NFL officials are hoping the busts will be recovered prior to tomorrow night's Bear-Packer game at Lambeau Field.

In the meantime, behind me, hundreds of Bear fans have been standing vigil outside the Hall of Fame, singing songs and carrying signs that say Bring Back Our Bears...I Heart George Halas...Goldilocks Did It!...and Cheese Stinks.

While the search for the missing Bears intensifies, it is a fact that, for the time being anyway, the Green Bay Packers have more players enshrined in the Pro Football Hall of Fame than any other team in the NFL.

Once again...it's being reported that a special FBI/Football Division SWAT Team is closing in on those responsible for stealing the Chicago Bear Hall of Fame statues...More to come on this story as it breaks...from Canton, Ohio, this is Adam Schefter, ESPN."

"Closing in?" mumbled Einstein. Distressed, he moved quickly to the kitchen window and looked out, searching for any activity.

"Zmienic kanał!" demanded Henrietta, waving her wooden spoon again. *Change the channel!*

His heart pounding fast, Einstein grabbed the TV remote off the counter and changed the channel in time for his mother to see Samoa Joe use his signature wrestling match move, *the Muscle Buster,* on his helpless opponent.

Watching the referee step into the middle of the ring and raise Samoa Joe's arm over his head, Henrietta shouted "Bravo!" and did a little Polish click step, while her son continued looking out the kitchen window with a worried expression on his face.

....

Looking out Papa's window, with a worried expression on his face, Michael's stomach was grumbling. "My belly wants to know why is the pizza taking so long?"

"Relax, Michael. The pizza place said 30 minutes," answered Nestor.

"It's been twenty-nine minutes now," complained Michael, looking at the big Packer clock on the wall.

Papa popped out of the kitchen with a stack of Packer paper plates and napkins and put them in the middle of the dining room table.

"Do you need help, Mr. Papadopoulos?" asked Killer politely.

"Thank you….uh…uh…well, I know you are called Killer by football boys, but what does your mama call you?" asked Papa with a twinkle in his eye.

My name is Kathryn…my mom calls me Kathy. But it's okay if you call me Killer."

Papa scratched his chin and thought for a moment. "Oh…why these boys say Killer? *Kah-tee* is beautiful name."

The quarterback smiled. "Once I punched a boy on the playground. He was picking on my little brother…

"After that, a lot of the boys started calling me Killer. And now, since I'm on the football team, I kind of like it."

"I see," nodded Papa. "Okay then, you like it…fine by me. I call you Killer, too."

"The pizza person is here!" shouted Michael, as he watched Vince's Pizza van pull in the driveway.

Papa peeked out the front window to see Vince's son, Junior, struggling to carry the eight-box stack. "Everybody in kitchen, and no talk, okay? This being a secret. If Squadron Leader Dan finds out… much-much trouble."

Michael, Nestor, Killer, Stinky Smothers and Hawk quickly and quietly slipped into the kitchen just as the doorbell rang.

Papa, looking back over shoulder first to make sure the coast was clear, opened the door and greeted the delivery person with a smile.

"Junior! Come in-come in!"

"Got your pizzas, Mr. Papadopoulos," huffed Junior out of breath and sticking his neck out around the pile of pizzas stacked in front of his face.

"Here-here, put down on chair," instructed Papa.

Junior placed his load on Papa's favorite recliner, sucked in a bunch of air. "Whew! Lucky for you I didn't crash on your sidewalk."

"Yes-yes…lucky for me," nodded Papa as he handed Junior three $20 bills. "Here. You keep change."

Junior cleared his throat. "Well actually, Mr. Papadopoulos, you owe me $5 more."

"Okay for you. I get more money," replied Papa, holding up a finger.

Then, grabbing a jar of change on the shelf by the television, Papa began dropping quarters in Junior's outstretched hand.

"You sure ordered a lot of pizzas, Mr. Papadopoulos. You having a party?"

"3-75…4-dollar…4-25…No-no…no party here," said Papa as he continued counting. "You know how they say it…pizza in the refrigerator is same as money in bank."

"They do?" asked Junior.

"4-75…FIVE-DOLLARS!" announced Papa. Then plunking down another quarter in Junior's palm he added. "And here, two-bits for you!"

As soon as the door closed and before Papa could yell, "Coast is clear," Michael was sitting at the table with his napkin in his lap.

By the time everyone else sat down, he was on his second piece of pizza. And, ten minutes later when Coach Yak came lumbering in the house, his Ohio State football jersey covered with greasy handprints, Michael had finished one entire pizza by himself.

"Where's my brother?" asked Stinky Smothers.

"Who?" snorted Yak.

"My brother!" repeated Stinky Smothers.

"Oh yeah..." Yak shook his head sadly. "I got a little tired of him talking and smearing grease all over."

"So-so wh-what did you do?" stammered Hawk.

Coach Yak grabbed a paper plate and sat down at the end of the table. "I told him - since the team back home was working out - this would be a good time for conditioning. I told him to run up and down that little road out back. He'll show up in a minute or two."

"This is my runway," said Papa, passing a pizza box to the Coach Yak. "I have runway behind hangar for Aphrodite."

"Runway? That's perfect!" chuckled the big coach as he took his first bite. "He's running on the runway!"

"Is the truck fixed now?" asked Nestor.

Coach Yak shook his head and waited to swallow the big bite of pizza before he spoke. "No...but I'll get working on it again. First thing in the morning."

At that moment, Stinky Smothers' brother burst through the front door, huffing and puffing.

"I did it, Coach! Ten times up and down that road!"

"This is my runway," corrected Papa.

"Right! I run way up and down it ten times," said Stinky Smothers' brother, as he sat down at the table next to Michael.

Before plopping a piece of pizza on his Packer paper plate, he studied it for a couple of seconds, then wrinkled his nose.

"This plate's okay. But do you have any with *Wreck-It Ralph* on it?"

"You better hurry up and eat before it's all gone," grumbled Stinky Smothers. "Michael is already on his second one."

"His second piece?" asked Stinky Smothers' brother as he took a bite.

"His second pizza!" crowed Hawk.

Everyone at the table burst out laughing, except Nestor, who was not laughing at all. He took a drink of milk and looked at his coach.

"What will we do if you can't fix it?"

Everyone at the table suddenly stopped laughing and even eating. Seconds passed in silence with everyone at the table looking at each other.

Coach Yak pulled out Agent Noodle's business card and studied it.

"I don't know," sighed Coach Yak as he shoved the card back in his pocket. "But don't worry. No one's going to prison. We'll figure it out."

"Yes-yes," agreed Papa. "We figure something. Now, eat-eat!"

"Good idea," said Michael as he opened another pizza box and piled three more pieces onto his plate.

....

It was 10:15 pm and the floor around Probationary Agent Elliot Ness was covered with peanut shells as he munched away, keeping his bleary eyes glued to the blinking red light on the monitor.

A few feet away, stretched out in on the Mobile Command Center sofa, KW was snoozing and smiling after having the biggest sales day in the 22-year history of KW's Nuts & Stuff.

Hearing the sound of crunchy footsteps, Elliot turned to see Agents Noodle and Sanders standing over his shoulder.

"What's the status on the GL-300 Tracker?" whispered Noodle, so as not to disturb KW.

"No movement, sir," answered Elliot with a quick nod at the monitor.

Noodle took a deep breath. "Confirm our distance to the target."

"Five miles southwest, Moscow Road."

Noodle looked at his watch. "Mobilize the team. We'll move in and secure the perimeter. We'll leave the chopper hidden in the cornfield."

"What about her? Should we wake her up?" asked Sanders pointing at KW.

Agent Noodle sighed. "Do you want to hear more stories about her cat spitting up hairballs or her six-toed cousin Cindy?"

Both Sanders and Elliot shook their heads firmly.

"Me, either," agreed Noodle. "Carry her outside. Put her in her wheelbarrow. Cover her with a blanket. Then roll her up to her shack and let's get moving. We've got to find those Bears or we'll be finding new jobs."

....

Papa, who gave up his bedroom to Killer, was sound asleep in his favorite recliner when his Packer wristwatch alarm beeped at 11:33 pm.

The noise woke Nestor, who was stretched out in an army surplus sleeping bag on the living room floor along with Michael, Hawk and the Smothers brothers. The massive Coach Yak was squashed up on the sofa and snoring.

"Pssst! Mr. Papadopoulos...your alarm is beeping," whispered Nestor, tapping the old man gently.

Papa blinked his eyes, then suddenly bolted out of his chair. "Sorry-sorry!" coughed Papa, slapping his wrist to stop the beeping.

"What's going on?" yawned Michael, lifting his head off his pillow.

"All okay, Hercules. Close eyes," insisted Papa. "Limburger Heads coming soon to dig holes in cemetery."

"Cemetery?" mumbled Hawk, still half asleep.

"No worry. I put on shoes and wait on porch," said Papa shuffling to the bench by the front door. "You stay and rest. My friends must not see you are here to save Bears. Okay?"

Nestor, Michael and Hawk nodded as they watched the old Greek pilot tie his shoes and put on his Packer jacket.

"You see 'em!" whispered Papa as he quietly opened the door and stepped out.

Nestor, instead of slipping back in his sleeping bag, went to the window and peeked around the shade.

"What's happening?" asked Hawk.

"Nothing. He's just sitting on the porch looking at the cemetery across the street," answered Nestor. Then, heaving a heavy sigh, he added, "You know what I think we should do?"

"I'm afraid to ask," groaned Hawk.

"Me, too," agreed Michael.

....

It was nearly midnight and fifty FBI/FD agents - 51 counting Probationary Agent Elliot Ness - were on their hands and knees crawling through a dark, dirty cornfield, closing in on the signal being sent by the GL-300 Tracker.

Finally reaching the edge of the cornfield, Agent Sanders, who was monitoring the blinking red light on his special FBI/FD shoe phone app, whispered into the speaker of his SWAT Team helmet.

"Target within 150 yards. Spread out along cornfield perimeter and maintain position. Over."

Sanders, seconds after signing off, was joined by Elliot and Senior Special Agent Roman Noodle, crawling up on either side of him.

"Target is in that white barn, dead ahead," reported Sanders.

"NVG-7 night vision goggles," ordered Noodle.

Instantly, Elliot reached into his backpack and pulled out what looked like a camera with binoculars attached and he slapped the device in his boss's outstretched hand.

Noodle gloated as he viewed the well-kept farm through his hi-tech goggles. "So, you kids and your extra-large coach thought you'd pull a fast one and hide out in a barn in Iowa, huh?

"Tellin' us some wild story about Limburger Heads and stink bombs. Well, let me tell you…the day a bunch of juvenile pipsqueaks pulls the wool over old Noodle's nose…is the day I turn in my FBI/FD NVG-7 night vision goggles."

"Should I give the order to conduct a search?" asked Sanders.

"No…let's wait 'em out," answered Noodle. "First time we see any activity around that barn, we nab 'em *bear-handed* and finish this thing."

"But they're just kids," said Elliot sadly.

Lowering the night vision goggles and letting them dangle by the strap around his neck, Noodle took a deep breath.

"For the last time, Probationary Agent Ness…somebody's got to go to prison."

At that moment, a rooster jumped up on the fence by the barn and let out a very loud ***Cock-A-Doodle-Doo!***

"11:59 pm…" mumbled Noodle, looking at his watch. "That cock's clock is a little off.

CHAPTER 12

September 2 – Midnight Monroe Wisconsin
19 Hours to Kickoff at Lambeau Field

Papa was pushing a wheelbarrow full of shovels toward his front porch when he saw the headlights headed his way.

Dairy Dan's pickup pulled in the driveway first, followed by Helmut and Nick and Rick Monroe in the Chalet Cheese Co-op delivery truck. Right behind them was Floyd, driving his Cavalier with Einstein in the passenger seat.

Snapping to attention, Papa saluted Dairy Dan as he stepped out of his truck. "Demetri Papadopoulos, ready to dig."

"STC! Seize The Cheese," said Dairy Dan, giving Papa a salute back.

With a yawn, Rick Monroe walked over to the wheelbarrow. "Let's get this over, so I can go back to bed."

One by one, the Limburger Heads shuffled over to Papa and the wheelbarrow and grabbed a shovel. Everyone except for Einstein, who was still standing by Floyd's Cavalier staring at the airplane hangar.

Floyd held up his shovel and waved it in Einstein's direction. But instead of joining the rest of the Pasteurized Brotherhood, he started walking quickly toward the airplane hangar.

"Hey, Wozniak! Where you going?" shouted Dairy Dan.

Without answering, Einstein disappeared inside the hangar, leaving the rest of the Limburger Heads in the driveway, scratching their sleepy heads.

"You guys wait here," huffed Dairy Dan, limping off in his ankle boot. "I'll go see what this is about."

300

Handing his shovel to Floyd, Papa followed Dairy Dan. "I go, too. Just in cases."

By the time the two of them hobbled to the hangar door, Einstein was coming out huffing and puffing with George Halas in his arms.

"It's imperative we destroy the evidence tonight," huffed Einstein, as he set Papa Bear down on the driveway. "If you would please assist me with the rest."

"Whoa-whoa, hold on," exclaimed Dairy Dan, grabbing his friend before he could go back in.

"Whoa-whoa," agreed Papa.

"You know the plan!" grumbled Dairy Dan. "It's *your* plan!"

"Yes! You know plan," nodded Papa.

"I've come to the conclusion the plan is in desperate need of an adjustment," insisted Einstein. "News reports indicate the authorities are closing in on us."

"Relax, Einstein. That big brain of yours is overheating," explained Dairy Dan. "Look around…do you see anyone closing in on us?"

They all stood there silently and listened to the crickets.

Dairy Dan shook his head. "There's no one here 'cept us Limburger Heads. Now, take a deep breath and let's go dig…as planned."

Floyd walked over to Einstein and handed him a shovel. "C'mon, Albert."

Einstein took a deep breath, pulled a flashlight out of his jacket pocket and the two of them started off toward the cemetery, leaving Papa Bear smiling at the airplane hangar door.

Rick ran over and picked up the statue. "I'll put this Bear back inside with the others. You guys go. I'll catch up."

"Good-good," said Papa, giving Rick a pat on the back. "You carry with care."

Rick disappeared inside the hangar as the rest of the Limburger Heads trudged across the street.

A full moon was out and the trees and gravestones were casting long, mysterious shadows. An owl hooted and swooped low, looking for a midnight snack.

"Hey, Floyd…you thought this place was spooky during the day," chuckled Dairy Dan. "How do you like it at night?"

Floyd shivered. "I'll be okay as long as that dog doesn't…" Before he could finish, the eerie sound of a dog howling burst through the chilly night air.

"**Oooooooooooooooooooooowhoo!**"

"O-o-okay, I admit it. I'm s-s-scared," gurgled Floyd, his hands shaking.

"That's Cheese Master Harvarti's old dog, Monterey Jack," said Helmut softy. "They say he comes out here every night and cries at his grave."

"Every night," nodded Papa. "Like clockworking. Get ready. He go again."

"**Oooooooooooooooooooooowhoo!**" howled Monterey Jack right on cue.

Einstein pointed the flashlight in the direction of the howl and there, some fifty feet in front of them, sat a sad-looking brown and tan bloodhound right next to a huge gravestone shaped like a cheese wedge.

"Shine the light down there," ordered Dairy Dan, pointing down a little hill from where Monterey Jack was holding vigil.

Following orders, Einstein directed the beam down at a clear, grassy area.

"That's it! That's the spot we picked out this afternoon," confirmed Dairy Dan.

"I told ole Harvey he was going to get some Hall of Fame company," chuckled Dairy Dan as he counted out steps and pounded six wooden stakes in the ground.

Taking off his jacket, Dairy Dan stepped up to the first stake and spit on his hands, "Okay, pick out your spot and let's get diggin'."

Putting his good foot on the edge of his spade, Dairy Dan plunged the point into the soft sod.

"**Oooooooooooooooooooooowhoo!**" wailed Monterey Jack.

"Stinkin' Bishop, how long can he keep that up?" shivered Floyd as he tossed his first shovelful of dirt over his shoulder.

Rick Monroe, who had just that moment jogged down the hill and joined the group, was greeted with a face full of rich, sandy loam.

"Watch it, Floyd!" complained Rick, spitting out chunks of earth.

"Whoops! Sorry, Rick! I didn't see you there," apologized Floyd. "But it does remind me of a kid I knew who used to eat dirt."

"That was me," admitted Dairy Dan. "But I don't do that anymore."

"Did you successfully complete your assignment, Mr. Monroe?" asked Einstein, stopping to wipe the sweat off his bald head with a handkerchief.

"Yup!" nodded Rick as he started digging alongside his dad. "I covered up Mr. Halas and put him back in the corner with the others where he belongs."

"Hall of Football Fame is where he belongs," muttered Papa under his breath.

"What'd you say Papa?" asked Dairy Dan, while continuing to dig.

"Oooooooooooooooooooooowhoo!" wailed Monterey Jack again.

Papa coughed and cleared his throat. "I ask how deep we dig hall of fame hole?"

"The official depth of a grave should be exactly 1.83 meters," informed Einstein.

"Did anyone bring their meter stick?" snarked Nick.

Dairy Dan jabbed his shovel in the ground and grunted. "Four feet should be plenty deep."

All of a sudden, instead of the dirt coming out of the hole Dairy Dan was digging, dirt started flying back *into* the hole.

"Hey! What's going on here?" yelled the Limburger Head leader.

Turning to look behind him, he discovered Monterey Jack with his front paws furiously attacking the ground near Dairy Dan, sending chunks of earth high up in the air.

"Look! He's helping us," said Rick.

"He can have my shovel if he wants," offered Floyd.

Then, just as suddenly as Monterey Jack began digging, he stopped. Lifting his head, the bloodhound sniffed the air, his tail at attention.

"What is it, boy? Is something the matter?" asked Helmut.

Monterey Jack, following his nose, walked back up the slope toward Harvey Havarti's cheese wedge monument.

"Ma-ma-ma-maybe he's hearing the ghost of ole Harvey calling," stammered Floyd.

"Whoo-whoo..." hooted the owl from an oak tree silhouetted by the moon.

"Harvey Havarti," repeated Floyd, answering the owl's question.

The Limburger Heads watched Monterey Jack as he poked his head behind Harvey's gravestone.

Helmut took a deep breath and swallowed hard.

"Maybe he *does* hear Old Man Havarti talking to him."

Monterey Jack took a couple more steps behind the huge, cheese wedge monument and all that could be seen of him was his wagging tail.

"Floyd! Find out what he's doing," ordered Dairy Dan.

Floyd shook his head. "No way! What if it's Harvey stickin' his skull out of the ground mad about all the noise we're making?!"

"I'll go see," volunteered Nick as he started up the hill, holding his shovel for protection.

But before Nick could make it halfway up the slope, Monterey Jack popped out from behind the cheese wedge made of stone and walked back toward the Limburger Heads chewing.

"What's he got in his mouth?" asked Helmut. "Did he dig up some body parts?"

Floyd, horrified, covered his eyes. "I can't look!"

Monterey Jack, his tail still wagging, walked back to the hole he was digging and dropped a narrow strip of meat on the ground and started licking it.

All the Limburger Heads, except Floyd who had his eyes closed, gathered around Monterey Jack and bent down to get a closer look.

Helmut sniffed the air. "You know what I think? I think it's..."

"Bacon," announced Dairy Dan, finishing Helmut's sentence.

"Bacon?" blurted out Floyd, uncovering his eyes. "I LOVE bacon!"

"For the love of Lombardi! Where did he get bacon out here in a cemetery?" grumbled Dairy Dan, scratching his head.

Before the question could be answered, a rustling sound came from the direction of Harvey's cheese wedge monument. Suddenly the owl swooped down from the nearby oak tree and flew off into the night with something clenched in its talons.

"Did you see that?" asked Helmut, his head snapping around. "That owl had a piece of bacon, too!"

Then, before anybody could say anything about *that*, another sound and some scuffling came from behind Harvey's grave and Nick's head snapped in the other direction.

"Look! Over there!" shouted Nick. "Kids! Running!"

"There are no kids out here!" huffed Dairy Dan. "It's just your imagination."

"I don't have an imagination," replied Nick.

"Just as I suspected," groaned Einstein. "It's the authorities closing in on us!"

"Authorities? You mean the police? Ha!" scoffed Dairy Dan.

"We're doomed! Operation Georgie Porgie is in peril!" wailed Einstein.

"Everybody, calm down," insisted Dairy Dan. "C'mon! Let's dig these holes and get out of here. Tomorrow, before the game, we'll come back and finish the job."

"Tell you what, Albert…how 'bout this? I'll stay at Papa's and stand guard," volunteered Floyd. "No one goes in. No one goes out. If I see anything suspicious, I'll sound the alarm."

"Good idea," agreed Dairy Dan. Then, throwing his arm around Einstein's shoulders, he added, "Now there, doesn't that make you feel better?"

"No-no…*I* stand guard, Squadron Leader Dan," offered Papa. "In Greek army, I am excellent guard."

Dairy Dan laughed, "When was that? 60 years ago? No, Papa. You've done your duty."

"I take duty again," pleaded Papa.

"You get your rest," insisted Dairy Dan. "Floyd can do it."

"We're doomed," repeated Einstein as everyone went back to their digging.

Licking his bacon-flavored chops, Monterey Jack walked slowly back up the little hill and put his hindquarters squarely down next to Harvey Havarti's huge cheese wedge gravestone. After a few seconds of watching the bumbling bunch of Limburger Heads toss dirt in every direction, he looked up into the moonlit sky and let everyone know how he felt.

"**Ooooooooooooooooooooooowhoo!**"

....

Sweaty and muddy and dead tired, the Limburger heads trudged out of a foggy Greenwood Cemetery, dragging their shovels behind them.

Dairy Dan looked at his Packer wristwatch as he limped toward his pickup parked in Papa's driveway. 5:05 am.

"Okay, meet back here at 4 this afternoon. We'll drag the Bears to the graveyard, bust 'em up and bury 'em. Then, we'll celebrate the successful finish of Operation Georgie Porgie when we go to Baumgartner's for kickoff!"

"Go Pack Go...", yawned Rick Monroe, giving a tired cheer.

"Oh, I almost forgot," grunted Dairy Dan, stopping just before he crawled up in his truck. "Helmut...if you have any stink bombs left, bring 'em. We'll bury them with the Bears and get rid of all the evidence."

Helmut nodded and waved his hand above his head.

"STC! Seize the Cheese!" crowed Dairy Dan.

"Seize the Cheese!" repeated the Limburger Heads.

A second later, Dairy Dan and Einstein in the Ford pickup and Helmut, Nick and Rick in the Chalet Cheese Co-op delivery truck, pulled onto 18th Street and disappeared into the fog, leaving Papa and Floyd standing in the driveway.

"Floyd...you go, too. Get rest," insisted the old Greek pilot. "I take guard duty. No one gets past Papa."

Floyd shook his head. "No Papa…you go in the house and sleep."

"But…"

"No buts Papa. I've got this! I'll just park my Chevy in front of your barn, stretch out nice and comfy in the front seat. I might even practice playin' my tuba."

Papa took a couple of steps toward the house, then stopped to watch Floyd parallel park his vehicle just inches from the airplane hangar, completely blocking the entrance.

Sadly, Papa turned and walked with his head down to his house. Arriving at the porch he stopped again, this time to study dozens of muddy footprints leading to his front door.

....

"Cock-A-Doodle-Doo!" crowed the rooster, greeting the 5am sun as it peeked over the Millers' farmhouse.

Senior Special Agent Roman Noodle, crabby from spending the past five hours crouched in a cornfield with his team of FBI/FD agents, looked at his watch and shook his head.

"Every ten minutes, like clockwork. All. Night. Long. Sanders! Dispatch a death squad and terminate that bird."

With a nod, Agent Sanders lowered the microphone on his helmet and started talking. "Agents Cassius, Marcus and Brutus…Special Assignment Code 13…"

"Whoa-whoa-whoa," interrupted Noodle. "What are you doing?"

"I'm dispatching the death squad to terminate that rooster," said Sanders.

"C'mon, Sanders. I wasn't serious."

Sanders' jaw dropped. "You were joking?"

Noodle scratched his chin and thought about it for a moment. "Yeah, how 'bout that? I made a joke."

"Good one, Senior Special Agent Noodle, sir," complimented Ness, happy the rooster was going to live to crow another day.

"Cock-A-Doodle-Doo!" added the rooster, flapping its wings.

At that moment, a light came on in the Miller farmhouse.

"Hey, look!" whispered Elliot. "Someone's up!"

"Good!" growled Noodle, rubbing his hands together. "What is the status of the GL-300 Tracker?"

Agent Sanders took off his shoe, slid the heel forward and checked the screen on his phone. "It still shows the target is located in the barn dead ahead. Confidence the missing Bears are inside *extremely high*."

"Okay, spread the word. The first time there's any movement in or out of that barn, we rush down and surround the place! Understood?"

Sanders and Elliot gave a salute and crawled off to alert the other FBI/FD agents snoozing in the cornfield.

Senior Special Agent Roman Noodle rubbed his hands together again, this time to generate a little heat.

Smiling, he mumbled to himself, "I made a joke..."

....

Killer covered her ears with her bed pillow and shouted to her teammates camped down the hall in Papa's living room. "Turn the sound down...it's too loud!"

Then, looking at the clock on the night stand, she bolted out of bed, threw her robe over her pink *Born to Stand Out* flamingo pajamas and flew out of the bedroom.

"Hey! Why didn't someone wake me up! It's past noon!"

At that moment, seven pairs of eyes blinked open and the sounds of yawns and heads lifting off pillows were coming from every corner.

"Good morning," greeted Hawk with a sleepy, smile.

"It's not morning anymore," announced Killer, pointing at the clock on the wall.

Coach Yak rolled off the sofa and scrambled for his shoes. "Oh no!" I gotta get out there and work on Woody. We need to hit the road!"

Nestor sat up in his army surplus sleeping bag and looked around the room. "What's all that noise?"

"No, not noise. Music," said Papa as he shuffled off to look out the window. "This is Comrade Limburger Head Floyd playing tuba. Look."

Immediately, everyone crowded around Papa and peeked out to see Floyd, sitting on the hood of his Cavalier, happily huffing and puffing on his tuba.

"You call that music?" muttered Michael.

"*Flying Car Polka*...just only tuba part. She is a very pretty song when all of band plays," explained Papa.

"How am I gonna fix the truck with him out there?" asked Yak.

Papa scratched his chin. After a couple of seconds, his index finger popped up. "I have idea. I take coffee to Floyd as for distraction. When he looks other way, you tippy-toes past."

"I don't know," frowned Yak. "I'm not that good at tippy-toes."

"Sure-sure...you tippy-toes," assured Papa, giving the 400-pound coach a pat on the back before shuffling off to make coffee.

"Time for breakfast," said Michael, following Papa right into the kitchen.

"It's past noon...it's lunchtime," objected Stinky Smothers.

"Maybe for you, but I'm not skipping breakfast," insisted Michael.

"I'm with you Michael!" chirped Stinky Smothers' brother as he turned to follow the hungry Hapburn. "You know what they say, breakfast is the importantest meal of the day."

Michael shook his head, "*They* don't know."

"Whaddya mean?" blinked Stinky Smothers' brother.

"*Every* meal is the most important meal of the day," declared Michael as the two disappeared into the kitchen.

Nestor sighed and sat down next to Coach Yak on the sofa where he was tying his shoes.

"I know I asked this before, but what if you can't fix the truck?"

Coach Yak reached in his pocket, pulled out Agent Noodle's business card again and handed it to Nestor. "If all else fails, we'll throw a *Hail Mary* and call the FBI," answered Coach Yak.

"FBI/*FD*," noted Nestor, handing it back.

"Right...*FD*," nodded the coach. "But it's gonna be our last-ditch, desperation move. We got ourselves in this mess and I want to get out of it by ourselves."

Nestor swallowed the lump in his throat. "Do you think we can?"

"Sure we can! What have I been saying all along?"

Nestor shrugged. "You mean about us being a team?"

Coach Yak nodded and smiled. "That's right! We're a team! T-E-A-M. T for TOGETHERNESS. E for EFFORT. A for ATTI-TUDE. and M..."

"M for MENTAL TOUGHNESS," added Nestor.

"Exactly!" agreed Yak. "We're going to get those Bears back to the Hall of Fame...we're going to win a state championship...and no one's going to prison!"

Papa walked back into the living room, carrying a plastic Packer travel mug, with Killer on his heels holding a small plate with chunks of cheddar cheese and a leftover piece of babka cake.

"Okey-dokey, you ready, Coach?"

"Ready," nodded Yak. "What's the plan?"

"I go out front door with coffee, cheese and cake...you go out *back* door. When I point at cemetery across street, you tippy-toes to truck," instructed Papa.

"Got it," said Coach Yak, grunting as he got up off the sofa and grabbed his Ohio State ball cap from the coffee table.

Papa tucked the travel mug under one arm and Killer handed him the plate and opened the door for him.

"You see 'em," he chirped as he stepped out on his front porch.

....

Coach Yak, hiding at the corner of the house, had his eyes glued on Papa as he shuffled down the driveway.

Floyd, still sitting on the hood of his red Chevy, happily huffing and puffing on tuba in the bright noonday sun...*OOM-PAH-OOM-PAH-PAH*...didn't notice the old Greek aviation carrying refreshments until he popped up right in front of him.

"Stinkin' Bishop! How nice!" chirped Floyd as he set his tuba on the ground beside him.

"No-no, no Stinkin' Bishop...I bring *cheddar*," corrected Papa. "And babka cake and coffee."

"Whoa! Are you up to something, Papa?" said Floyd playfully.

"Wa-wa-why you thinking this?" stammered Papa.

Floyd reached out for the treats and gave Papa a wink, "You know what they say...*beware of Greeks bearing gifts.* Get it?"

"Oh-oh, yes, trojan horse. Very funny. I am Greek and I bring you gifts," chuckled Papa nervously.

"They also say, *beware of dog*," added Papa, pointing at the cemetery across the street.

Seeing the signal, Coach Yak, all 400-pounds of him, quickly and quietly tippy-toed past the two Limburger Heads while they had their backs turned to the hangar.

"Beware of dog? Oh yeah, Monterey Jack," mumbled Floyd. "I still can't figure where he got that bacon."

"Bacon from pig," explained Papa. "Sometimes from turkey."

Floyd grabbed a hunk of cheddar cheese and tossed it in his mouth. "It's kinda spooky that dog hanging around Havarti's grave like that."

"Yeah-yeah, spooky," nodded Papa. "Speak of hang around...you no stay now. Go home. Rest up for big night. I guard Bears."

"No, I'm good," insisted Floyd, chewing on cheese and smacking his lips. "I got a text from Dairy Dan saying the guys are coming early. They'll be here at two o'clock."

Papa gasped. "Two o'clock? Why?"

Floyd took a gulp of coffee and wiped his mouth with his sleeve. "Yeah, two! He said Albert's all worried we're gonna get caught *bear-handed.* He won't be happy 'til we finish Operation Georgie Porgie."

Suddenly feeling weak, Papa leaned on Floyd's car.

"Wh-wh-when Squadron Leader Dan coming?"

"Soon. He wants to give me time to go home and clean up before the game tonight." Floyd popped the last bite of babka cake in mouth and kept talking.

"I can't wait for the game tonight! Our Packers are going to make those Bears wish they'd never been born! Go Pack Go!"

"Sure-sure, Go Pack Go," sighed Papa, brushing crumbs of flying babka cake off his face. "I go now to get ready. Big night tonight."

"Big night is right!" chirped Floyd.

Then, handing the plate and Packer travel mug to Papa, Floyd hoisted his tuba and went back to huffing and puffing. With the lively melody of the *Flying Car Polka* ringing in his ears, Papa shuffled back to his porch and into his house.

In a daze, he walked past Nestor, Hawk and Killer watching Sports Center in the living room and trudged into his kitchen, where Michael had finished with breakfast and was just starting lunch.

Sitting down at the table next to him, Papa put his head in his hands and groaned. "Oh, Hercules...we have more trouble."

....

With Sports Center on in the background, Nestor was nosing around looking at the collection of Packer posters and souvenirs Papa had jammed-packed in his living room. Killer was studying the Braves playbook and texting. Hawk, sitting next to the cute quarterback on the couch, was thinking out loud.

"I know we have a lot of stuff to worry about, but since we're so close to Lambeau Field, it would be fun to go over there. Actually, I'd like to visit a LOT of stadiums, wouldn't you?"

"Sure," answered Nestor, while he studied an autographed Bart Starr jersey hanging on the wall."

"I wasn't talking to you, dufus head," grumbled Hawk.

Ignoring his brother's snipe, Nestor moved on to a collection of Packer bobbleheads lined up in a china cabinet.

Hawk cleared his throat and started talking louder.

"Stadiums are really interesting, don't you think...ah...Killer?"

Hawk waited for Killer to stop texting on her phone and answer his question. When she did not, he took a deep breath and rambled on.

"But I like a lot of things besides stadiums. I like sports and movies, caramel corn and mosquito bites..."

"Mosquito bites?" repeated Killer not looking up from her phone.

Hawk smiled. "I was just checking to see if you were listening to me."

"Of course, I'm listening," replied Killer. "I just wanted to finish texting your mom."

"Oh!" cried Nestor. "I forgot about that! Mom's gonna be mad!"

"Don't worry...I've been texting her every time I text my parents," Killer informed him.

"Did you tell them all the truck was broke and we're stuck here?" asked Nestor.

"No. I didn't want them to worry. Here's what I said."

Killer passed her phone to Hawk and he read the text out loud. "Found the Bears. All good. Plan to drive home today. I'll text again later. I think Hawk wants to marry me."

"Hey! Why'd you say that?" groaned Hawk, his face turning red.

"That's funny," chuckled Nestor.

"I was just asking if maybe someday you wanted to get married... to...ah, ya know...to someone," said Hawk shrugging his shoulders.

As he was handing the phone back to Killer, a text tone rang out.

"Hey, she just wrote back," chirped Killer as she pushed the text icon on her phone.

Bears found - hooray! Safe travels.
Hawk wants to marry u? Cute! See u soon!

Killer was just about to read it out loud when an ESPN Special Bulletin popped up, turning everyone's attention to the television.

"Good afternoon. I'm Adam Schefter reporting from Canton, Ohio with breaking news on the six missing Bear Hall of Fame busts."

"Papa! You need to see this," shouted Nestor.

"Coming-coming," yelled Papa from the kitchen.

"Look!" said Nestor, pointing at the television.

"The Chicago Bears have issued a statement blaming their longtime rival, the Green Bay Packers, for the disappearance of the busts of their six legendary Bears named George, including team founder, owner and longtime coach George 'Papa Bear' Halas.

According to the statement, team officials are convinced this is the work of agents operating on behalf of the Packer organization in order to secure the bragging rights for having the most players enshrined in the Hall of Fame.

The statement goes on to say that if the missing Bears are not found and returned prior to the kickoff of tonight's Green Bay–Chicago football game at Lambeau Field, the Bears will refuse to take the field for the NFL's season opener. We'll have more on this ticking bombshell as details unfold. Adam Schefter, ESPN."

Hawk picked up the remote and shut the TV off. "This isn't good."

"No," moaned Papa. "Truck broke. Squadron Leader Dan and guys coming soon to break and bury Bears. Bears blaming Packers. No football game tonight. No, this is bad. Very, very, very bad."

Nestor looked outside to where Floyd guarding the entrance to the airplane hangar and blowing into his tuba. "What should we do?"

"If Coach can't fix the truck, there's only one thing we can do," declared Killer.

"Right," nodded Nestor. "We'll have to ask for help from those FBI Football guys."

"No! Not that mean Noodle guy! He wants to put me in prison!" howled Michael.

"It's going to be okay. I'm sure of it," cheered Hawk, trying to convince himself. "Any second now, Coach is going to come through the back door and yell: I FIXED THE TRUCK...LOAD UP THE BEARS AND LET'S GET OUT OF HERE!"

And at that very moment, they heard the back door burst open. The massive, hot and sweaty Coach Yak rumbled into the living room and shook his head. "I can't fix the truck!"

....

In her kitchen, Henrietta Wozniak was loading piping hot cabbage rolls into three Green Bay Packer heavy-duty Coleman coolers with wheels. Happy in her work, she was singing the Packers' fight song in Polish.

"How are you doing, Momma? You need any help?" asked Einstein as he walked into the kitchen.

"Prawie skończony!" chirped Henrietta. *Almost finished!*

"Excellent!" replied Einstein. "Dairy Dan is set to arrive in exactly

26 minutes and…" Einstein paused to glance at his watch and then continued, "…ten seconds. I want to be at the front door, ready to depart the moment his truck appears in our driveway."

"Będę gotowy!" hummed Henrietta. *I will be ready!*

....

Upon hearing Coach Yak's unhappy announcement, everyone in the house moaned.

"Oh no!" cried Nestor.

"This is bad!" shouted Hawk.

"You no fix truck?" gasped Papa.

Coach Yak wiped his forehead with his sleeve. "I can fix it. I just need a new part and more time."

Papa pointed at the Packer clock on the wall and shook his head. "No time is left! Limburger Heads coming soon! May gods help us!"

Heaving a huge sigh, Coach Yak pulled the card out of his pocket and handed it to Nestor.

"Gotta throw the *Hail Mary*. Send 'em a text and tell them to come NOW…*and hurry!*"

....

Probationary Agent Elliot Ness's heart was beating fast as he crawled through rows of corn to where his boss was stretched out asleep.

"Special Agent Noodle, sir…wake up! We have red zone activity!"

Lifting his head off the corn cob pillow he'd made for himself, Noodle opened his bleary eyes.

"Red zone activity?" yawned Noodle. "Where's Agent Sanders?"

"He's…*whoa!* Hold still, sir," ordered Elliot as he gave Noodle a hard slap on the cheek.

"Hey-hey, what's the idea? I'm awake!" complained Noodle.

"You had a corn borer larva on your face, sir. Don't worry. I got 'im."

Noodle reached up and wiped the squished worm off his face and frowned. "Oooh…icky!"

"Sir, we have activity in the red zone," reported Elliot, trying to contain his excitement. "An elderly white male, approximately 6-feet, 2-inches tall, bib overalls, toothpick in his mouth, entered the barn 30 seconds ago. GL-300 Tracker signal strong."

Suddenly, there was a scurrying and crackling sound. Noodle and Ness's heads snapped around to discover Agent Sanders crawling toward them through the cornfield, kicking up a mini-cloud of dust.

"We have activity in the red zone," said Sanders, gasping and trying to catch his breath. Then, looking at Noodle, he made a frowny face and added, "Sir, you've got something gooey on your face."

"A nasty corn borer," admitted Noodle, giving his cheek another rub. "But no worries, Sanders. Probationary Agent Ness got 'im."

"Good work, Ness," congratulated Sanders. "But, as I was saying, we have activity below...a male...approximately 60 years of age..."

"Yes, I know," interrupted Noodle. "I was being briefed just as you crawled over."

Then, looking at his watch, he added, "Give the order to the team. We move to secure the perimeter in exactly one minute."

Sanders quickly pulled off his shoe, slid back the heel and started punching in the code on the keypad.

"What size is your shoe phone?" queried Elliot longingly.

"Ten-and-a-half narrow," answered Sanders.

Elliot heaved a huge sigh as he watched Agent Sanders snap the heel in place and slid his foot back in his shoe.

"Do you think they come in a men's cap-toe oxford, extra wide?"

Special Agent Noodle scrambled around looking for his SWAT Team helmet. Locating it a few feet away from where he was napping, he flipped it over several times, inspecting it for corn borers.

Satisfied it was worm-free, he put it on his head, flipped down the visor, raised his hand and gave the command. "Time to move out!"

A second later, with military-like precision, fifty FBI/FD agents plus Elliot, all dressed alike in navy blue helmets, chest protectors, elbow pads, knee pads, shin guards and holding riot shields, rushed out of the cornfield and surrounded the neat and tidy white barn.

Then Noodle, his palms sweaty, crept ever so slowly toward the big barn door, waving at Sanders and Ness to follow him.

"On the count of three," whispered Noodle, his hot breath fogging up his visor. "We rush the barn, apprehend the suspects and locate the missing Bears.

Agent Sanders and Elliot nodded as Noodle closed his eyes, took a deep breath, swallowed, paused…and finally began his count.

"One…..two.…..…*three!*"

Noodle, Sanders and Ness busted through the barn door with their riot shields in front of them and 21-inch expandable batons held high over their heads.

"**FREEZE!**" shouted Noodle, fogging up the visor on his helmet even more. Then he added: "Help! I can't see anything!"

With a sigh, Elliot reached over and flipped up the visor on Senior Special Agent Noodle's helmet. "There really isn't much to see, sir."

Blinking, Noodle looked around inside the barn.

On one side of the barn was the trailer with the gleaming, brand new green and yellow John Deere tractor. On the other side, farmer Miller was sitting on a low, three-legged stool, milking a cow. And right in the middle was Doris Day, standing on top of a bale of alfalfa hay while she nibbled at its tasty sprouts.

Wiping his hands on his overalls, Mott Miller got up off the stool and walked over to Noodle and shook his hand.

"How do you do, sir? My name's Miller. Are you fellas from the Department of Agriculture? I saw you all out there in my cornfield inspecting my crops."

"Wh-wh-where are the Bears?" stammered Noodle. "We're looking for the Bears."

"Bears!" laughed Miller. "No bears around here. We do however get an occasional fox in the henhouse. And as far as my crops go… they're clean! You won't find nary a single corn borer in all 48 acres."

"I am sorry to inform you, Mr. Miller," broke in Elliot. "But I just killed a corn borer in your field a few minutes ago."

"No!" gasped the farmer. "Well, one corn borer is hardly considered an infestation. You're not putting a quarantine my crops, are ya?"

"We're not from the Department of Agriculture, Mr. Miller," explained Agent Sanders, stepping forward and showing his badge. "We're from the FBI Football Division."

The old farmer's eyebrows jumped in surprise. "I didn't know the FBI had a football division."

"Okay, enough of this *good ole boy* stuff," grumbled Noodle. "Where are you hiding that football coach and those kids who took the Bears?"

Mott Miller slipped the toothpick from one corner of his mouth to the other and shook his head. "I have no idea what you're talking about."

"We planted a GL-300 GPS Tracker on their vehicle and right now, the signal is coming from somewhere in this barn!" roared Noodle. "Ness! Check the tablet and locate the tracker!"

Setting his riot shield on the barn floor, Elliot unzipped a pocket on his bulletproof vest and pulled out a tablet.

While he was powering up his device, Doris Day jumped off the bale of hay and starting playfully head-butting the riot shield at Elliot's feet.

"Agent Sanders! Look at this!" cried Elliot, pointing at the image that appeared on the screen.

Agent Sanders rubbed his eyes and swallowed hard. "How is this possible?"

"How is what possible?" grumbled Noodle as he joined the other two agents staring at the device.

"According to this image sir, the GL-300 GPS Tracker is in the belly of this goat."

Agent Sanders pointed down at Doris Day, who was still prancing around, head-butting the riot shield.

Senior Special Agent Roman Noodle's jaw dropped. "The tracker is in this goat? But how?"

"Doris! Did you eat these gentlemen's *whatever it is?*" scolded the farmer, giving his goat an affectionate scratch on the chin.

"Baaaahhh!" bleated Doris.

Mott smiled and nodded at Doris, then turned to Agent Noodle.

"Yep, she ate it. So whatever that do-hickey 300 thing cost, tell me. I'll be glad to pay for it."

Noodle threw his arms up in the air. "Where are those kids? Where is that coach? And WHERE in heaven's name are those BEARS? We have NO clue!"

Just then, a text tone interrupted the FBI/FD agent's ranting.

"Sir, your shoe is dinging," said Elliot, pointing at Noodle's foot.

Taking a few quick steps to the milking stool, Noodle sat down, pulled off his shoe, slid back the heel and read the text message.

Nestor Hapburn

Hav found Bears. nEd help! Limburger Heads on thR way hEr NOW 2 crush & bury! 2707 18th St Monroe, WI. Pls hurry!

"Sanders! Find out how long it takes to fly from here to Monroe, Wisconsin," shouted Noodle as he put his shoe back on and took off toward the barn door.

Agent Sanders and Elliot gave a quick wave to the farmer and rushed out after their boss.

"Sure nice meeting you, fellas," called out Miller with a wave of his own. "Oh, and if you *do* run into anyone from the Ag Department, I'd appreciate it if you didn't mention your little run-in with the corn borer."

Outside, the FBI/FD SWAT Team was still surrounding the barn, holding their riot shields at the ready when Noodle burst out of the barn shouting orders.

"Everybody back to the Mobile Command Center, *double time!*"

Immediately, the SWAT Team turned and ran off in single file formation, like a bunch of ants on their way to a picnic.

"Sir, it's 47 minutes by chopper to Monroe," said Agent Sanders as he jogged down the road alongside Noodle. "So, those kids have the Bears?" he asked, fishing for more information.

"Apparently. And they're still sticking to that Limburger Head nonsense," added Noodle between breaths.

"Shouldn't we alert the local police?" suggested Sanders.

"What? And have some fresh-faced kid right out of the training academy get credit for cracking this case? No way!" growled Noodle.

A minute later, Noodle and his SWAT Team, all hot and sweaty, were back at the Mobile Command Center and the long convoy of black sedans lined up alongside the dusty dirt road in front of KW's Nuts & Stuff stand.

"Sanders! I want you and FBI/FD Probationary Agent Ness in the chopper with me," instructed Noodle, breathing hard. "Go tell the rest of the team to put the pedal to the metal and join us at 27-zero-7 18th Street, Monroe, Wisconsin."

Agent Sanders gave his superior a quick salute as Noodle and Elliot disappeared into Lester's cornfield, heading toward the helicopter.

Following a path of bent over corn stalks, they made their way out to the mashed down spot in the field where Noodle had landed...*only to find the helicopter nowhere in sight.*

Suddenly, deeper into the cornfield, they heard the sound of an engine trying to start.

"The chopper's over there, sir," shouted Elliot.

The two of them plowed through the cornfield at top speed in the direction of the engine sound. Within seconds, they were standing in front of their beautiful, black FBI/FD helicopter. And there in the cockpit was KW, yanking and twisting the controls.

"Hey! You're not supposed to be in there!" shouted Noodle, his face turning red.

"Oh! Hi!" greeted KW with a big smile. "You guys back already?"

"Get out of there! FBI/FD emergency!" yelled Noodle.

KW hopped down out of the helicopter and rubbed her finger under her nose. "I tried flyin' it...but the best I could do was get her to hop up and down a few times."

At that moment, Agent Sanders burst through the corn stalks with a confused look on his face.

"How did the chopper get over here?"

"I did it," said KW, proudly.

"Enough of this nonsense," snapped Noodle. "Sanders...Ness...in the chopper. We gotta go!"

"Can I go?" asked KW. "I'd like to see what buttons to push so the next time..."

"There is not going to be a *next time*," interrupted Noodle as he leaped into the cockpit. A second later, the engine roared to life and the helicopter blades started spinning.

KW held onto her straw hat with both hands and backed out of the way as dust and cornstalks whipped around in a whirlwind.

Then, as KW watched the helicopter rise straight up into the sky she shouted, "Wait! Don't go! I'll get ya some nuts! Flyin' and nuts go together! Like spaghetti and meatballs...and Bert and Ernie."

Elliot gave the nutty lady a friendly wave, as the chopper roared off on its rescue mission, leaving KW on the ground shouting to the heavens.

"Like mac and cheese...bacon and eggs...pot pies and schmierkase..."

....

"Help is on the way!" cheered Nestor, looking at a text from Special Agent Roman Noodle.

"Good," nodded Coach Yak. "How long before they get here?"

"They're here!" cried Hawk, peeking out the living room window. Coach Yak's jaw dropped. "What! Already?"

"Not those guys," cried Hawk shaking his head so hard his brain rattled. "*THOSE GUYS!*" he shouted, pointing a finger at what was happening outside.

Nestor, Killer, Michael, Papa, the Smothers brothers and Coach Yak all rushed to the window to see Dairy Dan's pickup truck whip in the driveway and screech to a stop in front of the airplane hangar, followed by the Chalet Cheese Co-op van.

A second later, the Limburger Heads were hugging and high-fiving each other as Henrietta Wozniak waddled around to the back of the Ford pickup.

Michael's eyes were glued to the wobbly woman. He watched her lower the tailgate and hoist three hefty coolers out of the bed. Michael licked his lips.

"We need more time," moaned Nestor, looking at the wall clock.

"More time, yes," agreed Papa. "Maybe I go out and...and..."

"Stall them?" blurted Killer, finishing Papa's thought.

"Stall! Yes! *That* is word! I go now and stall," nodded the old Greek.

As Papa walked out of the house and down his little sidewalk, nobody noticed Michael slip out the back door.

"You early," shouted Papa, giving the Limburger Heads a wave. "Why you hurry?"

"Papa," cheered the Limburger Heads, greeting him with welcome high-fives and pats on the back.

"Here you go," said Nick, as he handed Papa a shovel.

Papa shook his head. "No-no. I no go bury Bears...too sad."

"Sad? You should be glad, Papa," boomed Dairy Dan. "This is our moment of victory!"

Dairy Dan pointed at Henrietta pulling two coolers around to the front of the truck.

"Look! Ms. Wozniak brought cabbage rolls so we can celebrate the successful completion of Operation Georgie Porgie!"

Then Helmut Lunquist walked up and lowered a wooden crate marked DANGER in the middle of the group.

"And here's the cheese master with the leftover stink bombs," added Dairy Dan. "We'll smash the Bears, throw 'em in the holes we dug along with the stink bombs. After that, we'll have a little picnic, sing the Packer fight song, dance on the Bears' graves, then go to Baumgartner's for the game!"

Floyd clapped his hands happily. "Hot dog! That sounds great!"

Papa shook his head. "Bears say no game if Georges stay away."

"Oh, for the love of Lombardi! They're bluffing!" snorted the head Limburger Head. "They'll play!"

"Enough of this idle discussion. It's time to bring this operation to its long-awaited conclusion. Move your car, Floyd," ordered Einstein.

Quickly, Floyd hopped in his Chevy blocking the hangar and moved it, while Rick Monroe ran to the door and slid it open. As the Limburger Heads rushed inside, Henrietta waddled back to Dairy Dan's pickup to get the third cooler.

When she got to the truck, she discovered the lid of the cooler was ajar. With a shrug of her shoulders, she closed the lid and mumbled, "Jak dziwne." *How odd.*

Inside the hangar, everybody was stumbling around in the dark.

"Stinkin' Bishop!" exclaimed Floyd as he bumped into one of Aphrodite's propellers. "Someone turn on the lights!"

"Oh, sure-sure, sorry," babbled Papa. Walking slowly to his work-bench, he flipped on the light. Suddenly, complete darkness became blinding brightness bouncing off Aphrodite's shiny silver fuselage.

"Whoa!" yelled Nick, covering his eyes.

"I need sunglasses!" blinked Helmut.

After a few more seconds of stumbling around, Dairy Dan's eyes adjusted. He looked around and pointed to the burlap bags in the corner.

"Go! Everybody grab a Bear and…"

"Wait-wait. I have idea," interrupted Papa. "Better keeping Bears in potato sacks for keeping secrecy."

"Excellent thought, Papa," agreed Einstein. "Keep the Bears under wraps until we transport them to the gravesite. Understood?"

Nodding their heads, they each grabbed a burlap sack out of the corner and hauled it outside.

Dairy Dan folded his arms across his chest and took a moment for himself. There in front of him were six burlap sacks, three coolers on wheels and a crate of stink bombs. The *Pasteurized Brotherhood of Limburger Heads* were on the verge of completing the most daring and impossible mission in history. He was pleased.

Closing his eyes, he saw thousands of people cheering and ticker tape flying as he and the Limburger Heads paraded down Lombardi

Avenue and into Lambeau Field. A single tear rolled down his cheek as he imagined his name emblazoned on the stadium wall just below the scoreboard.

Dairy Dan Elliot, Green Bay's Greatest Fan!

"Oh, beautiful," he whispered. "They put me right between Bart Starr and Ray Nitschke."

"They did what?" asked Floyd, giving his leader an elbow.

Dairy Dan blinked and gave a little cough as he snapped out of his triumphant daydream.

With a snort, Dairy Dan reached down, tightened the strap on his walking boot and picked up the burlap sack in front of him.

"To the cemetery!" he announced.

At the same moment, each Limburger Head picked up the sack at his feet and started walking. Everybody except Papa.

"Wait-wait," sputtered the old Greek cargo pilot. "Sorry, Squadron Leader Dan. I can not go. My heart, she breaks."

Einstein threw his arms in the air. "Papa! Don't you want to witness the glorious defining moment of our crowning Cheesehead achievement?"

Papa sadly shook his head. "I love Packers. I do. But my heart, she tells me what I do is wrong and I must stop."

"But Papa! Think about..."

"Save your breath, Einstein," interrupted Dairy Dan. "If he wants out, that's fine with me. We don't need the old man raining on our parade."

"I wouldn't worry about that, DD," chirped Floyd looking up at the sun. "There's not a cloud in the sky."

Dairy Dan bent down and picked up the burlap sack at his feet and nodded toward the cemetery. "C'mon! Let's get this party started!"

Papa stood in the driveway as the Limburger Heads hoisted their sacks over their shoulders with grunts and groans and marched off across the street to Greenwood Cemetery.

As Nick Monroe walked past Papa, he reached over and gave the old Greek cargo pilot an understanding pat on the back.

"You see 'em," Papa mumbled to the group. Then turning to rush back into the house, he mumbled again...to himself this time.

"Aphrodite. She is our only hope."

....

Senior Special Agent Roman Noodle was at the controls of the FBI/FD McDonnell Douglas 530 Little Bird helicopter when he let out a groan.

"No-no-no! Not now!" he cried, as he pounded the navigation display monitor. "The GPS just went out!"

Agent Sanders gave the system a quick inspection. Unable to pinpoint the problem, he looked at his watch. "We've been in the air for twenty minutes now. By my calculations, we're still 30 minutes from our destination."

Noodle gave the monitor another pound, then shook his head.

"Argh! I guess we better find a gas station and ask for directions. Hang on! Going down for a landing."

"Wait!" burst out Elliot.

"What? **You** have a better idea, Probationary Agent Ness?" snapped Noodle.

"I don't mean to brag, but I did earn a Boy Scout merit badge for navigating in the woods without a compass," admitted Elliot. "I've been checking the charts and following our flight plan and I think I can get us where we want to go."

"Okay, Magellan," snapped Noodle. "Get us to 2707 18th Street in Monroe, Wisconsin."

"Sure thing, Agent Noodle, sir," agreed Elliot.

"Here. Sit up front," said Sanders, unbuckling his seat belt and moving to the back seat.

Quickly switching seats with Agent Sanders, Elliot looked at his map and gazed at the sky in front of them. "Okay. See that cloud straight ahead that looks like a bunny eating a carrot?"

Noodle leaned forward and pointed at the cloud "That one right there? That looks like a raccoon to me."

"Raccoon? No, I don't think so," said Sanders, leaning in from the back seat. "That's a beaver. See that long, flat tail?"

"Whatever you want to call it," conceded Elliot. "When we get to *that* cloud, make a sharp left."

Noodle nodded, "Got it! Sharp left at the raccoon."

"Beaver," corrected Sanders.

"Raccoon," insisted Noodle.

....

Monterey Jack poked his head around Harvey Havarti's cheese wedge gravestone when he heard the Limburger Heads trudging in his direction.

Thinking there might be more bacon in the deal, he meandered down to the holes he helped dig the night before and waited.

"Hey, look!" chirped Helmut Lunquist, pointing to the spot they were going to bust up and bury the Bears. "There's Monterey Jack!"

Hearing his name called, the old bloodhound wagged his tail.

"Never mind that dog," barked Dairy Dan as he hobbled along in his walking boot, dragging his burlap bag behind him. "Line 'em up and let's finish this."

"I agree wholeheartedly," added Einstein, dropping his sack in front of a hole and wiping his sweaty bald head dry with a hankie. "But first, I feel it only fitting and proper that we should take a moment to commemorate this historic event by vocalizing a *Seize the Cheese* salute to our leader, the very heart and soul of the *Pasteurized Brotherhood of Limburger Heads*, Dairy Dan Elliot.

"Who and wherefore, hither and dither, without his visionary vision of bestowing the ultimate acclaim, honor and distinction upon the Green Bay Packer franchise for having the lion's share of NFL legends enshrined in the Hall of Fame."

Floyd, standing at attention in front of his bag, wrinkled his nose and mumbled under his breath. "Lions? Who cares about the Lions?"

"And may I also state," continued Einstein solemnly, "that in the absence of this green and gold giant of a man, nary a one of us would be here at this moment, standing at the precipice of Green Bay Packer immortality.

"And now, with heads held high, I beseech thee to put your hand over your heart and declare with me..."

A tear trickled down Dairy Dan's cheek as Einstein, Cheese Master Helmut Lunquist, Nick and Rick Monroe, Henrietta and Floyd all shouted out: **"To Dairy Dan Elliot! STC! Seize The Cheese!"**

Pleased that all formal requirements of such a significant occasion had been satisfied, Einstein picked up the sledgehammer and handed it to Dairy Dan.

"The honor of striking the first blow for Packer pride is yours and yours alone! Remove the cloak of secrecy and begin."

Wiping the tears from his eyes and blowing his nose, Dairy Dan reached down and fumbled with the rope at the top of the bag. Finally, he managed to untie the knot and the brown burlap fabric slipped down onto the pile of dirt in front of the hole.

The Limburger Heads all let out one loud gasp!

Dairy Dan's jaw dropped and he rubbed his eyes.

Instead of a Hall of Fame Bear named George, there in front of him stood the king gnome with the blue hat and Band-Aid on his nose.

"A gnome?" shouted Dairy Dan in disbelief.

Quickly, the other Limburger Heads scrambled to untie the knots on all the burlap bags in front of them and discovered more blue- and red-hatted chess pieces from Mrs. McChesney's collection.

"Get a load of this one! A gnome riding on the back of a squirrel!" snickered Floyd, giving his knee a slap. "You don't see that every day!"

"Am I dreaming? Wha-wha-where are the Bears?" stammered Dairy Dan, staggering backwards, stunned and confused. "How is this even possible?"

His heart beating fast, he looked around at the Limburger Heads in disbelief and added with an angry roar, "For the love of Lombardi, HOW DID THIS HAPPEN?"

Flashback! 15 Hours Earlier
September 1 - Five Minutes to Midnight

"You see 'em!" whispered Papa as he quietly opened the door and stepped out.

Nestor, instead of slipping back in his sleeping bag, went to the window and peeked around the shade.

"What's happening?" asked Hawk.

"Nothing. He's just sitting on the porch looking at the cemetery across the street," answered Nestor. Then, heaving a heavy sigh, he added, "You know what I think we should do?"

"I'm afraid to ask," groaned Hawk.

"Me, too," agreed Michael.

"We need to sneak out and follow them," whispered Nestor.

Michael's eyes got as big as meatballs. "You mean you want us to crawl around that cemetery?"

"At night?" added Hawk, swallowing the lump in his throat.

"Sure! How else are we going to know what's going on?" said Nestor, quietly walking to the front door to put on his shoes.

Hawk peeked out the window to see the Limburger Heads pull into Papa's driveway and head off toward the cemetery carrying shovels.

"There they go," reported Hawk.

"C'mon, you guys! Get moving!" urged Nestor, standing by the front door.

Reluctantly, Michael and Hawk slipped on their shoes and followed their brother outside.

As the brothers stepped off the porch, the sound of a dog howling burst through the chilly night air.

"Ooooooooooooooooooooooowhoo!"

"I'm going back inside," said Hawk as a shiver shot down his spine. He turned and took a step toward the house when Michael reached out and grabbed him.

"If *I'm* going to that spooky graveyard," growled Michael. *"You're* going!"

"Stop arguing!" ordered Nestor. "And don't follow too close to 'em."

Crouched down, the brothers scooted across the street and into the shadowy cemetery, dashing between gravestones. Hearing voices and the sound of digging, they dropped to the ground and crept closer.

"There!" whispered Nestor, pointing to a huge, cheese wedge monument. "We can hide behind that."

On their bellies, the brothers army-crawled around the edge of the small hill - above where the Limburger Heads were busy tossing dirt - and slipped unseen behind the massive triangular hunk of marble.

"Hey look, the guy buried here was a cheese master. Har-vey Ha-Ha-var-ti," murmured Hawk, struggling to read the name in the dark.

"Cheese? Rats! I wish I would have brought a snack," mumbled Michael sadly.

Nestor put a finger to his lips. "Shhhh! I want to hear what they're saying."

Suddenly, a light flashed in Michael's food-obsessed brain. "Bacon!" he whispered loudly. Reaching back, he pulled three pieces of bacon-y smelling bacon out of his back pocket.

Peeking over the cheese wedge gravestone, Nestor saw the blood-hound that had been digging with the Limburger Heads immediately stop and sniff the air. With his nose pointed up, the big, floppy-eared dog strolled up the slope toward Harvey Harvarti's grave.

Nervous about the dog's approach, Nestor turned to his brother holding the strong-smelling bacon. "Where'd you get that?"

"From home. Breakfast. I just remembered I had it," whispered Michael, his mouth watering.

Just then, the bloodhound, his mouth watering, too, stuck his head behind Harvey's gravestone.

"Wh-wh-whoa!" sputtered Hawk as he wiped dog drool off his sleeve. "His face is leaking."

"He wants your bacon, Michael! Give it to him!" ordered Nestor.

"It's mine!" hissed Michael. "I need it!"

"Give him the bacon, Michael, and let's get out of here," insisted Hawk, as one of the Limburger Heads headed in their direction, holding a shovel like a club.

Nestor and Hawk both grabbed Michael's bacon-fisted hand and were trying to wrestle it away when, all at once, the drippy, drooling bloodhound shook his head.

Suddenly, the brothers found themselves covered in thick, ropy, frothy saliva.

Michael, wiping himself off, loosened his grip on the bacon. The meat fell to the ground and the opportunistic bloodhound scooped up two of the three pieces in his moist mouth and bounced back down the hill, his tail wagging.

"Gross," coughed Hawk, dragging his sleeve across his doggie-drooled face.

"Oooh, I've been slimed," groaned Nestor.

Then, spotting the third piece of bacon on the ground, Michael rejoiced. "He missed this one!"

Grabbing the piece of pork out of a pool of foamy spit, Michael held the prize over his head in celebration. Sadly for Michael, it was a very short celebration.

An owl perched in a nearby oak tree watching the action, suddenly swooped down and snatched the treat from the hungry Hapburn's upraised hand and flew off, hooting into the night.

Startled, the brothers scrambled out from behind Harvey's cheese wedge monument and took off at top speed away from the Limburger Heads. After splashing through a few puddles, bumping into a tree and tripping over a small gravestone, they tumbled onto Papa's porch, muddied and bloodied and out of breath.

"Do you think they saw us?" bleated Hawk, huffing and puffing.

"Maybe...I don't know," said Nestor, in between breaths. "But, we need to switch out the Bears."

Hawk wrinkled his nose, "Whaddya mean, switch them out?"

"The gnomes! We need to put the gnomes in the sacks and get the Bears out," explained Nestor.

"Get them out? And then what?" asked Hawk.

"I don't know...put them some place else, some place safe," urged

Nestor. "C'mon! Let's wake up the others and get this done."

"I need a snack," mumbled Michael.

"You can have a snack after," said Nestor, giving his brother a shove toward the front door. "Let's go!"

The brothers crashed through the front door, shouting instructions.

"Wake up, everybody! Wake up!"

"Get the gnomes...we need to switch 'em with the Bears!"

"Cake! I need cake!"

Coach Yak bolted off the couch from a dead sleep, yelling, "Bears? "Gnomes? Cake?"

Stinky Smothers leaped out of his sleeping bag with his eyes still closed and ran into the living room wall.

Stinky Smothers' brother covered his ears, muttering, "I don't want to go to school, mom!"

Killer, hearing all the commotion, jumped out of bed, threw her robe over her *Born to Stand Out* flamingo pajamas and flew out into the living room. "What's the matter? What's going on?"

"We need to get the Bears out of Papa's hangar and put the gnomes in! Now!" yelled Hawk as he tumbled over Stinky Smothers' brother in his sleeping bag.

"We gotta do it while those Limburger Heads are busy digging," added Nestor. "If we don't, we might not get another chance!"

"Okay," nodded Coach Yak as he put on his shoes and reached for his Ohio State ball cap. "Head to the truck and we'll unload the gnomes first."

Killer dashed off into the bedroom, while Coach Yak and everybody else, except Michael, scrambled to the front door.

"Michael! Where are you going?" shouted Hawk grabbing his brother's sleeve. "Outside is this way!"

"Yeah! But the kitchen is *this* way!" replied Michael, brushing away Hawk's hand. "I'll be out after I have a piece of pizza...or two."

Coach Yak reached back behind him and turned his star player around. "Hey, #99...have you forgotten? There is no *I* in team."

"But there IS in...*I am hungry*," groaned Michael as he followed the others outside.

At the broken-down Suburban, the Braves buzzed around as they unloaded Mrs. McChesney's chess piece gnomes.

"This one has a Band-Aid on his face," grunted Coach Yak, as he hoisted the King gnome off the truck and into Hawk's outstretched arms.

"I put it there! His nose got chipped after he tackled me," explained Hawk, hauling the King toward the hangar.

Coach Yak grabbed the blue-hatted Queen gnome and handed it to Nestor, who was next in line.

"True story, Coach," nodded Nestor, walking away. "That gnome tackled him."

Coach Yak took off his ball cap, scratched his head. After a few moments of trying to figure it out, he went back to unloading gnomes. The last one, the gnome riding on the back of a squirrel, he set on the ground for Stinky Smothers' brother to take.

"That gnome is almost as big as you! I'll tell you what...I'll carry it and you run ahead and open the doors for us," suggested Yak.

"Sure thing, Coach," said Stinky Smothers' brother as he sped off.

Passing his teammates carrying gnomes, he slid the hangar's metal doors open, slipped inside and turned on the light. Then stepping aside, he watched the gnomes parade past the big C-47 Sky Train and into the corner where the Bears were waiting in their burlap sacks.

"Take the Bears out, put the gnomes in and tie the bags back up," instructed Yak.

"Then what?" asked Hawk.

"I know!" shouted Killer. "We separate the Bears and make them harder to find. Take one and you hide it in a place only you know."

"But what if they torture us to try and find out where we hid 'em?" gulped Michael.

"Whaddya mean, torture?" mocked Nestor.

"I mean, torture!" repeated Michael. "Like what if they waved a double cheeseburger in front of my face so I could smell it, but they wouldn't let me take a bite?"

"That would be bad," agreed Coach Yak. "But that's a chance we have to take. C'mon, let's move!"

Immediately, they went to work, taking the Bears out of the burlap bags and stuffing the gnomes in. Then they lugged the Hall of Fame treasures out of the hangar, looking for spots to hide them.

Coach Yak carried George Musso to the house and hid him under the dining room table, adding a tablecloth so he couldn't be seen.

Stinky Smothers shoved George Blanda into the living room closet and threw a Packer parka over him.

Killer lugged George Connor into the bathroom, wiped a smudge off his cheek with a washcloth, then lifted him into the tub, pulling the shower curtain closed.

Nestor, spying some hedges surrounding Papa's front porch, slipped George McAfee behind the dense, dark green foliage of a Dwarf English Boxwood bush.

Hawk decided to disguise George Trafton as a lamp and putting him on an end table in the living room with a lamp shade on his head.

And Michael, taking care of *Papa Bear* as Papa wanted, hauled George Halas into the kitchen.

First, he checked the oven. Too small. Next, he looked under the sink. Too tight. Finally, Michael went to the refrigerator and pulled out a couple of shelves, plus a bowl of leftover macaroni and cheese.

Michael then hurried to the living room closet and rummaged around until he found a pair of earmuffs in the pocket of the parka covering George Blanda. Waving goodbye to George Blanda, Michael dashed back to the kitchen, snapped the earmuffs on George Halas's head, slid the smiling Hall of Famer into the fridge and shut the door.

Satisfied, Michael strolled into the living room to join the others with the bowl of cold mac & cheese just as Papa opened the front door and walked in.

"Hercules!" exclaimed Papa. "Why you not sleep?" Then, looking around, he rubbed his eyes and added, "Why everybody not sleep?"

Quickly, they filled in Papa on what they had been doing while he and the rest of the Limburger Heads were digging in the cemetery.

Papa was nodding and asking questions.

"You switch Bears with gnomes?"

"Right! It was Nestor's idea," chirped Killer.

"But where is gnomes' home?" asked Papa.

"Mrs. McChesney's front yard," answered Hawk. "She's nice. She let us take them. She doesn't want Michael or any of us to go to prison."

"But when Squadron Leader Dan and others take bags to grave-yard, they will find gnomes. And then..." Papa trailed off.

"But when they move them to the cemetery, we'll load the Bears in the truck and take off!" cried Killer.

"But truck is broke," shrugged Papa.

"But I'm going to fix it," answered Coach Yak.

Papa sighed, "But what if fixing doesn't fix?"

Coach Yak grabbed the bill of his Ohio State ball cap and pulled it down tight on his head. "Well, if the fixing doesn't fix it...then, we have REAL trouble."

Like a tree falling in the woods when no one's around to hear it, the room fell completely silent.

Silent until Michael blurted out inbetween bites, "Anybody want some of this mac and cheese? It's good."

Papa smiled and gave Michael a pat on the back. "No, Hercules. I am tired. I try to sleep now."

"Good idea," agreed Coach Yak. "I think we all better try and get a little more sleep. I gotta feeling we've got a pretty full day ahead of us."

With that, everybody slipped into sleeping bags, sofas and beds, closed their eyes and tried not to worry.

But Michael, before settling into his sleeping bag on the living room floor, took one last bite of mac and cheese, walked into the kitchen, opened the refrigerator and placed the bowl next to the smiling George Halas wearing his earmuffs.

"Here you go, Papa Bear," murmured Michael. "I saved some for you."

Back to the Present: **September 2 - 3:27 pm | Greenwood Cemetery**
4 Hours 33 minutes to Kickoff at Lambeau Field

The Limburger Heads were standing next to the holes they dug the night before staring in disbelief at Mrs. McChesney's gnomes.

"For the love of Lombardi, <u>HOW</u> DID THIS HAPPEN?" roared Dairy Dan. "**WHERE ARE THE BEARS?!**"

"**Ooooooooooooooooooooooowhoo!**" howled Monterey Jack.

Einstein Wozniak shook his head sadly. "It pains me to say this, but I fear that one Demetri Papadopoulos is likely responsible for this Hall of Fame catastrophe."

"No way!" cried Floyd. "Papa's a Limburger Head! He's one of us!"

"Not anymore," yelled Dairy Dan as he stomped angrily back and forth in his walking boot. "And now that I think of it, Floyd! Maybe **you** had something to do with this, too!"

Floyd's eyes popped out of his head in surprise. "W-w-what? **ME?**" babbled Floyd, pointing a finger at himself.

"Yes! **YOU!**" boomed Dairy Dan. "You were the one guarding the Bears! What did you do? Fall asleep on duty?"

"Stinkin' Bishop! I was awake the whole time!" objected Floyd. "No one went into Papa's barn and no one came out!"

"Cease and desist!" shouted Einstein, raising his hands up over his head. "This bickering back and forth is getting us nowhere!"

"The situation requires swift, decisive action. Operation Georgie Porgie has now become a *search and destroy* mission."

"Exactly!" agreed Dairy Dan. "We'll tear Papa's place apart if we have to, but those Bears must be found!"

"Tear Papa's house apart?" mumbled Nick Monroe sadly.

Rick Monroe pulled his dad aside and shook his head. "I don't think he means he wants us to *really* tear his house apart. Just maybe rearrange some of the furniture and stuff."

Right then, Henrietta opened a cooler and put a cabbage roll on a plate. "Czy ktoś chce bułkę z kapustą?" *Anyone want a cabbage roll?*

"Thank you, but not at the present time, Mother," replied Einstein politely. "We have a crisis on our hands."

Henrietta nodded and put the cabbage roll back in the cooler.

"Grab your shovels and sledgehammers!" commanded Dairy Dan. "And Helmut...you got the leftover stink bombs?"

"Got the stink bombs right here," replied Helmut, holding up the last two jars of yellow-green ooze. "You want me to throw 'em in a hole?"

"No. Bring 'em, just in case!"

"But, DD! They might not..."

"No buts," interrupted Dairy Dan. "Bring the stink bombs!"

Helmut shrugged his shoulders and stuffed the jars of glowing yellow-green ooze back in his backpack.

Floyd bent down and picked up a shovel and a sledgehammer.

Handing the sledgehammer to Helmut, he nodded toward the King Gnome with the Band-Aid on his nose. "That guy there sort of looks like your old boss, Harvey."

"He sort of does," agreed Helmut, giving the King a quick glance.

Dairy Dan hobbled into position at the head of the group shouting, "LIMBURGER HEADS READY?"

"READY!" yelled the Limburger Heads in unison.

"LET'S GO!" hollered Dairy Dan. "And when you find a Bear... don't wait! Smash it to smithereens on the spot! This is search and destroy! Understand?"

"YES, SIR!" they roared back.

Waving their shovels and sledgehammers in the air, the Limburger Heads marched toward Papa's house, singing the Packer fight song.

Monterey Jack, still sitting by the huge, cheese wedge shaped gravestone, watched the procession for a minute or two before deciding to get up and meet the new friends.

Introducing himself to each of the gnomes with a sniff and a nudge, he stopped at the King Gnome with the blue hat and Band-Aid on his nose and studied him a little longer. Seeing the resemblance to Cheese Master Harvey Havarti, his eyes brightened and his tail started wagging.

Monterey Jack gave the King Gnome a *glad-to-see-you* lick on the cheek and howled for joy, happy to spend time with an old friend. **"Ooooooooooooooooooooooooowhoo!"**

....

"New plan!" announced Papa as he burst into the house. Grabbing an old leather aviator helmet off a hook on the wall in the hall, he put it on his head.

All at once, everybody had something to say.

"New plan?" gulped Nestor.

"Why'd you put on that hat?" asked Hawk.

"Let's hear it!" shouted Killer.

"I'd like a hat like that," added Stinky Smothers' brother.

Papa rushed around the house, snatching up batteries, screwdrivers, pliers, water bottles and stuffing them into a green army duffle.

"Whaddya doing?" asked Coach Yak as he darted back and forth along with the old man.

Papa grabbing a flashlight blurted out, "We need supplies to fly."

"FLY?!" yelled everyone.

"Yes! Fly!" repeated Papa, buckling the chinstrap on his leather helmet. "We fly with Bears now. We save Bears from Squadron Leader Dan!"

"But what about the FBI Noodle guy?" asked Nestor. "He'll be coming soon!"

"Limburger Heads coming sooner!" wailed Papa. "Someone to keep watch now!"

"I'll do it!" shouted Stinky Smothers' brother.

"Good-good!" nodded Papa, as he handed Stinky Smothers' brother a rusty old cowbell currently serving as a doorstop on the floor. "Go to street. When you see Limburger Heads coming, sound alarm."

Stinky Smothers' brother saluted the old Greek Aviation officer and bolted out the front door, cowbell clanging.

"Coach Yakunshenko! Helping with me to push Aphrodite from hangar! Everybody, get Bears very fast and meet at runway!" Then, noticing Michael wasn't there, Papa asked, "Where is Hercules?"

"Don't worry Papa! We'll find Michael and we'll meet you outside at the plane," reassured Killer.

Papa smiled and patted the tough, little quarterback on the back. "Good-good! Get Bears, find Hercules and we fly with Aphrodite. Our new plan!" With that, everybody scattered.

"Do you really think we should fly?" huffed Coach Yak as he and Papa hustled toward the ramshackle hangar. "It might be better if we made like an O-line and threw some blocks. Four years at Ohio State and I never allowed a sack!"

Papa shook his head. "You are formidable man. But I am old and they are children. We need to fly them *and* Bears to safety," explained Papa as he slid open the airplane hangar's metal doors. "Squadron Leader Dan is very Packer passionate man. I have fear in my heart he can stop at nothing to have his dream."

With the hangar doors open, Papa pointed to the switch on the wall. "Turn on lights!"

Coach Yak rushed over and flipped the switch. Immediately, the darkness was replaced by brilliant, bright, shimmering shiny light bouncing off the silver body of the Douglas C-47 Sky Train.

Blinking from the light, Papa walked up to Aphrodite, reached over his head and touched her nose cone. "Are you ready now, beautiful? Today is day you touch clouds one time more."

Then, grabbing a thick rope off the floor, he fastened one end to a tow bar by the front wheels and the other end to the massive coach.

"**PULL!**" shouted Papa.

Coach Yak adjusted the harness around his shoulders, got down in a three-point stance, took a deep breath and with all the strength he could muster, he pulled.

One second, two seconds, three seconds...Coach Yak pulling and grunting and straining...but the huge cargo plane didn't budge.

"You can do this," encouraged Papa from the sidelines. "I help!"

Papa rushed behind Aphrodite, took a deep breath and gently blew. Magically, the titanic Sky Train started to tremble. One inch forward, two inches forward, three inches forward...Aphrodite was moving!

Slowly, the cargo plane built up speed.

Papa, clapping his hands, watched as Coach Yak pulled Aphrodite out of the airplane hangar and into the sunshine for the first time in forty years.

"*Whaaa*-HOOO!" shouted Papa, hurrying over to unharness the coach. "Thank Zeus and all the gods!"

"What about me?" huffed Yak, wiping the sweat off his forehead.

"Yeah-yeah, you do good, too!" nodded Papa with a smile. "Now you go round and open cargo hatch. Help kids load Bears. I make engines roar!"

Coach Yak lumbered around to the side of the plane and yanked open the doors to the cargo hatch just as Stinky Smothers showed up with George Blanda. Right behind him were Hawk, Nestor and Killer each with their Hall of Fame George.

With a huff and a puff, Stinky Smothers set his statue at Coach Yak's feet. "Here you go, Coach!"

"Good going," nodded Yak. "Tell you what! I'll hoist you up in the plane and you get the Bears in and buckled down."

Coach Yak locked his hands together and gave Stinky a leg up into the cargo hold. Then, like passing buckets in a fire brigade, Killer, Nestor, Hawk and Coach Yak passed the Bears up to Stinky Smothers.

Then with a finger snap, Coach Yak blurted out "I gotta get my Bear out from under the dining room table!"

"And where's Michael's *Papa* Bear?" added Killer.

"Yeah! And wh-wh-where's Michael?" sputtered Nestor, his head spinning around on his shoulders.

"Oh, brother," moaned Hawk. "This couldn't get any worse!"

Just then they heard the cowbell clanging furiously and Stinky Smothers' brother yelling.

"I SEE 'EM! THE LIMBURGER HEADS! **THEY ARE COMING!**"

"Okay, it's Hail Mary time!" shouted Coach Yak. "I'll get my Bear and you guys go long! Find Michael…and Papa Bear and meet back here! Time is running out!"

With the sound of the cowbell getting closer and closer, Coach Yak ran toward the house as Nestor, Hawk and Killer took off in different directions, hollering Michael's name.

Bursting through the back door, Coach Yak hustled to the dining room and pulled off the table cloth. There, peeking out from under the table, was Hall of Fame Lineman George Musso.

Falling to the floor, Yak reached under the table and dragged the statue out just as Stinky Smothers' brother burst through the front door, cowbell clanging.

"Whaddya doing down there, Coach?" cried Stinky Smothers' brother. "This is no time for hiding! This is a time for action!!"

Getting up off the floor with George Musso in one arm, Coach Yak scooped up Stinky Smothers' brother with the other and headed out the back door.

"Yeah!" crowed Stinky Smothers' brother, bouncing up and down in transit toward the cargo plane, the cowbell still in his hand. "This is what I'm talking about!"

At the same moment, Hawk and Nestor were inside the hangar, desperately searching for their brother when they heard Killer yell.

"I FOUND HIM! HERE HE IS!"

Immediately, the two brothers burst out of the barn and ran in the direction of her shouts to find Killer pounding on the window of Coach Yak's red suburban. "WAKE UP, MICHAEL! WAKE UP!"

Inside the truck, Michael yawned and calmly stretched his arms.

"Unlock the door, Michael!" shouted Killer, just as Nestor and Hawk arrived on the scene.

"What's he doing in there?" howled Hawk.

Nestor grabbed the door handle and gave it a yank, "Michael! Get out of there! We gotta go!"

Michael yawned again and gave everybody a wave. Then, holding an index finger in the air to tell everyone to wait a second, he fumbled with the lock. Finally, Michael opened the door and a paper plate with leftover bits of cabbage rolls slipped off his lap and onto the ground.

"What?! You were eating?" yelled Hawk.

"Sure," admitted Michael. "I saw the nice lady bring three coolers full of cabbage rolls. So, I had a few...then I got tired and took a nap." Rubbing his eyes, he looked around. "What's everybody doin'?"

"We've got trouble!" snapped Nestor, getting in his brother's face. "The Limburger Heads are coming right now and we've got load the Bears on Papa's plane and fly away!"

"Oh, cool," said Michael with another yawn.

"Michael, listen! We need to get your Bear and get him on the plane! Now! Where did you put him?" asked Killer.

"Refrigerator," mumbled Michael.

"Stop thinking about food, Michael!" shouted Hawk. "Where's Papa Bear?"

"I just told you. He's *IN* the refrigerator," repeated Michael. "But now that you mention it, I *could* use a snack."

"C'mon! Hurry! To the house!" ordered Killer, taking charge.

Killer, Nestor, Hawk and Michael took off running toward the house, but the moment they turned the corner of the airplane hangar, they skidded to a stop.

"Oh no," moaned Nestor. "Look!"

Dropping down to the ground, the bunch of Braves looked on in horror to see Dairy Dan and the Limburger Heads pounding on Papa's front door, peeking in windows and shouting.

"We know you're in there, Papa! Open the door! Save yourself! You can't save those Bears!" yelled Dairy Dan, banging his shovel on the cement porch.

"Demetri Papadopoulos! In the name of the *Pasteurized Brotherhood of Limburger Heads*, I hereby order you and your six Hall of Fame hostages to surrender now!" shouted Einstein, cupping his hands to his mouth like a megaphone. "Failure to do so could result in your social ruination and ostracization!"

"Albert! Don't you say that to Papa!" scolded Floyd, shaking his finger. "You're gonna make him feel bad!"

Floyd cupped his hands to his mouth. "Don't worry, Papa!" He shouted. "We won't hurt your ostrich! In fact, I didn't even know you had an ostrich! Bring him out...we'd like to meet him!"

Nestor, Hawk, Michael and Killer watched as the Limburger Heads surrounded Papa's home, continuing their angry shouts and threats.

"What will we do?" whispered Hawk. "The last Bear is still inside."

"Hey, there's that nice lady," said Michael.

Henrietta was sitting nearby on a cooler waving a cabbage roll in the air and hollering in Polish. "Hej stary, wyjdź. Mam gołąbki!" *Hey old man, come out. I have cabbage rolls!*

Suddenly, a plan popped into the tough little quarterback's brain. Grabbing a short stick, she drew a big square, a small square and some Xs and Os in the dirt.

"Here's the house. Here is the cooler," explained Killer. "Nestor, this X is you. Hawk, this X over here is you. And this X on this side is you, Michael."

All three nodded, not saying a word.

"I'll call the signals. On hut one, Nestor, you sprint straight across the front of the house and get as many of those Limburger Heads as you can to follow you. On hut two, Hawk rolls out to the cooler, grabs two cabbage rolls, then runs to the runway and gets on the plane.

"Michael..."

Michael's eyes grew big as he waited to hear what Killer would say.

"On hut three, you follow me through the back door and into the kitchen. I'll grab Papa Bear out of the refrigerator, hand him off to you and then you GO!

"Just like Twinkie Off Tackle," clucked Michael. "I hand Papa Bear over to Hawk on the plane and he hands me the cabbage rolls."

"Exactly!" said Killer, proudly looking at the play she drew up. "Okay, everybody. Got it?"

"Got it!" shouted the Hapburn brothers.

Then, erasing the cabbage-roll-out play in the dirt with her hand, she stood up, ready to break the huddle.

"Team on three...one...two...three..."

"**TEAM!**" They all shouted in unison. And with that, they hustled around the corner of the airplane hangar to stand in clear view of the Limburger Heads, who were still storming around Papa's house and pounding on his front door.

"Where did those kids come from?" shouted Rick Monroe.

"Hey! We know them!" yelled Floyd. "They're the kids from the Hall of Fame game! What are THEY doing here?"

Dairy Dan stopped pounding on Papa's front door and hobbled from the front porch and pointed at Michael. "You're the one who helped us steal the Bears!" snarled Dairy Dan.

"Yep! That would be me," chirped Michael, giving a friendly wave.

"And now, we're here to steal them back!" shouted Killer defiantly.

Einstein Wozniak stepped forward and raised his hand. "I would strongly recommend you reconsider that proposition, young lady. Otherwise, the likelihood that a person or persons could get seriously injured in the melee that ensues would be extremely high."

"Yeah, right! What he said!" agreed Floyd.

"Enough of this nonsense," yelled Dairy Dan. "Where are the Bears? WHERE'S PAPA?"

Suddenly, the roar of an engine filled the air.

"Whoa! What's that?" shouted Nick Monroe.

"Aphrodite!" cried Helmut. "Papa going to try and fly that old plane!"

Out of time, Killer clapped her hands and started calling signals as the Hapburn brothers got down in a three-point stance in front of her.

"POUND OF HAMBURGER...CUP OF ONIONS...CUP OF RICE..."

"They're lining up to run a play!" howled Dairy Dan, the former high school linebacker for the Monroe Cheesemakers. "Limburger Heads! All-out blitz!"

"PINCH OF PARSLEY...HEAD OF CABBAGE...LET'S GET COOKIN'! **HUT ONE!**"

Nestor took off running across Papa's front lawn.

"Nick, Rick...get that kid!" ordered Dairy Dan.

"HUT TWO...

Hawk gave a head fake toward the house and then made a mad dash toward Henrietta and the cooler.

Dairy Dan pointed at Hawk. "Floyd! Helmut! Cover him!"

Waiting another split second for the Limburger heads to scatter, Killer took a deep breath and shouted...

"HUT THREE!"

Killer and Michael sprinted toward Papa's back door with Dairy Dan and Einstein giving chase. Younger and faster, the two Port Clinton Braves ran into the house way ahead of the out-of-shape Limburger Heads and locked the door behind them. Killer ran to the refrigerator, swung open the door and there – happy and waiting with his earmuffs on - was Papa Bear George Halas.

Grabbing the chilled but smiling Hall of Famer from the shelf, she handed him to Michael, just as Dairy Dan and Einstein started pounding on the back door.

"Now what?" whispered Michael.

"To the window! Let's see if Hawk has the cabbage rolls," answered Killer, rushing out of the kitchen into the living room.

"Yeah! That's important," agreed Michael.

Out in front, Nestor and Hawk were twisting and turning, doing a brilliant job of escaping the grasps of the lumbering Limburger Heads, while looking for a chance to raid the coolers filled with cabbage rolls.

"How we gonna do this?" panted Hawk as he sprinted alongside his brother. "I need a second to get in a cooler without them chasing me."

"Look out!" said Nestor, between a huff and a puff.

"Look out?" repeated Hawk, confused.

"We run a crisscross pattern...and then..."

Hawk waited for Nestor to catch his breath and continue.

"...when l yell *look out*, we drop to our knees...they trip over us and crash into each other..."

"Oh yeah! Like me tripping over the King Gnome!" gurgled Hawk.

"Right!" huffed Nestor with a thumbs-up as he and his brother rolled out in opposite directions.

As the brothers looped wide apart, Nick and Rick followed Nestor and Floyd and Helmut trailed Hawk. Then, subtly and quickly, they led the two exhausted mini-mobs in a high-speed dash toward each other.

Nestor patiently waited as the two groups got closer and closer. And just at the very moment, as they were about to crisscross paths, he shouted..."**LOOK OUT!**"

Nestor and Hawk immediately dropped to their knees to become stumbling blocks. Unable to stop, Nick and Rick and Floyd and the cheese master tripped over the brothers and went airborne, crashing into one another in a bone-busting, head-to-head collision.

In a flash, Hawk and Nestor were up and speeding toward the cabbage roll coolers, leaving the moaning, groaning Limburger Heads on the ground in a tangled-up pile.

The short, round Henrietta, standing on one of the coolers to have a better view of the action, applauded as Nestor and Hawk swooped by the other two coolers. Grabbing two cabbage rolls each, they took off in the direction of the roaring airplane engines.

Seeing what had occurred, Henrietta climbed down off her cooler, flipped open the top, grabbed a cabbage roll herself and shook it in the air, shouting, "Hej! Wroc! Wez troche wiecej!" *Hey! Come back! Take some more!*

"They've got 'em!" shouted Killer, watching from Papa's window.

At that moment, they heard glass shatter in the kitchen, fumbling with the door lock and angry voices.

"Limburger Heads coming in the back door!" cried Michael, scooping up George Halas and tucking him under his arm like a football.

"This way out!" yelled Killer, scrambling to unlock the front door. "Go! And don't stop until you've got Papa Bear on the plane."

Michael burst onto the porch like he was shot from a cannon, just as Dairy Dan and Einstein burst out of the kitchen.

"That kid's got a Bear!" snarled Dairy Dan, plowing through the dining room, knocking over chairs.

Spotting a big umbrella leaning by the wide open front door, Killer grabbed it, ducked down next to a small table and waited for the big, lumbering dairy farmer to pass. Just as Dairy Dan was about to step out on the front porch, Kathy Kopecky brought the umbrella down – with a walloping whack -- on his sore foot.

"Watch your step!" hollered Killer.

"**Owwwwwwwww!**" hollered Dairy Dan and he tumbled onto Papa's porch and onto the sidewalk.

Einstein, who was right behind him, immediately flipped over his fallen friend. Rubbing his knee, Einstein moaned, "This is not only exceptionally embarrassing; I am also finding it exceedingly painful."

Jumping from her hiding spot, Killer vaulted over the two Limburger Heads on the porch and caught up to Michael, who was going as fast as he could lugging the heavy Hall of Fame statue.

"C'mon, Michael!" shouted Killer, slowing down to run beside him.

"Don't wait for me!" panted Michael, "We'll see you at the plane!"

Kicking it into another gear, Killer nodded and waved and sped off as the Limburger Heads, now off the ground, were again giving chase.

Michael, struggling under the load, ran slower and slower. The Limburger Heads, bruised and battered but running free, got closer and closer.

At one hundred yards, a whole football field away from Aphrodite, Rick Monroe was right on the heels of the determined Port Clinton running back.

"Tackle him!" shouted Dairy Dan. "We're right behind you!"

At fifty yards, Rick reached out and grabbed Michael's shoulder. Michael, feeling the Limburger Head's grip tighten, let his football instincts take over.

Putting on the brakes, Michael stopped dead in his tracks, sending his would-be-tackler tumbling to the ground ten feet ahead of him.

With Rick between him and Aphrodite, and Nick, Floyd and Helmut closing fast from behind, Michael started running toward the sideline, hoping to find a teammate willing to throw a block or two.

And he did. There, charging onto the playing field to join him was the All-American Lineman from Ohio State, Carl Yakunshenko.

"I've got your back!" yelled Yak. "Zig-zag to the middle toward me."

Not bothering to even get in front of him, Coach Yak, reached out with a massive forearm and knocked Rick Monroe down to the ground as he rushed past.

"Illegal block in the back!" shouted Rick, his mouth full of dirt.

Next, Nick Monroe took a desperation dive at Michael's feet, but Michael executed a well-timed 360-degree spin, making him miss.

"Cut behind me!" bellowed Yak, as he worked to get in a position to take out the rest of the bull-rushing Limburger Heads.

Stretching his arms out full length, the extra-wide Coach Yak was now extra-extra wide and he flattened Floyd, Helmut, Einstein and Dairy Dan with one devastating clothesline block.

Floyd tried to hop out of the pile and continue the chase, but Yak reached out with his huge hand and grabbed him by the ankle.

"Holding! 15-yard penalty!" yelled Floyd as he fell back down on the jumble of people.

Now, with no one left standing between him and the airplane, Michael put his head down and took off, with Papa Bear George Halas still tucked under his arm.

"Go, Michael! Go!" shouted Yak. "Don't wait for me! I'll hold them off for as long as I can!"

Tangled up on the ground and trying to break loose, Dairy Dan spotted Helmut's backpack lying a foot away. Stretching with a free hand, he unzipped the backpack and out rolled a jar of glowing, green-gold ooze.

Shoving the stink bomb toward Einstein - who, after much effort had squirmed away from the pile of Limburger Heads - Dairy Dan hollered one last desperate command.

"Einstein! Stink bomb! Throw it!"

"B-b-but what if I hit him?" stammered Einstein.

Dairy Dan, his face beet red, partly from running and partly from the massive Coach Yak sitting on him, bellowed...

"For the love of Lombardi! Throw it! He must be stopped!"

Taking a deep breath, Einstein picked up the stink bomb and heaved it as far as he could in Michael's direction.

Suddenly, all the pushing and shoving and grunting and groaning stopped as the tangled mess of men watched the glowing, green-gold missile fly, tumbling end-over-end toward its intended target.

Michael, not wanting to fumble, was holding Papa Bear with both arms now and heard the stink bomb buzz over his head.

A split second later, the stink bomb landed in front of Michael, exploding on contact with the hard-packed gravel runway.

KA-BOOOOOM!

Instantly, a thick mushroom cloud of the most foul, rank, reeking, horrible smelling cheeses appeared. It smelled a million times worse than a locker stuffed with sweaty, sour, stinky socks.

And Michael vanished in the middle of it.

"Great toss!" cheered Dairy Dan from the pile. "Aaron Rodgers couldn't have thrown it better! Hurry, while he's down and out.... somebody go get that..."

Dairy Dan stopped mid-sentence as he saw Michael, still on his feet, stumbling out of the stink cloud and running toward the roaring engines of the plane.

"What?! Why didn't he pass out?" demanded Dairy Dan.

"I tried to tell you, DD!" howled the cheese master. "Stink bombs may not work outside! Too much fresh air!"

When he was only a few feet from Aphrodite, Hawk, Nestor and Killer ran to meet Michael.

"Wow! Way to go, big brother!" shouted Nestor.

"You did it, Michael!" chimed in Killer.

"Here! Let me help you! Give me Papa Bear!" chirped Hawk.

"Give me my cabbage roll!" grinned the ready-to-collapse running back.

"Seriously?" said Killer, trying not to laugh. "Get on the plane first! We gotta go!"

They all gave a quick look down the runway to see Coach Yak pushing and grabbing and doing his best to stop the Limburger Heads from giving chase.

"What about Coach?" asked Nestor.

"He said for us to go! He'll hold 'em off for as long as he can," huffed Michael, still breathing hard.

Hawk grabbed Papa Bear and handed him up to Stinky Smothers, then they all scrambled up into the cargo hold.

When everyone was on board and all the Bears were securely strapped down, Nestor ran up to the cockpit to where Papa was busy checking all the buttons and gauges on the instrument panel.

"Take off, Papa! We're ready!" announced Nestor.

"Papa Bear and Hercules here?" asked Papa.

"Onboard!" answered Nestor.

"Coach?"

"He said not to wait! He's holding 'em off, so we can get away!"

"Okay! Coach knows best," nodded Papa. "Everyone goes buckle up! Aphrodite, she wants to fly one time more!"

Nestor flew back to the cargo hold with Papa's instructions as the ancient Greek aviation officer spit into his hands and rubbed them together. Then, grabbing the throttle, he gently pushed it forward.

Aphrodite's engines, shaking off forty years of dust, roared louder and the C-47 Sky Train starting rumbling slowly down the runway. The Limburger Heads, finally busting over and around Coach Yak's blocks, were running behind trying to catch up.

Papa adjusted his weathered leather aviator helmet and pushed the throttle full forward. Faster and faster, the old cargo plane bounced down the runway.

"Up-up-up, old girl," encouraged Papa gently. "You can do it."

Charging forward at her top speed and running out of runway, Aphrodite's wheels were still on the ground.

In the back of the plane, strapped in tight, Hawk was nervous.

"What's wrong? Do you think we're too heavy?"

"Maybe I ate too many cabbage rolls," mumbled Michael.

"Maybe she's forgotten how to fly," added Stinky Smothers' brother.

"That's it! Aphrodite just needs to remember," shouted Killer. "On the count of three, everybody stretch out your arms like wings and raise your feet off the floor."

"How's that going to help?" frowned Stinky Smothers.

"I don't know," shrugged Nestor. "Just do it."

"What about the Bears?" blurted Stinky Smothers' brother.

"They don't have any arms," reminded Nestor.

Stinky Smothers' brother nodded. "Oh yeah, I forgot."

"Everybody ready?" shouted Killer. "One...TWO...**THREE!**"

At the very same moment, they all stretched their arms out wide and lifted their feet...and then it happened.

They all felt a lighter-than-air sensation as Aphrodite's nose inched up ever so slightly. Within seconds, she was airborne, flying above the trees with Greenwood Cemetery below.

"We're flying!" sang Killer.

"Yahoooo!" cheered Papa from the cockpit!

"Ooooooooooooooooooooooooowhoo!" howled Monterey Jack as Aphrodite passed overhead.

With their noses all pointed up at the sky, the Limburger Heads gave up the chase.

"There they go," groaned Helmut, breathing hard.

Dairy Dan, heartbroken that his dream of Packer glory had just disappeared into thin air, dropped to his knees and let out a moan. "That junk heap got off the ground. I can't believe it."

Standing around, huffing, puffing and exhausted from their epic tussle, Rick pointed at large lump laying on the runway, right where the C-47 Sky Train had left the ground.

"What's that over there?"

Curious, the Limburger Heads and Coach Yak walked over to inspect. As they plodded down the runway, Floyd gave the Coach a poke and issued a complaint.

"You were holding! Cheater."

Arriving at the steaming hot piece of debris, Einstein circled it a few times and gave it a kick. It was two tires attached to a metal shaft.

"It appears Papa is lacking an essential part of his aircraft."

"Oh no," croaked Yak. "How are they going to land without the front wheels?"

Before anyone could answer, the whir of helicopter blades overhead caused everyone to look up.

There, descending in front of the group, was a jet-black chopper with the letters FBI/FD on the side, kicking up a huge cloud of dust.

Dairy Dan shook his head. "You're kidding me. Now what?"

September 2 - 4:56 pm | End of the Runway at Papa's House
3 Hours 4 minutes to Kickoff at Lambeau Field

"2707 18th Street," exclaimed Elliot, pointing to Papa's house on the ground. "Put her down right there!"

"Are you sure Probationary Agent Ness?" grumbled Senior Special Agent Roman Noodle. "This will be the third time we've landed."

"I'm positive!" confirmed Elliot. "This is the place!"

"Suspicious activity below. Possible suspects," announced Agent Sanders, pointing to where the Limburger Heads and Coach Yak were scrambling around Papa's airplane hangar.

"All right! We're taking her down!" informed Noodle.

Hands over their ears and squinting through the swirling dirt and dust, the Limburger Heads watched the helicopter land a few feet away from where Aphrodite had taken off.

Dressed in their riot gear, Noodle, Sanders and Ness jumped out of the chopper before the helicopter blades stopped spinning, rushed up to the ragtag group and announced their presence with authority.

"FBI/Football Division," shouted Noodle. "Hands in the air!"

Too tired to escape, the Limburger Heads and Coach Yak raised their arms up over their heads and waited.

Flipping up the visor on his helmet, Noodle frowned and barked |at Coach Yak. "Where are the Bears?" demanded Noodle. "And where are those kids of yours?"

"What took you so long to get here?" complained Yak.

"We took a wrong turn at the raccoon cloud," explained Elliot.

"Beaver cloud," corrected Sanders.

Noodle held up his hand for quiet. "Where are the statues?"

"These are the guys who stole 'em," answered Coach Yak, pointing at the bunch of Limburger Heads.

Disgusted, Floyd shook his head and whined, "Stinkin' Bishop! Not only are you a cheater, you're a tattle-tale, too!"

"They were going to bust them up and bury 'em in that graveyard across the street," said Yak, nodding toward Greenwood Cemetery.

"To stop them, we had to put the Bears on a plane and they took off just now."

"Took off?" hollered Noodle. "Took off to where?"

Einstein raised his hand. "I'd like to interject my thoughts here."

"Go ahead," nodded Noodle. "Interject."

Einstein coughed and cleared his throat.

"The Douglas C-47 Sky Train appeared to be bound north by northeast at a very low altitude. Given the pilot's predisposition for Packer football and the high probability that the aircraft will be capable of flying only a short distance based on its age, condition and available fuel, I would conclude that the Bears and all occupants are bound for Green Bay."

Noodle gave his chin a scratch.

"Okay, so we fly to Green Bay, intercept them at the airport and take possession of the Hall of Fame statues. Case solved."

"What do we do about these guys?" asked Sanders, pointing at the bunch of Limburger Heads still standing with their arms in the air. "We can't take them with us. There's not enough room in the chopper."

Giving his chin another scratch, Noodle took off to the helicopter and came running back with a big roll of yellow crime-scene tape.

"Wrap 'em up with this," instructed Noodle, tossing the roll to Probationary Agent Elliot Ness. "All of 'em except the big guy. He's going with us."

"Hey! No fair! How come he gets to go?" objected Floyd, pointing at Coach Yak. "He cheated!"

Elliot, moving quickly, herded all the Limburger Heads together in a circle and wrapped them around the middle, with their arms pinned down to their sides, in a tight, tight bunch.

Agent Sanders did a quick inspection and nodded his approval. "Nice work, Ness. Very good."

"To the chopper," shouted Noodle. "Let's go!"

"What about us?" objected Dairy Dan. "What are we supposed to do?"

"Don't move!" answered Noodle as he hustled off. "We'll be back!"

"Then what?" cried Dairy Dan.

"Someone's got to go to prison," shouted Senior Special Agent Roman Noodle over his shoulder.

The Limburger Heads watched as Noodle, Sanders, Elliot and Coach Yak climbed up into the helicopter, stirred up a cloud of dust and flew off.

"Prison? But what about my job at the cheese co-op?" moaned Helmut, blinking specks of dirt out of his eyes.

"I suggest you call in sick tomorrow," answered Einstein.

"I wonder if they show Packer games in prison?" sighed Rick.

Suddenly Floyd's eyes brightened. "The Packer game! Hey, what time is it right now?"

"I can't move my arms to see my watch," complained Nick.

"Judging by the current location of the sun, which as you can see is barely visible on the horizon," observed Einstein, squinting into the western sky. "My best calculation would be it is now approximately 5:31 pm Central Daylight Time."

"Great!" shouted Floyd.

"Great? What's great about any of this?" grumbled Nick.

"The Packers' game! We've got two and a half hours 'til kickoff."

"So?" said Nick. He tried to shrug, but he was tied up so tight with crime tape, he could barely move his shoulders.

"So, I think we got enough time."

"Enough time for what?" asked Rick.

"Enough time to shuffle over to Baumgartner's to see the Packers-Bears game!" chirped Floyd.

The cheese master shook his head. "That guy told us not to move."

"It's only a few blocks away. What difference would it make?"

Dairy Dan thought about it for a few seconds, sighed and then finally nodded his head in agreement.

"That's a good idea, Floyd," said Dairy Dan, managing a hint of a smile. "Let's go to Baumgartner's for one last party before we go to prison. After all, there's nothing like a Packer victory to make everything a little bit better."

The Limburger Heads let out a cheer and started moving slowly in one big, taped-together bunch, taking baby steps down Papa's driveway to the street, singing the Packer fight song.

"*Smash their line with all your might, A touchdown Packers, Fight, Fight, Fight!*"

Henrietta Wozniak was singing, too. In Polish. "Walka! Walka! Walka!" *Fight! Fight! Fight!*

September 2 - 5:41 pm
In the Helicopter Somewhere Between Monroe and Green Bay
2 Hours 19 minutes to Kickoff at Lambeau Field

Coach Yak, squeezed into the back seat with Probationary Agent Elliot Ness, reached forward to Senior Special Agent Roman Noodle in the pilot's seat and tapped him on the shoulder.

"There's one more problem I need to tell you about," said Yak, using his shouty voice, so he be could be heard over the noisy chopper blades.

"Now what?" cried Noodle, using *his* shouty voice.

"That plane that took off, with my kids and your Bears, lost its front wheels. They can't land!"

"What?! Does the pilot know that?" asked Sanders.

"I'm not sure. It happened just as they lifted off," replied Yak.

"This is bad! This is **REAL** bad," announced Noodle. "Probationary Agent Ness, establish radio contact with the aircraft and alert them of this emergency."

Elliot, all squished up in the back next to Yak, squirmed around to free one of his hands and grabbed the microphone above his head.

"Don't bother," said Yak, shaking his head. "That old plane...I'm sure the radio doesn't work. I've got my phone...I'll text them!"

Yak twisted and squirmed around until he was able to free his phone from his back pocket.

Moving his thick, meaty thumbs surprisingly fast, he pounded out a message, hit the send key, heaved a heavy sigh and waited.

"What do we do now?" muttered Sanders.

Suddenly feeling nauseous, Yak moaned, "I think I'm going to throw up."

Mashed up in the back of the helicopter with the massive football coach and nowhere to run, a look of terror flashed over Elliot's face as he closed his eyes and begged, "Please, don't!"

September 2 - 6:02 pm
In the Cargo Plane Somewhere Between Monroe and Green Bay
1 Hour 58 minutes to Kickoff at Lambeau Field

Nestor, Michael, Hawk, Killer and the Smothers brothers were bouncing around in their seats in Aphrodite's cargo hold with the Bears, happily revisiting their narrow escape from the Limburger Heads, shouting to each other to be heard over the roaring engines.

"I can't believe we did it!" cheered Nestor, popping up and down with a jolt as the C-47 flew through some bumpy sky.

"Whoa!" shouted Stinky Smothers' brother, banging the back of his head on the metal wall. "We musta hit a pothole!"

"Looks like you won't be going to prison, Michael," laughed Hawk.

"That's good. We need him playing in our game on Saturday!" shouted Killer.

"Anybody got a snack?" yelled Michael.

"That's right...we've got a game on Saturday," chimed in Stinky Smothers. "What about Coach?"

"Yeah! What about Coach?" agreed Hawk. "Last I saw him, he was blocking and tackling those Limburger Heads."

"I'm sure Coach is okay. He can take care of himself," assured Killer. "We'll text him when we land."

Just then, a text tone rang out and Nestor pulled out the phone.

"**OH NO!**" burst out Nestor as he handed the phone to the Braves' quarterback. She read the text out loud.

Coach Yak
Bad News! You can't land! Front wheels fell off your plane! Tell the old man! Don't worry. Noodle is working on a plan. TEAM!

"What? We're stuck up here?" shouted Hawk.

"No snacks?" added Michael.

Stinky Smothers shrugged his shoulders. "Well, we're not stuck up here forever. At some point, we'll run out of gas."

"Not good! Not good! Does this mean we're gonna crash?" babbled Stinky Smothers' brother. "I wished I'd brought my football helmet."

"Nestor! Run up and let Papa know," ordered Killer, once again taking command of the situation. "There's something we can do. We just need to figure out what."

In a flash, Nestor unbuckled and ran to the front of the plane.

"Papa! Emergency!" shouted Nestor as he burst into the cockpit.

"No, no…everything okay! We hit bumpy air. Aphrodite, she just shaking off her rust," crowed the old Greek pilot. "I think in my head, thirty, forty minutes and we see lights of Green Bay airport."

"But Papa, we can't land!" added Nestor.

"Can't land?" repeated Papa, wrinkling his brow.

Nestor nodded his head extra hard and fast.

"I just got a text from Coach. He said our front wheels fell off! We can't land without wheels, right?"

Papa scratched his chin and sighed.

"This is true. Wheels make landing much better."

"So…what should we do?" cried Nestor.

"I think," Papa paused and scratched his chin again. "I think…"

But before he could finish telling what he thought, Kathy Kopecky came running into the cockpit yelling…

"**PARACHUTES!**"

"**SIZZACTLY!**" agreed Papa. "Parachutes!"

"I counted them," added Killer. "We've got twelve!"

"Yes! Aphrodite has twelve!" confirmed Papa.

Excited, Killer continued. "So we strap the parachutes on and we fly over Lambeau Field…and we jump out!"

"Yes!" nodded Papa.

"And then we land nice and easy right there on the 50-yard line!" finished Killer, throwing her arms up in the air in victory.

"YES!" cheered Papa. "You are making the most greatest Lambeau leaping of all time!"

"I don't know," croaked Nestor. "Jump out of a plane? That sounds dangerous. Will the parachutes even work? I mean, how many years have they been sitting there? They could be rotten. Or packed wrong."

"No worries," declared the old pilot confidently. "I pack them all myself. Forty years ago."

"See, Nestor! No worries! Papa packed them himself!" cried Killer.

"Right…forty years ago!" sighed Nestor.

"Okay, I've got it! We strap the Bears to parachutes first and push 'em out," suggested Killer. "If the parachutes open, the rest of us jump!"

"Okay. Good. But there are seven of *us*, six Bears and only twelve parachutes. We're a chute short," said Nestor doing the math.

Killer bit her lip and heaved a sigh. Suddenly, a light flashed in her brain.

"Michael! Michael can hold one of the Bears in his arms!"

"Yes-yes!" agreed Papa. "Hercules is strong!"

The C-47 cargo plane suddenly bounced up and back down as it hit another airborne pothole and Killer and Nestor bumped heads.

As Aphrodite's metal moaned and creaked, Papa leaned forward in his seat and whispered softly so no one else could hear, "Just short time more, beautiful. Fly just short time more."

"Okay!" burst out Nestor. "We leap into Lambeau! I'll text Coach!"

"Let's do it!" cheered Killer, rushing off to tell the others.

"Parachutes on everybody! Bears, too!" shouted Papa. "Lambeau Field…we coming over!"

September 2 – 6:21 pm
In the Helicopter 25 Miles from Green Bay
1 hour 39 minutes to Kickoff at Lambeau Field

No one was talking, so when the first three notes of the Ohio State fight song suddenly rang out, it startled everybody.

"Whoa, that scared me," crowed Coach Yak, grabbing his phone to read the text that just popped in. "Oh no! They've got parachutes! They're planning to jump over Lambeau Field. This is bad!"

"No! This is good!" declared Noodle. "A Lambeau *sky-high* leap! Probationary Agent Ness, radio the Green Bay FBI/FD office. Tell them to send 100 agents to the stadium now!"

"Have 'em bring every safety net they can lay their hands on and meet us on the field," added Special Agent Sanders.

"Roger that!" exclaimed Elliot, punching buttons on the system.

Coach Yak blinked. "You've got a hundred agents in Green Bay?"

"It's the Football Capital of the World! It's the Home Office of the Federal Bureau of Investigation/Football Division," proclaimed Noodle, puffing out his chest.

"I don't know. Kids? Jumping out of a plane?" said Coach Yak, swallowing hard. "I told their parents I'd take good care of them."

"You got a better idea?" snorted the Senior Special Agent.

Coach Yak heaved a big sigh and sat silently; his thinking hounded by the loud, constant chuff of chopper blades spinning.

With the sun dipping below the trees in the west, a golden glow, slowly growing brighter, appeared in the sky to the north.

"There they are! The lights of the stadium," announced Sanders.

Pushing the throttle forward, Noodle let out an uncharacteristic whoop. "Lambeau Field, Green Bay, Wisconsin…here we come!"

....

The area known as Green Bay, Wisconsin was originally inhabited by Native Americans of the Menominee and Winnebago tribes.

Because of French and British interest in the fur trading industry, a trading post was established in Green Bay in 1745 by Charles Michel de Langlade. The French residents at the trading post called the town *La Bey*. The British fur traders referred to the settlement as *Green Bay* because the waters along the Lake Michigan shore had a greenish tint in the spring.

As British settlers in the area grew to outnumber the French, the French term gave way to the British designation of *Green Bay*.

Today, Green Bay is the third largest city in the state of Wisconsin and it is the third largest city on Lake Michigan's west shore, behind Chicago and Milwaukee.

The Greater Green Bay Metropolitan Area has a population of more than 300,000 people and, while its robust economy can be traced to its long history of thriving meat-packing plants and paper mills, the city is best known as the home of the Green Bay Packers.

Earl *Curly* Lambeau, a player and the first coach of the Packers, founded the football franchise in 1919. Looking for money to buy uniforms and equipment, he was given $500 by his employer, the Indian Packing Company, in exchange for Curly's promise to name the team for its sponsor.

The Packers team is the only community-owned franchise in all of North America's four major leagues, which includes football, baseball, basketball and hockey. Over the years, the team has had a total of five stock sales. The very first was in 1923 when the Packers raised $5,000 by selling 1,000 shares at $5 each.

Despite being the last of the small-town teams, which were more common in the early days of the National Football League, *and* having the smallest TV broadcast market in the league, the Green Bay franchise has sold out every home game since 1960.

In addition, the Packers have one of the longest season ticket waiting lists in professional sports, with Cheeseheads waiting years and years...*and years*...to purchase a season pass to the games played in historic Lambeau Field.

The stadium first opened on September 29, 1957 and rises out of the heart of a Green Bay neighborhood. Lambeau Field has a seating capacity of 81,441 and is the 4th largest stadium in the NFL.

Imagine that.

81,441 *passionate Packer football* fans, walking through the gates and packing Lambeau Field from the bottom to the tip-top row, waiting for the kickoff.

And not just *any* kickoff. The kickoff of the *first* game of the season.

And not just *any* season opener. The season opener against their longest-standing and bitterest rival, the Chicago Bears, the dreaded *Monsters of the Midway.*

The Packer faithful from all parts of Wisconsin, the #1 cheese-producing state in America, coming together expecting to *see* the start of a Super Bowl season.

But instead, they *hear* the distant sound of a helicopter approaching.

September 2 - 7:12 pm   Lambeau Field North Entrance
48 minutes to Kickoff

An ESPN video crew was bustling around, setting up equipment next to the Vince Lombardi statue outside the North Entrance of Lambeau Field.

ESPN NFL Insider Adam Schefter was blinking into the bright lights and adjusting his tie, waiting for Flipper, his videographer, to start his count-down.

"Ready?" shouted Flipper from behind the camera.

Adam nodded and Flipper raised his hand above his head and starting counting.

"Five-four-three-two-one...rolling..." Flipper pointed at his on-camera talent and the ESPN superstar began.

"Adam Schefter, reporting from outside historic Lambeau Field, where we are hopefully going to see the kickoff the NFL season between longtime rivals the Green Bay Packers and the Chicago Bears.

I say hopefully because, while the Bears ARE on the field warming up, they say they will NOT play the game until the six missing Hall of Fame Chicago Bear busts, all named George, have been returned.

As Adam Schefter continued his report, a green and gold Packer tour bus pulled in next to the Lombardi Statue and started unloading passengers in full view of the camera.

Last off the bus was the driver, slurping from a big plastic souvenir cup and strolling directly toward the bright lights.

Standing behind Schefter, the bus driver waved at the camera with a big toothless grin and pointed at the Packer cap on his head.

Feeling someone breathing down his neck, the ESPN reporter turned to the bus driver and complained, "Do you mind?"

The bus driver shook his head. "Oh no! I don't mind!" Thrusting the plastic cup in Schefter's face, he spluttered, "Wanna sip-a-soda?"

"Look, whoever you are," sighed Schefter. "If you would just move over th…"

"The name's Sharky!" exclaimed the bus driver, interrupting the sports announcer and pointing to the name embroidered on his shirt.

Suddenly, a loud roar filled the sky and discarded candy wrappers, paper napkins and trash tornadoed up into the air. The startled Sharky whipped around, splashing his extra-large soda all over Schefter.

Drenched head-to-toe in red pop, Schefter dropped his microphone and stumbled away in search of a towel.

Sharky, seeing a helicopter overhead, scooped up the microphone, looked into the camera with a juicy, pinky-gummy smile and finished Adam Schefter's report.

"In an exciting new development, we have just spotted an FBI Football Division chopper flying over Lambeau Field! Could this mean a break-through in the case of the missing Hall of Fame Bears? More to come on this story as details unfold! From Green Bay, this is Sharky for ESPN."

Instantly, the lights went out. Flipper moved from behind the camera, walked up to Sharky, took the microphone and patted the bus driver on the back.

"Nice job."

Sharky didn't respond. He was too busy watching the jet-black helicopter hovering overhead.

September 2 - 7:16 pm
In the Helicopter Hovering over Lambeau Field
44 minutes to Kickoff

"There's no place to land," exclaimed Agent Sanders.

Senior Special Agent Roman Noodle scanned the thousands of cars surrounding the stadium and all the people partying in-between.

"Guess we'll have to put down on the field," he announced.

Maneuvering up and over the bright lights of Lambeau, Noodle moved the helicopter directly above the 50-yard-line and did a slow 360-degree spin searching for a spot to put down.

"The players are on the field warming up," boomed Coach Yak.

"They'll get out of the way," chuckled Noodle as he lowered his whirlybird onto the big, bold Green Bay **G** painted in the middle of the field.

The Packers and the Bears, stretching on the field, were shocked to see a helicopter landing right next to them and they scattered to the sidelines.

Tired of being squeezed in the back seat next to the super-sized coach, Probationary Agent Elliot Ness popped out of the helicopter first and was greeted by a man in a black-and-white striped shirt with an **R** on his back, running toward him with an angry look on his face.

"You can't land that thing here," shouted the referee, as he pulled a yellow flag out of his back pocket and threw it in the air.

"But the parking lot's full," replied Elliot, shrugging his shoulders.

"Let me handle this mess, Ness," snorted Noodle, jumping out of the chopper and rushing over to join in the discussion.

"Who are you?" snapped the referee, who was now surrounded by the rest of his team of officials, all dressed in striped shirts, with varying letters on their backs.

"Senior Special Agent Roman Noodle, FBI Football Division,"

answered Noodle, flashing his badge and announcing his presence with authority.

"I didn't know the FBI had a Football Division," whispered the official with a **U** on his back.

"Me, either," mumbled the official with **DJ** on his back.

"Well, I'm sorry, Agent Noodle," hissed the referee, shaking a finger at Noodle's nose. "We've got a football game gonna start here shortly and no way can we have a helicopter on the field! I'm in charge here and I say move it!"

Noodle, standing nose-to-nose with the ref, shouted back. "Well *I'm* in charge now...and I say the chopper stays!"

"Goes!" yelled the referee.

"Stays!" yelled Noodle.

"GOES!" "STAYS!" "**GOES!**" "**STAYS!**"

"TWEEEEEEEEEEEEEEEEEEEEET!"

The shrill blast of a whistle came from Coach Yak, who had finally squeezed out of the helicopter - with the help of Agent Sanders - and was lumbering over to the fracas.

"Step aside, Noodle. I'll handle this," said Yak calmly, his whistle dangling from the lanyard around his neck. "I'm a football coach. I speak these guys' language."

Noodle, steaming, reluctantly walked back to where Ness and Sanders were standing, while Coach Yak huddled with the team of officials and explained the emergency situation.

After a few minutes, as Noodle impatiently watched, he saw Coach Yak point up to the sky and then at his watch. The referee scratched his chin and nodded. Picking up the flag, he and the other officials cleared the field of remaining players, then trotted to the sidelines.

Just as the last of the players and coaches were trudging back into the tunnel, an army of FBI/FD agents in navy blue windbreakers busted past them, carrying safety nets onto the grassy stadium floor.

"They're here!" cheered Elliot.

"Spread out!" shouted Noodle, throwing his arms out like the wings of a plane. "When those Bears come parachuting down, your job is to catch them!"

"Don't forget the kids!" reminded Coach Yak.

"Oh, yeah! Catch the kids, too!" hollered the FBI/FD boss.

The agents scattered out, end zone to end zone, covering as much ground as possible.

"Four to each net!" yelled Sanders as he positioned his team.

In the stands, 81,000 fans were finding their seats with jaws dropped, as they watched the mad scramble on the field.

A few minutes later, everyone was in place. The fans in the stands. The Bears and Packers peeking out from the tunnel. The officials on the sidelines sitting anxiously on the benches. One hundred FBI/FD agents with a firm hold on 25 circular safety nets. Everyone ready to see something that had never, in the whole history of the world, happened before.

His hands on his hips, Noodle surveyed the field.

"This is good," he nodded.

Probationary Agent Elliot Ness, noticing one last safety net lying next to the helicopter, ran over and grabbed it.

"I guess this one is ours," said Elliot.

"Looks like we could use another one in that area," noted Noodle, pointing at the north end zone.

Standing at midfield, Noodle, Sanders, Elliot and Coach Yak each took a hold of the safety net and together they marched down the field.

"This is good," said Noodle, stopping a few feet from the goalpost.

There, holding the net, the four of them stood in silence, looking at each other. After nearly an *entire* minute, Sanders took a deep breath and sighed. "Now what?"

Noodle blinked his eyes. "Now......we wait."

September 2 - 7:31 pm
In the Cargo Plane 13 Miles from Lambeau Field
29 minutes to Kickoff

"But I don't want to jump out of a plane," moaned Stinky Smothers' brother as Nestor was helping him put his parachute on.

"I don't either, but we've gotta do it," explained Nestor, pulling the straps tight across his teammate's chest and fastening the buckle.

"Yeah! You've got two choices," added Stinky Smothers, as he worked on buckling his own parachute. "You can either jump out of the plane or *crash* with the plane."

"Those are bad choices," grumbled Stinky Smothers' brother.

A few feet away, Killer, Michael and Hawk were busy strapping parachutes on the Hall of Fame Bears.

"I'm sorry, but could you tell me again what we're doing?" asked Hawk, trying his best to stay calm as he tightened the harness around George Blanda.

"First, we shove a Bear out that door there," explained Killer. "If the parachute opens, we know it's okay. Then, we *all* jump out! Great, right?"

"Yeah, great," mumbled Hawk, swallowing the lump in his throat. "But aren't you a little scared?"

"A little scared? No, I'm not a little scared," said Killer, stretching a strap under George McAffee's chin. "I'm a whole lot scared."

"Why is this attached to the parachute?" asked Michael, holding up a heavy cord with a metal fastener at the end of it.

"Oh, Papa told me about that. See that thing that looks like a clothesline up there?" asked Killer, pointing at a metal cable running from above the cargo door all the way to the back of the plane.

Michael, Hawk, Nestor, and the Smothers brothers, all listening carefully, nodded.

"You snap that hook to that clothesline and then, when you jump, the parachute is supposed to open automatically," explained Killer.

"Supposed to?" repeated Hawk nervously. "But what if it doesn't?"

"Flap your wings," suggested Michael. "Maybe you'll find out you can fly."

"I can't reach the clothesline! It's too high!" yelped Stinky Smothers' brother, standing on his tiptoes and jumping toward the cable.

"I'll hook it for you," offered Hawk.

Then, feeling a gentle tug on his arm, Hawk turned around to see Killer and her dark brown eyes looking up at him.

"I'll think you'll have to hook it for me, too," she said with a shrug of her shoulder.

His face suddenly turned red, and, fighting the urge to ask the little quarterback to marry him, Hawk mumbled, "S-s-s-sure. Okay."

"**ACHOOOO!**" sneezed Michael, as he grabbed the last parachute and looked around to see who was missing one.

"Don't tell me your cold is coming back," moaned Nestor.

"No colds allowed," teased Killer. "You have a football game to play Saturday."

"It's not a cold. I'm just allergic to starvation," explained Michael. Then spotting Papa Bear without a parachute, he headed toward him.

"No, no, no, that last one is for Papa," protested Nester.

"That is Papa!" said Michael, pointing at the smiling statue.

"Not *that* Papa. The Papa flying the plane. He needs a parachute," explained Nestor.

"But what about him?" sniffled Michael, rubbing his runny nose with his sleeve.

"I guess we better tell him," said Killer.

"Tell me *what?*" grumbled Michael.

Killer paused, took a deep breath, then started talking. "We've only got 12 parachutes and there are seven of us and six Bears. So, we thought you could hold one of the Bears."

Michael's jaw dropped. "What!? You want me to jump out of a plane AND hold one of these super-heavy George guys?"

"Sure! You're Hercules," insisted Hawk.

"Did Hercules ever jump out of a plane holding a two-ton statue?" complained Michael. "I don't think so!"

"Michael, do it and I'll call Twinkie Off Tackle the first three plays of the game on Saturday," bribed Killer.

"Four times," countered Michael without hesitation.

"Okay. Four times," agreed Killer.

"But Michael, that's only if we don't get killed," added Nestor.

"Yeah, right," nodded Michael. "If we die jumping out of the plane, no Twinkies."

"Go!" laughed Killer, pointing to the front of the plane. "Take the parachute to Papa while we get ready."

With that, they all moved toward the C-47 Sky Train's cargo hatch, dragging the Hall of Fame statues with them as Michael took off toward the cabin with Papa's parachute.

Just as Michael got to the front of the plane, Aphrodite hit another pothole in the sky and he bounced into the cockpit where Papa was putting duct tape along a crack on the windshield.

"Why are you doing that?" asked Michael. "Is something wrong?"

"Oh, no, no, no, Hercules. No worries," chittered Papa, bending over and putting some duct tape over a crack in the floor. "Aphrodite, she holds together long enough."

"Here! I brought you your parachute," said Michael.

Papa pointed at the empty co-pilot seat. "Thank you. Put there."

Michael tugged on Papa's sleeve. "Aren't you going to put it on?"

"Sure, sure," said Papa, sitting down in his captain's chair and checking the altimeter to see how high they were flying. "But I jump not with you."

"What do you mean?" asked Michael, his eyes big as saucers.

"Promise you not have sadness," sighed Papa. "But wheels falling off, metal creaking and cracking. Taping this, taping that…"

Michael swallowed hard. "Are you saying…?"

Papa nodded. "Yes. Aphrodite, she will be crashing. I must stay by her and fly her to the place where she does not hurt the people. She feels very bad sadness if she hurts the people."

"But what about you?" protested Michael. "We don't want *you* to get hurt!"

Papa smiled. "Great Lake Michigan very close. Aphrodite and me, we fly to this lake. I jump. She splash. Nobody hurt."

"You'll jump into Lake Michigan?"

"You no worry! I swim like fishes!" said Papa proudly, pounding his chest with his fist. "But first, Hercules, you must save you and the friends and the Hall of Fame Bears, am I right?"

Michael stood there silently, his eyes looking down at the floor.

"Yes! I am right!" cheered Papa.

Then the old Greek cargo pilot put his hand under Michael's chin and lifted it up and pointed out the window.

"Look now. See glowing in sky? These are lights of Lambeau."

That instant, an engine sputtered and died, tipping the C-47 sideways with a jolt.

"Whoa!" yelled Michael, grabbing the seat to keep his balance.

A split-second later, Killer and Nestor stormed into the cockpit.

"What was that? Why are we flying tilted?" shouted Killer.

Papa turned the control wheel and the plane rolled back to a level position. Looking out the window, he saw smoke coming from the right wing. "Okey-dokey. Engine died now," reported Papa calmly, pointing over his shoulder. "See? Propeller stop spinning."

"What?" yelled Nestor. "What are we gonna do?"

"No-no-no, no worry. Aphrodite, she have *three* engines," reassured Papa. "Everything okay. Just only to fly few more minutes now. See glowing lights?"

"There it is," gulped Nestor, nervously. "Lambeau Field."

"Yes, yes! Football palace of the gods," proclaimed Papa.

"Papa's not going with us," moaned Michael.

"But, Papa!" burst out Nestor. "What will you…"

"I stay okey-dokey," interrupted Papa. "After you parachute, I fly Aphrodite by Lake Michigan and jump just only before she crash."

"Crash?" cried Nestor.

Papa nodded. "Yes. But crash on water much better than crash on land. No people hurt."

"But Aphrodite, you love her," groaned Nestor.

Papa nodded his head again. "This is true. I love her. But even though she will crash, we are happy."

"Happy?" questioned Nestor with a tilt of his head.

"Yes," beamed Papa. "After many, many years, she flies! She is touching the clouds one time more…and she saves the day."

"That's right!" agreed Killer, giving Aphrodite's metal insides a tender touch. "She did save the day!"

Papa smiled. Nestor bit his lip. And Michael, wanting a snack, knew not to mention it.

"Okay, okay, the plan I tell you now," began Papa. "I fly Aphrodite way down low...

"Good. I like low," admitted Michael.

Papa pointed at the altimeter. "It is okay at 3,000 feet."

"*Three-thousand feet?*" whined Michael. "You call that low?"

"We fly by Lambeau Field three times. First time, Bears go out. When parachutes open, we fly by again and you make your Lambeau leaping.

"Third time, Aphrodite and me, we fly by stadium to see all have landed," added Papa. "Then my sweet Aphrodite and me, we fly to the lake for our swim!"

Nestor stood there, worried. "But what if the parachutes don't..."

"Don't say it! Don't even think it!" interrupted Killer, covering Nestor's mouth with her hand.

"I tell you now about things. You listen careful with me," insisted Papa firmly. "You push Bears out by parking lot...they drift with air and land on football field. Also too, *you* make jump by parking lot. You are not making wait for stadium to be by you...no, no, no! Over stadium, *it is too late*. You understand these things?"

"We understand, Papa. We'll jump over the parking lot," said Killer, giving Papa's hand a squeeze. "And thank you."

"You all have much bravery," beamed Papa, squeezing Killer's hand back. Then, pointing ahead at the lights growing brighter, he added, "Lambeau Field comes very close. Go now! Good luck!"

"Good luck to you!" cried Nestor, Michael and Killer.

As they took off, they heard the old man call out from behind, "YOU SEE 'EM!"

....

"What happened? Why were we flying sideways?" asked Stinky Smothers' brother when the trio scrambled back to the cargo hold.

"We lost an engine," blurted Nestor.

Stinky Smothers' brother stood there with a puzzled look on his face. "Did you help him find it?"

"We're almost over Lambeau Field. We better open the door," announced Killer.

Grabbing the lever on the huge metal door, Michael slid it open.

Suddenly the rush of wind and the roar of the C-47 Sky Train's two remaining engines had everyone covering their ears.

Dropping to his knees, Hawk took hold of Hall of Fame Center George Trafton and wrestled him forward. "This guy volunteered to go first!"

"Perfect!" shouted Killer, giving the Bear an encouraging pat.

"Everybody grab a Bear and line up behind Hawk," instructed Nestor as he pushed linebacker-tackle George Connor into position behind his brother.

Following orders, Michael and Stinky Smothers rushed to grab a Hall of Fame George and got in line.

Stinky Smothers' brother, grunting and groaning and struggling to add lineman George Musso, finally gave up and looked at Michael.

"This one must be fatter than the rest. He's really heavy."

"He probably is," agreed Michael, reaching out with one arm to drag Mr. Musso over to the open door with the others.

Leaning out of the airplane with a firm grip on a metal brace bolted next to the opening, Killer, with her short, dark hair blowing, squinted into the wind and studied the ground three-thousand feet below.

"Get ready!" yelled Killer, spotting the parking lot surrounding Lambeau Field. "Hawk! When I say GO...push your Bear out!"

Closing in on the parking lot, the C-47 dipped a little closer to the ground. And holding on tight, Killer leaned out a little further to get a better view.

"Wait...*wait*...***wait***..."

Then...when they were directly over the thousands and thousands of people crowded around cars, trucks and vans, laughing and singing and tailgating in the parking lot…Killer shouted, *"GO!"*

....

Perched at the very edge of the open cargo door, with the ground three-thousand feet below, Hawk gave George Trafton a bear hug and swallowed the football-sized lump in his throat. Then, with all his might, he pushed the Hall of Fame statue out of the plane.

Holding their breath and peeking out, Hawk, Killer, Nestor and Michael watched as the Chicago Bear legend plummeted toward the earth like a rock.

Suddenly, the ripcord attached to the metal clothesline tightened and snapped. With a *whoosh*, a huge, beautiful umbrella appeared in the sky.

"IT WORKED!" cheered Hawk.

"THE PARACHUTE OPENED!" sang out Nestor.

"HOORAY!" shouted all the Braves.

Then, checking to see that they were still flying over the parking lot, Killer yelled, "Hurry! Push 'em all out!"

In an instant, Nestor shoved off George Connor. Michael quickly gave George Blanda the heave-ho. Stinky Smothers pushed out George McAfee and Stinky Smothers' brother, with Michael's help, tossed George Musso off the plane.

"Great job, everybody!" cheered Killer as she watched four more parachutes whoosh open and the Bears drift down toward the stadium.

Then feeling the wing dip slightly and the C-47 starting to circle around a second time, Killer's smile turned serious. Clearing her throat, she coughed out, "Okay. I guess it's our turn next."

....

"Get ready! Here they come!" shouted Senior Special Agent Roman Noodle, pointing up at the five billowy parachutes floating down.

"It's kind of pretty," gushed Probationary Agent Elliot Ness.

"Yeah, it is," nodded Agent Sanders.

Squinting through the stadium lights at the parachutes, Coach Yak burst out, "It looks like it's just the Bears! Where are my players?"

"The plane is coming back around," replied Sanders, pointing as the plane made a wide, banked turn. "Bet they jump on the next fly over."

Eighty-one thousand people in the stands and 100 agents spread out on the grass of Lambeau Field all had their eyes glued to the sky as the Hall of Fame Bears floated through space.

"Don't let them hit the ground! Catch 'em in the nets!" yelled Noodle.

George Trafton was the first to drift peacefully over the stadium wall. Clearing the seats in the south end zone, two groups of four FBI/FD agents charged over to where the Bear was landing. Looking up instead of where they were going, they crashed into each other at full speed and tumbled helplessly to the Lambeau Field turf.

"Ohhhhhhhh," groaned the crowd in horror, thinking all was lost.

Then, from out of nowhere, a third bunch of agents scrambled to the rescue, catching the Hall of Fame statue dead center in their safety net at the two-yard line, a split second before it smashed to the ground.

Seeing the impossible grab, the fans in the stands went wild and the four agents on the field celebrated with a touchdown dance.

"Go, TEAM!" shouted Coach Yak with excitement.

Then, one right after the other, parachutes with Hall of Fame Bears were descending all over the field. George Connor was caught on the twenty-one yard line. George Blanda landed at midfield. George McAfee was snagged safely at the thirty-three and George Musso drifted to the north end zone, happily hauled in by Noodle, Ness, Sanders and Coach Yakunshenko.

Setting their safety net gently on the ground, Senior Special Agent Roman Noodle grabbed the Hall of Fame statue and carried it over to the Bears sideline to the officials waiting there.

"There's not a scratch on him, I'm pleased to say," stated Noodle.

The officials huddled up and, after a short discussion, they called for the rest of the statues to be brought over for inspection.

After buzzing around the Bears like bees in a hive, spending a few minutes looking at the replay and then talking to more officials in the booth, the crew chief walked to the sideline and stood at attention, facing the stands.

Turning on his microphone, he addressed the fans.

"There is no flag for roughing the Hall of Fame Georges. However, one George, Papa Bear, is still missing. Until he is returned, there will be a delay of game."

Blowing his whistle, the crew chief jogged over to the rest of his team gathered around the statues. Noodle marched back to Yak, Elliot and Sanders, who were still standing at the ready with their net in the north end zone.

"Okay, we've got one more Bear to get," declared Noodle, looking up at the sky as the C-47 cargo plane circled back toward the stadium.

"And six kids!" exclaimed Coach Yak. "Don't forget my kids!"

"Oh yeah, right," nodded Noodle. "Those kids."

"What about the pilot?" added Elliot.

"You mean, the old man?" asked Noodle.

"Yeah," shrugged the probationary agent.

"What about him?" snorted Noodle.

....

One engine dead and the other two sputtering, Papa was anxiously flipping switches and checking his gauges on the instrument panel, trying his best to keep Aphrodite flying just a little bit longer.

In the cargo hold, three thousand feet over Lambeau, the terrified Braves were nervously getting ready to make the highest leap in Packer history.

"Who-who-who wants to go first?" stammered Nestor, backing away from the open door.

Everyone stood silently. Michael looked at Stinky Smothers. Stinky Smothers looked at his brother. Stinky Smothers' brother looked at Nestor. Nestor looked at Killer and Killer looked at Hawk.

Hawk, swallowed hard and shrugged his shoulders.

"I'll do it. I'll jump first," gulped Hawk, holding his hands tightly together so they wouldn't shake.

Immediately, Killer rushed over and standing on her tip-toes gave Hawk a peck on the cheek.

Hawk, turning red, reached up and touched his face with his hand.

"Hey, that's not right," complained Stinky Smothers' brother. "A player kissed by a quarterback?"

"I'll guess I'll go after Hawk," volunteered Nestor, raising his hand.

"Hooray, Nestor!" cheered Killer. "I'll go next. Everybody else, line up behind us. And remember! We need to jump over the parking lot to land on the field."

Stinky Smothers grabbed his brother by the shoulders and drove him behind Killer. Taking a deep breath, Michael bent over and grabbed the smiling Papa Bear George Halas with a grunt and got behind Stinky Smothers.

"Remember the deal," croaked Michael. "I jump holding the statue and we run Twinkie Off Tackle the first five plays of the game on Saturday."

"The deal was four times, Michael," corrected Nestor.

"I'll call it five times," agreed Killer. "But you gotta jump!"

"Yeah, yeah. I'll jump. I'll jump," moaned Michael, standing at the back of the line, happy, crabby and scared all at the same time.

At the front of the line, Hawk closed his eyes and tried to imagine being back home playing in the Braves' first real game on Saturday in True Lay Stadium.

He was playing safety on defense, the football flying high in the air and coming right toward him. Reaching his arms out, he grabbed it… INTERCEPTED! A clear field in front of him, he started running full speed toward the end zone. He passed the 30-yard line…then the TWENTY…the **TEN**!

Just as he was about to cross the goal line, he felt a hand shake his shoulder… "Hawk. **HAWK!** It's time! We're over the parking lot," announced Nestor.

Hawk's eyes snapped opened. He looked down and he saw the ground three-thousand feet below.

"Oh, I almost forgot. I guess I better………" And then, leaping out of the open cargo plane door, he put an exclamation point on his sentence, yelling… **"JUUUUMP!"**

Hawk suddenly found himself in mid-air flying free. One second… two seconds…three seconds and just about the time he was wishing with all his might that he was back on the plane with something solid under his feet, it happened.

WHOOSH!

His chute opened and Hawk started floating gently down toward Lambeau Field. Looking above him, he watched Nestor and Killer jump and then he laughed out loud as their parachutes whooshed open just like his.

"YAHOOOO!" cheered Hawk, happier than he'd ever, ever, ever been before.

Back on the plane, Stinky Smothers' brother was standing frozen stiff at the front of the line, refusing to jump.

"C'mon, you gotta jump!" yelled Stinky Smothers, giving his little brother a shove from behind.

"No-no-no…I-I-I-I'll go after you," stammered Stinky Smothers' brother as he stepped back from the open door.

"Go, Stinky!" shouted Michael. "We're running out of parking lot!"

Closing his eyes and holding his nose like he was jumping into a swimming pool, Stinky Smothers leaped out hollering…"Okay, here I GOOOoooo!!"

Stinky Smothers' brother peeked out to see Stinky's parachute whoosh open and he watched as his brother floated nice and easy toward the ground.

"Hey, his parachute opened, too," announced Stinky Smothers' brother, sounding a bit surprised.

"Right!" huffed Michael as he set Papa Bear down for a second to give himself a rest. "Now, it's your turn. Go! Jump! Now!"

"Nope! Can't! Too late! Look…we're over the stadium now!"

"Oh no! Now what?" moaned Michael. "I better go tell Papa."

"Yeah, tell Papa. Papa Bear and I will wait here," nodded Stinky Smothers' brother.

Taking a deep breath, he watched Michael speed off to report the problem to the pilot. Then, sitting on the floor next to the smiling George Halas, Stinky Smothers' brother got nose-to-nose with the statue and looked him in the eye.

"Why are you so happy? Don't you know? We got serious trouble."

....

"Here they come!" shouted Coach Yak as the parachutes appeared.

Noodle squinted into the sky, yelling excitedly. "Good-good-good! It looks like they're headed toward us! Everybody get ready!"

The one hundred FBI/FD agents on the field, the 81,000 fans in the stands and the humongous crowd tailgating outside the stadium all had their noses pointed in the air as the four billowy silk umbrellas sailed earthward.

Lifting his knees to his chest so his feet wouldn't smack into the top of the stadium, Hawk glided over the stands and sailed down on Lambeau Field.

"Woo-hoo! What a ride!" hollered Hawk as he landed dead center in a safety net a foot out of bounds at the five yard-line.

With the crowd roaring its approval, the FBI/FD agents holding the safety net set it on the ground and Hawk scooted off and slipped out of his parachute harness. Sprinting down the sidelines, he skidded to a stop at the fifty and watched his brother come down on the big Packer **G** in the middle of the field.

"We did it, Nestor! We're alive!" yelled Hawk, as he ran to meet him with a hug.

"Yeah! How about that!" cheered Nestor. Then, pointing a little further down the field to where Kathy Kopecky was landing, he added, "Look! Killer made it, too!"

The brothers took off running, weaving in and out and back and forth, trying not to crash into the FBI/FD agents scattered everywhere on the field.

After some happy hugs and high-fives, Hawk, Nestor and Killer looked up to see parachute #4 still a few hundred feet up in the air.

"That's Stinky," said Nestor, worried. "But what about…"

"Yeah," interrupted Killer. "Where's Stinky Smothers' brother? Where's Michael?"

"And Papa Bear?" cried Hawk. "Why didn't they jump?"

"There's Coach Yak!" cried Nestor, pointing at the north end zone.

Once again, they took off down the field, dodging FBI/FD agents. Crossing the goal line out of breath, they greeted their distressed coach, all talking at once.

"Coach! Big trouble! The plane's not flying good," shouted Hawk.

Nestor waving his arms wildly and yelled, "Coach! An engine blew! Papa's fixing cracks with tape and it's running out of gas…"

"Coach! Michael and Stinky Smothers' brother are still on the plane and it's going to crash in the lake," cried Killer, adding more problems to the pile.

Trying his best to stay calm, Coach Yak got down on a knee and threw his arms around his players, gathering them in a huddle.

Looking each of them in the eye, he asked, "First…are you okay?"

"We're good, Coach," blurted out Hawk as they all nodded.

"Okay, good," said Yak, taking a deep breath. "Now remember what I keep preaching…there isn't anything we can't do as long as we work together as a team right?"

"RIGHT!" they all yelled.

"So, we need to stay positive and tackle one problem at a time. Whaddya say?" offered Coach Yak, finishing his mini-pep talk.

"Sounds great, Coach! And I know the first problem we should tackle," said Nestor, pointing to the sky. "Look up there! Stinky is headed for the goalpost!"

Everybody's heads snapped up to see Stinky Smothers and his parachute now only one hundred feet above the field and on a direct collision course with the thick, metal goalpost in the north end zone.

"Oh no!" exclaimed Killer. "He's going to smash right into it!"

Just then, the official with the **R** on his back came running over, yelling, "Warning! Warning! If that kid breaks the goalpost, I'm throwin' a flag! Fifteen-yard penalty for unsportsmanlike conduct!"

Up in the air, Stinky Smothers was twisting and turning, trying his best to change directions. "Whoa! I can't steer this thing!" he shouted.

"Careful, Stinky!" yelled Hawk up into the sky. "If you break the goalpost, we're getting a 15-yard penalty!"

As the parachute got closer and closer to the goalpost with the two spear-like uprights threatening to skewer Stinky like a shish-kabob, Killer covered her eyes and groaned. "I can't look."

She didn't open her eyes again until she heard Stinky hollering from the heavens. "**HELP! GET ME DOWN!**"

Looking up and blinking into the stadium lights, Killer saw Stinky Smothers kicking and screaming and dangling ten-feet above the field. His parachute, hanging from the goalpost, was a big, tangled mess.

"Hang on, Stinky," roared Coach Yak. "We're coming!"

"I have to go to the bathroom," whined Stinky.

"All right, team!" shouted Yak, calling for his players to gather around him. Then, nodding at Senior Special Agent Roman Noodle, Agent Sanders and Probationary Agent Elliot Ness, he added, "Over here, guys! We need you, too!"

Dropping the safety net they were holding, Noodle, Ness and Sanders rushed over to join the group.

Waving his outstretched arms to quiet the fans roaring wildly in the stands, Coach Yak knelt down in the middle of the huddle. "Here's the play! We build a human pyramid under the goalpost."

Pointing at the FBI/FD agents, he explained it. "Me, you, you and you are the base of the pyramid." Elliot, Noodle and Sanders nodded.

"Nestor and Hawk, you climb up on our shoulders and get a good grip on each other. Killer, you're at up to the top of the pyramid. You should be high enough to unbuckle Stinky. Once he's out of the parachute, you both climb down the pyramid to solid ground."

Then Yak clapped and hollered: "Let's do it! Team on three! One... **Two...THREE!**"

"**TEAM!**" they all shouted in unison as they broke the huddle.

Quickly, Yak rumbled over to where Stinky was dangling in midair. Planting himself next to the goalpost, Noodle, Sanders and Elliot circled the massive coach and locked arms to form a sturdy base.

"Hurry! I can't wait much longer," cried Stinky.

"Hold on another minute, Stinky," yelled Nestor as he and Hawk climbed up to create the human pyramid's second story.

Killer, waiting for her turn, called up to the top, "You guys ready?"

"READY!" shouted Nestor and Hawk.

Not wasting a second, Kathy Kopecky sprang into action. Like an expert rock climber, she placed her first foot on Noodle's knee, her second step on top of Coach Yak's Ohio State ball cap, and her third and fourth steps were on Nestor's shoulder and Hawk's beat-up beak.

"Sorry about your nose, Hawk," apologized Killer as she carefully balanced herself before reaching up toward Stinky.

"That's okay...it doesn't hurt...much," snuffled Hawk.

Carefully balancing herself, she stretched out her arms, grabbing Stinky's harness and unbuckled his parachute.

"Thanks!" cheered Stinky as he slipped out of the tangled mess of straps and strings. In a flash, he climbed down the human pyramid, stepping recklessly on fingers, toes, ears and, of course, Hawk's nose.

Once the ground, Stinky ran directly to an official shouting, "Which way to the lavatory, sir?"

"Down that tunnel, turn left into the Packer locker room," yelled the referee, pointing at the southeast corner of the stadium.

Stinky sprinted off, waving his arms and smiling to the cheers of the crowd. Behind him, the human pyramid was disassembling even faster than it was built.

"Great job, team!" shouted Coach Yak, clapping his hands. "Four kids down safe and sound! Two more to go!"

"We're still missing that last Hall of Fame Bear," growled Noodle, rubbing the ear Stinky Smothers had used as a step.

"And don't forget about the pilot," added Elliot.

They all looked up in the sky as the sputtering C-47 cargo plane made a wide, sweeping turn, getting ready to fly over Lambeau Field for the third and final time.

CHAPTER 13

September 2 - 7:47 pm   In the Cargo Plane over Lambeau Field
13 minutes to Kickoff

Demetri Papadopoulos was at the controls of his Douglas C-47 Sky Train, doing his best to keeping it flying when he felt a tap on his shoulder. Snapping his head around, he was startled to see Michael standing next to him.

"Hercules! You still on plane? You no jump?" asked Papa, wrinkling his forehead in confusion.

"No…me and Stinky Smothers' brother and Papa Bear, we're all still here. We didn't go. We waited too long," explained Michael.

"Good, good! Better wait than jumping late," said Papa. Then pointing at his fuel gauge, he added, "But now you make Lambeau leaping this time. You must. Aphrodite, she has very little gasoline."

"Don't worry, Papa. We'll jump this time," said Michael, turning to run back to the cargo hold. Then, suddenly stopping, he turned around, cleared his throat and asked, "You're going to be okay, right?"

"Oh! Sure-sure," said Papa. "No worries. I am a-okay fine."

Michael, turning to leave a second time, stopped himself again and stuck out his hand. "You are my hero, Papa."

Smiling broadly, Papa shook his young friend's hand. "You are *my* hero, Hercules."

Giving the old Aviation Officer's mitt an extra squeeze, Michael took off to join Stinky Smothers' brother, who was still sitting next to George Halas a few feet away from the open cargo hold door.

"Okay, this is our last chance," announced Michael, reaching up to hook his parachute to the static line. "If we don't jump this time, we're crashing in the lake with the plane, understand?"

"Yeah, yeah," muttered Stinky Smothers' brother. "But I wish I was running through a brick wall instead of jumping out of a plane."

"So, start running and pretend you're busting through a brick wall," suggested Michael.

Stinky Smothers' brother shrugged his shoulders. "I guess I could do that. You got a football helmet I can put on backward?"

"Just close your eyes," said Michael as he peeked out the cargo hold door at the ground below. "We're almost over the parking lot again. Get ready to go."

Stinky Smothers' brother took a deep breath and started to stand up, his knees shaking, when suddenly Aphrodite hit another pothole in the sky. Banging his head on the inside of the plane and bouncing up and down, he landed hard on his bottom.

"Y-Y-You go first," stammered Stinky Smothers' brother, rubbing his head.

"I'm not jumping until I know you are off this plane!" insisted Michael. "C'mon! We're over the parking lot! We gotta go NOW!"

"I'll go! I'll go! Just let me watch you jump first, so I know it's okay, okay?"

Heaving a heavy sigh, Michael bent down and picked up smiling Papa Bear George Halas. "Okay. I'll go, then *you'll* go, right?"

"Yeah, sure," nodded Stinky Smothers' brother.

"You promise?" asked Michael, looking his teammate dead in the eye.

"Promise," said Stinky Smothers' brother, carefully standing back up and getting in line behind Michael.

"Okay, good! Let's do this!" exclaimed Michael, stepping up to the open door.

Pausing a second to make sure he had a Herculean bear hug on the Hall of Fame statue, he leaped off the plane yelling, "**TWINKIES! HERE I COME!**"

Stinky Smothers' brother peeked down and out the cargo plane door and watched as Michael's parachute *whooshed* open.

"Time for me to jump," mumbled Stinky Smothers' brother to himself, his whole body shaking with fear. "Time to jump...time to jump...time to jump."

But, instead of doing his leap over Lambeau, he backed away from the door, groaning and shaking his head, "I'm not jumping...I'm not jumping."

He was slowly scooting backward when a second engine sputtered and died. With a sudden jolt, the C-47's left wing dipped down hard, tipping the whole plane on its side.

Losing his balance, Stinky Smothers' brother rolled through the open cargo plane door. As he tumbled out, his parachute snagged a metal rivet sticking out of the floor and ripped a bowling ball-size hole in the billowy silken lifesaver. Instead of opening with a *whoosh*, the damaged parachute *wheeeeeeeeeeeeeesched* open.

With air pouring through the hole, Stinky Smothers' brother was falling at breakneck speed and quickly catching up with Michael and Papa Bear, who were floating happily toward Lambeau...completely unaware of the pending disaster above.

Down below, everyone was watching in horror as Stinky Smothers' brother came hurdling down through space.

"They're headed right for each other!" shouted Hawk.

"Michael! LOOK! Stinky Smothers' brother!" yelled Nestor.

"Point up!" hollered Killer, thrusting her arm skyward. "Point up!"

Coach Yak, realizing what his little quarterback wanted everyone to do, sucked in all the air his 400-pound frame could hold and let out a roar.

"TEAM! POINT UP ON THREE! ONE...TWO...THREE!" First, Nestor, Hawk, Killer and Coach Yak pointed up. Then, Noodle, Sanders, Elliot and the 100 FBI/FD agents on the field threw their arms up. Finally, every one of the 81,000 fans packed into the stands pointed up, too.

Michael, still a few hundred feet in the air, but close enough to see the puzzling sight of thousands of people pointing to the sky, looked up over his head.

"Oh. This isn't good," mumbled Michael, seeing his teammate plummeting from above. "He's going to smoosh himself flatter than a pancake."

Instantly, a stack of flat pancakes with butter and syrup dripping down flashed in Michael's brain. Then, just a second or two left before Stinky Smothers' brother zoomed past him, he groaned, "Sorry, Papa."

Letting go of the Hall of Fame statue, Michael leaned to his left and stretched as far as he could, just managing to snag the human meteor by his waist.

"Gotcha!" grunted Michael as he wrapped his arms firmly around Stinky Smothers' brother, completing the process of the catch.

"Oh! Hey! Hi Michael!" chirped Stinky Smothers' brother opening his eyes in surprise. "See? I told you I'd jump!"

Back on the ground, Coach Yak leaped almost an inch in the air and was high-fiving his players. "He caught him! He caught him!"

"And he's going to prison! He let go of the statue!" barked an angry Noodle as he watched Papa Bear George Halas tumbling end-over-end from the sky. "It's gonna get smashed to pieces!"

With no time for talk, Probationary Agent Elliot Ness sprang into action. Pointing at the corner of the north end zone, he shouted, "Quick! To Section 106! Follow me!"

Grabbing a safety net, Elliot leaped into the stands, followed by Hawk, Nestor, Killer and Agent Sanders. Coach Yak tried to climb the wall, but couldn't.

"Everybody back!" ordered Elliot, waving the fans away.

They scattered immediately and the rescue team, their eyes glued to the sky, stumbled around the stadium seats trying to place themselves exactly where Papa Bear would land.

"Over here," shouted Elliot, tugging the safety net toward the aisle. "A little more...a little more...THIS LOOKS GOOD!"

"Okay, everybody! Get a good grip! Stretch it tight!"

Holding on to the safety net with white knuckles, Hawk, Nestor, Killer, Sanders and Elliot looked up to see the gravity-sucking Hall of Fame statue plummeting to earth at super-scorching speed.

"Here comes Papa George!" yelled Hawk.

A second later, the bronzed bust SMACKED dead center in the outstretched net. After a couple of serious bounces, Papa Bear came to rest, lying face-first on the thick canvas.

Carefully carrying the safety net down to the rail, Elliot and his rescue team passed it to Coach Yak and Special Agent Noodle on the field. Then, jumping out of the stands onto the legendary Lambeau turf, they gathered around and stared at the priceless NFL treasure lying face down on the net.

Nestor and Noodle knelt down on the net. Gently lifting the statue, they set it on its base to reveal the smiling face of the legendary George *Papa Bear* Halas.

"Look! He's still smiling!" shouted Hawk.

"He sure is!" chimed in Coach Yak.

"And look up there!" added Killer, pointing at the parachute about to land a few feet away. "Michael and Bob!"

"Bob? Who is Bob?" asked Hawk, wrinkling his nose.

"Stinky Smothers' brother!" she shouted as she ran to greet the last two returning heroes.

Hawk and Nestor sprinted over to the visitor's sideline where Killer was waiting and watching as a team of FBI/FD agents positioned themselves to make the catch.

Floating gently toward the field, Michael and Stinky Smothers' brother plopped down in the safety net and hopped off to the ground.

"That was fun!" shouted Stinky Smothers' brother.

"I'm hungry," blurted Michael, blinking into the Lambeau Field lights in search of a hot dog vendor.

The stadium crowd exploded with cheers as Nestor, Hawk, Killer, Michael and Stinky Smothers' brother were swarmed by the FBI/FD agents. Lifting the Port Clinton players to their shoulders, they carried them in triumph around the field.

Suddenly, the pro players burst out of the tunnel. A few Bears' players grabbed the Hall of Fame statues and joined the Lambeau parade. There were Packers hugging Bears. Bears hugging Packers.

The officials were pouring Gatorade on each other's heads. Noodle, Sanders and Elliot Ness were holding a safety net while the big, happy Coach Yak jumped up and down on it like a trampoline.

Finally, Stinky Smothers came running out of the tunnel, holding a length of toilet paper over his head, yelling, "I got Aaron Rodgers' autograph! I got Aaron Rodgers' autograph!"

It was one loud, gigantic, wild and crazy, super-sized victory celebration in the stands and on the field.

It was so loud, no one could hear the old Douglas C-47 Sky Train, its last engine sputtering, as it struggled to fly off into the dark, cold night.

September 2 - 7:57 pm In the Cargo Plane over Lake Michigan
3 minutes to Kickoff

Papa was twisting and turning knobs and controls, trying to keep his plane in the air as the city lights of Green Bay below were replaced by the inky, black nothingness of Lake Michigan.

Glancing at the fuel gauge that was now below *E*, Papa sighed and reached for his parachute.

"You do it, Aphrodite…you touch the sky one more time and save the day," said Papa softly. "You go only minutes more. Then…then, you can rest."

Sadly, the old Greek pilot stood up, slipped the parachute over one arm and started to walk back to the open cargo hold door to jump out.

Just as he was about to take the first step, he stopped.

"Aphrodite! I have idea! I stay and we go for swim together!" Papa chirped, dropping his parachute to the floor and kicking it to the corner.

Just then, the C-47 cargo plane hit an air pocket and bounced up and down.

"Good! I am much happy you agree," nodded Papa. Quickly sitting back down in the pilot's seat, he returned to feverishly turning and twisting the controls.

Pushing the yolk forward, he and Aphrodite started their descent.

"No nose dive. Nose dive no good," said Papa, thinking out loud in a whisper. "Going down nice and flat. Flat, flat, flat."

Aphrodite, her one last engine coughing and sputtering, dropped down closer and closer to the big lake. Barely above the water, Papa pulled back on the yolk, lifting the C-47's nose ever so slightly.

"Okay! Now we make splash!" shouted Papa, just as Aphrodite's tail section touched down first.

Skipping hard across the top of Lake Michigan, the old Douglas C-47 Sky Train was now a boat with water wings.

"WAHOO!" cheered Papa. "We floating Aphrodite! We floating!"

Flipping a switch to shut off the engine, Papa gave the control panel a kiss, then grabbed an old transistor radio out of his toolbox.

As he was climbing through an overhead hatch to get to the top of his cargo plane, Papa heard the happy sound of a tugboat horn.

A few minutes later, the SS Kathryn Keaggy pulled alongside the C-47 with the Captain and crew scrambling on deck to come to the rescue.

"Ahoy there! Are you okay?" hollered the Captain through his megaphone.

"Sure-sure! Okey-dokey!" shouted Papa from his perch on top of his plane.

The Captain turned to a few crew members, giving instructions. Instantly, there was a flurry of activity with men grabbing ropes and hooks and life jackets. Satisfied his orders were being followed, the Captain shouted through the megaphone again.

"Hang on! We'll get you on board. Then, we'll tow your plane!"

"Thank you for towing. I stay with my plane! She make a good boat!" replied Papa.

The Tugboat Captain shrugged his shoulders, waved and went back inside the wheelhouse.

Zipping his jacket up to his neck and pulling his leather aviator helmet tight over his ears, Papa made himself comfortable on top of the C-47's nose cone as the SS Kathryn Keaggy blew her horn and began tugging Aphrodite toward the twinkling lights of Green Bay.

Reaching into his pocket, Papa pulled out his transistor radio and turned the dial to WTAQ 1360 just in time to hear Packer Announcer Wayne Larrivee's warm voice float over cold Lake Michigan...

"What a show we've had already, football fans! A helicopter landing at midfield! Hall of Fame Bears falling from the sky! A victory parade around legendary Lambeau Field and now, we're just a minute away from the kickoff of another exciting NFL season!"

Papa laid back on Aphrodite and looked up at the stars. With a smile, he whispered, "Go Pack Go!"

September 2 - 7:59 pm Monroe, Wisconsin
1 minute to Kickoff

Still tied together with yellow crime-scene tape and still taking baby steps together, the Limburger Heads turned the corner on 16th Avenue, singing the Packer fight song for the 623rd time in a row.

"There it is! Baumgartner's!" cheered Floyd, nodding toward the cheese store and tavern in the middle of the block.

"Finally!" whined Helmut. "I thought we'd never get here."

"My throat's dry," coughed Rick Monroe. "I need a root beer."

"I concur. I am in need of a thirst-quenching beverage myself," agreed Einstein.

"Stop breathing in my ear, Floyd," complained Nick Monroe.

"Wonder if the game's started," snorted Dairy Dan. "Shuffle faster!"

Henrietta Wozniak shook her head and moaned out, "Szuram tak szybko jak potrafie." *I am shuffling as fast as I can.*

Speeding up just a little, the herd of Limburger Heads scuffled their way down the street, stopping at Baumgartner's front door.

"This is great," moaned Nick, struggling to move his shoulders. "We're all tied up. We can't move our arms. How do we get in?"

"Over here," ordered Dairy Dan, dragging the bunch to the window. Moving a few feet to see inside the jammed packed tavern, they discovered all eyes were glued to the television above the bar.

"Stinkin' Bishop! The Packers are lining up for kickoff!" cried Floyd.

"We gotta get in!" yelled Dairy Dan, banging his head on the glass.

In a flash, the bartender bolted over the bar and ran out to the sidewalk, waving his arms. "Hey! Hey! Hey! Stop that! You're gonna bust my window!"

"Sorry, Chris!" apologized Dairy Dan, recognizing Baumgartner's owner. "But the game's starting! We're tied up and we can't open the door."

"Oh, it's you guys," muttered Chris, rolling his eyes.

"Yep! It's us!" chirped Floyd.

"Floyd! Where's your tuba?" asked Chris. "The Taleggio Trio is playing tonight."

Wrapped up in the tight bunch of Limburger Heads, Floyd did his best to shrug his shoulders. "Nope. Can't do it tonight, Chris. Goin' to prison."

"I see," said Chris, scratching his chin. "Well, I guess the trio will have to try and get by with just the three."

Then opening the door, the owner stepped aside and watched as the Limburger Heads squeezed through the entrance and shuffled over to a table.

"Look at those beautiful uniforms," smiled Dairy Dan, pointing with his nose at the television screen showing placekicker Mason Crosby setting the football on the tee. "Nothing like Packer football! Isn't that right, Mr. Wozniak?"

"Without question," nodded Einstein, his shiny bald head glowing. "Green Bay Packer football is absolutely…most definitely…the highest caliber of regalement known to mankind."

On TV, Crosby waved to let the referee know he was ready to kickoff. Smiling, Dairy Dan shouted to Chris behind the bar. "One root beer, please…seven straws!"

With a salute, Baumgartner's owner shouted back. "ONE ROOT BEER … SEVEN STRAWS … COMIN' UP!"

CHAPTER 14

September 2 - 8 pm Lambeau Field
Kickoff!

On the Packer sideline, Coach Yak, Nestor, Hawk, Killer and the Smothers brothers were watching the teams line up for the kickoff. Michael, his back to the field, was looking in the stands for someone selling hot dogs or pizza or nachos.

On the other sideline, FBI/FD Senior Special Agent Roman Noodle was carefully inspecting the six Hall of Fame Bear busts, searching for nicks and scratches as Agent Sanders and Probationary Agent Elliot Ness looked on.

On the field, the Packers' kicker waved to the ref and approached the ball.

Putting the full force of his powerful leg into it, Crosby booted the football high and deep and out of the end zone. The first game of the new season...the game pitting the NFL's oldest rivals against each other, the game 81,000 Cheeseheads in the stands and millions of crazed football fans nationwide had been waiting for all year long... *THE* game had finally begun.

CHAPTER 15

September 2 Lambeau Field
After the Kickoff

"Look at that!" shouted Hawk.

"Look at what? A hot dog vendor?" hollered Michael, his head spinning in circles.

"He kicked that ball 80 yards!" crowed Hawk.

Nestor, jumping up and down, high-fived Killer. "I can't believe we're actually here! On the sidelines! Lambeau Field!"

"I'd rather be where the food is," grumbled Michael, pointing to the stands.

Mesmerized by the wild, back-and-forth action the field, Coach Yak and his players sat on the bench and cheered for both teams. The first two quarters flew by and, at halftime, the score was tied 17-17.

As the Packers and Bears ran down the tunnel to their locker rooms, Sanders and Ness were trotting across the field behind Noodle, who was waving his arms and yelling, "Hey, Coach! Coach!"

"Wonder what he wants?" muttered Yak, watching the FBI/FD boss jogging in his direction with a navy FBI/FD duffle bag.

Hawk shrugged his shoulders. "Maybe he's coming to get Michael and take him to prison."

Kathy Kopecky wrinkled her nose. "He can't do that. They've got the Bears back! Everything's okay now."

"Everything's NOT okay! I'm still hungry," complained Michael.

"You know what? I'm hungry, too," laughed Nestor. "It's halftime. Let's go find a concession stand."

"Now you're talking!" exclaimed Michael, turning to leave.

Coach Yak held up a meaty hand, "Hey, wait a second, guys. Let's see what Macaroni wants and then we'll *all* go get something to eat."

"Macaroni sounds good," whispered Michael, licking his lips.

Noodle, not smiling, arrived on the Packer sideline, huffing and puffing. Setting his duffle on the ground, he held his arm up and waited to catch his breath before he started talking.

"Coach, I just wanted to thank you and your boys for all your help."

Then, noticing Killer with her hands on her hips and a frown on her face, Noodle cleared his throat and started over.

"I-I-I mean, I just wanted to thank you and your **PLAYERS**..."

Hearing this, Killer nodded her head and smiled.

Noodle continued, "...for all your help. We've got the Bears loaded in the chopper and we're taking off. They'll be back in the Hall of Fame tomorrow."

"But what about us?" bellowed Yak. "We've got football practice tomorrow at 2 o'clock and our truck's broken. How do you expect us to get back home?"

Noodle scratched his chin as Sanders leaned over and whispered in his ear.

"According to Agent Sanders, our hi-tech mobile command center has just arrived," stated Noodle. "How about we have FBI/FD Agent Ness drive you back to Ohio? We can hitch your truck to our van and tow it back home, too."

"Sure...that would work," nodded Coach Yak.

"The mobile command center is parked outside the North Entrance by the Vince Lombardi statue," said Sanders, shaking Coach Yak's hand. "Follow Agent Ness and you can get on the road. If you leave now, you'll get back to Port Clinton in plenty of time for practice."

"Got it!" nodded Yak.

Just then he felt a poke in his ribs. Looking down at his side, he saw Michael standing there.

"Oh yeah, I almost forgot," said Coach Yak, snapping his fingers. "We'll meet you at the Lombardi statue in 15 minutes. I need to get the team something to eat! Turns out jumping out of planes works up an appetite."

With that, everybody shook hands and the two groups separated with Coach Yak shouting, "Let's go get some food! Order whatever you want, as much as you want! We've got some celebrating to do!"

With cheers of happiness, Michael, Nestor, Hawk, Killer and the Smothers Brothers ran off with their coach, following the smells of Italian sausage, chicken tenders and popcorn.

Standing in a circle, Elliot looked at Noodle and then to Sanders and then back to Noodle.

"Senior Special Agent Noodle, sir, d-d-did I hear you right?" stammered Elliot. "When you said I'd drive the coach and his kids to Ohio…"

"Don't argue with me, Agent Ness," interrupted Noodle. "You're driving that bunch back home. That's an order!"

"Hold it right there! You didn't say it again!" exclaimed Elliot.

"Didn't say what?" barked Noodle, scratching his head.

"When you told the coach I'd drive them home, you said AGENT Ness! You didn't say PROBATIONARY! I was listening carefully and you didn't say…"

Holding up his arm to stop Elliot in mid-sentence, Noodle pulled a box out of his duffle bag and handed it to the wide-eyed agent.

His hands shaking, Elliot lifted the lid of the box to reveal a pair of shiny black shoes. A split second later, one of the shiny shoes starting ringing.

Grabbing it out of the box, Elliot slid the heel forward and put the shoe to his ear.

"Welcome to Federal Bureau of Investigation Football Division **Agent** Ness!" said the voice on the other end.

Spinning around quickly, he saw the smiling face of Agent Sanders, holding *his* shoe phone to *his* ear.

"I made it? I'm part of the team now?" gushed Elliot. "Wow! I can't believe it! I-I-I don't know what to say!"

"Don't say anything," barked Noodle. "Just put your shoes on and get going. You've got some driving to do, rookie."

"Yes, sir!" sang out Elliot, giving his superior a snappy salute.

Springing into action, Elliot jumped out of his scuffed-up oxfords and slipped into his official issue FBI/FD shoe phone shoes.

"Perfect fit," cooed the brand-new agent.

Still smiling, Agent Sanders tossed Elliot the keys to Mobile Command Center.

"No speeding!" yelled Noodle.

Elliot took off running as Noodle and Sanders stood there and watched. Bending down to pick up his duffle, FBI/FD Senior Special Agent Roman Noodle blinked back a tear.

"You okay?" asked Sanders.

"Of course, I'm okay! Why wouldn't I be?" snapped Noodle. "C'mon! Let's get to the chopper and get those Bears back where they belong."

Wiping his nose on his navy-blue FBI-FD windbreaker, Noodle started walking across Lambeau Field, followed by Agent Sanders who was happily high-fiving the players coming onto the field for the second half.

September 3 – 11:30 am On I-80 Somewhere in Ohio
3 hours from Port Clinton

Riding along in the front seat of the Mobile Command Center, Coach Yak looked at his watch.

"We're behind schedule," he grumbled.

"Yeah, it took more time to hook your truck to the back than we thought," admitted new FBI/FD Agent Elliot Ness. "Oh, and don't forget. We had to wander around that cemetery in the dark, gathering up those gnomes."

"That dog tried to bite me," complained Yak.

"I know, right? He seemed pretty attached to that blue gnome with the Band-Aid," agreed Elliot as he checked their current location and destination on the GPS monitor.

"But," Elliot added with confidence, "if we don't make any more stops, we should get to your practice right on time."

Coach Yak unbuckled his seat belt and walked to the back.

"We're running behind, so no stopping for lunch," announced the super-sized coach.

"That's okay, Coach," chirped Killer, looking up from the Braves' playbook she was studying. "We still have plenty of snacks left from last night."

"Speak for yourself," objected Michael. "I only have two bags of chips, a box of Goldfish and…"

Michael stopped for a second to count his beef jerky treats.

"One-two-three-four-five…only SIX Slim Jims."

"I have an extra Slim Jim," announced Stinky Smothers' brother. "You want it?"

"Sure! Toss it to me!"

Stinky Smothers' brother flipped the Slim Jim to the always-hungry running back, who caught it with one hand and piled it on top of his stack of snacks.

"Thanks, Bob," said Michael. "Every little bit helps."

"Who do we play on Saturday, Coach?" asked Nestor.

"Oak Harbor Rockets," replied Yak as he headed back to the front.

"The Rockets? Ugh, they really beat us last year," moaned Stinky Smothers.

Closing her playbook and her eyes, Kathy Kopecky leaned her head against Hawk's shoulder and yawned. "That was last year. *This* year, we've got Nestor's secret snack plays."

"That's right," smiled Nestor, suddenly finding himself yawning, too. "Those Rockets are in for a big surprise."

"Remember, Twinkie Off Tackle first six plays," yawned Michael, leaning his head on Killer's shoulder.

Nestor, his eyelids getting heavy, leaned his head on Michael and mumbled, "First four plays."

Within minutes, everybody in the back of the Mobile Command

Center was sound asleep. Everyone except Hawk, who was wide awake looking out the window at the wide-open countryside.

Suddenly, there was the black and white Holstein again, standing out in front of a white barn holding another sign.

U R InViTED to mY BIRTHday PaRTY.
- LucKEY

"Whoa!" shouted Hawk, "Look at that!"

Hawk, moving and twisting around to look behind him, created a chain reaction and everyone, leaning on each other's shoulders, flopped over and woke up.

"What-what?" burst out Nestor, his eyes blinking open.

"Are we home?" asked Killer, stretching out her arms.

Michael, grabbing a snack off the top of his stack snorted, "Is it time to eat?"

"No!" shouted Hawk excitedly. "Back there, in that field! I saw that cow again holding a sign!"

"You were dreaming," yawned Nestor.

"No! I was wide awake," argued Hawk. "The cow invited me to a birthday party!"

"A birthday party?" repeated Nestor, wrinkling his nose. "You were definitely dreaming."

"How about me? Am I invited?" asked Stinky Smothers' brother.

Just then, they heard a text tone come from inside Killer's pink duffle on the floor.

Zipping open her bag she reached in and pulled out her cell phone. "Hey! It's from Frankie," chirped Killer.

"Frankie Flat-Nosed Fitzwater," grumbled Hawk, a little jealous. "What does *he* want?"

"Wow! Frankie and Billy DelSesto found the buried treasure in Portage Park!" exclaimed Killer.

"They did?" asked Nestor. "What was it? A big chest of jewels? A sack of old coins? Ancient Egyptian artifacts?"

Killer made a frowny face and shook her head. "No. A gold tooth."

Stinky Smothers laughed. "A gold tooth?"

"Yeah. Frankie says the people at the Ottawa County Museum think the tooth might have belonged to U.S. Captain Oliver Hazard Perry from the War of 1812."

"If it is," she added, "they might have a parade down Main Street." She shrugged her shoulders and put the phone back in her duffle bag.

"Teeth are important," declared Michael, ripping open a bag of potato chips.

"I agree," said Stinky Smothers' brother.

Hawk sat back down, mumbling to himself. "A birthday party... for a cow?"

Looking out the window, he sighed.

"And I'm invited?"

TIGER STADIUM TIME MACHINE
Stadium Adventure Series Book #3

Hawk, Nestor and Michael agree to feed the neighbors' cat while the couple is off on a Florida vacation. Poking around the basement during their first day on the job, they stumble upon two wooden seats from old Tiger Stadium in Detroit.

Stadium seats that had been converted into a TIME MACHINE!

By the time the brothers discover that traveling back in time is dangerous business, it's too late! Hawk, Nestor and Michael get separated from each other – *lost years apart* – with no way to get home.

Visit *stadiumadventureseries.com* and sign up to receive a notice when Book #3 is available!

And be sure to read Book #1 *Freaked Out at Wrigley Field*

ROGER D. HESS has always been a writer.
He's worked as a journalist, a greeting card writer,
a screenwriter, a speech writer and a ghostwriter.
He's been an award-winning copywriter in
advertising and marketing and a crackerjack
public relations expert, pounding out hundreds
of press releases for major news outlets.
Now, he's a novelist.

He is also a husband, a dad, a grandpa and…
a stadium lover. Every year, he squeezes in
as many visits as possible to ball parks,
football stadiums, hockey arenas large and small.
For him, happiness is a ticket in one hand
and a hot dog in the other.
And it's at that point, the adventure begins!